FROM OUT OF THE DARK . . .

I froze almost mid-stride in the thick, ominous blackness. I was sure there were things creeping at me. I
was sure I heard faint sounds all around me.

Then the lights came on again, too faint to be anywhere near the level I wanted, but at least a thousand
times better than absolute darkness. And, to my horror, I saw that instead of one archway leading into
the room and one leading out, the walls were now
covered with archways, some lit, some as black as
the darkness I'd so recently been through. I didn't
know which way I'd come in, couldn't tell which
passageway led out again, but knew beyond the
faintest doubt that if I chose the wrong one I'd deeply
regret it.

And then I heard it, a sound that froze the blood
in my veins. Something was moving in the darkest
passage to my right, something that shuffled and
dragged part of itself, something that breathed with
a gargling, burbling sound, something that was definitely coming for me!

MISTS OF THE AGES

SHARON GREEN

DAW BOOKS, INC.
DONALD A. WOLLHEIM, PUBLISHER

1633 Broadway, New York, NY 10019

DAW Book Collectors No. 756.

Dedication:
This one, with apologies, is for, in alphabetical order:
Robert Adams and Pamela Crippen Adams,
Alexis Gilliland and Dolly Gilliland,
Joel Rosenberg and Felicia Hermann Rosenberg.
Six people who are delightfully easy to like.

First Printing, September 1988

1 2 3 4 5 6 7 8 9

Printed in the U.S.A.

Chapter 1

I stood in the middle of the very posh office, looking around by the light of the faint glow coming from the eight-foot desk, trying to *feel* where the hidey-hole was. With the building shut down for the night most of the maintenance systems were on low-power standby, leaving only the security checks fully active and alert. If you stop to listen you can hear maintenance systems, but security nets can only be detected by instruments or nerve endings. I'd used both to get through the net, and now stood in low-power silence trying to detect where the safe spot had been put.

Even the heavy shadows couldn't hide the position of the wall vault from me, and I had to turn my back on the corner before it would stop jumping up and down in my face, waving its arms trying to get my attention. Sometimes the talent of finding things like that makes itself more of a handicap than a help, getting in your way when it's the really obscure location you're trying to pinpoint. The wall vault would have illegal documents and negotiable securities and a good chunk of cash and possibly even jewelry and drugs that were exchangeable for cash, but I had no use for frivolities and no time to waste picking them up. I was after something a lot more delicate in nature and valuable in potential, a special prize that would *not* be kept with everything else.

Turning away from the wall vault faced me toward one of the rows of windows, the one that had been on my left when I'd entered the office. The second row had faced me when I'd come in and now decorated most of the wall to the right. Corner offices had been high status just about forever, but wouldn't have been quite as popular if the occupants had to *wash* all those windows they were so proud of. The thought made me grin into the near dark I stood in, a little female humor injected into an otherwise dull time, and then I began laughing softly instead of grinning. What I had thought of as a joke was my subconscious noticing something the rest of me hadn't, and I was forced to admire the skill that had almost gotten it past me. The safe spot in that office was *very* well situated, but "almost" doesn't make the mark.

I moved carefully around the desk and approached the second window-section from the left, every sense I had extended and alert. It seemed possible that some part of the floor would be pressure sensitive, and I found out rather quickly that it certainly was. Once I discovered that, it was back to the desk to check for the controls that would not be part of the general systems, but once found the switches weren't difficult to neutralize. They couldn't be turned off without activating a different set of alarms, of course, something a large number of my contemporaries had learned the hard way, but setting them to neutral didn't produce the same results.

Neutral was off enough to suit my purposes, and let me turn away from the desk to examine what I'd found. The window-section that had caught my attention was no window-section, and with the system deactivated I was able to get a good look at the four-foot by four-foot safe spot. The repeater screen that covered it most of the time was excellently made, but that very excellence had been its greatest flaw. The other windows in the office were filthy with the usual city grime that settles on everything no matter how often washing is done, but that section of window was measurably cleaner. The system designer hadn't been stupid enough to leave it spotless, but had erred on the short side when it came to "dirty enough." Most people would never have noticed something like that, but that's what makes me more valuable than most people.

There was a fairly complex maze lock on the safe

spot entry, but maze locks, as they say, are only good for keeping out the honest. Opening it took no more than a few minutes, and then I was able to slide the entry down out of my way so that I might look at what it normally hid. Only four of the dozen or so compartments were filled, two with off-planet bank notes that might well have been counterfeit, a third with a large, tightly-stoppered vial filled with something bright yellow that glowed very faintly, and a fourth with a narrow envelope which was clearly from an expensive set of stationery. I took the envelope and folded it, stuffed it inside a pocket of my belt, then put the safe spot entry back where it belonged.

Returning everything to normal took almost as long as deactivating it had, but under those circumstances it wasn't a waste of time. Once I'd rechecked the last set of circuits I'd worked, I connected the final lead that meshed everything back into place, then was able to disconnect my diddle box, allowing the next intrusion signal generated to go to the security force board instead of a dead-end panel in the box. I'd been taught to cover the possibility that I wasn't as good as I thought I was and would therefore set off *some* kind of alarm during the prowl, and found it wise to never forget the lesson. Seero had taught me that, just as he'd taught me all the rest, but I'd learned on my own that there were times when all the caution in the Empire just wasn't enough to make a difference.

I left the building through a maintenance duct that led to the parking level of the building next door, stayed out of range of the scanners until I was back in a normal, street-type bodysuit, then ambled to my jump-around with all the nonconcern of any woman who knows she's parked in a total visibility area. Not only are there no blind spots in a t.v. area, anyone stepping or driving into the section activates real-time monitoring by the duty guards. If an emergency happens they can get there *fast*, and they usually make the effort to move. There are cash bonuses and public recognition each month for the fastest response to any activated emergency, and any team logging twelve wins gets put on a roster of perpetual commendation.

Gryphon was a world that knew the benefits in paying
for what it wanted, and what it wanted was maximum
effort from the people whose job it was to protect others. Substantial annual salaries attracted the best, bonuses and public commendations kept them; with those
who couldn't afford to have the notoriety, stroking was
arranged on a somewhat more discreet level.

My jump-around unlocked itself at my approach, and
I unobtrusively checked the back before getting in and
starting it up. I didn't really expect to find anyone
hiding in the back seat, but when you know how to
get around t.v. areas and approach locks, you tend to
remember that others can do the same. No one should
have known where I was and what I was doing, but
that didn't mean no one did; the faster you learned
should-haves can turn quickly into dids, the better your
chances became of surviving.

I had casually thrown my shoulder bag to the front
seat beside me, but once I was out of the parking level
and skimming along a concourse, my main priority
became getting the contents of the bag properly seen
to. I wasn't due to deliver the envelope I'd taken for
another two and a half hours; simply carrying it with
me would have been possible but not terribly bright. I
was scheduled to visit some old friends during the time
I had free, but not everyone around them would also
be friends. If you make a habit of wiggling your backside at the Fates, you can't really complain when they
arrange a suitable response to the gesture.

Not being the sort to make gestures for no reason,
by the time I reached the nightclub district I had my
prowling suit, tools, and belt all neatly tucked away
in the safe spot in my jump-around. No hiding place
is really safe if its location can change as soon as you
turn your back on it, but many times half measures are
better than none at all. Even if someone managed to
steal the jump-around, they would only be close to the
rest, not have it.

And having the jump-around stolen wasn't that far
out of the question, not in *that* neighborhood. Once
off the concourse I drove more slowly, paying attention to the darkened, dirty streets and watching those

who roamed about on them. On the outer fringes of
the district were most of the nightclubs the city
boasted, and the foot traffic moved easily under bright
lights with easy companionship and enjoyment. About
three blocks beyond that the district changed, and although there were still clubs they weren't the sort to
announce their whereabouts with lights and laughter.
Those who patronized this sub-district usually had
money and the urge for anonymity, a combination
which encouraged the presence of those who most liked
to take things whose absence would not be reported to
the proper authorities. If you're only going to steal
what's safe, I don't understand why you'd bother, but
that's a personal prejudice. Others don't look at it the
same, which is really too bad.

The parking lot of the Dark of the Moon Club sat
beneath the delicate blue glow of its name sign, at
least three-quarters of it neatly and quietly filled. I
pulled into a spot between a limo and a new-model
sports job, which was the best I could do in the way
of protective prevention. In company like that, my little jump-around was hardly worth looking at, and that,
hopefully, meant it would still be there when I came
out.

Getting out of my transportation brought me the stale
but familiar smell of the air in that district, air that
seemed to be holding itself as still as possible to avoid
being noticed. It was an attitude that seemed to be
shared by a lot of the denizens of the area, and one
that had never failed to annoy me. I could understand
not wanting to be noticed at certain times, but to spend
your life slipping from shadow to shadow, afraid to be
touched by the light of day, afraid to be seen by anyone who might take note and remember—I had grown
up in that area and learned a lot of things there, but
that particular attitude wasn't one of them. I enjoyed
standing tall no matter who was watching, and if the
day ever came that I couldn't, I would know my life
was coming to an end.

Walking through the dark to the modest front entrance of the club didn't take long, and I smiled when
I remembered the days there had been scanners which

checked out all new arrivals. What the club had offered then was blatantly illegal rather than just mildly so, and they'd had to be careful not to be surprised by unexpected visits. When the club had changed hands its policies had also changed, and it had become a place where people could meet friends and sit and talk in relative comfort, or indulge in certain vices that affected no one but themselves. Those of us who became old time regulars after the change preferred it that way, and with the amounts of money the club was now making legally, it wasn't likely to change back again. When I reached the front entrance I pushed inside to the outer foyer, and the maitre d' on duty glanced up from his station, then suddenly grinned.

"Well, will you look at that," he drawled in greeting, nothing left of his usual professional aloofness of manner. "We must be starting that age of miracles the preachers keep telling us is on the way. Inky has finally decided to come home."

"You may be a dear, Mal, but home isn't necessarily where the heart is," I answered, not letting the familiarity of the noisy dining room behind him reach all the way through to me. "All I'm back for is a visit, and to ask myself what I ever saw in this dump. I don't expect to do it a second time."

"You'll change your mind," he said, the grin softening to a smile, which also softened his handsome features. "Home is where your friends are, where you can be yourself with others like you. We all knew why you left, doll, and we all understood. Now that you're back again, everything will be the way it used to be."

"Not quite everything," I corrected, almost losing it so far that I told him not to call me doll. That was what Seero had most often called me, and Seero was dead.

"No, not quite everything," he agreed, losing his smile as he remembered. "But things do change, and the rest of us are still here. Tris, Riccom and Sharp said to send you back as soon as you showed up."

"I'm willing to bet they said *if* I show up," I countered, deliberately pushing away the air of gloom that was trying to descend like a falling building. "I didn't know if I'd be able to make it, so I didn't commit to anything definite. All I promised to do was try.''

''Which is why they said *when*, not if,'' he countered back, the grin beginning to return. ''We know the people we can trust from those we can't. I'd be there with them myself if I didn't have to work, so I'll have to catch you next time. They're waiting in the quiet corner.''

As expected. I nodded my thanks to Mal and headed into the room his station guarded, paying no attention to the people at the curtain tables which crowded almost every inch of floor. About a fifth of the tables had nothing of a distortion field around them, double that number had shadow curtains to tease passersby, and all the rest were completely hidden by fields that let no one see who was at them, what those people were watching, or what the watchers were doing. How you set your table depended on what you had come to the club to see and do, and very few of the table patrons were there for wholesome entertainment. The club had a full spectrum licence, though, which meant even opera and ballet were available, and some of the tables were automatically set to those frequencies. Doing it that way meant no one could prove what anyone had chosen to view unless they were right there beside a particular individual, an anonymity which meant quite a lot to some of the regulars.

I was almost across the floor to the booths when Tris spotted me, and then Riccom and Sharp were turning around, adding their grins to Tris'. Most of the booths in the quiet corner were taken, which was usually the way it went. Our kind of people preferred keeping their conversations private even if they were only discussing the weather, a topic that wasn't often at the head of the list.

''Inky!'' Sharp exclaimed as soon as I was inside the silencing field and could hear her, the delight in her voice all too obvious. ''I knew you would make it, and I told these doubters so. Have you any idea how long it's been?''

''For me, it's been almost a year,'' I answered, sit-

ting down in the place Tris had moved from to make
for me. "How long has it been for you, Sharp?"

"You're not amusing," she stated while Tris and
Riccom chuckled, her pale, delicate face flushing faintly
with embarrassment. "I wasn't referring to the amount
of calendar time, and you know it. What I was trying
to say was that we missed you."

"And I missed you three," I admitted without hesitation, telling them nothing but the truth. "If all
you're after now is rekindling old friendships, I'm all
for it. If there happens to be an irresistible business
deal you're dying to include me in on, I think I'm late
for another appointment."

"Why do you have to be such a stinker?" Sharp
demanded in annoyance while the chuckling around us
changed to outright laughter. "Most people in the trade
would give up their vices for the chance to work with
us. Did you hear us asking you to give up even a small
vice?"

"I don't think she has any vices to give up," Tris
remarked, his green eyes studying me where I sat. Tris
was good looking in a smooth-featured way, and his
physical grace had been the cause of some problems
for him. When it came to enjoying himself he preferred doing it with females, but some people had difficulty accepting that. When Tris was propositioned
politely by the wrong gender, his refusal was just as
polite; if the suggestion then turned to insistence, Tris
reached for a knife.

"She certainly doesn't look like she has any vices,"
Ricco agreed with Tris, his blue eyes even more
amused than the other man's green ones. "Have you
ever seen such an innocent, open face, hair that black
in such a plain, unassuming style, black eyes so large
and guileless that you could trip and fall right into
them? I'll bet most places she still has to prove she's
old enough to drink."

I offered Riccom a wordless gesture that made all
three of them laugh, but it wasn't anything they hadn't
been expecting. They'd never let me forget the time
Ricco and I had gone together to make an assessment
of the possibility of approaching a target Seero had

been interested in. The point of entry to the target would have been through the posh bar next door, and Ricco and I had dressed to the eyebrows so they'd let us in. We'd made our entrance in a grand way, letting our attitudes say we didn't own the place only because we didn't go in for petty-cash investments, and the maitre d' guarding the entrance was very impressed. He inspected Ricco from light brown hair to broad shoulders to zilf-hide shoes, smiled faintly in total approval, then began to apologize. It took a minute for us to understand that the man was apologizing for the regrettable fact that they couldn't serve children in their establishment, and then Ricco had broken up. He'd laughed so hard we'd had to leave before we were thrown out, and I hadn't had to ask what was so funny. Since I was five months older than Ricco I *knew* what he found so funny, but I'd never been quite up to sharing the joke.

"I love talking about old times, don't you?" Sharp asked me with a wide grin still in place, one hand brushing at her reddish brown hair. She was a small woman but very rounded for her size, and looked even smaller sitting beside Ricco. "We used to have such fun together, Inky, but the fun doesn't have to stay in the past. If you come back to us, we can have the same all over again."

"We might have fun, but it would never be what we once had," I disagreed, deciding it was time we got the matter settled out loud. "You three worked with Seero for a couple of years, but I was raised by him. If he hadn't kept his word to my mother to look after me, I would have ended up in one of those orphan shelters after she died. He forced me to go to school, bribed me into learning something there by refusing to teach me anything *he* knew unless I got good grades, and always had the time to listen if there was something I needed to talk about. He was always *there* for me, Sharp, but when *he* needed *me*, all I could do was stand by and watch him die."

"You were there?" she asked, sharing her disturbance with the glances she sent Tris and Ricco, getting the same back from them. "We thought Seero was out alone that night. But Inky—his getting killed was an accident, something no one could have prevented. His line slipped, and even if you'd been right next to it you couldn't have . . .''

''His line didn't slip,'' I corrected flatly, watching her pale as her eyes flinched away from my gaze. I knew what I looked like when I thought or spoke about that night, and innocent was about as far from it as it's possible to get. I was about to go on when a buzz sounded, letting us know someone was entering our field, and then a harried waiter was beside the booth, putting a cup of javi on the table in front of me. If I'd wanted something to eat I would have used the booth menu to order it directly from the kitchen, but javi, unless refused when you first come in, is brought automatically to everyone. Our part of the crowd of regulars had developed that custom for the club, and it had slowly spread until everyone was doing the same. We all waited until the waiter was gone out of the field again, and then Ricco leaned forward.

''What do you mean, Seero's line didn't slip?'' he demanded, his big hands on the table's edge, his expression harsh with confusion. ''It was all over the news the next day, and the thuds read a statement about it. 'Death by misadventure during an attempted felony' was the way it was put, and that was after they'd investigated. Are you trying to say it was a cover-up?''

''I'm trying to say they weren't there,'' I answered, reaching for my cup of javi. Black was the way I drank it, as black as my hair, and preferably as strong as my resolve for revenge. ''Ricco, you and Sharp and Tris have a decision to make. I can tell you the whole story, or we can simply drink javi and reminisce about old times. If you decide on the story, I can't guarantee the safety of any of you.''

That time even Sharp didn't have anything immediate to say, and their three expressions were almost identical. In the life-niche we and others like us occupied, there was a great deal of truth to the proverb, ''Ignorance is bliss.'' Too often just knowing about something put you in line for erasure, and it made no

difference whether or not you intended using, selling
or even giving away the information. Knowing it meant
you *might* pass it on, and that was more of a chance
than the people involved were willing to take. It wasn't
considered polite to tell people things without first
warning them you were going to do it, so I'd given
the warning. What happened after that was entirely up
to them, and Tris was the first one to acknowledge it.

"I think I'd like to stay and hear about this," he
said after a minute, stirring where he sat to my left.
"Seero once did something for me I'll never forget,
and if there's a question on how he died, I want to
know about it. I can meet you two later, somewhere
else."

"The hell you can," Ricco said in a flat-voiced way,
leaning back in his seat opposite me as he looked at
Tris. "You aren't the only one Seero did things for,
which means I'm not in the mood for a walk. But it
also doesn't mean we *all* have to stay."

He and Tris turned to Sharp with that, telling her
they had no intentions of making any decisions for her,
and for an instant she didn't seem to know what Ricco
meant. Then she understood they were saying she
could leave, and she was suddenly made of indignation rather than flesh.

"Ricco, is your head as muscle-bound as your
body?" she demanded, bristling up like an inside-out
pincushion. "If you two think you owed Seero, you
ought to hear *my* story. I happen to know he didn't
even tell Inky, which means I owe him for that, too.
If anyone misses what she has to say, it isn't going to
be me."

"That's it, then," Ricco said with a shrug, moving
his eyes back to my vicinity. "We're all in and we're
all ears. Let's get a pot of javi ordered, and then we
can start."

"Let's start by *not* ordering a pot of javi," I said,
reaching over to catch his arm before he activated the
menu. "Seero once told me that most people know
they're opening a circuit through the silencing field
when they order, but think the circuit is dead once the
menu-acknowledge light goes out. All it really means

is that the light is out, not that the circuit is closed. Let's let that waiter bring us refills when he manages to get around to it.''

"You think the thuds could have this place tapped?'' Tris asked with a frown, exchanging glances with Ricco. "Even if they *were* covering something up when they called Seero's death accidental, how could they get in here? And after all this time, why would they bother?''

"It isn't the police we have to worry about,'' I answered, speaking to all of them. "It's the Twilight Houses that are involved, and they can get in anywhere. Are you still sure you want to hear about it?''

"More than ever,'' Sharp said as she rested her forearms on the table, nothing left of the empty-headed high-lifer she enjoyed pretending to be. "If the thuds put Seero out of the way, I could understand it even while hating it. The Twi Houses are another matter entirely.''

Ricco nodded his agreement while Tris simply sat and waited, so I shrugged and shifted sideways on the seat.

"As we've already noticed, this was almost a year ago,'' I began, toying with my cup as my mind went back to that soul-tearing night. "Seero had intended going out alone, but when I showed up with nothing of my own scheduled, he invited me along. The stroke was set up as a solo and that's the way he intended keeping it, but he didn't mind the idea of having company on the ride back. He also intended having something to show off, and you know how he enjoyed showing off.''

They all smiled faintly at the reminder, also remembering how we used to tease him about it, but no one interrupted.

"The location of the stroke was in one of those open high-rise enclaves that pretend to be closed, the kind that keeps out no one but the innocent people who live there,'' I continued. "For anyone with a little skill there are a dozen private ways in, and Seero took one of them. He intended using the top of the north tower to reach one of the penthouses in the south, so as soon as he left I found a way into the west tower. I wanted to watch him without being in the way, you understand, which I might have been if I'd gone up with him to the north.

"By the time I reached the roof of the west tower, he'd already set his line onto the balcony wall of his target apartment," I said, raising my cup to sip from it. "A minute later he was moving up the line by shifting his coasters an armspan at a time, making it look as easy as he always did. Going back it would be downhill, of course, and he'd simply hold on and let gravity do all the work. He reached the balcony, dropped down to it after locking the coasters in place on the line, then went to half-kneel in front of the balcony doors. He already knew what sort of a lock was on them, and even Mal could have gotten it open without a key."

That time they chuckled, knowing how badly Mal did with *anything* that had a lock. If anyone was ever born to be honest Mal was it, a point finally brought home to him the time he'd lost his key ring. After finding it impossible to get into his jump-around he'd had to walk home, and then had discovered that we, who were his neighbors and who kept a spare set of his keys, were out. He'd decided then and there that he'd be damned if he'd simply sit down and wait until we got back, so he began trying to pick the lock on his door.

By the time Tris and I got back there he'd apparently been at it for hours, and had reached the point where he wouldn't have used a key even if he'd had to spend the rest of his life out in that hall. It was do or die with no other acceptable options, and Tris and I were trying to decide whether or not to mention something rather important to him when Ricco showed up. Ricco, having no idea about what was going on immediately congratulated Mal, and when Mal looked up at him blankly, Ricco reached over and opened the door with a simple turn of the knob. At some point or other Mal had managed to pick the lock, but the tragedy of it was Mal hadn't *noticed*. It took quite a while before we were able to get Mal to stop crying, but once he was back to normal his mind had been made up. He still considered himself one of us, but he never tried breaking into anything again.

"I watched Seero fade through the balcony doors, and automatically checked the time," I went on with a sigh, wondering if Mal knew how really fortunate he was. "Seero's maximum time on a stroke never went beyond nine minutes, no matter what he had to leave behind. Better to get out and come back some other time, he always said, rather than stay that extra minute or two and maybe lose all your some-other-times together. At any rate I knew it wouldn't be long before he was out again, but it turned out to be a lot less than not very long. It couldn't even have been a minute before he reappeared, and he immediately tried jumping for the coasters."

"Without stopping to relock the balcony doors?" Sharp asked with shock in her voice. "I can't believe Seero would overlook anything that important."

"He didn't overlook it," I said, answering the question for all of them. "He didn't stop because they were right behind him, too close, as it turned out, for him to get the coasters moving before they were on top of him. They had hand weapons out and ready, so all he could do was drop back down to the terrace."

"But he wasn't supposed to have been killed with a hand weapon," Ricco pointed out, his expression strange. "Did the thuds cover up that part of it?"

"They didn't use the weapons, they just covered him with them," I said with a headshake. "At first it was only the two heavies who stopped him, and I was sure they were private security, which would have meant Seero was caught. Then three men and a woman stepped out on the balcony, four faces I recognized instantly in the light coming from inside, and I began to think everything would be all right. I knew for a fact that Seero had done strokes for at least two of them, and they would therefore understand he could be counted on to keep quiet about whatever he'd seen or heard. One of the men spoke to Seero with an amused smile on his face, turned and said something to the others, then gestured away the two heavies with the hand weapons. From where I stood, it looked like Seero had been told he was free to go.''

When I paused to swallow at my javi, none of them jumped in with prompts or questions or comments. They knew what was coming, and although they had already decided to listen, they were in no hurry to hear it.

''I watched Seero go back to his line with what seemed to be reluctance, and couldn't understand why he wasn't acting as relieved as I felt,'' I continued beyond the pause. ''After thinking about it I've decided he knew what was coming, which is another thing those four will regret. Seero jumped for the coasters, had them unlocked in a moment, then slid away from the balcony. He was about halfway across when one of the heavies reached up to the line anchor with something too small for me to see, but which must have been made of plastic. It broke the holding field that kept the anchor firmly attached to the wall, and suddenly Seero wasn't sliding down the line, he and the line were falling toward the inner face of the north tower. He tried absorbing most of the shock of contact with his legs, but the angle of descent was too steep and he was moving too fast. He slammed into the building between two terraces, the impact so hard I could hear it, and then he was gone from the line and falling toward the ground so many stories below. When I looked back to the terrace, the four and their heavies had already disappeared.''

By then I was staring down into my javi cup, wishing it held something a lot stronger than javi, feeling the new silence that surrounded me. All the expectation from earlier had disappeared, leaving behind a limping, wordless plea for some sort of explanation.

''I don't understand,'' Tris said after the gap had grown almost awkward, his voice filled with confusion. ''If they knew Seero and didn't even have a completed stroke to complain about, why did they wipe him? And how did he end up in a Twi House meeting place to begin with? He was always so careful about checking a layout before going in.''

''They must have been discussing something they

considered more important than Seero's life," I answered, looking up to see the way all three of them stared at me. "They could have decided to depend on his silence the way they had in the past, but chose instead not to bother. As for how Seero ended up in the middle of a meeting between the heads of four Houses who never in the past got together on *anything*, that one is easy. He was set up."

"Is that a guess, or do you know it for certain?" Sharp asked, her voice very soft in contrast to the look in her eyes. "If it's confirmed, give us a name."

"I didn't have to guess," I said, running a finger around the rim of my cup without looking down. "On the way to the stroke Seero told me who had put him onto the target, and the idea made him chuckle. The man who considered himself Seero's greatest rival had worked for months digging out the location of this shady political bigshot's city address, had confirmed what artwork and other valuables the apartment held by visiting it as a repairman or some such, and had only been waiting for the bigshot to be out of town. As soon as that happened he started getting ready to go—and while he was moving around managed to slip and fall because of a small pool of salad oil that had been spilled by his roommate on their kitchen floor. He ended up with a very painful sprained ankle, which meant he needed someone he could trust to take over for him. He'd hated the idea of calling Seero, but Seero was the only one he knew who could be relied on to play it straight."

"And the reason he didn't simply wait until he was healed, and then go ahead *without* a reluctantly-taken partner?" Tris asked, filling in the line as he and the others knew it must have gone. They weren't wrong, and my nod acknowledged that fact.

"The bigshot had sold the apartment, and would be moving his things to an in-city estate as soon as he got back," I supplied. "If the stroke didn't come off right then, all those months of work would be worse than wasted. Better half the rake than losing it all."

"And Seero believed him," Sharp stated, her dark eyes furious. "Just as we all would have, because of the one bit of truth he used: Seero *was* the only one among us who could be counted on to play it straight. There was no way *anyone* would have thought it was a trap.''

"The slig must have found out about the Twi meeting while he was sniffing around," Tris said, coming to the same conclusion I had. "There's never been even a whisper about a connection between that politico and the Houses, so the slig must have counted on their wiping Seero to keep *that* quiet, if for nothing else. They must be into him below his underwear if they used his apartment for their high-level hush-hush. Seero never had a chance, not with the kind of heavies they use to keep those meetings private. Give us the name of that slig, Inky. We want to pay him a visit and tell him how much we admire his planning ability.''

"I don't think we *can* pay him a visit," Ricco said, the first words he'd spoken in a while, his light eyes directly on me. "It was Tardin who did that to Seero, wasn't it, Inky? Tardin the slime, who could never forgive Seero for being better than him. Am I wrong?''

"No, you aren't wrong, Ricco," I allowed, feeling myself smile for the first time since that conversation had started. "Tardin was the one who set Seero up, but I don't think he'll ever be doing something like that again, do you?''

"Tardin was convicted of those murders!" Sharp said with a hiss of shock, her stare now on the wide-eyed side. "It made all the news progs, and more than half the editorial slots! Everyone wanted the courts to forget the law and sentence him to a lifetime of torture instead of simple execution. The evidence against him was so overwhelming, not even his court-appointed lawyer believed him when he screamed he was innocent.''

"That was because of how sickening the crime was," Tris said, giving me the same sort of thoughtful look Ricco had been maintaining for the last couple of minutes. "When the victims are children it's bad enough, but when they're also physically handicapped children who have managed to win outstanding awards despite their handicap— And when they aren't simply killed, but put through what the autopsies showed— It was all they could do to find thuds to guard him. Most of them wanted to join everyone else and tear him apart.''

"And all those of us who knew him wondered was how he'd kept that much twisting from showing sooner," Ricco said, closing the circle he'd opened. "I don't think it would bother any of us to find out he was framed, Inky, but what about the one who really is guilty? With Tardin tagged for the thing, they stopped looking for anyone else."

"Why look for a dead man?" I asked, letting my smile broaden. "One of the earlier victims had a relative none of the news progs found out about, a half-brother who had loved the little girl very much. The half-brother had a lot of friends and acquaintances, and I don't think I have to tell you what it's possible to pick up when almost everyone on the street is watching and listening for you. Seero had introduced me to him a few years ago, so when it was time to take a good look around a certain apartment, I was the one he asked to do it. Finding those grisly trophies the slime had kept wasn't hard, but once they'd served the purpose of telling us we'd located the right sicko, no one had any more use for them. My acquaintance took charge of the sicko, and when I explained why I wanted the trophies, he thought my taking them was a good idea. It even turned out that one of his friends was the woman who cleaned Tardin's apartment, the very woman who accidentally found all that horror and immediately called the police."

"Finding Tardin's name on the membership list of that group of fanatics who want all handicapped newborns put to sleep really sealed the lid on it," Ricco said, a grin finally breaking through on his face. "Was he really a member, or did your acquaintance have another friend?"

"That time it was a friend of *mine*," I answered, watching Tris and Sharp stir where they sat, as though waking from a daydream. "She owed Seero a lot more than one, and computer files will whistle the latest hit if she asks them to. Getting them to accept Tardin's name as a long-time member of that group took about ten minutes.''

''No wonder you kept refusing to work with us,'' Sharp said, satisfied acceptance in her voice. ''You were too busy doing things that really needed doing. But now that it's just about over, you shouldn't be busy any longer. Tardin's appeal was denied last week, which means his execution is set for the forty day minimum. Why don't we all celebrate by pulling off a really spectacular stroke?''

''That would be a good idea except for one thing,'' I said, quickly interrupting the agreement coming from Tris and Ricco. ''I won't be ready to celebrate until there isn't even a foundation left of four certain Houses. Tardin may have been the one who set Seero up for wiping, but he wasn't the one who actually did the job. Until that happens, I expect to have quite a lot to do that's best done alone.''

''You don't mean you're taking on four of the Twilight Houses!'' Tris said in almost the same hiss Sharp had used earlier, his expression full of outrage. ''Inky, that's crazy! I can understand refusing to take commissions from them, or maybe even cheering on the thuds, but actively working against them? They'll wipe you the same way they did Seero, and you won't ever be able to say you didn't ask for it! If Seero was still around, he'd be the first to tell you to forget it.''

''If Seero was still around, there'd be nothing to forget,'' I pointed out, raising my cup to finish the last of the javi. ''I only told you three about this so you'd know why it isn't smart associating with me. I haven't been sitting around with my feet up for the past few months, and although I've been careful not to be sloppy, it's only a matter of time before they find out who's been stroking them. When that happens, you don't want to confuse them by standing next to their target. They usually settle confusions like that by taking out everyone in sight.''

''They seem to have a thing about playing it on the safe side,'' Sharp agreed with familiar dryness, but there was more frustration behind the words than amusement. "Damn it, Inky, all you'll do is get yourself killed, and no one will be able to help you! Do you expect us to just sit back and let it happen?"

"The only way you can stop me is by tipping the Houses," I said, taking a deep breath before making the effort to shake off the gloom that had grabbed me again. "If you decide to do that, hold out for as much as you think the information should be worth, but stay out of reach both before and after you collect. They're already feeling the pinch, and I'm told they're not in a very good mood."

"Told by who?" Ricco asked, as annoyed as Sharp and Tris by the suggestion I'd made. "I can believe you've been stroking them, and I believe they don't know who's doing it. Seero always said you were the best he ever taught, and if you ask me you're even better than that. You're also not suicidal, so I'm willing to bet you're not doing this alone. Who do you have who's telling you about their mood, and what are they doing with the rake from your strokes?"

"I don't think you really need to know that," I said as I looked around at the three with a friendly smile. Sharp and Tris were startled by the guess Ricco had made, but he always had been the swiftest on the uptake. "Let's just say I've found the perfect place to drop what I come across, and it's possible I may even be around to some day celebrate cracked foundations. I'm not counting on the possibility very heavily, but it could happen. And now I really do have another appointment."

"Was this your way of saying good-bye to us?" Tris demanded as I began getting ready to leave the booth, his tone almost harsh. "You don't want us getting killed along with you, so you took some time out to cut the ties? That was really thoughtful of you, Inky, but what if one or two of us don't *want* to say good-bye? What if we're willing to take our own chances with getting killed?"

"I'm sorry, Tris, but this is *my* way of getting killed," I said with a glance around, trying not to laugh. "If you or Ricco or Sharp decide you're interested, you'll have to find your own way. You know how I've always hated sharing things.''

I put my left hand on his arm to keep him from saying any more, then reached my right hand toward Sharp and Ricco. Both of them took it, Sharp with tears in her eyes, Ricco almost as broken up as Tris, but I refused to let any of their sadness touch me.

''I'll say this as plainly as I can, so I won't ever have to repeat it: stay out of the argument!'' I told them, looking at each of them in turn, starting with Tris and ending with Ricco. ''I've got *myself* covered to a certain extent, but the coverage isn't enough for four. I'd hate to make it through all this, only to find that one or more of you three didn't. And don't forget, if one of you trips, you might take me down right along with you. If for no other reason, will you let *that* make you back off and forget all about it?''

Once again I let my eyes touch each of them, and despite their reluctance they didn't refuse me the nods of agreement I'd asked for. They'd given me their words to stay out of it, but Tris felt it necessary to add one last comment as I freed my hands and stood.

''If you ever change your mind about wanting company, you know where you can find us,'' he said, then gave me a smile that was trying very hard to become a grin. ''Don't forget how bad I am at thinking of my own ways to get killed.''

There was nothing to do but laugh at that, and then wave once before turning and walking away. Tris was most probably feeling the short time we'd lived together, but he'd get over it and then he'd be fine. I'd made sure they would all be fine, but that was something else they didn't need to know about. When the Houses finally found out I was the one stroking them, not knowing where I was would be no protection at all for people who were named as friends of mine. What I'd arranged *would* be protection, but they definitely would not have enjoyed hearing about it.

On the way out I said good-bye to Mal without giving him the chance to press me as to when I'd be back, then left to keep an appointment which centered about the delivery of an envelope.

Chapter 2

My new associates had very little imagination, which meant they insisted on my meeting them in their own offices. It might have been true that none of their people could have betrayed them even if they'd wanted to, but that didn't make me any happier about becoming a familiar figure to the workers on all four of their shifts. I was used to having no one or almost no one know what I was into; Stellar Intelligence didn't believe in running it the same. As far as they're concerned, if everyone around you doesn't know what you're doing, you probably shouldn't be doing it. Needless to say, the difference of opinion made our association even more pleasant than it would normally have been.

I left my jump-around parked in a street-level square a couple of blocks from my destination, preferring to lose it among the various vehicles of neighborhood night-shift workers over sitting it down all alone in plain sight in front of the building where the offices were. It wasn't exactly common knowledge that the Empire offices building also housed Stellar Intelligence, but among those who did know, very few cared. S.I. was a branch of the Empire administration that supposedly concerned itself with nothing less than things like treason on a planetary scale, and that, of course, made it nothing to worry about to anyone who wasn't plotting the overthrow of the Empire. I'd found out differently one night, and the revelation had modified my plans in an interesting way—if you consider that sort of thing interesting.

The Empire building was as brightly lit and as full of people going in and out as it always was, which means I accessed their underground parking area through a service conduit that bypassed their security system, then made my way to the upper floors from there. My getting into the building like that was more of a game than a necessity, especially since S.I. hadn't yet gotten around to finding the route. The other end of the conduit was supposed to be completely inaccessible, and they still believed that; for people who shouldn't have believed anything they hadn't checked personally, it was sad to see how trusting they were. It was also one of the reasons I wasn't precisely thrilled to be working with them, but they were definitely the lesser choice between evils.

The lift took me up to the fifty-fourth floor, and when the doors opened I stepped out to see the transparent wall on my left that told me I'd found the offices of the Empire Messenger Corps. Beyond the wall was a rather unplush reception area which contained a brittly-pretty girl behind a desk polishing her nails, and a bored-looking man in the blinding-red uniform of the Messenger Corps leaning against the wall not far from her. When the lift doors closed behind me the girl stopped polishing and the man stopped looking bored, but neither one tried to say anything until I'd pushed through the entrance panel in the transparent wall. At that point, the girl grinned wide.

"Raksall's expecting you, so you can go right in," she said, sounding nothing like what her looks would lead someone to expect. "And by the way, thanks for earning me a little extra cash. Again."

She made no real effort to look at the man in the red uniform, but she didn't have to. Her final word had let him know he was being laughed at, and his expression said he wasn't enjoying the experience.

"It's not a joke," he said in a near growl, his dark eyes sending accusation in my direction rather than toward his partner in disguise. "If *she's* getting into the building in a way we don't know about, there can be others doing the same thing. Betting on whether or not she makes it through without getting caught isn't as good an idea as trying to find out how she does it."

"Our current assignment doesn't call for finding things out," the woman said, her grin still in place as she swiveled her chair to turn her in the man's direction. "And if you think betting is such a bad idea, why wasn't I the only one doing it?"

The man looked down at her without answering the question, but also without visible enjoyment of the ankle-length, veed-to-the-waist work dress the woman was wearing. She had no trouble at all filling out the standard red and white dress, but men seem to lose interest in such things when their pride—or wallets—have been brutalized.

"Is Raksall in her office?" I asked, more to change the subject than because I wasn't sure. "I'm still a little early."

"She expected you to be late instead, but she came in on time," the woman told me, and then her expression went solemn. "It may be the next thing to immorality to mention it, but I think *she* earned some extra cash, too."

The man came away from the wall with his fists to his hips at that, and even though I was no longer the target for his killing stare, I still headed on back to the offices beyond the corridor leading out of the reception area. S.I. people seemed to be much freer souls than I'd expected them to be, but I wasn't involved with them to make friends. We had a joint business venture going, they and I, and in that area things weren't doing badly.

There were as many people hurrying around the inner S.I. office as the rest of the building suffered from, all because of the need of the place to be fully staffed at all times. When you have to deal with information and requests coming in from hundreds of planets and going out to the same number, you run every minute of the local day and night or you don't run at all. I usually preferred night hours because of how much more peaceful they were than the daytime, but in that place it was like middle of the morning any time you got there. I ignored the bustle as best I could, made my way across the floor to the office I wanted, and simply walked in.

Raksall looked up at the sound of the door opening, her transparent desk showing all of the stylish orange and brown business suit she wore. The legs of the pants were so full they even looked like a full-length skirt while she was sitting down, and the tight-waisted jacket was more frilly-lace-concealing than straight-line form-revealing. Using lace instead of body lines was the very newest rage in fashion, and it surprised me not at all that Raksall was already wearing it.

"Well, well, early instead of late," my S.I. contact said with an amused look, leaning back in her chair while I closed the door behind me. "With everything you had on your schedule tonight, I thought it would be the other way around."

"I have a feeling you thought it would be the other way around because of the number of guards stationed all over the building," I came back, walking forward to my usual chair and then sitting in it. "They were trying to spot me coming in, but somehow they missed."

"I've learned there's nothing of the 'somehow' about it when people miss seeing you," she said, her stronger amusement now showing in a grin. "If we hadn't had Fieran's luck, we wouldn't have stumbled over you the first time. I hope it went just as successfully earlier tonight."

"They're not quite as clever as they think they are," I said with a smile of my own, reaching down to the wide black shimmer-belt I wore above my semi-skirt. "If you don't have a pair of gloves, I recommend leaving the thing in the belt until you can get a lab to check it for you. They had it in a safe spot, but I have the distinct feeling they decided to play it double safe. If unprotected skin touches that envelope, I'd rather not be around to see what the results are."

"That means they're beginning to try doing something about you," she said, her grin gone as she reached across the desk to take the belt. "What you've gotten from them over the last few months hasn't been used against them yet, so they must think that ridding themselves of you will make sure it never is. I'd say it's time you let up on them for a while."

"And I say if I let up on them, what I've done so far will be wasted effort," I countered, watching how carefully she handled the belt. "You're the one who told *me* how straight-line all this evidence has to be, how an Empire court will accept it if there aren't any carefully timed gaps in the gathering of it. You said if we can prove these Houses are constantly and consistently involved in large-scale illegalities rather than occasionally dabbling over the line of the law, the Empire court will accept jurisdiction as the only certifiably unbiased source of justice for the people. We both know their bought bodies on this world won't even let them be accused here let alone convicted, and the chance of throwing them to an Empire court was the only reason I agreed to work with you people. If you try backing out now . . ."

"I'm not trying to back out of the deal," she interrupted in annoyance, the look in her brown eyes half impatient and half concerned. "I promised we'd break those Houses for you if you helped us get the evidence we need, and that promise stands. I'd just like to know how well you'll uphold *your* end of the bargain if you get yourself killed. None of our own people ever managed a fraction of what you have in locating the sort of damaging proof we can't go ahead without. If the enemy succeeds in stopping you, where does that leave our effort?"

"Before the question becomes relevant, they have to succeed in stopping me," I answered, working hard to control the furious anger that had suddenly risen inside me. "You told me stolen evidence is just as good in an Empire court as whatever is gotten on a warrant, as long as it's documented as true and isn't unreasonably out of date. If I back off now, you know we'll have a gap, and that gap could get them off. If this is how dedicated you law-and-order types are, I would have been better off going with my original idea."

"Your original idea was to use the other Twilight Houses to destroy the four you're after," she said with

a brusque gesture of dismissal, still annoyed. "You
may or may not have succeeded in that, but when you
came to this building to see if the Empire had any file
information you could take for the other Houses to
use, you walked into one of *our* security areas. We
had to use a Question Beam to find out what you were
after, but once we did, didn't we agree to drop all
charges against you? Didn't we decide together it
would be better to eradicate those Houses completely,
rather than simply helping the other Houses to absorb
them?"

"Is that what we 'decided together'?" I asked,
making a rude face as I leaned back in my chair. "I
thought what we decided was that I'd be better off
getting evidence for your group, instead of vegetating
in a heavy detention center while those four Houses
went blithely on the way they *had* been going. If I'd
known you scared this easy, I would have opted for
the heavy detention."

"Since I'm not the one whose life is on the line,
scared doesn't enter into it much, does it?" she countered, ignoring what I'd said about how I'd been co-
erced into the partnership. "And I'm not trying to tell
you to back off for good. I want these people as badly
as you do, but throwing away the life of the only one
able to get me my evidence doesn't make much sense.
What you picked up for us four days ago from the
Larcher House was a coded list of scheduled ventures
involving drugs, prostitution, soul-selling, air smug-
gling, puppet-stringing—at least a third of everything
they're into. Since we've got to take the time to doc-
ument that stellium-mine of a list, there won't be anything of a gap showing in our evidence trail. And don't
forget what you got for us tonight. If that works out
the way I expect it to, what's in that envelope will
give the Empire court no choice but to step in. When
politicians *that* big are owned by a House, trying to
find an unbiased planetary court is an exercise in fu-
tility."

"All of which is a reason for you people to sit back
a while, but doesn't in any way apply to me," I said,
refusing to buy the wiggler oil she was so good at

selling. "That list you're so hot about involves only one of the Houses, which leaves three more for me to go after while you're playing with the first. In case you've forgotten, it's all four I want, not just a token one or two."

"But you can't get all four if one of them gets you first," she said through her teeth, her fist clenched and her short blond hair almost bristling. "If you leave them alone for a while they'll *have* to dismantle their traps, or take the chance of losing one of their own, with legitimate business, to something meant to get *you*. Can't you under—"

Her little speech of useless repetition probably would have gone on until she ran out of breath, but she was interrupted by something other than my impatience. A single knock came at the door, and I turned in time to see a man walking in. He was of average height and build, wearing the tight trousers, tight-waisted jacket, and severely cut shirt that was the masculine equivalent of Raksall's outfit, but his was a conservative yellow and tan. He had brown hair and eyes and a narrow, humorless face, was carrying a file of some sort, and I'd seen him once or twice during my previous visits to those offices.

"I'm sorry, Filster, but we're in the middle of an important discussion here," Raksall said to the man, making an obvious effort not to be too short with him. "I'll let you know as soon as I'm through, and . . ."

"This can't wait until you're through," the man Filster said, coming forward after having closed the door behind himself. "When you're through, the girl will disappear the way she always does, and I need her here for this."

"For what?" Raksall demanded, letting the river of annoyance inside her wash over the man who was pulling up a chair to *her* side of the desk. "She isn't an operative who shifts from one department to the next and therefore needs to know everything going on everywhere. She has a limited association with *my* department, so what could you possibly have that concerns her?"

"I have a Situation," the man answered, the word

so clearly capitalized that his glance at Raksall was unnecessary. "I queried the main files in search of someone to suit my needs, but rather than offering me a choice of our own operatives, I was given the suggestion of that girl. After considering the matter, I was forced to agree with the decision."

His narrow-faced sourness showed how unhappy he was over being forced into whatever it was he was talking about, but I wasn't in the least curious as to what that could be. I'd already done what I'd come to that place to do, and wasting any more time there would have been—a waste of time.

"I think I'll be going now," I said to Raksall as I got out of my chair. "From what you said I'm assuming you and your people will be too busy for a while to come up with any target assignments, so I'll take care of finding my own. If I happen across anything interesting, I'll be sure to let you know."

"Just a moment, young woman!" the man Filster said in a very stern way as I turned toward the door, interrupting whatever Raksall had been about to come up with. "You and I have a matter to discuss, which means you're to sit back down and listen to me. I didn't come in here just to watch you walk away."

"I don't much give a damn *what* you came in here to do," I told the disapproving frown I was getting, liking the man as much as he obviously liked me. "You and I don't have anything to discuss on any subject I can think of, and I really would prefer keeping it that way. Have a nice evening."

"How about your four friends?" he countered at once as I began turning away from him again, his tone unpleasantly triumphant. "*My* department is the one responsible for assigning operatives to make sure the Twilight Houses don't try to use them in an effort to locate you. I've had no trouble finding enough people to assign up until now, but with a Situation demanding all the attention and manpower I can give it . . ."

He let the sentence trail off without finishing it, and when I looked at him his smug expression was all but pure enjoyment. They really did enjoy threatening without using the words, those people, and I was beginning to dislike the habit more than I'd thought was possible.

"Part of my agreement with your group covers the protection of the four people my efforts put in the most danger," I said, speaking primarily to a Raksall who was mostly mad but partly upset. "If that aspect of the deal falls through, so does the rest of it. You may need me to get the Twi Houses, but I can do my own getting with people who don't have your problems. Would you like to tell me which way you want it?"

"We want it *our* way," Filster said with narrow-faced aggressiveness before Raksall could answer me, a gleam of satisfaction still inexplicably in his eyes. "If you don't do your getting with us, you won't do it at all, especially not from the cell of a heavy detention center. You are a *thief*, young miss, and we have enough evidence against you in your dossier to keep you in a cell until long past the time the designation 'young' is no longer appropriate. What will happen to your friends during that time, I have no idea. If you aren't identified as the one who robbed the Houses, they may well survive without any sort of difficulty."

Or they may not, his tone suggested, the man ignoring the way I straightened where I stood. He seemed to know as well as I that if the Houses found out I was the one who had been stroking them, also learning where I was would not keep my closest friends safe. There was still what I'd taken to sustain interest in my background, and until they had that back no one I'd known would be safe.

"Inky, a department with a Situation has priority over all other departments until the Situation is being handled," Raksall got out with difficulty, her intention probably to smooth things over despite her own raging anger. "If you discuss the matter with Filster and can prove to him you can't be of any help, he'll just have to look elsewhere. Let's listen to what he has to say, and afterward you and I can talk for a minute or two."

And get things back to where they were, she didn't

bother adding, at least not aloud. At that point I had lost my appetite for dealing with any of them, and if it hadn't been for Tris, Sharp, Ricco and Mal, I would have walked out of there and let them *try* to catch me. But I did have my friends to consider, so I went back to the chair and sat.

"Your wisdom is exceeded only by your graciousness, young miss," Filster said when I crossed my legs, his tone as dry as abrasive powder. "Despite your obvious opinions to the contrary, I'm not enjoying this any more than you are. With that glowering expression you're now wearing, you look more than ever like the innocent child you most certainly are not."

"If all you came in here to do was insult her, Filster, you can just get out again," Raksall said with a hard look in her eyes, her voice thick with the anger she was feeling. "And however this turns out, don't think for a minute that I won't be reporting you. Even having a Situation is no excuse for ruining another department's dealings with essential associates."

"For all the control you have over her, even 'associate' is too binding a descriptive word," the man came back with complete unconcern, paying more attention to his papers than to his co-worker. "You can report me as much as you like, as long as you're ready to tell the same board why so essential an 'associate' of yours does as she damned well pleases. And would either of you mind if we got on with this now?"

He finally raised his dark eyes to look at each of us in turn, but not even Raksall had anything else to say. She made herself more comfortable in her chair with her fingers laced together in front of her, and the look in her eyes that promised the man more argument to come at a later, better time didn't bother him in the least.

"About five standard years ago, the planet Joelare announced the opening of its new vacation continent, and within a year it was on the 'must' list of three-quarters of the people in the Empire," Filster said, keeping his eyes on me even as he lectured. "The planet has an anomaly area that does cover just about an entire continent, an area of perpetual fog, and the section was considered a waste of good world-space until someone came up with the idea of turning it into a tourist attraction. They had a hell of a time doing the necessary building and developing, but when it was finally completed they had the Mists of the Ages.''

He paused then, as though expecting Raksall or me to comment, and when we didn't he smiled faintly.

"What are the Mists of the Ages, you ask?" he said in the lightest tone he'd used yet. "I thought everyone already knew about them, but since you don't, I'll explain. Towns, villages, and even cities were built in the fog, each area depicting a different historical period from the past of dozens of the worlds of the Empire. No one really *knows* yet why so many human and humanoid-populated worlds arose independently to eventually reach the stars and become the core-worlds of the Empire, but that doesn't mean people aren't interested in what other people lived through before they reached contact capabilities. Joelare hasn't been settled long enough to have picturesque historical eras of its own, so it used everyone else's. With tours ranging from basic to aristocratic, everyone chooses what he or she can afford, and everyone has a fabulous time.

"Or so claim the press releases," Filster went on, impatient disapproval suddenly back in his voice. "Approximately six standard months ago, odd reports began being filed. People who were supposed to have been on the tours were reported missing by friends or relatives, but a couple of days later the reports were canceled. The missing people weren't really missing, they'd only been enjoying themselves so much they'd extended their tours beyond their original intentions. Some of the reports, however, weren't canceled; the missing people really were missing, and eventually turned up dead. They'd wandered off on their own into areas which were restricted because of dangerous conditions and had had accidents that turned out fatal. What was left of each body was returned to its home world, and then *those* reports were officially closed.''

"I'm not seeing what you consider so odd," Raksall said to the man, interest rather than criticism narrowing her eyes. "People *do* enjoy themselves so much they extend their vacations, and people do die when they wander into places they shouldn't be. All natural-habitat resorts have restricted areas; that's why you sign a release when you vacation in spots like that. If you're properly warned and the restricted areas are clearly marked, your getting killed doesn't entitle your estate to sue."

"Everything you say is absolutely correct, but you haven't seen the reports," Filster answered with a shake of his head. "The computers considered them all together, did a little records checking, then kicked the matter out with gongs clanging and blazing red Situation flags flying. Thirty of the canceled missing persons reports stated that the people involved couldn't possibly have simply stayed past their intended time; they had previous, very important commitments, and weren't the sort to forget those commitments. When it turned out they *had* only stayed a little longer, the ones who had filed the reports were bewildered. The objects of their concern had laughed off the entire matter, and none of the thirty showed even the faintest regret for what they'd done. That was the point the computers checked the cash and credit accounts of those thirty and the other 'missing' vacationers for the additional payments they should have had to make to Joelare for their extended stays, and then the alarms went off."

"The payments hadn't been made?" Raksall guessed, her brows higher than they had been. "That would make even an adding machine suspicious."

"Which is probably why most of the additional payments *had* been made," Filster said, grudging respect only very faintly coloring his continuing disapproval. "Where there were no funds or available credit to meet the payments, suits had been filed against the defaulting parties. All nice and proper and legal, except for two things: the suits were in perpetual continuance despite the fact that not even token payments had been made, and most of those who *had* paid hadn't really been in a position to *take* those extra days. They'd strapped themselves badly by doing it, and were right then working their backsides off trying to make up the losses.''

''I'd hate to be the computer who had to specify a Situation like that,'' Raksall said, one finger to her lips as her mind raced behind distracted eyes. ''Is there something in the mists on Joelare that causes reliable people to become uncaring spendthrifts, and if so, do the friendly natives running the show know about it? If they *don't* know about it, why aren't they pressing for payment from everyone? If they do know about it, are they taking advantage of an existing situation, or causing the situation to begin with? If the reaction is a natural phenomenon, why aren't more people suffering from it? And as a temporary last, how, if in any way at all, do the dead bodies fit in?''

''A neat summation as to why we have a Situation,'' Filster said to her, his attitude indicating anyone in Raksall's position would have been expected to do the same. ''There are people being hurt and taken advantage of *somehow*, but we don't yet know who is innocent and who isn't. It's also been pointed out that the number of people actually reported as missing is guaranteed to be a lot less than the grand total in that category. Some planetary authorities operate under the absurd conviction that people who never deviate from schedule even once in their lives, can't be considered missing until a prechosen amount of time has passed. Places like that would have nothing in the way of reports filed.''

''So the questions asked need immediate answers, and then we'll know what we're dealing with,'' Raksall said with a slow nod. ''If it turns out the people of Joelare decided to help hurry the return on their investment by convincing certain people to stay longer and therefore spend more money, our branch of the Service won't be involved any longer. What we need to do is get those answers.''

''Which is the reason I'm in *your* office now instead of my own,'' Filster said, back to looking at me rather than Raksall. ''We need someone to go in there who will not only not arouse any suspicion, but who also has the ability to check records and files that are out of easy reach. Mists of the Ages is run from a central location situated itself in the mist, which means the very finding of it won't be a matter of checking the address and then walking in. Our computer tells me your—associate—over there has a definite talent for finding things, so she's the one I want."

By that time Raksall was sharing in the stare directed at me, and I didn't need to hear her saying anything to remember the "we" she'd used with Filster. After hearing his problem, she was no longer blaming him for barging in on us and was also no longer inviting him to look elsewhere for help. I'd somehow had the feeling things would work out like that, but they and the computer who had suggested me all had equally randomized circuits.

"Anyone with a little intelligence can be expected to find things," I said after a decent pause, making it seem as though I'd considered his request. "What isn't quite as reasonable is hauling someone off the streets and expecting them to be able to do the sort of job you people are trained for. Not only wouldn't I know where to begin, I wouldn't even know when to look unsuspicious. They'd have me spotted five minutes after I got there, and that would be the end of my playing snoop. My talent is in extracting things from places people have them hidden, not inserting myself in places people don't want me to be."

"Your talent is in stealing," Filster contradicted with no change of expression, his dark eyes still directly on me. "You specialize in preying on those who have managed to acquire possessions of worth, and haven't enough social conscience to feel shame over such a thing no matter how badly your victims are hurt by it. I despise parasites like you and your sort, who live well themselves by causing misery for others. If I had any choice in the matter I'd see you all in heavy detention, but instead of that I'm forced to work with you. I need information stolen from a place others can't get near, and for that you are *exactly* right. If you refuse to do it, the trash you call friends will be en-

tirely on their own, just as they really deserve to be.
Make your decision now, and make it fast.''

If I'd been in the habit of showing enemies how I
felt, I probably would have shivered from the pure
hate and disgust coming at me. The man's eyes were
all but glowing with it, and I couldn't ever remember
feeling so sick. People won't understand, Seero had
always told me, sometimes not even if you explain.
Don't waste your time, little Inky, just let them go on
believing as they like. It won't change what we're doing, it will just make it a little harder. Filster made it
harder, all right, but not just a little.

''Inky, if you think about it, you'll find this is all
probably for the best,'' Raksall said, the pitying embarrassment so thick in her voice that I hated her.
''You need to take some time off from our own project
anyway, so why don't you see what you can do with
Filster's? We know you're not a professional, but that
might be just the thing to get you past any safeguards
they may have erected. We'll give you what information and help we can, and your friends—you have *my*
word that they'll be perfectly all right. You can look
at it as a paid vacation, and by the time you get back
we can probably get on with our work again. —What
do you say?''

In actual fact I didn't say anything, primarily because I couldn't. I also couldn't quite meet Filster's
eyes or look Raksall directly in the face, not the way
Seero would have been able to. He had always been
so serenely sure that what he did was right, so gently
willing to forgive anyone and everyone the awful
things they might say about him. I didn't have the
same inner strength, but at least I was able to refuse
the urge to make excuses for myself. Making excuses
only means you think you're doing wrong, Seero always used to say, and if you think what you're doing
is wrong, you shouldn't be doing it. The only wrong
I saw was in what I was about to do, but I couldn't
betray four people whose safety was my responsibility. I nodded my head stiffly, agreeing to the demand
they'd made on me, then stood up and got out of there
as fast as I could.

The lobby of the Empire building had dozens of public call squares, every one of them undoubtedly monitored. I chose one at random and made the call I had to, setting in motion a sequence of events all the monitoring in the Empire couldn't have followed. Then I walked out one of the lobby doors, and went to the place I was then calling home.

Chapter 3

The S.I. didn't believe in wasting time. I'd intended dragging my feet for a while, at least until the completion of the events I'd started the night before with a no-view call, but Filster began taking immediate advantage. I don't know if he realized I'd let myself be followed back to the place where I was sleeping those days, but the very next morning one of his people was pounding on my door. The racket woke me to see it wasn't even noon yet, which gave me second thoughts about how wise I'd been in using myself as a diversion. I pulled on a bodysuit without bothering to add shorts or a skirt, yanked the door open, and glared at the large blond-haired, blue-eyed man standing right outside.

"Don't you people have any sense at all?" I demanded in a hiss, working to keep my voice down. "Are you trying to let everyone in the Empire know we have a deal going?"

"How did you know I was sent by a mutual friend?" the man asked mildly, his squarish face openly surprised. "Since you're staying in this over-night for working girls, you—and everyone else—were supposed to think I was an early customer looking for some fun."

"Don't you think they *know* I'm not wiggling for the trade?" I asked in turn with a lot of the weariness I was feeling, wondering again how people of their supposed caliber could be so innocent. "The ones who run this place make it their business to know what's going on; if they slip, they could be *out* of business."

"Then we'll just have to say I'm your boyfriend," he decided with a grin, totally unbothered by anything I'd told him. "Just because you don't get paid for it, doesn't mean you have to pretend you never do it. Aren't you going to invite me in?"

I gave it up with a shake of my head and simply stepped back out of the way, and he walked in while looking around in curiosity. He was the sort of really big man I usually find attractive when I'm not three-quarters asleep, and he was dressed like a long-haul jockey whose usual run takes him through the wilds: leather jacket, leather boots, hugging zilf-skin pants and bright svalk singlet. Wilds jockeys make large amounts of money and aren't shy about spending it, which some people think is what puts the swagger in their walk. What really does it is a knowledge of just how good they are, undoubtedly the same thing that did it for my visitor.

"You know, this isn't bad," he decided by the time I got the door closed, his all-around inspection of the predominantly pink room finally turning his back in my direction. "The carpeting and walls are clean, the mirrors are shiny and clear, the bed is big enough for three, and the leather is out of sight while it isn't being used. What more can you ask from a temporary lay-over?"

"Watch your language," I said with a yawn, heading for the counter with the javi spout and cups. "Females not doing the trade aren't usually allowed to stay in places like this, but I have friends who owe me favors. Its greatest benefit is that I'm not the only one coming and going at all hours of the day and night."

"Now *you* watch *your* language," he said with a small laugh, following me over to the counter. "If you're in the mood to pour two cups of that, we can sit down with them while I tell you what I came to tell you. After that you can get dressed and start getting on with it."

"What's the hurry?" I asked, turning to hand him the first cup of javi I'd filled. "According to our mutual friend, the game-playing has been going on for at least six months. Since whoever they tick will eventually be paid back, what difference can another couple of days make?''

''They'll get paid back if we can prove the Joelare natives are game-playing,'' he corrected, his blue eyes serious as he took the javi. ''If we can't prove it, all we'll be able to do is make the Mists people check cash and credit before anyone is allowed on future tours. Those who can't afford extra time on the planet will then either be separated from their tours at the proper time, or Mists won't be permitted to bill them. That will still leave their previous victims in the hole, and that might not even be the worst of it. We still have those dead bodies to think about.''

With my own cup filled with javi I was able to try frowning at him, but he was already heading for the comfortably stuffed chair only a few feet away. He sat down, began settling himself, then moved his head quickly from side to side, a sure sign that he'd just noticed he was in the only chair in the room. When he was certain of that, he looked up at me.

''It seems these rooms weren't furnished with conversation in mind,'' he observed, his grin faint but definitely there. ''We'll either have to move to the bed where there's room for both of us, or you'll have to sit in my lap.''

''That's the benefit in having carpeted floors,'' I countered, folding into a cross-legged position opposite his chair. ''They give you all the extra options you need. Now, what's all this about dead bodies?''

''Some of those who were reported missing on Joelare turned up dead instead of late,'' he said with a supposedly disappointed sigh, forcing himself to get back to business. ''Any place like the Mists of the Ages is bound to have areas of high danger, and tourists are notorious for going past flashing lights and screaming sirens without ever seeing or hearing them. Going on vacation seems to turn normal people into instant idiots, so just having bodies isn't what bothers us. The disturbing part centers around the fact that there isn't much left of most of the bodies they send back to the home worlds, only enough to make a positive I.D. A certain percentage of those bodies are going to be true accidental deaths, but what about the rest?''

''You mean you think they might have been deliberately killed?'' I asked, putting both hands around my cup to fight off the sudden chill I was feeling. ''Possibly because they found out what was going on?''

''Possibly, but somehow it doesn't feel right,'' he grumbled, raising his cup to sip from it while distraction showed in his eyes. ''It isn't unheard of for people to kill to protect the secret of what they're doing, but this Mists whiz isn't all that big and profitable, and it isn't being run by professionals. In most instances amateurs try to *buy* silence rather than resort to killing, and most people offered bribes will accept them. It's a piece that doesn't fit in the puzzle we're trying to work, and even though it's colored the same it might fit in another puzzle entirely. You'll just have to keep your eyes open when you get there.''

''Assuming I don't end up in that second puzzle, and have my eyes closed for me in some permanent way,'' I said, looking up at him with very little enthusiasm. ''I keep telling you types I wasn't trained for this, but none of you want to hear me.''

''We hear you,'' he disagreed with a shadow of amusement behind his expression. ''We're just having trouble believing what we're hearing. You claim to be afraid to get involved in this, afraid of getting killed. For someone who refuses to let up the pressure on four Twilight Houses, any of which would be more than happy to arrange a messy, permanent send-off for her, you're unexpectedly worried about checking into the doings of a whiz run by nervous, almost-innocent amateurs. You consider us unreasonable for feeling the least bit skeptical?''

''If nothing else, the way you dismiss amateurs makes me nervous,'' I came back, disliking his entire attitude. ''I'd hate to tell you how many competent pros are killed or almost killed because of them. And this thing between me and the Twilight Houses is entirely different. With them it's a personal matter, and I really don't care if they end up getting me, as long as I get them at the same time.''

"With us, *everything* is a personal matter," he said, the amusement gone as he leaned forward just a little. "We hate seeing people being taken advantage of in any way at all, and we've sworn to stop it every time we can. But letting them get us when we get them doesn't make much sense, not if we want to go on getting them. That's why we're as cautious as it's possible to be, and glad to be giving you a vacation from your personal vendetta. We don't like the idea of losing you, and this should keep it from happening. While you're gone we'll be looking after your friends, so you don't have to spend even a minute worrying about them. All you need to do is use that talent of yours, and get us the evidence we need against whoever is doing things to innocent, unsuspecting people."

"My talent for stealing," I said as I looked away from him, remembering the way Filster had said it. After thinking about it I'd decided Filster was actually the most honest of all of them, saying aloud what the others had probably only been feeling. None of them understood or even particularly wanted to, which was the reason I'd made the call that began setting up escape routes for Mal, Sharp, Tris and Ricco. When everything was set the four would be slid into the routes, and then they would be gone from the planet with no possible way of tracing them. I'd set up the routine as an emergency exit before the first time I'd stroked any of the Houses, before I'd gotten involved with the S.I. I'd thought the S.I. could be counted on to keep those closest to me safe, but S.I. worried most about victims, not about those who created victims. It would take a few days, but then my friends would be really safe, and after that I could do as I pleased.

"Your talent for stealing," my visitor mused in a calm, even voice as I sipped my javi, making no comment on the fact that I still wasn't looking at him. "That's the way Filster put it, along with everything else he said. The man is really good at the job he does, but he has no true understanding of people. To him, if you aren't prey you have to be a predator, and he can't forget what predators did to his family. He doesn't see *himself* as a predator, only as prey fighting back, so he's incapable of understanding any other mode of existence. You'll find it easier forgiving him for what he said if you tell yourself the rest of us don't see it the same.''

"I don't tell myself much of anything," I said, finally bringing my eyes back to him. "Talking to yourself is a bad habit to get into, especially in my line of work. Was there anything else, or are you ready to leave so I can go back to bed?''

"Sorry, but you don't have time to go back to bed," he informed me, the grin accompanying the words the least little bit forced. "I still have to tell you about the special ring I have for you, and about the people who will be showing up to help you. After that you have to get your things together in time to catch a shuttle. Your liner to Joelare will be ready to load passengers about three hours from now.''

"You people really don't waste any time," I muttered, not terribly pleased with the way things were going. If I could have put them off for the couple of days necessary until my friends were gone from the planet, I would then have been free to refuse to go at all. The four should no longer be where they had been, not since a very short time after I'd made the call, but they were still on Gryphon and would be for another day or two. If S.I. really tried, they could keep them from leaving, which meant I would have to work S.I.'s job before I'd be free to melt into shadow.

"We try not to waste any time, but it doesn't always work," the man in the chair above me said, still trying for a grin. "If it did, you and I would be exchanging more than information, and from a lot closer than three feet. I usually don't have quite this much trouble making friendly suggestions, but Filster has a knack for ruining things for everybody. What say we put off the briefing for an hour or so, and use the intervening time to—re-cement good relations?''

He watched me as he sipped his javi, nothing showing in the way of anxiety over the question he'd put. As attractive as he was he had no real reason to be anxious, but I prefer getting to know someone before getting into bed with them. Many people consider that narrow-minded of me but, as my choice of occupation showed, I didn't much care what other people thought. And I also didn't feel the need to be any closer to the people of S.I. than I already was.

"I don't have that sort of relationship with S.I., so there's nothing to re-cement," I told him, wondering in passing if the idea had been his own, or if he'd been instructed to make the suggestion. "We have a very limited association, your group and me, and that's the way I'd like to keep it. If I have a shuttle to catch, you'd better tell me whatever it is you're supposed to tell me."

"I think I'll have a long talk with Filster when I get back to the offices," he said sourly, letting his eyes move over me in a very deliberate way. "And if I can't get you to change your mind once you're back from Joelare, I'll have a second talk with him. Not all of our people are full-time agents, you know, and after this thing with the Houses is done, you'll probably be made a different kind of offer. Not that I don't prefer my own sort."

His grin came all the way out with that, showing he was still in there selling. As hard as he was trying, he probably *was* under orders to get me into bed, which was an even better example than Filster's of what his people thought of me. I knew well enough how innocent I looked, but leave it to S.I. to equate innocent with gullible. I stirred impatiently where I sat, too disgusted to let myself say anything, and he finally got the message.

"All right, all right, strictly business," he conceded, briefly holding up his free hand. "We have almost no information on the Mists of the Ages and certainly no details on the headquarters building you'll be looking for, but one thing we *were* able to accomplish. We had the Division of Records send the Mists board a supposedly new form to be used when sending Information Request responses, but the form was really a flat-circuit transponder. We expected it to be filed with the rest of their records, which should have been what was done. Unless we're a lot more unlucky than usual, their main offices are somewhere to the east of the major entry point to the Mists, so we've booked you on the tour that goes that way. Once you're down and moving in the proper direction, you'll use this ring to guide you nearer.''

He reached into his leather jacket and pulled out a flat, dull silver band that looked well-worn and tarnished, then handed me the thing. The circular ring was about a quarter of an inch wide and very plain except for three small pieces of plastic that were supposed to look like jewels. When paste isn't even good enough to make you think it's glass, you have a real example of junk, and all I wanted to do with it was send it back to the two-for-a-slug vending machine it obviously came from.

''Don't just look at it, put it on,'' my visitor directed, sounding somewhat amused again. ''I know it probably offends your every esthetic sense, but that's only because it's in disguise. It's not jewelry, it's a homing device for the flat-circuit transponder and will keep you from getting lost in the fog. When you want to know which way to go, clench your fist and hold it up in front of you. If you need to bear left the left jewel will flash, right and the right jewel will do the same. Once you're dead on, the central jewel will flash, and then you just keep walking until you run right into it.''

''Walking,'' I echoed, hoping hard the thing wouldn't fit as I put my cup down then reluctantly slipped the ring on my right ring finger. ''And running right into it. Every time you open your mouth, you make this all sound better and better.''

''It'll work out beautifully,'' he assured me with confidence, supported, no doubt, by the fact that the monstrosity fit my finger perfectly. ''That ring will also identify you for the ones who will be working with you, two of our associated part-time agents who help us out when the need arises. They were already on their way when the computer decided your talent fits in exactly with theirs, so they were alerted to watch for you. When they think it's safe, they'll come over and introduce themselves.''

''Safe,'' I couldn't help echoing again as I re-

claimed my javi, wondering if there ever really was
such a thing. "What sort of talents do they have that
I fit in so well with them? Arson and mayhem?"

"You intend getting a lot of mileage out of what
Filster said, don't you?" he asked with a strange lightness, leaning back in the chair to cross his legs.
"Beating people over the head with mistakes seems to
come natural to some females, but it wasn't my mistake in the first place, so I think my head's taken
enough. I also think we'll both be better off if we consider that part of our discussion closed."

For a field agent he was getting awfully pushy, but
all I did was shrug at the order thinly disguised as a
suggestion. How I reacted or didn't react to things was
none of his business, especially since his being there
hadn't been my idea. If he was trying to disassociate
himself and the rest of S.I. from Filster, he'd eventually find out he didn't do much of a job of it.

"The two people you'll be working with have never
worked together before either," he went on after a
moment, realizing that my shrug was all the answer
I'd be giving to his comment. "The woman was chosen because it was realized the Mists headquarters
would be guarded by the most sophisticated electronic
devices available, and her specialty area is electronics.
There's nothing so advanced that she doesn't know
about it, but a number of her own gadgets can't be
matched or countered by anything. Once you reach the
building she'll be able to get you into it, especially if
you're able to spot parts of the system she might otherwise miss."

"And the other is a man?" I asked, my inner mind
suddenly very interested in the woman I'd be meeting.
There were a couple of very important places begging
to be stroked, but had proven untouchable because of
security devices that couldn't be gotten around. I always knew where those devices were, but had never
found anyone with the knowledge of how they could
be neutralized. If the woman turned out to have that
knowledge . . .

"Yes, the other is a man," the field agent said,
again sipping at his javi. "He was included because

of the dead bodies, the ones there was so little left of only identification was possible. All sorts of explanations accompanied the bodies as to how the people died, but the various home-planet medical authorities were able to confirm the causes of only a few. The third member of your team is a medical specialist, one who concentrates on research but at the same time knows more than a little about other branches of medicine. If you happen to come across another body, he'll be able to tell us if the death was natural, accidental— or caused.''

"As long as the body in question isn't me, I hope he has fun," I said with a small shiver. "Far be it from me to criticize other people's tastes in leisure-time activities, but he must have had a very limited social life in his youth if pathology is one of his hobbies. Is that it, or do we have more to talk about before I can start packing?''

"Except for handing you these papers, reservations and fund vouchers, that's all the business I have," he answered, reaching into his jacket again for the packet in question before passing it over. "Now, about our date for when you get back. I thought we'd start with dinner and dancing, maybe visit a club or two, and then I can show you my apartment. It took me a while to get it fixed up the way I wanted it, and I think you'll like it.''

"Of course I will," I answered smoothly as I rose to my feet, giving his renewed grin a very small smile. "I always enjoy seeing apartments people have put a lot of money into. I certainly hope you won't be off on a run through the wilds by the time I make it back.''

"I can guarantee I won't be," he answered, the direct look he gave me as he also stood showing that he knew what I was hinting at. "I haven't met a woman yet I was afraid of, and you're no exception. Since I actually do make runs through the wilds, you might as well stop trying to scare me. Whatever happens, I don't expect to have any trouble handling it.''

I discovered that he no longer had his cup when he put his arms around me, and then he was giving me the sort of kiss that can't in any way be described as

shy or passing-friendly. He seemed to have taken my
threat to strip his apartment as a challenge, and if he
really did do runs through the wilds, he couldn't be
the sort who let challenges go unanswered. My hands
were not only trapped between us, they were also filled
with papers and a javi cup, which made it almost impossible to push or pull away from his demanding lips.
I squirmed around trying to get loose, upset over the
way he was making me kiss him, and then, suddenly,
I no longer was.

"Now I'm really looking forward to that date," he
said softly, letting me go so that he might put a finger
to my face. "Make sure you take care of yourself during this thing. I don't like being stood up."

He grinned and kissed me lightly one last time, and
then he was striding toward the door. I watched him
until he was gone and I was alone again, and then I
slowly shook my head, answering him even though he
was no longer there. No, I would *not* be going on a
date with him when I got back, not for anything he
would find it possible to name. I had just found out
how attractive I really considered him, and even if I
intended continuing my association with S.I.—which
I didn't—he would not be any part of it. I'd have
enough interest brought into my life by the efforts of
the Twi Houses; letting him add to that would be worse
than suicidal.

I went back to the counter with my javi cup, thought
about packing, then said to hell with it and refilled the
cup. I didn't have all that much to pack, and I needed
the javi to help me get my reactions down from biological and back up to intellectual. I had almost forgotten that he had most likely been assigned to get me
interested in him, which went to show how thoroughly
S.I. had investigated me. They knew I liked big men
so they had provided one for me to become interested
in, an interest that would keep me with S.I. for as long
as they needed me. Associate, free-lance worker,
whatever they wanted to call it, I'd be theirs to use
any time they needed my abilities.

I left the packet of papers on the counter and took
my cup to the chair my visitor had used, still enough

bothered by what he'd done that the thought of revenge was very satisfying. He'd tried romancing me
to get what his bosses wanted, but no matter how positive a report he wrote, subsequent happenings would
not prove a match to it. We'd see how wide a grin he
wore when I not only didn't continue with S.I., but
used whatever I could get from their electronics expert
for myself. I didn't really care *who* was ultimately responsible for the destruction of the four Houses that
had killed Seero as long as I was the one who made it
possible, and as soon as I returned to Gryphon that's
what I would be getting on with. The destruction of
four Houses. Without the help of the mighty S.I.

I sipped my javi as I felt the pleasure in thinking
about what I would do, then ran into something a little
less satisfying. I liked knowing the identity of the person I decided to teach a lesson to, and the bastard who
had been here hadn't even told me his name.

Chapter 4

Being a member of the bodysuit generation is a benefit
to more than your cash account. Considering how light
and thin bodysuits and their accessories are, you can
pack a month's worth of changes in a single, medium-
sized grip, and still have room left over for odds and
ends. I'd moved into the over-night with the single grip
and that's the way I moved out again, only not to go
back to my apartment. I took a public glide directly to
the shuttle port, surrendered the grip when the man
confirming my presence at the port demanded it, then
went to the appointed place where the shuttle was expected to land at any minute. I had no doubt that the
shuttle was *ready* to land, but it's less hassle traveling
from planet to planet than it is taking off from or landing on one. We who waited in the all-weather shelter
waited fifteen minutes longer than they'd told us we
would have to, were finally rewarded with the sight of
our transportation arriving, then were allowed to
board. Another fifteen minutes after we were settled
the shuttle began taxiing up the runway, and that meant
the worst of it was behind us. It took no time at all
before we were high enough to switch from thin-air
flying to no-air power assist, and then we were matching with the liner.

If it wasn't such a pain getting off the ground, I
would enjoy everything about traveling. Liners move
so fast it isn't possible to even come close to imagining their speed, but no one on board ever feels the
slightest hint of motion. Multiple light speed and artificial gravity all come from the same math the big

brains say, but as far as my understanding of it goes, they might as well say it's done with magic. Before they found the math everyone was told it wasn't possible to travel at light speed or beyond, but now we can do almost anything we please. Except, of course, get off the ground on time.

Once aboard the liner I was shown to the cabin that had my grip in it, was handed a five-dimensional fold-up that showed liner layout and scheduled mealtimes, and then was left alone. If I'd needed help with the fold-up I would have had it for the asking from the steward who showed me to my cabin, but services like that are added to the cost of your trip, something the inexperienced traveler doesn't realize. I wasn't in any way short of funds, but I do have this thing about paying tribute when it isn't absolutely necessary. I took time out to sneer at S.I. for having missed finding *that* little whiz, at the same time trying to fold the fold-up with the meal schedule out and, by pretending I had six-foot-long arms, finally managed to do it. I hadn't had the chance to eat before it was time to head for the port, so when I saw we were just about right on top of a scheduled meal, I tossed the fold-up onto my bed and headed out.

Cabins on liners tend to be somewhat on the small side, but with the extra amount of fun space that gives you, no one really minds. There are game rooms and lounges and bars and soda fountains and sensor rooms and libraries and exercise halls and just about anything you can name, all there for the use of passengers. Only a very few, very exclusive entertainments aren't included in the price of your ticket and if you've developed a taste for those things you can usually afford to pay extra for them. If you can't afford them but want to do them anyway, you're best off trying to get some help. Those who don't too often wind up in *my* field, which doesn't really crowd the rest of us. Stealing, like anything else, takes training and ability; if you try to do without those requirements, you soon find yourself doing without your freedom.

The wide yellow ship's corridors weren't really crowded, not even with the number of people heading

for the dining area. I ambled along with everyone else,
looking forward to the meal, noticing how many other
people were wearing bodysuits like mine. The bodysuit covers you from shoulders to feet bottoms and
down to the wrists, stretches to fit easily no matter
what sort of contours you have, comes in every color
there is, and is so light you hardly know you're wearing one. Most of the people I walked among wore
contrasting shorts as an accessory just as I did, but
some wore skirts, or vests with their shorts or skirts,
or fancy collars and cuffs along with everything else,
or maybe just jewelry. One woman with a spun svalk
suit of orange-red had blue-white ice gems decorating
it, her hair dyed to match the gems and her walk insisting the gems were real. There were quite a few
men around the woman, all trying to capture her attention, all working very hard to pretend they weren't
having trouble deciding which to watch, the jewels or
her body.

I, myself, had no trouble deciding which I wanted
to look at, and not being into women was only a part
of it. I was curious as to whether those gems were the
genuine article, but not because I had any designs on
them. It happened that ice gems were something of a
hobby with me, and I enjoy comparing the ones I own
with what other people put their money out for. A
glance ahead showed me we were almost to the dining
hall, but if I maneuvered myself into the proper position, I ought to have at least a minute or two to check
on their authenticity. Phony ice gems are easy to spot,
even without a loupe.

By increasing my pace I was able to begin moving
through the crowd, half an eye on where I was going,
the other eye and a half on the jewels. To avoid trouble
I was also trying to pretend I wasn't looking at the
gems at all, and all that watching-not-watching activity took too much of my attention. The clumsy clod
was right on top of me before I caught the first glimpse
of him, and by then it was too late. I couldn't keep
from moving toward him just as he moved toward me,
his attention obviously elsewhere, and then we col-
lided the way jump-arounds sometimes do, glancingly

but hard enough to notice. I "oofed" as I bounced off
him, staying on my feet only because of my trained
balance, but his problem wasn't keeping erect. He'd
been holding his fold-up liner guide when we came
together, and the crash sent it flying out of his hand.

Now, reflexes are supposed to be the things that keep
us alive in hostile environments, but in civilized sur-
roundings you're expected to learn to control them.
The clod who ran into me had apparently never learned
that; without stopping to think about it, he jumped
to catch the fold-up before it hit the deck. Why he
bothered, I have no idea; the thing isn't really five-
dimensional, it only feels that way when you have to
refold it. Whatever his reasons he did move fast
enough to accomplish his aim, but when his oversized
foot came down on my normal one I screeched, immediately losing interest in admiring his agility. He
bobbled the fold-up at the sound, but finally he had it
and then was kind enough to take his monstrous weight
off the extremity he had just crushed.

"Sorry about that, but maybe next time you'll learn
to watch where you're going," a deep voice came as
I balanced on one foot, trying to clutch at the mangled
other. "If you hadn't been trying to plow through the
crowd, you wouldn't have run into me."

"*I* ran into *you?*" I demanded in outrage, finally
looking up at the mindless fool. "*You* were the one
too busy ogling the scenery to watch where you were
going, and you were also the genius who thought the
fold-up would break if it hit the floor. I thought they
knew better than to let your sort out without a han-
dler."

His jaw tightened at the insult and his big hand
closed harder around the fold-up he held, but there
wasn't much he could say. He was really big with
longish red hair and a mustache down to his chin to
match, hard gray eyes in a square-jawed, masculine
face, and a wide-muscled body that his tunic and leg-
gings didn't do anything to hide. Adding soft ankle-
boots to that let you see at a glance that he was from
Rober Tay, the arena world, the place that specialized
in breeding and training fighters for their sand arenas.

Every world in the Empire followed the top-named fighters in their tries for the golden circlets, then bet on their favorites in the multi-circlet challenges. Many fighters died before they won anything at all, others were crippled and permanently disqualified, but only rarely did any of them retire for good without one of those reasons forcing them to it. The most commonly attributed reason for that was supposed to be total lack of human intelligence, and the fact that most fighters traveled with attendants started people calling the attendants animal-handlers instead. It wasn't the sort of comment you usually made to the fighter himself, not if you had any interest in finding out what your natural life span would turn out to be, but he had gotten me mad in more ways than one, and I didn't really mind returning the favor.

"If my—'sort'—needed handlers, you'd be regretting that question right about now," he said at last, a definite growl in his voice to match the coldness in his eyes. "And if I was ogling anything, that's only because I'm used to going after the best in sight. It's also the reason I didn't happen to see *you.* But try coming back when you're all grown up, maybe I'll change my mind. Until then, though, I'd appreciate it if you'd keep your suicide attempts at least twenty feet away from wherever I happen to be."

His gray eyes swept over me in a quick, dismissive way, and then he was striding toward the dining hall, leaving me to stare furiously after him. Our argument had collected a small crowd, and half of them were chuckling while the other half looked after the departing fighter as though he were crazy. For my own part I *knew* he was crazy, especially for thinking I didn't know what I looked like. Most men had no trouble at all finding me attractive, so his considering me substandard was hardly a crushing blow to my ego. What was getting me so mad was his crack about my not being fully grown, a point I was justifiably touchy about. As I watched the fool disappear into the dining hall, I promised myself he would end up regretting having said that.

It took another minute or two of flexing my foot,

and then I was able to use it to make my own way into the dining hall without limping. I looked around the paneled and carpeted room as I entered, hoping there were some empty tables left, and spotted a small one straight back and to the right, just in front of the projection-screen wall. The screen on that side was showing a typical Adexian rainstorm, complete with chain lightning and three-hundred-mile-an-hour winds, which made it a perfect match to my mood of the moment. I headed for the table, reached it before anyone else, and claimed it by sitting down.

I couldn't have been studying the table-top menu for more than two minutes, when I was interrupted by the presence of someone hovering at my left elbow. I gave the presence about thirty seconds to see if it would go away, and when it didn't I looked up ready to *ask* it to go away. I was in no mood for company, but the nastiness I'd been about to speak disappeared at sight of the girl who stood there, almost wringing her hands. She wasn't very tall but was definitely on the chubby side, had long blond hair streaked with purple to match her bodysuit, and had the largest, widest brown eyes I'd ever seen. She looked to be just short of terrified, and I couldn't imagine what was bothering her.

"Is something wrong?" I asked, glancing over my right shoulder to check on the storm. It wasn't any worse than it had been when I'd arrived, and surely the girl knew it wasn't really there. The wall may have looked like a window, but even liners aren't big enough to carry storms for the viewing pleasure of their passengers.

"I—know this—is an awful—imposition, but is that—seat taken?" the girl forced herself to say, the words coming out like a request for charity. "I'm—supposed to meet—someone here, but he hasn't—arrived yet, and I really couldn't—take up a table all—by myself—"

"No, the seat isn't taken," I assured her quickly, coming close to feeling my own pain over her very painful embarrassment. "You can sit here until your friend comes, and then the two of you can find a table together."

"That's really good of you," the girl said in almost a whisper, moving to the chair opposite me with a shy but brightly warm smile. "I'm—bad at speaking to strangers, so I appreciate this more than you know. I'm Lidra Kament."

"It's nice to know you, Lidra," I said, returning her smile. "Would you like a cup of javi or something while you're waiting? I'm about to place my order, so I can just add whatever you want to it."

"You really are nice," the girl said in a very soft voice, a shadow of unexpected amusement lurking somewhere behind her words. "Most people I do this to don't even look in my direction, let alone ask me questions or offer me things. I'll order when our third gets here, but just for form's sake you'd better tell me your name."

I forced myself to pay attention to the menu I was ordering from instead of jerking my head up to stare at the girl, but once I'd pressed the proper boxes I did look up. There wasn't a chance anyone had heard what she'd said to me, and after the routine she'd gone through when she'd first appeared, no one would wonder why they couldn't hear her and certainly wouldn't make the effort to listen. I know I hadn't expected to be found by my coworkers quite that soon, and my expression must have held a trace of my surprise.

"There are times you do get lucky with liner connections," the girl Lidra said with a hidden grin, her voice still so low I was almost reading her lips. "Since we knew you were due to come on board at Gryphon, I synched with the frequency of your ring when the shuttle came back and spotted you that way. Chal and I met completely by accident too, and once we all find we're going to the same place, we can decide to pal around together. Now will you please share your name out loud?"

"By the way, I'm Dalisse Imbro," I said, putting my palms on the table as I leaned back in my chair, trying to decide if I liked what had happened. "Most people call me Inky, because my favorite color is black. What's *your* favorite color, Lidra?"

"No matter how it looks, it really isn't red," she

answered, now appearing the least bit uncomfortable.
"I wasn't trying to embarrass you, Inky, this is just
my standard contact routine. People deliberately tune
out of conversations they find distasteful, and having
them ignore what we're saying is better than using a
damper field to make it happen. We'll find enough
need for that sort of thing later on."

"I suppose we will," I allowed, accepting the explanation in place of an apology. I'm not very good at
apologizing myself, which may be why I don't think
much of people who start out by glibly saying the word
'sorry.' If you're really sorry, the word isn't quite that
easy to say. And there was no denying that her way
of making contact was clever, which led me to add,
"I'm glad you decided to sit here, Lidra. My friend
was supposed to go on this vacation with me, but at
the last minute she got sick. It hasn't even been an
hour, but I'm already learning how lonely a solitary
vacation can be."

"Then *I'm* glad I stopped here, too," the girl said
with that not-quite-hidden grin, relief clear in her large
eyes. "Even if we don't happen to be going to the
same place, Inky, at least we can hang around together
here on the liner."

We had enough time to discover—with great surprise—that we were both going to Joelare, and then
my food was brought. Lidra watched without comment
while the dishes were set in front of me, but once the
waiter had gone on his way she produced a strange
grimace.

"If you make a habit of eating that sort of junk
food, you won't be living very long," she said, an
odd kind of amusement behind the criticism. "That
stuff will kill you faster than an enemy. If you have
any doubts, wait until Chal gets here. He'll be glad to
tell you all about it."

"He isn't one of those," I groaned, understanding
why she'd been amused, then I determinedly took another bite of my grilled meat-round on a bun. "Well,
he can be as finicky as he likes about his own food,
but if he tries changing *my* eating habits I'll defend
myself. Once he loses the contents of his pouch or

pockets a time or three, he'll get the message and leave me alone.''

"I haven't known him very long, but I have the feeling he may not be that easy to discourage," she said with a small laugh, her dark eyes dancing. "When we first met he thought I really was as heavy as I look, not realizing there's some of my equipment I don't want anyone putting hands on without my being there. He was already into a very gentle lecture before I knew what he was doing, and I actually had to show him the truth before he let up on me. There *is* a way to distract him from nutrition, a way I discovered to be very enjoyable, but you may not share my tastes for that sort of thing.''

The expression in her eyes had turned very amused, but as I looked at her I had the sudden impression she was more an experienced, self-controlled woman than a young, flighty girl. She'd been fishing around in my direction for reactions, trying to find out as much as she could about me without coming straight out and asking, but was being as fair as possible in her game-playing. Before checking my preferences and habits she was telling me her own, and there's not much more you can ask from a near-total stranger.

"I'm not above enjoying myself, but I don't believe in buying freedom from pestering," I said, beginning to share her amusement. "I was raised by someone who never tried running my life; he only made sure I knew what all my options were before I came to a decision about something. The only problem with being raised like that is it doesn't prepare you for everyone else in the universe, three-quarters of whom *know* what's best for you and are determined to see you do things their way. I have an abysmally small amount of patience when it comes to that sort, which they tend to find out if they hang around very long.''

"I have a feeling poor Chal is in for it," she said, her attempt at a sigh buried beneath delighted laughter. "Just try keeping in mind that he's basically a very decent person—and that we're probably going to need him, one way or the other. He's— Oh, wait a minute. Here he comes.''

Her chair had her facing the doors leading into the dining hall, and when I turned I saw a man coming toward us who wasn't quite what I'd been expecting. He was fairly tall and broad-shouldered, had very light brown hair with light-colored eyes, and sported a tan that most sensor stars would have envied. He was dressed in light-blue slacks and white, long-sleeved shirt, a style favored by some of the more conservative planets of the Empire, which meant he also had to wear shoes. Bodysuits relieve you of that necessity unless you intend going some place where there's likely to be mud or snow or some such, but the length and ease of his stride said he didn't mind wearing them. He grinned a grin at my companion that turned his face downright handsome, and snagged an empty chair from a nearby table as he passed it, giving himself something to sit in when he joined us at our table.

"Wait till you hear," he enthused in a voice he wasn't able to hold down much, his excitement almost enough to make him bounce where he sat. "Lidra, you won't believe who's on board this liner!"

"Chal, I'd like you to say hello to Dalisse Imbro, known to a certain select few as Inky," the girl said with what was turning out to be usual amusement, her hand making a graceful gesture in my direction. "She and I met in the same lucky, accidental way you and I did, and believe it or not, she's also going to Joelare."

"Well, what a surprise," the man said, turning his head to give me a nod and a grin. "Someone else going to the Mists of the Ages. I certainly hope you suggested we all go together, Lidra. With three of us, we should have a wonderful time. Now, don't you girls want to hear the news?"

"What news is that, Chal?" Lidra asked with a glance toward me, one that had something of a shrug in it. "From your reaction, I'm ready to believe the newest Miss Empire is on board with us."

"Better than that," Chal answered with a laugh, apparently too sure of himself to be bothered by teasing. "I just found out that Serendel is on board, something no one was expecting. He seems to have picked

up the liner at Forge, the port of call just before
Gryphon.''

''Are you serious?'' Lidra asked him as she leaned
forward, the widening of her eyes destroying all traces
of the sophisticated woman she had only just started
to show. ''Serendel is my absolute *favorite,* and I'd
kill for an hour alone with him! Chal, are you sure it's
true?''

''He's been seen by any number of people,'' the
man assured her with confidence, enjoying her reaction as he leaned forward to put his arms on the table.
''Serendel has always been my favorite too, but if *I*
ever got an hour alone with him, I don't think he'd
enjoy it as much as he would yours. I don't believe
what they've published about his diet, and I'd give my
next year's research budget to get a piece of him under
my trans-field microscope. Under ideal conditions, the
piece would still be attached to him.''

''Who are you two talking about?'' I interrupted to
ask, mostly to divert Chal from what he'd been saying. If you're a mass murderer and you chop people
up, planetary governments pull out all the stops in an
effort to get you. If you're a research scientist, though,
you can chop up just about anyone you like, and every
official in sight will smile and nod in approval.

''You can't mean you don't know who *Serendel* is!''
Lidra said with the next thing to outrage, she and Chal
both looking at me now. ''Where could you possibly
have been hiding these last four years? Serendel is the
best of the five triple-gold winners, and most people
believe he'll take the crown this year. Do you know
how *few* glads have taken the crown after only a triple?''

''So he's a Rober Tay fighter,'' I said with no enthusiasm at all, lifting my cup of javi before leaning
back in my chair. ''I think I have heard something
about him, but I don't pay much attention to arena
doings. I usually have a pretty heavy schedule, and if
I were going to back any of them, it would probably
be Farison.''

They continued to stare at me for a few seconds,
their expressions an identical sort of blankness that

declared my insanity without words, and then, an instant later, were happily back to being caught up in
their enthusiasm.

"How could he have been on the liner for three days
without anyone finding out about it?" Lidra asked
Chal, the ardent worshiper eager for the latest word
about her god. "Everyone in the Empire must know
what he looks like, even if he doesn't happen to be in
fighting leather."

"He must have stayed in his cabin after coming
aboard," Chal answered with a matching eagerness,
the two of them proving that even above-average intelligence is often no proof against low-taste diversions. "If he disguised himself on the shuttle up and
had his meals delivered by chute instead of waiter, no
one would have been the wiser. If I know anything at
all about fighters, three days of being locked up gave
him a case of screaming cabin fever. That has to be
why he suddenly showed himself."

"But not just ordinary cabin fever," Lidra said in
the tones of revelation, her finger and stare pointing
toward Chal. "If he came aboard in disguise, he could
have come out of his cabin in the same, anonymous
way. If he came out as himself, he must be after something he can get most easily by *being* himself! Oh,
Chal, if I only knew where he was!"

"Sorry, Lidra, but if you're right, he's already found
what he was looking for," the man replied, his totally
unapologetic expression reinforcing my belief about
those who started sentences with the word "sorry."
"Take a look over there, and you'll see what I mean."

Chal turned his head toward the back of the hall
rather than pointing, and when the girl followed his
gaze she made a sound of deep disappointment. Having nothing better to do I looked in that direction as
well, and saw the pretty woman in her red-orange
bodysuit with the ice gems—sitting at a table with the
clumsy hulk who had nearly run me over and crippled
me!

"You don't mean *that's* your magnificent Serendel?" I asked, the sight of him annoying me all over
again. "That big fool with the red hair?"

"Yes, the big fool with the red hair who has every woman in the room—including me—drooling over him," Lidra turned back to say, a dangerous edge to her voice and near-murder in her eyes. "Do you have any final words you'd like to utter before I kill you where you sit?"

"Not a one," I came back, returning her stare over the rim of my cup. "If my continued existence depends on my saying something nice about *that* jerk, I'd rather keep quiet and have it end."

"You sound as though you have something personal against him," Chal remarked with obvious curiosity, his hand patting Lidra's arm in an effort to calm her. "Don't tell me you were silly enough to bet against him, and now blame him for whatever money you lost?"

"Money has nothing to do with it," I answered with a snort, clanking my cup down on the table. "I was on my way here for a meal, minding my own business, when the damned fool ran right into me. He was so busy staring at the object of his desire he almost broke my foot, then had the nerve to insist the collision was *my* fault. If he was that hot, he should have had an escort sent to his cabin."

"I think it's against the laws of the glad guild for any of them to pay for it," Lidra said in a breathless sort of way, her eyes wide again. "You mean you actually came close enough to him to get stepped on? Why can't *I* ever have luck like that?"

"Lidra, remember what his fighting weight is," Chal put in, chuckling at the face I was making in response to the girl's ridiculous comment. "If our new friend here really was stepped on, she's lucky she can still walk. Just to be on the safe side, after we eat I'll check the foot over. And biologically speaking, Inky, you can't blame him for being that—eager. He really has no choice in the matter."

"I can blame him for anything I like," I came back, uninterested in listening to excuses for the man, even supposed medical ones. "If other men can control themselves, so can he. The plain fact of the matter is, fighters don't *care* to control themselves. They're so used to having women throw themselves all over them, they get to the point of thinking it's owed them.''

"My dear girl, it *is* owed them," Chal said with a lot of amusement, leaning back in his chair as he looked at me. "Our species may have advanced to the point of conquering the stars, but our genetic references are just what they were when we huddled around tribal fires, fearing the dark and the creatures it held. Female codes demand that they seek out the strongest and most successful of the males, to insure as far as possible the strength and success of their offspring. Male codes insist that they take the most attractive females—the definition of attractive varying with cultural needs and biases—and that as often as possible before they're rendered incapable of adding to the race through death or crippling. The drive is strongest among those who face physical danger on a regular basis, which means, of course, among the glads. The rest of us know we have time, so we're not driven by the same urgency. Serendel could die in his very next challenge, and his body won't let him forget that. I'm really surprised he was able to hold out for as long as three days.''

"It's too bad *I* wasn't around when he lost the fight," Lidra said glumly, elbow on table and face held in palm. "There aren't many men in this Empire I would choose to have children by, but he's certainly one of them. And I want to have my kids soon, while I'm still young enough to have fun with them. I suppose I'd better face the fact that if Inky couldn't distract him, I'd have no chance at all unless I used one of my gadgets. That means you're still at the top of the list, Chal, so don't forget about applying for leave after this thing is over. Now that we've finally met, there's no sense in wasting time.''

"I won't forget," the man said softly, looking at the girl with a very faint smile she didn't happen to see, and then he was back to looking at me with another expression entirely. "And now that you've mentioned it, I wonder why Serendel *wasn't* distracted by Inky. She's attractive enough by any standards you'd care to use, so why didn't he choose her?'

"Can't we find anything else to talk about?" I asked, the annoyance I'd been feeling beginning to reach for new heights. "My reservation in the Mists calls for a three day tour, what they call a half-week. I understand that many of the tours are for even less than that, which doesn't make sense. Why would they limit a tourist's stay like that?"

"Maybe it has something to do with the constant fog," Lidra answered, allowing herself only reluctantly to be distracted from the previous topic. "When you leave a day-night schedule—even an artificial one—for nothing but gray that varies only a little, something inside you could start getting anxious. Different people are probably able to take the sameness for different amounts of time, but maybe most people are quick to reach the point of screaming to be let out and have to work up to being able to take more. Since the Mists people would like to have you come back again to tour a different section, they try to get you out the first time before the screaming starts."

"I hope it's also before the mold sets in," I muttered, trying to keep my distaste only among the three of us. "Wandering around in damp, constant fog isn't my idea of a fun time, no matter what they've done to pretty it up. I hope you two are in good enough shape to keep up with the pace I intend setting."

"The pace you'll be setting depends on how the tour is set up," Lidra told me, her tone of voice back to being one step above inaudible despite the fact that her expression hadn't changed. "They'll be sending us through the section we're booked for, and it has to have *something* besides fog. And let's not forget the contention that it's so compelling some people have *insisted* on staying longer. That's one of the points we're supposed to be verifying."

"Well, if you hear *me* deciding to stay longer, you won't have to wonder if they've gotten to me," I told her, sure she heard the dryness no matter how softly I was speaking. "At that point you'll *know,* and hopefully will have enough time to yell for help before you go the same route. It's just too bad any help will be too far away to help."

"But it won't be," she said, and the amusement was back to lurking in her eyes. "It's highly unlikely that we'll need them, but a destroyer stuffed with Empire shock troops won't be far from the planet while we're on it. If it turns out we do need them, all we have to do is call. For you, that consists of covering all three of the jewels in your ring, then pressing down on them three times in a row in rapid succession. You do it nine times with a ten second pause between each set of three, and before you know it the place is being overrun. Chal and I have different means, but the results will be the same. Our friends don't want to lose any of us, not if they can possibly help it."

"That certainly does make me feel loved," I commented, experiencing a need to say something about the awe and gratitude with which I was being filled. The field agent who had given me the ring must have known about its additional ability, but he hadn't mentioned it. Either he was counting on Lidra to give me all the data I needed—which is one hell of a way to design a briefing—or he didn't care to see me too overburdened with unnecessary knowledge. When you trust someone, you don't tend to pick over the available information before passing it on, which said quite a lot about how far S.I. trusted me.

"Now I know why Serendel didn't choose Inky," Chal said suddenly, his light eyes filled with the satisfaction of a puzzle solved. "I've been seeing it all along, but only just now noticed it when her expression changed. I think the best words I can use to describe it are innocent and wholesome."

"Watch it, Chal," Lidra warned with a laugh. "As close as she is, if she throws that cup at you she's not likely to miss. I can see what you mean about the way she looks, but what does it have to do with Serendel? Is he supposed to be turned off by innocence and wholesomeness?"

"If all those articles are right about his sense of decency, he is," my almost-target answered with a grin, keeping an eye on the cup I still held without letting it discourage his fun time. "If a man has any standards at all, one of the firmest will be on the point of 'ruining' a 'nice' girl. If he gets serious about that nice girl, that's another story, but if all he's looking for is horizontal exercise, he'll choose an already experienced female. If you look at it right, his rejection of Inky could mean he's really quite attracted to her."

"Chal, that's disgusting," I told him while Lidra laughed, failing to see what they both found so amusing. "I may like my men big, but I also insist that they have personalities and intelligence. Since the mighty Serendel doesn't qualify on those last two points, he can be attracted in someone else's direction. As for me, I think I can use a nap to make up for the sleep I lost hurrying to catch this liner. Maybe by the time I wake up, you two will be ready to talk about something other than your favorite fighter."

"Haven't you checked your planetary-destination schedule yet?" Lidra asked as I started to get out of my chair, a faint amusement still with her. "If you shift over right now, what you just ate was dinner, with a night's sleep ahead of you. Chal and I are already on the schedule, and we were going to spend some time in the game rooms after our own dinner. Why don't you join us, and turn in for the night later?"

"Thanks anyway, but I don't think so," I said, really in no mood to be entertained. If I'd still been on Gryphon I could have done some work during that night, but liner nights are good for nothing but sleep. "If I don't get my rest I stop looking pure and wholesome, and that would be a crime against humanity or something. Suppose I meet you two here for breakfast?"

"Maybe a good night's sleep and a fortifying breakfast will bring you back to your senses," Lidra said, the gleam in her eye downright evil. "Anyone who thinks Farison would have a chance against Serendel needs *something* to bring them back to reality."

Chal laughed outright at that, but all I did was shake my head and turn away without saying anything else. Glad-groupies are impossible to argue with, and I should have known better than to even think about trying. What I wanted right then wasn't an argument, but the privacy of my small cabin. I needed some time alone to curse everyone who thought I was sweet or wholesome or innocent-looking—or still hadn't grown up—and to think about what I would do first once I had gotten back to Gryphon. I strode out of the dining hall, trying to decide which of the Twi Houses I would do best allying with, and thought nothing further about all the people I'd seen hovering around the area where Serendel sat, happily drinking in the sight of him.

Chapter 5

The next ship's morning found me wide awake and feeling really good, which lasted until I met Lidra and Chal in the dining hall. They'd taken a larger table not far from where we'd sat the night before, about fifteen feet from the right-hand wall window which now showed a violently spectacular vista of volcanic eruptions. My two new acquaintances were paying more attention to their food than to the supplied scenery, but when I came up to the table they actually took a second or two out to smile and nod.

"Morning, Inky," Lidra said around a mouthful of cereal as I sat. "There isn't much time, so you'd better order and eat as fast as you can."

"She can order fast, but you'll have to let her take her time with the eating," Chal put in, the words more of an order than a comment. "She won't enjoy it very much if she has indigestion, which is what *you'll* get if you don't stop swallowing without tasting. And by the way, Inky, how's your foot feeling this morning? I didn't get a chance to look at it last night the way I wanted to."

"My foot is fine," I answered as I ordered juice and javi and two slices of pro-pure. "I know you're probably disappointed, but they won't be able to add me to your idol's maim stats. And what am I supposed to be hurrying-but-not-hurrying for?"

"If she takes her time eating, she'll miss the opening warm-ups," Lidra said to Chal, ignoring the question I'd asked. "Even more to the point, *we'll* miss them. If we don't stay here until she's through and then drag her along, do you think she'll go anywhere near the gym?''

"Getting her sick won't help in changing her mind," Chal returned as he took another spoonful of his soft-boiled eggs, obviously unimpressed with Lidra's arguments. "And speaking about getting sick, you really will have to add to your breakfast order, Inky. Pro-pure isn't a food, it's a supplement—and an artificial one at that. If you don't want to die from malnutrition, what you need in your body is food."

"Food doesn't do well in my body while I'm working out, Chal," I answered with a sweet, innocent smile as I looked at him. "Throwing up isn't my idea of fun, and the pro-pure is all protein with enough electrolytes to get me through the session. After that I'll be able to eat all the greasy hot-fries and grilled meat-rounds I like. And what's supposed to be happening in the gym?''

They immediately began choking, Lidra with laughter and Chal with outraged indignation, the result of trying to talk and swallow both at the same time. A waiter came over with my order while they were still fighting to stop coughing, so I was able to drink my juice without being bothered. By the time I put the emptied glass aside and reached for the first slice of pro-pure, though, Chal had recovered enough to be able to split his stern-stare between Lidra and me.

"You don't have to encourage her, Lidra," the girl was told, an obvious effort to banish her continuing amusement. "If she starts thinking what she said was cute and clever, she might even go so far as to try it. Inky—Dalisse—I know you're not a child, so I won't spend time lecturing you. All I'll say is that what we're about to do is very important, too important for any of us not to be in peak condition. To be sure of that I'll order all of our meals from now on, and then none of us will have to worry."

"The hell you will," I countered as Lidra almost choked again, the good mood I'd been in beginning to thin in the presence of his "helpful" attitude. "You, more than anyone else, should know, Chal, that species survival depends most heavily on the ability to

adapt. *Anyone* can keep going on the best and health-
iest foods available, but it takes true survival ability
to thrive on the junk food most prevalent in our society
today. If you're interested in continuing on with the
rest of the species, my friend, you'd better hurry up
and start adapting.''

Chal stared at me wordlessly with his mouth moving
just a little, but Lidra put her head back and laughed
like hell. I didn't know if she was laughing at what
I'd said or at the way Chal was taking it, but it didn't
really matter. This time I was able to finish the slice
of pro-pure and half my javi in relative peace, and then
Chal managed to pull himself together.

"That has to be one of the most ridiculous arguments I've ever heard," he stated, annoyed with Lidra's ongoing chuckling, but apparently determined to
ignore it. "You can't possibly believe that any more
than I do, and even beyond that . . .''

"What has belief got to do with truth?" I interrupted to ask, still blandly innocent. "If I jump off the
top of the Empire building on Gryphon while believing
I can fly, will that stop me from splattering when I hit
the pavement? Some things can be affected by belief,
but Ultimate Truth isn't one of them. And isn't eating
right considered to be an Ultimate Truth?''

"I always thought it was just plain good sense,"
Chal came back, finally understanding that the
straighter he played it, the worse off he would be. "I
can prove it's good sense by the kind of physical shape
I'm in, which happens to be excellent. Can you and
your Ultimate Truth say the same?''

"Well, I *am* a little on the underdeveloped side," I
admitted with a sigh that caused Chal's eyes to briefly
flicker down from my face to the top of my bodysuit.
"That's why I work out, to see if I can't improve on
the physical shape *I'm* in. If you and your good sense
think you're in better condition than me and my Ultimate Truth, why don't we test the theory by working
out together for a while? You may have noticed I already have on my exercise bodysuit.''

"Don't be silly, of course he hasn't noticed," Lidra
said with a small laugh that brought a grin to Chal.

"Why would he notice a skin-tight black suit that seems to be promising to go transparent if it's stared at for a while? And don't try to tell me you're wearing anything under that. If you were, you wouldn't have brought that large an eyeball collection to the table with you. Or are you going to pretend you didn't notice all the stares when you walked in?"

"As a matter of fact, I didn't," I said, feeling the least bit uncomfortable over the way Lidra was teasing me. "Getting stared at sometimes is just one of those things that happen. As long as it doesn't happen at the wrong time, there's no sense in making a fuss over it. But I still don't have an answer to my question. Are you up to working out with me, Chal?"

"With Lidra sitting here right next to me, I refuse to answer that question," he came back, his grin and words making the girl chuckle again. "Whether or not I'll join you in the gym is another matter entirely. I can't see any reason *not* to join you—except for the fact that there probably won't be any room for us to work out, together *or* individually. The crowds will be too thick."

"That's the reason I was trying to hurry you," Lidra said, her amusement finally withdrawn in favor of faint wariness, possibly due to the frown I could feel myself wearing. "Someone else will be working out in the gym this morning, and if half the ship doesn't show up to watch, you can bet they're nothing less than dead. Seeing it on the specials is nothing like seeing it when you're right there."

"Don't tell me," I said, my tone so flat it could have been used to land a shuttle on. "Your idol is putting on a show for the benefit of the lowly masses, and you can't wait to ooh and ahh. I hate to tell you this, but I left every one of my hoorays back on Gryphon, right next to my yays and lookatthats. I think you two had better count on going without me."

"But we won't do that," Lidra came back, a sleek assurance edging aside the wariness she no longer seemed to need. "We're supposed to be a team, and teams like ours should stay together while they're learning each other. If you end up in the sticky, it helps to know what to expect from the people around you. We can't get to know each other if you keep going your own way, so this time you'll go ours. If it'll make you feel any better, you can criticize Serendel while we defend him—if you can *find* anything about him to criticize.''

"We won't be together long enough for me to list everything there is to criticize about him," I countered, just to let her know I was taking her up on her offer. The girl was right about our needing to learn to know one another, especially when our lives could conceivably depend on that knowledge. I had experience going out with teams, and didn't have to be told how important it was to know beforehand which way everyone would jump if the stroke went sour. "And you sound as though you've worked with strangers before," I added after a moment.

"I certainly have," she said with a grimace, reaching for her cup of javi. "If the first time hadn't been against intellectual types rather than heavies, it could also have been the last time. My teammate was supposed to be the best with computers ever born, an opinion he managed to slip into every conversation we had, and he did seem to have very little trouble cracking the access code of our targets once I got him past the electronics they had on guard. The only problem was, when someone unexpectedly showed up in the offices, I turned around to find him gone, leaving me to get out or get caught on my own.''

"What did you do?" Chal demanded, his frown showing more than faint disapproval. "If I'd been there, he would have needed specialists once I caught up with him."

"He almost needed them when *I* caught up with him," Lidra returned with a snort, sharing his feeling. "If he'd stayed he couldn't have helped, but at least he would have made me feel less abandoned. What I did at the time, though, was the only thing I *could* do: I turned invisible."

"Now, that's a trick I'd like to learn," I said with a grin, pushing aside the empty pro-pure plate to lean my forearms on the table. "Some people will swear I already know how, but there's a difference between talent and true invisibility. Are you into giving lessons?"

"I'm afraid lessons won't do it," she said with a laugh, only glancing at the odd expression on Chal's face. It was part amusement and part admiration, but his mad against her former partner was still there as well. "One of my gadgets caused the invisibility, but it's really very simple to build. It's based on the principle used by privacy curtains, but generates a 180 degree reflecting surface rather than simply distorting a preset field of vision. Designing the function is easy when you compare it to the time you need to spend recircuiting, but even the recircuiting only takes about a week."

"Oh, is that all it takes," I said in a way that made Chal laugh as I sat back again. "If I'd known it was that easy, I would have done it years ago."

"Well, you should have asked me," she said with a smoothly innocent expression, taking the teasing better than I had. "I wouldn't have minded telling you. Are we all ready to go now? If we wait much longer, we won't even get in the doors."

I groaned at the reminder and reluctantly finished the last of my javi, then got to my feet under protest and let them drag me out. There were any number of things I'd rather have been doing instead of watching a fighter work out, but if it was that important to my new teammates it would hardly kill me to go along with them. With the number of people bound to be there it wasn't likely I was in danger of needing to speak to the big fool, after all, and once he had left and had taken his admirers with him, I'd be able to use the gym for my own workout.

There was a thin stream of people moving through the main corridor heading for the gym, so we simply joined them and went with the flow. The overwide double doors of the room were standing open when we got there, and we entered to see that half the ship really had shown up. An area of about twenty feet by twenty had been roped off to the far left of the gym, and the buzz of the crowd surrounding the area sounded child-level excited. There was enough room left over for a couple of people to be involved in their own workouts, but even as we came to a stop to the right of the incoming flow of new arrivals, one of those exercising gave it up to go and wait with those who had come for a show.

"Oh, good, he hasn't gotten here yet," Lidra said in a low voice, eyeing the crowd with excitement of her own. "Remember to stay as close to me as you can, you two, but don't go past the line of my shoulders. I'll be using a hemispherical repellent field to get us as far front as we want to go, and you're best off staying out of it. It won't hurt you, but it's everyone else we want to make uncomfortable enough to move, not one of us."

"I'm glad to see you come well-enough equipped to get the job done," I commented, having no intentions whatsoever of asking her what a repellent field was. "It's a good thing this isn't a real vacation, or you might have gotten caught short."

"I make it a practice *never* to leave home without the essentials," she answered with a smugness Chal and I both found funny, waving one hand in airy dismissal. "I was tempted to leave some of it behind in my cabin on the chance that Serendel might look my way, but that sort of off-again on-again poundage is too hard to explain. I guess I'll have to settle for *me* looking at *him*. Are we ready to move?"

"Why don't you two go ahead, and I'll join you once he gets here?" I suggested, having taken a minute to look around the unoccupied part of the gym. "I really hate standing in crowds doing nothing, and I see a mat over there where I can get some loosening up in. Then once the show is over, Chal and I can see which of us follows the most profitable eating regimen."

"But if we go ahead without you, how will you get through?" Lidra asked, turning to glance at the waiting spectators. "People like that sometimes get huffy if all you do is try to crowd them. An attempt to get ahead of them is usually considered a capital crime."

"Only for those who don't know how to move through crowds," I said with all the assurance she seemed to need, at the same time giving her a grin. "The man who raised me had a lot of friends, and they all felt they were under some kind of geas to teach me everything they could of their various specialties, even if I never intended using any of it. Every one of them considered me a star pupil, so I don't think you have to worry."

"I guess I'll just have to take your word for it," she grudged, but was already on the way to matching my grin. "And if it does work out right, maybe *you* could give *me* some lessons. That way I can think about catching Serendel's eye next time."

She gave me a small wave and then headed off with Chal following, which meant I was able to aim my own steps toward the deserted mat to the right of the doorway, not too far from the wall. This corner of the gym looked almost bare, with nothing but mats and climbing ropes and wall peg lifters and such between a couple of private-looking doors. The more sophisticated equipment was over near where the exhibition would take place, and a lot of it had people sitting or standing on its benches and frames to allow them a better view. It was a pure waste of good equipment, but happily I didn't need it just for loosening up.

I walked to the center of the mat and immediately bent over, stretching my arms down to where my palms were flat on the rough surface I stood on, then sending them back between my ankles as I stretched even lower. For some reason I was remembering how Seero used to tease me when I said I had to loosen up, insisting that I didn't *have* to, I only wanted to. I started out with the flexibility most people had to work up to, he'd always told me, and then went on from there to places most, including him, couldn't reach. I could almost hear him chuckling as he watched, telling me my palms-to-the-floor handicap ought to be my having to stand on two-inch-high blocks. . . .

I straightened up and then folded into sitting on the mat, trying to drive those thoughts away from me. It had been a long time since I'd last stopped to *feel* my loss, to send out my need for the close companionship and warm support I'd known for all those years—only to find the usual place of it forever emptied. Seero had always been there for me, *always,* and like a silly child I'd assumed he always would be. I couldn't yet cope with the thought of his being gone, not on an emotional level, so I hadn't even tried. All I'd done had been to look at those who had thrown his life away, and swear they would feel the same loss they'd given me, the same helplessness while knowing exactly what was happening. I needed to get on with fulfilling that vow even more than I needed to breathe, but there I sat, on my way to investigating something utterly unimportant, wasting the time I should be spending on what was really vital . . .

I took a deep breath, spread my legs and stretched my body down to the mat left, right and center, then bent my legs back at the knees so that my heels were close to my thighs. Letting all that burning impatience get the better of me would be stupid, most especially since there wasn't anything I could do about it just then. For the most part I'd have to wait it out, but if Lidra thought I'd be letting the tour people set my pace in the Mists, she wasn't as bright as she was supposed to be. Ours would be the fastest tour in the history of the Mists of the Ages, and that would include finding and breaking into their headquarters building.

Slowly, using muscle control, I began letting my body bend backward toward the mat. Lying flat while your legs are bent at the knees gives strength and stretch to your thigh muscles and tone to your body, and isn't anywhere near as painful as some people claim. You may be able to feel some strain if you pay attention to it, but relaxing is easier if you look at something else while you're doing it. I looked up at the gym ceiling hanging a full thirty feet above me, seeing the network of narrow and wide metal beams spanning the room about ten feet below that, consciously relaxing my muscles once I was flat down on the mat. I intended staying like that only a minute or two before raising myself again just as slowly, but suddenly something besides the ceiling appeared high above me.

I didn't know where he'd come from, but from my place on the mat he looked almost as tall as the network of beams I'd been inspecting. He was dressed in nothing but the heavy leather of a fighter, knee-high boots, narrow groin-cover, wide brown chest plate, bracers from wrist to elbow, and a brow-band. Around his waist was a swordbelt, and at his side hung a legendary multi-blade, the weapon allowed only to the best of the best. Glads started out with uniswords, worked at mastering them, then, if they lived, moved on to trithrusters. You had to be a double-gold winner at the very least in order to merit a multi-blade, and Serendel was supposed to be the best of the three-circlet winners. He put his fingertips to his swordbelt as he looked down at me, and faint amusement filled his cold gray eyes.

"I think I understand now why you blundered into me yesterday," he said, his wide-legged stance an arrogant challenge even when his words were nothing but mild. "If you do that on any sort of a regular basis, it's a miracle you can ever walk straight."

"Since *you* were the one who ran into *me,* I wonder what *your* excuse is," I retorted, staying down just for the hell of it. Some people claim that simply watching others do the stretch is painful, and if Serendel was one of those, he deserved every twitch. "Maybe you ought to trade in your equipment for a sonic tapping cane."

"If I were blind, I wouldn't have been in so much of a hurry that I couldn't have kept you from tripping under my feet," he returned, that long red mustache rising slightly with the increase of his amusement. "And if you've come to watch the show, little girl, remember what I said about staying back away from me. Someone with balance as bad as yours needs all the distance from danger she can get."

He turned and walked away then, coming up on the crowd from a direction they obviously hadn't been expecting him to appear, and I was so mad I sat up again without taking it slow. Someone with balance as bad

as *mine?* From a man who couldn't be trusted not to
stampede in the middle of a group of innocent people?
He had a hell of a lot of nerve making cracks about
me, especially in view of the way everyone stepped
back out of his path, opening a broad aisle for him to
stomp up. *That* was the sort of thing he was used to,
people scrambling to get out of his way, and too bad
about anyone who didn't.

I sat there on the mat with my fists to my thighs,
fuming mad, watching as the crowd closed up behind
him before surging forward a very little bit. They
couldn't wait for the big show to start, the sort of
exhibition of skill a top fighter put on even when he
was only warming up or practicing. It was too bad
nothing was likely to interrupt that exhibition, making
him look like the stumbling incompetent he was.

"You'd better stay back away from me," I mim-
icked in a mutter, hot enough to boil over. "Remember what I said about that."

What he'd said was twenty feet, but if he'd asked
my opinion, I wouldn't have settled for less than a
hundred. Twenty feet was a good deal closer than I
ever wanted to be to him, unless it was to watch him
hang by the neck from a rope—

The thought broke off as another one came to me,
an idea that brought a sudden grin to my face. So he
wanted me to stay twenty feet away from him, did he?
I raised my head slowly to look up at the network of
metal beams above me, thought about it for at least
ten seconds, then smoothly rose to my feet.

The crowd had already started their oohing and ahh-
ing and applauding as I turned to look for a climbing
rope, showing that the big hero had undoubtedly begun warming up. I knew I'd promised to join Lidra
and Chal as soon as that happened, but maybe they'd
be satisfied if all I did was spot them and wave. They
wouldn't be able to claim I hadn't watched the workout the way I'd said I would, because my seat was
going to be the best one in the house.

The climbing ropes were anchored into the ceiling,
so all I had to do was choose the one that fell closest
to the metal framework and unhook the bottom of it

from the wall. It was a heavy rope that looked sturdy enough, but I still hung my full weight from it for a minute while I was close enough to the ground that a fall wouldn't matter. Seero had taught me to distrust everyone's rigging but my own, and not to expect miracles even then. Things can happen even to an unbreakable line, and if you don't really believe that, you'll never find it possible to be prepared.

The climbing rope seemed as solidly anchored as possible, so I began pulling myself up it, hand over hand. It didn't take long to reach the framework the rope hung beside, and swinging over to it with my legs was also no problem. The metal beam was a narrow one, no more than a couple of inches wide, but I'd walked smaller and with a lot less light. I stood with the help of a ceiling-set corner brace, glad that the framework was as steady with me on it as it looked from below, then started moving toward the brace on the other side. The metal was hard under my feet and a little too smooth, but I still made it all the way without slipping.

When I reached the second brace I took a minute to look down, which confirmed the fact that no one had spotted me yet. Everyone's eyes were locked to Serendel, watching with fanatic pleasure as he swung his multi-sword on its lowest setting, moving through a glad drill that was meant to warm him up. The drill demanded grace rather than strength, finesse rather than attack, and watching him it was almost possible to believe he'd negated most of his own weight as well as his sword's. Most big men weren't that quick—which is not the same as being fast—and I thought I could see why so many people expected so many great things from him.

But none of that changed my own intentions. The man wanted me at least twenty feet away from him, so that's what he would get. Past the brace I held to was a triple line of metal framework, three times the width of what I'd walked and more than wide enough for what I planned. I swung around the brace to its other side, got both feet onto the triple beam and then, with my arms only a small distance from my sides, walked to the spot I'd been aiming for all along. It was about two-thirds of the way along the beam, and when I got there I bent carefully, then stretched myself out along the metal.

Grandstanding on a beam that high off the ground isn't very smart, but as I pretended to make myself comfortable on my right side, I knew that right then I preferred feeling satisfied to feeling intelligent. The fighter was about ten feet ahead of my position and twenty feet down, which, if I remembered my school math correctly, meant I was a little better than twenty-two feet away from him. Since I'd done just what he'd asked me to, he couldn't very well complain, could he?

Everyone applauded when Serendel finished his warm-ups, and then gasped in delight when the fighter whirled his sword over his head to reset its weight. The jewels in its fingerguard blazed with a light that was almost life, and everyone watching undoubtedly wondered exactly how much weight the sword was now being allowed to manifest. During multi-blade combats the glads themselves usually had that question, wondering just how much it would take to stop the strike coming at them. It wasn't unknown for a fighter to defend against an attack that seemed to have everything behind it, only to find that the multi-sword striking his was set at minimum and therefore was immediately bouncing off. What usually happened after that was seeing his opponent ride the bounce away in an arc that brought the sword back faster than he could defend against, most often with maximum weight returned to it, and that ended the bout in a bloody and very final way. Knowing when to change the weight of the sword, how much to change it, and performing the changeovers smoothly were skills the fighters worked very hard to master; those who made it survived and prospered, while those who didn't had their names added to the lists of the fallen.

I was leaning on my right elbow and supporting my head with the hand, watching with supposed full attention while I kept my balance with my left hand on the beam, when someone finally spotted me. One of the people on the far side of the crowd happened to glance up, did a double take, then started nudging others around him as he pointed. Even more eyes began coming to me then, the nudging and pointing spreading left and right away from its starting point, and before very long it had migrated around the circle to those who stood with their backs to me. When more and more people began turning around, looking up and gasping, it finally came to the star of the exhibition that he was losing his audience. He finished a run-through of a series of attacks and counters, frowned when he saw how many people had their backs to him, then finally looked up.

"By the five-pointed crown of Lethen Highwinner!" the fighter blurted, letting his point fall almost to the deck plates as he saw me. "What in hell are you doing up there?"

"I'm watching the show," I called back, making sure I didn't let the speaking shift me off balance. "You *did* tell me to stay at least twenty feet away from you, and this was the only way I could do it and still get to see something. That isn't all you're going to be doing, is it?"

"Get the hell down from there before you fall and break your neck!" the magnificent Serendel ordered in a growl, resheathing his sword before putting his fists to his hips. "How in the name of sanity did you get up there in the first place?"

"I used a climbing rope," I answered innocently, moving my head in the general direction of where the rope still hung. "If heights bother you, you don't have to look at me, you know. Just turn your back and pretend I'm somewhere underfoot, and then you'll be able to get on with your practice."

The man's head came up in annoyance as most of the crowd chuckled, his appreciation of my comment a lot less than theirs. They were interested and amused because they thought I was challenging the fighter, the way any number of misguided fools did with glads on a more or less regular basis. What only the fighter himself realized was that I was *answering* a challenge, not offering one, and he didn't seem to care for it much.

"You're not interested in coming down right now?" he asked once the laughter had quieted, his tone suddenly as smooth as the glint in his eyes. "Well, in that case there's something that should be taken care of, and since you're way up there, I'll see to it for you."

I didn't understand what he was talking about any more than the other people in the room, but they got out of his way fast enough when he stepped over the rope around his practice area and began striding across the floor. I sat up on the beam, shifted my feet under me before standing carefully, then turned to walk back the way I'd come. I had a very strong hunch I needed to be back to where I'd started from as fast as humanly possible, and when I reached the end brace I saw I'd been right but was already too late. The miserable fiend had reached the climbing rope before I got to the brace, and even as I watched he finished hooking it tight to the wall in its original position. Pulled that far out of line I couldn't reach it from the framework of beams, something my adversary had known would happen even before he'd done it.

"There we are, now everything's neat and tidy," he said as he turned from the wall, looking up to send me the faintest of grins. "Leaving a rope just hanging down like that can cause someone to get hurt, and I really hate seeing people get hurt. You be sure and let me know as soon as you're ready to come down, and we'll see about untying that rope again."

This time the laughter was in support of *him,* half a dozen people going so far as to applaud as well. The upstart's challenge to their hero had been answered with style, and the foolish female would be stuck up on the beams for as long as he wanted her there. They also seemed to be hoping he would make her ask him nicely before he let her down, and I really did feel sorry that their hopes would end up being dashed. The foolish female would have stayed in the metalwork until she died of thirst and hunger before asking their

hero for anything, but happily for her, staying and dying weren't going to be necessary.

Serendel had already turned and started back to his
practice area when I swung around the brace, then began walking the single beam back toward the center
of it. I couldn't afford to spare attention for anything
but what I was doing and planned to do, but I heard
the muttering and gasps of the crowd telling me they
were still watching. The highest point I'd ever formally dismounted from was fifteen feet, but I knew
there had been an informal time or two when I'd bet-
tered that. I hadn't had the opportunity to measure back
then, but if twenty feet was more than I could handle,
I'd certainly find out soon enough.

By the time I reached the center of the beam, I had
driven all doubt away, setting myself firmly into the
proper confidence and concentration for dismounting.
I had all the room and time I needed, all the balance
and ability, so I turned head on in the center of the
beam, kicked off it backward, caught it with my hands
as I dropped, then sent myself swinging below and
past it into the empty, open air.

I don't think dismounting will ever stop making me
feel as though I can fly. Flipping over in the air slows
your rate of descent and gives you control of the drop,
but while you're doing it you feel as though you don't
have to land, you're simply doing it because you've
decided to. I turned twice in the air and twisted, and
then I was down on the mat I'd been stretching on,
my landing crouch a little deeper than proper form
approves of, but doing nothing to keep me from staying erect. Once I was sure I would continue that way,
I turned my head toward my trusty opponent.

"I think I'd like to come down now," I said, working to sound as helpless as possible. "Would you
please see about untying the rope?"

Serendel was frozen in place less than ten feet way,
everyone else silent and gawping behind him, and then
the cheering and applause erupted, making it sound
like there were a thousand people in the room. I wasn't
used to being cheered and applauded—audiences tend
to be minimal or absent entirely when I perform—and

I was so distracted by the unexpected enthusiasm that Serendel was standing right in front of me before I even knew he'd moved.

"I have to ask you to forgive me for the boorish way I've been insulting you," he said, looking down at me with an odd expression in those cold gray eyes. "I can see now our collision couldn't have been anyone's fault but mine, which means I must offer a belated apology. From now on, please feel free to come as close to me as you like."

If I'd been distracted a minute earlier by the cheering and applause, his apologizing sent me into virtual shock. Never in a million years had I expected him to say something like that, which is most likely the reason he had my hand before I so much as realized he'd taken it. I felt the touch of shock again, only stronger, when he actually bent over it and kissed it, and it was all I could do to keep from staring after him like a gaping idiot when he turned to go back to his practice area. Never in my life had I seen anything like that—not to mention having it done to me—and it took a minute to realize that Lidra and Chal hadn't followed the crowd back to where it had come from.

"So that's what it takes to get his attention," Lidra said, her amusement still very much with her. "The equivalent of diving off a rooftop. Okay, no problem. Next time it'll be *my* turn to be kissed."

"Before or after you get out of traction?" Chal asked with a chuckle, looking at me with very bright eyes. "Inky here was obviously born to fly, but we lesser mortals have to make do with being chained to the ground. And in case you were wondering, Inky, our competition date is off. If that's the kind of shape eating greasy hot-fries and meat-rounds puts you in, I don't even want to know what decent food would do. The Empire isn't yet ready for the perfect woman."

"Why, Chal, I thought you said *I* was the perfect woman," Lidra protested with pretend insult, her pout just about as believable as her claim, her hand coming up to take his arm. "If the Empire isn't yet ready for me, whatever will I do with my time?"

"We'll figure *something* out," the man reassured her with a grin, patting the hand that held to his arm. "But until we do, we still have an exercise session to watch. Are you ready, Inky? With the sort of personal invitation you were given, you won't need Lidra's repellent field to get you right up to the front line."

"Why don't you two go ahead without me," I suggested, for some reason very embarrassed by what had happened. "I don't find much interest in watching other people exercise, and it would be rude if he caught me yawning in boredom. He apologized for that misunderstanding yesterday, you know."

"For the—'misunderstanding,' " Lidra said dryly, apparently trying to hide some sort of new amusement. "Yes, we know, we saw him do it. Don't you just love the way fighters apologize? It makes you want to start an argument, just to give him another chance to do it. If you're sure you don't want to come with us, meet us later in the dining hall for lunch. We can tell you how it went over a nutritious meal of hot-fries and meat-rounds."

I smiled and nodded while Chal laughed, and then we separated to go our individual ways. I left the gym and got back to my cabin as quickly as possible, then sat down in a chair to look at the hand that had been kissed. It was such an odd feeling to have been treated like that, to have been made to feel that I'd been raised in palaces rather than on the dusk side of respectability. I'd never regret the way I'd been raised or what Seero had taught me, but somehow I wished we *had* lived more often among those who inhabited palaces, so that I would have learned what to do when a man kissed my hand. There *had* to be something to do besides standing there staring like a moron, but I suppose it takes time and experience to learn what.

I folded my legs under me and leaned back in the chair, regretting the fact that we'd be getting to Joelare in less than another two ship's days. If the time were going to be longer I would have seriously considered Serendel's offer, but with no more than a day and a half to work with, all I could do was forget it. My co-workers and I had things to do on Joelare, and after that I had things of my own to occupy me on Gryphon. That meant I would be wisest avoiding all contact with Serendel for the rest of the trip, to keep from starting something I might not want to see end.

I sighed as I closed my eyes, called up a picture of the man in his fighting leathers to look at, and spent some time wondering if I would ever see him again.

Chapter 6

The rest of our time on the liner went by as quickly as I'd known it would, and my only major chore turned out to be putting up with Lidra's teasing. She understood well enough why I'd decided against getting involved with Serendel; it would be more than awkward if the fighter decided to pay my way to wherever *he* was going, just to give us more time together. Fighters did that sort of thing on a regular basis with women they found attractive, and what kind of excuse could I use as a reason for refusing? Previous reservations? He'd be sure to insist on paying me back for them. Lack of interest? Then why did I get involved with him in the first place? No, the only option I had was to stay away from the man, that or tell him what we'd be up to on Joelare.

Since Lidra understood the point at least as well as I did, she didn't let herself be more than disappointed that she and Chal would not be introduced to the fighter the way they'd been looking forward to. What she did do, though, was give me a detailed description of all Serendel's public movements, including the fact that there were times he seemed to be surreptitiously searching the crowds around him. This, to Lidra, was Highly Significant, an action she didn't hesitate to interpret.

"He's obviously looking for *you*," she proclaimed once, delighted to be privy to limited, inside information. "Every time I see the poor thing doing it, my heart goes out to him."

"I'll bet that's not all you'd like to have going out

to him," I couldn't help saying, her pious pity quickly getting to be more than annoying. "And chances are what he's really looking for is that elegant female he appropriated the first day out of his cabin."

"Why would he be looking for *her?*" the very innocent question came, changing Chal's grin to chuckling. "She showed up at that first practice right after you left, carved entirely out of smug self-satisfaction and obviously thinking she was making an entrance. When no one even glanced at her she started getting annoyed, but when she tried to get through the crowd and no one would let her by, she went furious. I didn't have a directional pick-up handy, so I couldn't hear what she said, but she must have convinced the people around her that she was entitled to be in front because she was sleeping with the guy. They must have believed her because they finally let her through."

"But not very willingly," Chal added, laughing softly at the memory. "I don't think they would have minded if it had been you trying to get past them, and some of them actually seemed to resent her. After that she gave up on the entrances, and strutted into places on Serendel's arm."

"Why do you people feel you have the right to approve or disapprove of your hero's personal life?" I asked, suddenly resentful of the supporter mentality. "He didn't *ask* any of you to support him, so what gives you the right to tell him who he should or shouldn't be sleeping with? Unless one of you is scheduled to be his bed stand-in, it's really none of your business."

"But of course it is," Chal answered at once, beating Lidra to it, neither of them the least bit insulted. "His being as good as he is *forced* us to be his supporters, and now that he belongs to us we want nothing but the best for him. He's *entitled* to it, you see, and if he doesn't find it for himself, we don't mind helping out. It's the least we can do in appreciation of what he does for us."

"And since we female fans can't have him for ourselves, we're damned well going to see him with someone we can stomach," Lidra said, one hand smoothing her purple-streaked hair. "That slinker he picked up is okay as a bed-bunny in the absence of anyone better, but there's nothing she can do that the rest of us couldn't, so why should *she* have special privileges? What you did, on the other hand, *was* special, which is the reason most of us would rather see him with you. We know we can't compete with an accomplishment like that, so we can accept your being with him in place of one of us. That's not to say we like it, but we *can* accept it."

At that point I sat back in my lounge chair and sipped at my javi, far from satisfied but deciding not to pursue the point any further. The whole thing felt too much like the sort of prearranged lifestyles some elements of the Empire still insisted on, the kind that sewed you into what other people thought was best for you. I'd been outraged the first time I'd heard about the practice and had known that those people were lucky they'd never tried their nonsense on *me*. Telling them what to do with themselves would have been the least of my reactions, and somehow this approval of me for Serendel felt almost like the same attitude. Lidra, Chal and I had been taking our meals in various lounges rather than in the dining hall despite the fact that it cost more that way, preferring the cash outlay to the possibility of running into Serendel. At first I'd been disappointed that it had to be done like that, but after our conversation concerning approval, I was more relieved than disappointed.

When the shuttle took us down to Aeon, Joelare's newest port, Lidra and Chal finally found something other than their hero to talk about. We left the vehicle with at least twenty other people, gasping out our awed delight with the port's decor, admiring the fairyland castle which was their entry-admin building for those booked into the Mists of the Ages. People who were coming to Joelare for reasons other than tourism had to make do with an ordinary customs building of metal and glasstic, but we who were the chosen were escorted into the Castle of Beginning.

". . . where all you lucky people will be given orientation information about your individual tours," our chief guide burbled as she walked ahead of us, smiling and gesturing at our destination. Assistant guides or aides were also among us, carrying any hand luggage we were willing to part with, cautioning us to watch our steps, and taking food and drink orders from anyone who felt themselves in dire need.

"Costumes like mine and other tour area variations will be available for you as soon as we have your measurements," she went on in great enjoyment, pausing to turn once in front of us to let us see the many-layered gown of gold she was wearing. The skirts were so wide she probably needed double doors to get into a room, the front of the dress dipped so low her upper measurements could have been taken by eye, and the three-quarter sleeves on the thing trailed so much white lace it was surprising she was able to lift her arms.

"What if gold isn't our best color?" a mild but very deep voice asked, the voice of one of the men with us. We all laughed at the way he'd avoided asking the most obvious question, and even our guide enjoyed the effort.

"I was about to add that masculine equivalents of this gown will be available for viewing on the castle servants," she answered with a laugh as she resumed walking, the first real laugh we'd heard out of her. "If you'd rather, though, we can have the gowns made up in any color you like. As our guest, the choice will be entirely yours."

The man acknowledged her comment with a deep-voiced chuckle of appreciation shared by most of the rest of us, but some of us weren't very happy with the entire idea. We weren't even near the Mists yet, but some of us were already impatient to be leaving.

"Oh, Inky, stop looking so sour," Lidra said to me with no effort at keeping her voice down, her exasperation with my attitude clear to anyone who heard her. "Dressing up in costumes will be *fun*, as long as you make yourself forget you couldn't cancel your reservations without losing your deposit money. It isn't *their* fault your friend got sick at the last minute, so what's the sense in deciding beforehand that you aren't

going to enjoy yourself no matter what? As long as
you're paying for it, you might as well enjoy it.''

"I may have to pay for it, but I sure as hell don't
have to enjoy it," I countered, also making no effort
to keep my voice down. "If I've got to be here *I'll*
decide what I will and won't wear, not some overpaid
flunky with an underactive imagination."

Lidra sighed and simply shook her head, but that
didn't mean she wasn't satisfied with the way the conversation had gone. We'd decided back on the liner
that a reluctant guest would be the best thing for me
to be, especially if everyone was made fully aware of
my attitude. There would be times I'd need to be away
from the tour group or dressed in a way that would let
me work, and being tagged uncooperative right from
the start would get us past the need for later excuses.
Chal had helped us build a logically consistent story,
and I was a lot happier with it than I would have been
with pretend enthusiasm.

"You don't need to watch your steps on the draw-
bridge, the entire area is shielded," our guide said,
moving first onto a wide ramp of golden vapor. "Once
you enter the Mists there will be areas you mustn't
move through except with your journey scouts, but
you'll be warned about them well in advance, and the
warnings will be repeated on a regular basis until after
the area is behind you. You will, of course, be told
more about that later. Right now, please follow me."

The first people to follow the woman felt a need to
test the solidity of the vapor with one foot before trusting the rest of themselves to it, but after them no one
else bothered. The golden vapor was as solid underfoot as you would expect a force field to be, and we
climbed the ramp without difficulty through a golden
arch that led us to a wide entrance hall of marble and
rainbows. The hall was roofed over with something
transparent that took the outer day's sunshine and di-
vided it into its prismatic parts, and I had to be careful
not to gasp with everyone else. The hall was absolutely beautiful, and there wasn't anyone there who
didn't appreciate it.

"Just show your reservation slips to the attendants

moving among you, and they'll direct you to the proper Customs section," our guide told us after a moment, having given us a chance to stare at the loveliness. "You'll relax in comfort while our Customs people clear you, and then you'll be allowed the choice of starting for the Mists as soon as your wardrobes are ready, or spending the night here in the castle and starting in the morning. Those of you on A and AA class tours won't be supplied with wardrobes, and will therefore be able to leave as soon as you've gone through Customs. We know none of you will want to waste even one extra minute reaching the Mists, and we can't blame you. We hope you all enjoy your stay at Mists of the Ages, and look forward to welcoming you back many times in the future."

The woman gave us a final smile and then went to stand at the far side of the room, all finished with her part of the job unless someone had a question they wanted to ask. The attendants who moved among us were both male and female, the men wearing knee-pants and hose and more-or-less elegant coats and such, the women wearing long-skirted gowns that for the most part were nearly the equal of our former guide's dress. Eight closed doorways were spaced around the otherwise empty hall, and each of the doorways had one additional attendant standing in front of it. From what I could see, the door attendants were dressed somewhat differently from those who circulated among us, and then one of the latter was up to Chal, Lidra and me, checking our slips with a glance.

"Portal number three, counting from the left, is your destination, my lord and ladies," the man said with a bow, sweeping his arm in the proper direction. "If you should be interested in the period my costume represents, just ask about the tour through sectors six, eleven and twenty-one."

He bowed again before moving on, and Lidra and I turned briefly to watch him go. His costume had been mostly tights with the addition of a large, intricately decorated codpiece, and the tights were as tight behind as they had been in front. I'm not quite sure what our expressions were like, but Chal put a hand on each of our shoulders from behind.

"Don't even think about it," he said in a low voice, but not so low that we couldn't hear the flat finality in it. "After we finish our fun time here you girls can go wherever you like, but don't even think about suggesting we go through his sector on the way. Anybody who tries to get me into a get-up like that will have a fight on his hands."

"Why, Chal!" Lidra said with surprise, turning to look at him. "That's the second time you've talked about committing violence. I thought you were dedicated to healing the hurt, not causing them the problem in the first place."

"When you're willing to fight, you usually don't have to," he answered with calm confidence, the look in his eyes the same. "And just because my greatest joy comes from curing the sick and hurt, that doesn't mean I have to stand helplessly by while people take advantage of me and those around me. I don't usually go out looking for people to mangle, but if you two don't get that calculation out of your eyes, I'll be happy to make your cases an exception."

"We surrender," Lidra said with both hands raised before her while I laughed. "You're bigger and stronger and nastier than we are, so there won't be any side trips. I just think it's such a pity. Women who haven't seen your behind don't know what they're missing."

Her glance was very bland when she slid it away from him, and most likely the only thing that saved her was the fact that she immediately began walking toward the "portal" which had been pointed out to us. It was possible that Chal would have strangled her if she'd stayed within reach, and the embarrassed flush on his face as he and I followed her said it might still happen as soon as they were alone together.

When we reached door three it was opened for us by the attendant standing in front of it, a man wearing a leather skirt that came down to his knees and leather sandals that laced all the way up his legs. For the most part his chest was bare, except for two straps of leather

that crossed it, then spread out very wide over his
shoulders. Both shoulders were completely covered
and the leather extended a least two inches beyond
them, an odd sort of arrangement I'd never seen before.

"Now *that's* something I can live with," Chal remarked as we entered the room, gesturing back toward
the attendant with his head. "Especially if you girls
get costumes just like it."

That time it was Chal's turn to grin while Lidra gave
him a stare that promised a lingering death, which
made me the only one left to look around. The room
we'd entered was open and airy while still giving the
impression of privacy, but above that it was very in-
terestingly furnished. The carpeting under our feet appeared to be open, blue-green water, the sort you sail
on and swim in, but rarely walk on. Chairs and
couches were white, fluffy clouds, billowing a little
where they hung, and large fluttering birds hovered in
the air beside the couches and chairs. Two servants in
costumes made up of gauze and wings stood on two
of four tiny islands spaced around the room, while two
more servants dressed the same way were offering trays
of food and drink to the four older people already in
the room and seated on the clouds.

"Well, will you look at that," Lidra said from behind my right shoulder, Chal to her right. "It does pay
not to be on a class A or AA tour, doesn't it? If they're
not willing to give them costumes or a bed for the
night, they certainly won't be giving them something
like this."

"I've got to try one of those clouds," Chal said,
for all the world like an eager tourist. "I've always
wanted to stretch out on one, but I'm too practical not
to know I'd fall through. If I fall through here, I can
sue."

"If you don't drown first," Lidra said, looking
down at what our feet rested on. "Are those fish I see
swimming down there? Maybe we *would* be better off
sitting down. The idea of being submerged is not one
I care for at the moment."

She headed for one of the cloud-couches without

adding anything to what she'd said, but Chal and I still got the message. Lidra had never told me exactly how much of her electronic equipment she carried with her, but from her reaction to the ocean-carpeting, most of it must have been of the non-waterproof sort. I thought briefly about swimming while wrapped up in a working electrified fence, shuddered a little, then followed along to the couch.

The cloud felt just the way a cloud should feel, soft and billowing but still firm enough to support us. We had barely made ourselves comfortable when one of the winged servants came over for our food and drink orders, telling us we could name just about anything and it would be supplied—for a price. Standard for our tour at that particular moment was a beverage and sandwiches, but we would be given an assortment of the sandwiches and could eat as many as we liked. One of the other tours included a free choice of edibles and drinkables at no extra charge, and before the servant left to get our food and javi we were told which one it was. Lidra waited until the servant was out of easy hearing range, and then she shook her head.

"They do believe in advertising in this place, don't they?" she asked, one hand brushing at her purple-streaked hair. "I wonder what they try to sell you if you've booked the best they've got?"

"Possibly a life membership," Chal suggested, too pleased with his section of cloud to really care. "I think those people over there ordered more than the sandwiches. If our standard dinner isn't a good deal above snack level, we ought to consider spending the extra money ourselves."

Lidra made a noncommittal noise and I shrugged, but I was seriously considering going along with Chal's suggestion. The man had been annoyed with me for teasing him when he found out I usually *did* eat well-balanced meals rather than junk, but I'd been arguing a principle rather than a belief. If I wanted to eat junk food I should be free to do it, whether or not I actually indulged in the freedom. Chal had refused to see that, insisting I was only trying to be difficult, but I still intended joining him in any superior meals that were

offered. After all, with S.I. paying for it, there was no
reason I shouldn't.

By the time our food and drink had been brought,
there were two new arrivals over with the older people. The two men were dressed in svalk pants, hose,
ruffled shirts and patterned svalk vests, and they chat-
ted comfortably with the newly arrived guests as they
checked and stamped their papers. Customs inspection
is something you go through no matter which world
of the Empire you visit, but some are a little less fanatic about it than others. Joelare officials seemed to
be downright human, which was a pleasant surprise.

Our javi cups had been refilled two or three times
before it became our turn, and the two men called for
javi of their own before they settled down near us.
They studied our papers so thoroughly they couldn't
have missed anything that was there to be found, and
then one of the two men looked up at us with a smile.

"I see you three young people each came here on
your own," he said, looking very satisfied with that
idea. "Did you meet on the liner the way those two
couples over there did? Yes, I thought you might have.
People do that all the time, coming here as strangers
and leaving as friends. Right now you'll probably think
I'm boasting, but our world *does* bring people together
and make fast friends of them. It's sharing the experiences you have ahead of you that does it, and even
if you never come back you won't forget the time.
Very few worlds can say the same, and that makes us
rather proud."

"And also pleased to welcome you here," the second man said, adding his own smile. "You list nothing but clothing and a few convenience devices on
your declaration statements, but for safety's sake there
are specific questions we need to ask. Are any of you
taking a prescribed medication of any sort? We've
found there are certain substances that don't react well
with the vapor of the Mists, and we can tell you
whether or not a given prescription is one of them. It
isn't necessary to ask about *illegal* substances, and for
good reason. Anyone taking one or more of the current
crop of dustings and fixings will find they don't get

along with the Mists at *all*. If throwing up every ten minutes for your entire tour appeals to you, we wouldn't think of asking you to forgo the pleasure.''

Lidra, Chal and I exchanged glances while the two men grinned at us, that more than anything else assuring us they were telling the truth. If they hadn't been, they would have been working to get us to believe them, not telling us to go ahead and try it for ourselves. It was an interesting way of doing things, but I found myself faintly curious.

''I'm not taking anything of any sort, but I have a question for *you*,'' I said, keeping my tone mild but not looking in any way impressed. ''Did you make the same point to our older companions over there, or do you save the speech for the Empire's flowering youth?''

''Oh, we make sure to announce it to people like them first,'' the second man told me, neither one of them looking the least insulted. ''Kids *know* they're doing something wrong, so all but the really lost among them will try for caution if not moderation. Many so-called grownups, though, know the laws aren't made for *them,* so why should they bother with caution beyond surface appearances? Some are so deeply into it they become violently ill in the Mists, and end up in a hospital for the rest of their vacation. It's one of the reasons for these ironclad releases you'll be signing. When you look through them, you'll find other reasons.''

My two companions and I were then handed small leather books, and each of us got the book with our name on it. Inside were a number of pages with questions and statements, and if a question didn't call for a specific answer, the directions ordered us to sign our full names instead. We were also handed indelible markers, and then the first of the men signaled for more javi.

By the time I was ready to hand the book back, I'd shared all of my personal preferences, most of the things I'd tried doing during my life, some of the things I thought I could do in the future, and no longer remembered how to spell my name. The thing was a good deal more than just a release in the event of an accident, and once the two men had glanced through what we'd written, one of them told Chal he had nothing to worry about, then the two of them thanked us with smiles and went on their way.

"Phew!" Lidra said as she let herself fall back against our cloud, holding her right hand up in a claw. "Did anyone notice if that thing held them blameless in the event of an acute case of writer's cramp? If it didn't, I'm seriously considering calling my lawyer."

"What aren't you supposed to worry about, Chal?" I asked, turning my head to see the way he massaged his right hand with his left. I'd already flexed my fingers back to normal, but still half-wished Lidra wasn't just fooling around about suing.

"I listed the medication I'm taking, and apparently I don't have to worry about it getting into a fight with the Mists," Chal answered, his light eyes very open and innocent, no more than a friendly smile on his face. "It's really nothing more than a general health enhancer with a complex base, my doctor tells me, but there was no sense in taking chances by keeping quiet about it."

I nodded vaguely and performed a small shrug, just as though I were dismissing the whole thing after understanding almost nothing of what he'd said, but to describe me as curious would be like describing the room we sat in as faintly unusual. I hadn't known Lidra and Chal long, but the one thing I was absolutely certain of was that neither of them took any sort of medication, necessary or unnecessary, legal or illegal. Lidra was like me in that she could never remember to take something even when she was sick, and Chal believed almost fanatically that to become dependent on a drug in anything but the most extreme emergency was as good as cutting your own throat. For him, the key to true survival health was to strengthen the body's own defenses, not ignore them in favor of artificial supplements. With that in mind I *knew* Chal wasn't taking anything, so why had he said he was?

I would have enjoyed being able to ask someone other than myself, but even though I'd never done that sort of S.I. sneaking around before, I wasn't simple-minded. Since we didn't know whether or not we were being listened to by people out of sight, we had to assume we *were* being listened to and therefore had to watch what we said. That, at least, was the way *I* saw it, and my companions seemed to be operating under the same set of rules. I shifted around on the cloud, about to wonder aloud what would be coming next, but the appearance of a woman in the same sort of golden gown as our original greeter and guide saved me the trouble.

"My lords and ladies, I bid you all a good day," the woman announced with a practiced smile, apparently unaware of the fact that she sounded as though she were leaving rather than arriving. "I'd like to take my own turn at welcoming you to the Mists of the Ages, the vacation land you'll never forget. I'm Filla, and after you answer a few questions for me, I'll be glad to answer any *you* might have. To begin with, have you all decided whether or not you'll be staying in the castle tonight? If you haven't, please take a moment or two to make the decision now."

"What do you think, girls?" Chal asked as quiet conversation arose among our four fellow tourists where they sat. "I'd rather stay with you two than take off on my own, so which way do you want to do it?"

"I'd rather leave now and get it over with that much faster," I answered, still sticking with my impatient-and-unhappy pose. "Hanging around here will just drag it out longer, but I don't want to go on alone either. If you two decide to stay, so will I."

"Come on, Inky, being in a hurry is dumb," Lidra said with a shake of her head, adding a sigh for good measure. "We'll be spending a total of three days here, and staying over until tomorrow morning doesn't mean the three days begin *then*, because they've already begun. Starting tomorrow morning only means we spend less time in the Mists. Didn't you read the brochure?"

"No," I answered a second time, trying not to show how stupid I felt for not knowing that. "My friend was the one who talked me into all this, and I'd never

even heard of the place. Does that mean you want to
stay over?''

"Hell no," she came back with a grin, sitting up
straighter on her piece of cloud. "Since we came to
see the Mists, why waste time sitting around in *this*
place? Let's get going as soon as we can."

"Then that's our decision," Chal said, getting to
his feet. "I'll go over and tell her."

As he walked away I could see the other four people
were still talking it over, but our decision wasn't just
made, it was also justified. We weren't likely to find
much of anything to investigate out in the open and
right at the port, so Lidra had come up with a reason
as to why we didn't want to stay there. My own try at
justification had been on the flimsy side, but at least I
now had a reason for asking about the place. And a
reason for not knowing about most of what was going
on. Lidra and Chal were supposed to have filled me in
on the liner ride, and probably would have if most of
their time and conversation hadn't been taken up by
their favorite fighter. I felt a brief flash of annoyance,
but getting mad at the two would have been useless.
If those S.I. people had briefed me properly I wouldn't
have needed anyone else doing it, but they'd been in
too much of a hurry to get rid of me to come up with
so much as a brochure. If I'd had any intentions of
continuing to work with them, that alone would have
made me stop to think about it.

By the time Chal finished talking to the woman, one
of the men from the other group was on his way over
to her with their own decision. The woman thanked
them both with a smile, then turned to include the rest
of us in on the conversation.

"My lords and ladies, the group of four will remain
our guests for the night," she said, sounding as though
everything had worked out exactly the way it was supposed to. "If the smaller group will follow me, I'll
get them started toward the costuming area. As soon
as that's done, I'll be back to take accommodation and
dinner orders from those who will be staying. Ladies?''

The last word was addressed to Lidra and me, and

I didn't know about her, but I found it—inappropriate.
I had always considered a lady to be someone who did
nothing but stand or sit around looking cool, aloof,
and untouchable, totally useless and helpless and very
pleased to have it like that. Seero had tried more than
once to tell me I was wrong, but that was a point we
had never agreed on. He'd said it was possible for a
woman to be a lady no matter what she looked like or
did, but that was silly. How could you be a lady if
you didn't look or act like one?

The woman in the golden gown led us to one section
of a light blue wall, which slid out of her way when
she stopped in front of it. Beyond the now-opened
doorway was a thirty-foot corridor of rich brown wood,
and the woman pointed toward the narrow wall at the
other end of the corridor.

"Just walk straight at it, and it will open for you,"
she said, giving us another professionally warm smile.
"The dressers there will have your costumes, and once
you're into them you'll be ready to go. Your measurements were taken electronically when you first entered
the castle, so what was made up for you should need
no more than minor adjustment."

"What about the luggage we brought with us?" I
asked, stopping Lidra and Chal as they began to enter
the corridor. "Your costumes may be absolutely wonderful, but if I should decide I'm not in the mood to
wear one, I don't want my only other choice to be
skin."

"Your luggage has already been passed through
Customs, and will be sent with you to the places you'll
be staying in the Mists," she answered, her pleasant-
ness still intact. "Whether or not you wear a costume
will, of course, be your choice alone, but I certainly
hope you don't decide against them. Only those who
are costumed can be considered part of the scene, and
missing the interaction will take half the fun out of
your vacation. Without a costume all you can do is
watch, and unless there are physical reasons for that
sort of a decision, I don't recommend it. Please step
ahead now, and do enjoy your trip."

With my question answered there was nothing to

keep me standing there, and the woman did have the decency not to turn away from us until after we reached the other end of the corridor and the door there slid open. As we stepped through I could also see her stepping back, letting the wall on her end close again, the gesture possibly meant to keep us from feeling trapped. That had been something of a narrow corridor, and I could see how some people might feel uncomfortable in it.

The room we stepped into from the corridor was not only normal, it was downright dull. The plain brown walls to right and left had nothing but closed doors to decorate them, and the lighting came from ordinary overheads. The man and woman who waited for us with smiles wore bodysuits like Lidra's and mine, both of them having added shorts and vests, and they were briskly firm about separating Chal from us. The man took him to the first room on the left, and the woman led the "ladies" to the first door on the right.

"Your costumes are in the two cubicles, girls," our newest guide said, throwing open the door to show us a large mirrored room with curtained alcoves to the far left and right. "The lilac set is for you with your blond hair, dear, and the rose-red is meant to go with your black hair, honey. Once you're into the outfits, ring the bell between the cubicles, and I'll come in and check the fit."

The woman gently bustled us inside, then closed the door behind us, so Lidra and I shrugged at one another and went to check out our "outfits." It was to be expected that we each went to the other's alcove, but once we traded I stood by the closed curtain and studied what had been made for me. The color was a very delicate rose-red, all right, but it was also a female version of the costume the door attendant outside our Customs room had been wearing. Rather than being leather it was made of svalk, the knee-length skirt neatly pleated, the top a sleeveless cross-over wrap, the whole thing belted with a side-knotted scarf. The sandals that went along with them had soft leather bottoms and svalk upper parts and lacings, and didn't look as though they would be all that uncomfortable. Taken together it wasn't a bad little outfit, and it came to me that I would have to try their costumes at least once before I could safely "decide' I didn't want any more of them. It would obviously be best if I did that trying in the beginning, where nothing of interest to us was likely to be found, and then I would be set for later on. The decision was a logical one, not to mention easy, which meant I barely hesitated before starting to get out of my bodysuit.

Once I had the sandals laced, I stood up from the alcove's cushion stack and went out to see what I looked like. I knew I'd probably like the way the costume fit, so I made sure to set my expression into something closer to resignation than enjoyment before I looked into one of the mirror walls. It was a good thing I'd had the foresight to do that; as I turned just a little in front of the mirror, frowning slightly at my reflection, on the inside I was grinning in full appreciation.

"Hey, look at you!" Lidra said as she stepped out of her alcove, her eyes going from me to my mirror image. "If I look half that good, I may never leave this place. What do you think?"

She came up to me on my right and began posing in front of the mirror, more than just passing satisfaction in her voice. It wasn't hard seeing she looked a good deal slimmer than she did in a bodysuit, and then I suddenly understood what her question had really meant. She hadn't been asking whether or not she looked good, but whether or not her equipment was showing. I inspected her as closely as I could without being too obvious about it, but didn't see anything that looked remotely like equipment. At that point I would have loved asking where the hell she'd put it all, but even if I'd been able to, her laugh of delight would have come first.

"I think I've decided to burn all my bodysuits as soon as I get home," she said, examining the back of herself with the help of the double reflection from the other mirror wall. "Someone once told me they make you look thirty pounds heavier than you really are even if you're only five pounds overweight, but until this minute I didn't believe it. Look at these shoulder scarves, aren't they adorable? Like the leather on that door attendant's costume, only these don't stand out and they're much softer."

She fluffed out the short scarves that, like mine, were tied around the two-inch-wide shoulder straps of the tunic top, and no one looking at her would have guessed she was interested in anything but her appearance as a woman. Standing next to her I could see the way her eyes rested just a little longer on certain parts of her reflection than on others, the expression in her gaze very direct and almost coldly calculating, but if I hadn't been looking for something like that, I never would have seen it. I wondered just exactly how much experience she did have at doing jobs like that, but that was another question I couldn't ask aloud.

"I suppose I can live with it for a little while," I grudged, looking again at my own costume with outer lack of enthusiasm. "If I get tired if it, I *will* change back to my own clothes, even if that keeps me from being part of the 'scene.' Whatever that's supposed to mean."

"I really do think we have to get you a brochure to read," Lidra decided, still very much into admiring her reflection. "It only gives you very broad hints about things, but having the hints lets you understand what's going on once you see that release we signed. For instance, didn't you wonder when you got to the question that asked whether or not you were a virgin?"

"It was under the physical health section," I answered with a shrug, looking at her reflection rather than at her. "Most of the questions in that section were intrusive, so why would I wonder about one more?"

"Because *that* particular question is significant," she said, looking very positive. "People have to be in good physical health to come here because there's a lot of walking *'and such'* involved, the brochure says, but if you answered that you weren't a virgin, the way I did, you were asked one more question. Did you happen to see it?"

"Yes, I saw it," I allowed, smiling inwardly at the way she'd put her own question. "They asked if I would mind being intimate with men who were strangers, but who were also professionals. If I cared to answer no to *that* one, they were offering a guarantee that I wouldn't be hurt. There was also something about the tour being more interesting if I were a 'full participant.' "

"Well, of course there was," she said, now looking somewhat exasperated as she turned away from the mirror. "Don't you see? They've recreated scenes from the histories of some of the planets, but you can bet none of the tours take you through a lazy free-day afternoon at nap time. They'll be showing *significant* happenings with lots of action, and being a full participant has to mean we'll be right in the middle of it, having it happen to *us!* We'll be full participants in whatever they stage, and I don't mean simply being jostled in a crowd! They'll provide *sex,* girl, and probably lots of it!"

"You know, I think that word 'sex' sounds familiar," I said, turning to meet her stare with one finger to my lips. "Is that when a couple of people get together and spend most of their time yelling at each other?"

"You're an absolute riot," she said, now examining me sourly as she folded her arms. "And no, that's not the definition of sex, that's the definition of marriage. *Did* you opt for full part, or didn't you?"

"Sure I took it," I said, tossing my head a little as I turned back to the mirror. "When this thing is over and I still haven't enjoyed myself, I don't want them to have any easy reasons why that they can smugly point to. Sex is all right, but it's hardly such a big deal that it's guaranteed to make me change my mind. And I don't think I have to ask whether or not *you* chose it."

"No, you certainly don't," she answered, only her head turning back to the mirror, her mood now thickly self-satisfied. "You can be as stubborn as you like about not enjoying yourself, but I intend having *fun.* I've never tried a man with professional training, and

I'm really looking forward to it. I want to know if those groups that say all men should have the same are right.''

"I wonder if they offered female professionals to the men,'' I commented, this time not even glancing in her direction. "If so, Chal might soon be deciding all *women* should have training the way *those* groups insist.''

Her annoyance was so thick I could feel it *without* looking at her, but she didn't get to vocalize any of it. A knock came at the door, immediately followed by the entrance of the woman who had directed us to our costumes, and that was the end of casual conversation. The woman examined Lidra and me with a frown, briefly tugged and smoothed at our costumes, then announced with a smile that no alterations seemed to be necessary. Now that our sizes had been confirmed extra outfits would be produced and made available when they were needed, and the clothing we'd taken off would be cleaned and returned to our personal luggage. Since everything was satisfactorily taken care of, we were then free to leave the fitting room and really begin the Great Adventure.

It took some doing not to react to the capitals in the woman's voice, but we made it out of the room without insulting her and rejoined Chal, who was waiting for us. His costume was exactly like the one the door attendant had worn, all leather with straps across the chest, and on him it looked even better than it had on the attendant. Lidra hummed low in interest when she saw him, but I was the only one who heard it. Chal was talking to a boy in his mid-teens who was wearing a page costume when we came out, and only when the boy had finished what he was saying did Chal turn to us with a grin.

"Say, you girls look great even if you do have more than simple chest straps,'' he said, then gestured to the boy at his right. "This is Tad, our newest guide, and he'll be sending us on our way as soon as he gives you two your watches.''

"Watches?'' Lidra asked for the two of us, apparently as surprised and curious as I was. "What watches?"

"People always say that, and in just that way," the boy Tad responded with a grin, handing Lidra and me plain leather bands no more than an inch and a half wide. "You'll need some way of telling the time once you're in the Mists, and ordinary timepieces don't do well in them. If you use these, you'll know exactly what's happening. Just smooth them closed around your wrist, and then follow me."

The leather band was very soft and flexible, and once I'd smoothed it closed around my left wrist I looked at the face of the timepiece embedded in the center of it. Rather than give the date and local time, it showed days, hours and minutes, all of it going backward. It took no more than seconds to realize the countdown had started at three full days, and even as we stood there the minutes disappeared into the past and were then no more. With a couple of hours already gone, it was clear Lidra had been right about when our vacation had started, which meant that when Tad began leading the way past the fitting rooms, we followed along without much foot-dragging.

An ordinary door at the end of the fitting area brought us to a wide, well-lit section of stairway that led downward, the stairs themselves curving around out of sight to the left. We continued to follow Tad as he followed the stairs, and after a few minutes of walking we reached the bottom. It was fairly clear we were well below-ground at that point, but the area was brightly lit and painted with cheerful pastel colors that suggested a party atmosphere. There were leather couches and chairs spaced along the two walls to the right of the foot of the stairs, a sign made of dancing black letters on the wall to the left that said, "The Castle of Beginning," and something that looked like a wall with windows and doors straight ahead. It wasn't immediately clear where we were supposed to go from there, but Tad answered the question before it was asked.

"That right there is what will be taking you into the Mists," he said, gesturing toward what I'd thought

was a wall with windows and doors. "I was supposed
to have sent you on your way immediately, but while
coming down I was told to have you wait a minute or
two. There's someone else starting this tour right now,
and it will be more convenient for everyone involved
if you all travel together. He was given his costume
in another fitting room, so there won't be much of a
wait at all. In appreciation for your patience, the management has arranged to compensate you for the loss
of time."

His smile accompanied a gesture to his wrist, which
naturally made us look at our new watches. The first
thing I saw was that the countdown had stopped, and
then the minute window blinked twice before advancing for a count of five. After that it blinked another
two times then froze again, which obviously meant we
were now on hold. The countdown had stopped while
we were waiting as we'd been asked to do, and to
thank us for being patient we'd been given a bonus of
five whole minutes extra. I was seriously considering
mentioning how impressed I was with their generosity,
but Lidra beat me to it with a comment on a different
subject.

"Then that button in your ear is a communicator,"
she said, sounding pleased and impressed. "Is it one
way or two way?"

"One way is all it has to be," the boy said as I
looked up to notice for the first time the button Lidra
had mentioned. "I don't usually spend enough time
with guests that I'd be likely to need to pass things
back up the line, but if I have to I can use one of the
house phones. I'm sure you didn't notice them, but
every area you've been in has had at least one. Like
here, for instance."

He moved between us to go to the wall that had been
to the right of the stairs, and pushed aside one light
orange section of it to show a quietly modest light
orange phone. I felt the urge to ask if the bright yellow
and light pink sections also had matching phones behind them, but decided that wouldn't be very discreet
of me. From their reactions I was fairly sure Chal and
Lidra hadn't known there was anything behind the light

orange section of wall, which meant it would be best if I joined them in ignorance. Our page guide reclosed the section and began turning back to us, then put his hand to his ear and turned to the stairs instead.

"See, they weren't exaggerating," he said, and at that point we also became aware of the sound of two sets of footsteps descending. "A couple of minutes was what they said, and a couple of minutes was all it was. Now you can be on your way, and the man won't have to travel alone."

If the boy had been facing in our direction he might have seen the glance exchanged between Chal and Lidra, a glance that didn't have much in the way of welcoming fellowship in it. Since we three were supposed to be virtual strangers to one another, we couldn't very well refuse the company of another stranger without having it look very suspicious. That left us with no option other than to accept him, at least on a temporary basis. If his presence couldn't be turned to a diversion once we reached our objective, we'd have to find some way of getting rid of him.

Waiting with bated breath for someone to appear has never been one of my favorite pastimes, so I turned away from the stairs the others were watching to glance again at the sections of the wall that were obviously meant to be pushed aside. I really would have enjoyed knowing what was behind those sections even if it was nothing but light switches and thermostats, but I couldn't very well walk over to them and open them up to look. I was seriously considering camouflaging my knowledge by trying all of the differently-colored sections in order, starting with the pale brown right next to the light orange, when I heard the sound of a gasp. The origin of noises like that are often hard to figure out, but it hadn't sounded like Chal or Lidra, and that left no one but the boy Tad. I turned around, immediately curious as to why *he* would make a sound like that, and just as immediately found out. My two companions were doing nothing more than staring in silence, but our page couldn't seem to control himself.

"I know you!" he said excitedly to the man who was coming down the last of the steps, another shining-eyed teenage boy trailing adoringly behind. "You're my absolute favorite, and I've memorized every stat they ever put out about you! Can I shake your hand, just to be able to say that I did?"

The man reached the bottom of the stairs and put his hand out for the boy to take, but only part of his attention was on the exchange. The rest of it was involved in the faint smile he wore, the smile he'd developed when his gray eyes had turned in my direction. For my own part I didn't know *how* to feel, now that it was clear the fourth of our party was the one and only Serendel.

Chapter 7

"I think I'm starting to become a believer," Lidra said in something of a mutter, the gloating delight so thick in her voice she might as well have shouted. "My mother always told me that if I was a good girl I'd be rewarded, and was she ever right! After this I'll be willing to eat *everybody's* vegetables, not just my own."

Chal smiled faintly as he glanced at her, but he didn't seem to be as amused—or as pleased—as I'd expected him to be. Lidra, her stare still glued to Serendel, missed Chal's reaction, but didn't miss it when Serendel looked at her with a frown.

"I'm sorry, but I'm afraid I didn't hear that," he said, honestly puzzled. "Were you talking to me about vegetables?"

"No, not really," she said with a small cough and a swallowed laugh, gesturing aside everything she was very glad he hadn't heard. "We're delighted you'll be joining us, Winner, and we promise not to chew off more than one of your ears with questions. Don't we, Chal?"

"We certainly do," my other teammate answered, this time more amused as he put a hand out. "I'm Chal Arnor, and this is Lidra Kament. As I'm sure you've already noticed, we're also fans of yours."

"I usually prefer fans to enemies," Serendel said with a grin as he took Chal's hand. "Or, to be more precise, fans of *mine*. I once found myself sharing ground transportation with a small army of one of my main rival's supporters, and I didn't know if I would

make it to my destination in any condition to fight.
Between looks meant to kill and acres of frozen silence, I almost ended up with poisoned frostbite.''

"Oh, you poor thing," Lidra commiserated even
while she chuckled in enjoyment of the story. "But
this time Chal and I are here to protect you, so don't
let it worry you a single minute that Inky has declared
for Farison. We won't let her hurt you."

"Inky?" Serendel said with a puzzled look, and then
he seemed to remember the first face he'd seen. He
looked in my direction with his brows raised, hopefully missing the blush I could feel in my cheeks over
what that miserable Lidra had told him, and Chal
cleared his throat.

"To complete the introductions, that's Dalisse Imbro, known to those around her as Inky," Chal said,
sounding suspiciously bland. "Since she isn't much of
a fight fan she hasn't really declared for Farison, but
above that, I think you two have already met."

"You might say we've run into each other once or
twice," the big man answered, speaking to Chal but
still looking at me, definite amusement now in his
eyes. "We've never before been formally introduced,
though, so I appreciate having it done."

"Excuse me, my lords and ladies, but I'm afraid
it's time for you to leave now," our page Tad interrupted with obvious reluctance, one hand to his ear.
"If you'll follow me into the car, I'll get you settled
for the trip."

"Or," Lidra muttered low as the boy moved past
us, " 'get them going, you idiot!' His boss apparently
has very little appreciation for the art of conversation."

"Which may be a good thing for us," Chal added
in a matching murmur. "Our watches have started
again, which means time flies swiftly before us. We
can yak all we like once we're on our way."

"Oh, Chal, you're so practical," Lidra told him
with a sigh, an utter condemnation Serendel found
more amusing than Chal did. Our male teammate might
have been tempted to defend himself against the
charge, but just then Tad pressed a switch in the recess

he'd uncovered beside one of the doors, and what I'd thought was a wall opened and lit up inside to show what looked like a wide lounge. We followed the boy inside, and he gestured around to the chairs, dispensers, consoles and carpeting.

"We hope everything here will make this short trip a comfortable one," he recited, the speech one he'd clearly made any number of times before. "Drinks and snacks are available from the dispensers, music from the consoles, and even news or fiction, if you should want them. When this car stops, you'll have reached the Mists of the Ages. I hope you have the best time ever, Winner Serendel!"

The last line was said faster than all the rest, and after the universe's quickest bow, the boy got himself out of there before his blush set the room on fire. We all chuckled as the door slid back in its place to close us in, and then we felt a small, very smooth lurch.

"Well, it looks like we're on our way," Chal said, rubbing his hands together. "Would you like something to drink, Inky? Serendel?"

"How about me?" Lidra asked before Chal could get any answers, her tone puzzled. "Were you under the impression I got left back at the castle?"

"I couldn't be that lucky," Chal returned, his back as stiff as his leather shoulder pieces as he walked toward the drink dispenser. "Since you obviously don't think much of people who are practical, I was sure you wouldn't want to be offered a drink by one. If you can't manage on your own, you'll have to stay thirsty."

"Men!" Lidra muttered darkly with her fists on her hips, glaring at the back that was still toward us. "Say even a single word to them, and they get all bent out of shape. And from a distance they look so solid! I think I'd better make sure I don't die of thirst on this trip."

She glanced at us to excuse herself and then followed Chal to the dispenser, apparently with the intention of fence-mending and bridge-unburning. That left me in the middle of the car with the fourth of our number, and I suddenly discovered that the trip wasn't going as comfortably as it was supposed to. I looked around at the fifteen foot square that was our underground transportation, seeing dark walls rushing by beyond the sealed windows, and then my most immediate companion stirred.

"I think it's going to be a while before we see those drinks," Serendel observed, his voice held low. "Would you like to sit down while we're waiting?"

His big hand gestured toward a cozy grouping of six chairs around a polished-wood table, and I think if I could have refused the suggestion I would have. I felt like an idiot practicing to be an awkward adolescent, and I didn't understand why that was. Serendel was hardly the first man I'd ever met, and being asked if I'd like to sit down was hardly the most intimate suggestion ever made me. I finally managed to force a smile and a nod, walked over to the chairs and picked one, then sat down. I discovered I'd been hoping Serendel would choose a place a few chairs over when he sat down right next to me, but at least things could have been worse. If the chairs had been couches instead, I probably would have stayed on my feet.

"I'm finding out why so many women wear bodysuits instead of skirts," Serendel said once he was settled, his eyes on his costume as his hands smoothed the bottom of it. "If I get to the point of sitting down without paying enough attention, I'm guaranteed to be accused of advertising."

He looked up at me with a grin, and I couldn't help smiling at his problem. Svalk makes a skirt that's much easier to live with than the leather variety, but I suppose it's harder to feel manly in svalk. My own skirt lay obligingly relaxed around my knees, and didn't need smoothing of any sort. With that in view I decided it was time I pretended to be adult, and made my own contribution to the conversation.

"My friends and I were surprised to see you," I offered, hanging onto the smile I'd gained. "We thought we were the only familiar faces coming to the Mists of the Ages."

"One of the prices of fame is sometimes having to sneak around," he answered, a look of apology appearing briefly in his eyes. "If that crowd on the liner had found out what my destination was, right now we'd be up to our ears in watchers. I never knew how many people can afford and are more than willing to abandon their own plans to follow around after their favorite, not until the first time it happened to me. It ruined the quiet couple of days of relaxation I'd planned, and even ruined the time for the other people at the resort. After that I learned how to make private arrangements with liners and resorts, and I'm usually gone before anyone notices. This time the liner captain used a later run to bring me down with some of the freight, which is why you and your friends were delayed. I hope it wasn't too long a wait."

"We managed to live through the extra two minutes," I said, trying to control the outrage I felt. Having to sneak around like a criminal just to get some privacy simply wasn't right, not for someone who didn't thrive on that kind of treatment. If it had been me, I would have refused to live like that, would have told those people to get away from me and stay away. I probably wouldn't have been liked very well, but people take me as I am or they don't have me at all.

"And I don't know how you can stand it," I went on, finding it impossible not to mention the point. "You can't scratch at a private itch without having twelve people offering to help. If it was me, I'd be insane in about a minute and a half."

"It's not quite *that* bad," he said with a chuckle, his gray eyes now empty of apology. "For the most part they're really good people, and because they're so involved with my life it usually doesn't occur to them that I'm not actually a member of their immediate family. Ninety percent of them will gladly and willingly give me privacy any time I ask for it, without feeling in the least insulted. It's that last ten percent you have to watch out for, the ones who think their support means they own you. Not only don't they take hints, they have to be shoved out of the way before you can close your cabin door. Real fans don't like their sort any more than the fighters do, but there's

nothing any of us can do about them short of extermination."

"What's wrong with extermination?" I asked, liking the sound of it. "The Empire would end up being
a much better place, and if fighters aren't equipped to
do the job no one is."

"You're overlooking one small problem," he answered with a laugh, shifting just a little in his chair.
"There are laws against doing things like that outside
of an arena, no matter how soul-satisfying we'd find
it. Do you think they'd be suicidal enough to push
fighters the way they do if they *weren't* protected by
the law?"

"That's only one of the things wrong with the law,"
I told him firmly, not about to be talked out of my
opinion. "It protects the guilty instead of the innocent,
which isn't the way it was supposed to be. If the ones
who made the laws were forced to live *with* them rather
than above or around them, you'd see how fast things
would change."

"If it makes you feel any better, I agree with you
completely," he said, trying not to look *too* amused
at my outrage. "I'd love to put one of the lawmakers
in my position, and then see how long the pests would
last. I'd give it until the first time the man saw an
attractive woman he really wanted to meet, but
couldn't get anywhere near her because that ten percent was constantly in the way. Some women don't
mind the unending hoopla, but the really special ones
often dislike being crowded and jostled. When they
stay away from you after the first meeting or two, you
sometimes wonder if it's the crowds—or you."

Those light gray eyes were no longer filled with
amusement, and somehow the conversation had
changed from what it had started out as. I discovered
that my outrage had disappeared along with his amusement, a cowardly move if I ever saw one. Outrage
never seemed to be there when you really needed it,
but fluster and awkwardness were always quick as a
bunny when it came to showing up. I really didn't
know *what* to say, and when he saw my hesitation he
smiled faintly.

"Farison isn't just a good fighter, he's also a very lucky man," Serendel said, trying to make the words sound light-hearted. "His followers don't believe in letting themselves be lured away from him."

"But I'm not really a follower of Farison," I blurted, not even thinking about what I was saying. "I've hardly seen him fight, no more than once or twice, but he happened to look better than the ones I *did* see more of. On the liner— It wasn't *you* I was staying away from, it was an involvement—with so many people around, and so short a trip—"

"Now *that's* what I was hoping to hear," he interrupted my rambling with a grin, his sadness evaporating so fast it might never have been there in the first place. "It's crushing to think a pretty girl is avoiding you because she can't stand looking at your ugly face. I do hope you noticed there aren't any crowds around now."

He leaned toward me with that and reached for my hand, his grin so infuriating I would have happily smacked him in the face with something. Instead of moving my hand out of reach I simply curled it into a fist, and that got his attention the way my silence hadn't.

"You did that on purpose," I stated, so hopping mad my voice was absolutely steady. "You made me feel sorry for you in order to take advantage of me. I dare you to deny it."

"I had to do *something* to make you talk to me," he protested with light-eyed innocence, not a trace of guilt in him at having been caught. "After you stopped yelling at me on the liner you avoided me completely, and when we met again just a few minutes ago, you looked like you were about to go back to the avoiding. I just thought I'd let you know I don't *want* to be avoided."

"I'll file your preference in with the rest of your stats," I said, standing up before he could reach for my hand again. "If you happen to get curious about how *I'm* looking at it, try making a wild guess."

I turned my back and walked away then, giving him help with the guess he'd be making. I really hated it when people tried to take advantage of me, which they usually did because they thought I was innocent. Seero had always told me I was lucky to look the way I did, as it helped me to find out very quickly who was trustworthy and who wasn't. I, myself, had never considered the talent that much of a convenience, and I was still so annoyed I almost ran directly into Chal and what he was carrying.

"Hey, look out!" he squawked, stopping very short to avoid the collision, his hands holding the spill-threatening drinks away from his costume. "I have your cup of javi right here, Inky. You didn't have to come after it yourself."

"Thanks for the javi, Chal," I said, taking the cup out of his hand with a brisk nod. "I'll be drinking it over here by myself, so you and Lidra enjoy your own drinks."

I gave him a second nod and then marched away, barely glancing at a Lidra who stood silently beside him with brows raised high. To the left of the drink dispenser was another cozy grouping of chairs, one that looked more attractive than the first in that I would be using it alone. I sat down with my back to the others, crossed my legs, and sipped at the javi.

"What in hell is going on?" Chal demanded, coming around to where he could see me. "One minute you're sitting over there, having a quiet conversation, and the next you're practically running me down to get to another seat. Do they charge more for that part of the car, or what?"

"You *could* say the price of sitting over there is higher than I care to pay," I agreed with a judicious nod, giving the javi most of my attention. "That doesn't mean you two have to do without, not on my account. I'm perfectly capable of spending the trip time alone, and in fact I think I'd prefer it."

"I have a feeling we've been through this conversation before," Lidra said, coming to stand beside Chal, each of her hands holding a glass. "Don't tell me: you and Serendel are back to looking for your own private arena."

"Don't include me in on that," the big man himself

said, making it unanimous as he stopped beside Lidra.
"All I was trying to do was get acquainted, but apparently I picked the wrong track to take. It looks like
I owe everyone another apology."

"Chal and I spend enough time apologizing to each
other," Lidra said, looking up at Serendel with a grin.
"I don't think we have room for anyone else's apologies, so why don't you save what you have for Inky?
And by the way, this drink is for you."

"It's cream-clear," he said in surprise after taking
the glass and sniffing at it. "How did you know it's
my favorite drink? Winners never state preferences like
that one way or the other. If we did, it would be like
forcing everyone who follows us to eat or drink the
same."

"Which is against fighter codes," she said with a
nod, sipping at her own drink. "The only thing is,
you didn't start out as a triple-gold winner, and someone did an interview with you after your second or
third successful showing. The interviewer mentioned
she spent two hours drinking cream-clear with you,
which led me to suspect it might be one of your favorites. How much did I have to lose by taking the
chance?"

"Absolutely nothing," he agreed with a grin that
matched her earlier one, raising his glass to her. "I
gladly toast one of the ninety rather than one of the
ten, and tender my thanks for your consideration. And
by the way, even though there isn't enough alcohol in
cream-clear to affect an infant, the toast is still valid.
The codes are clear on *that* point, too."

The three of them chuckled as they all drank to
whatever ritual fighter-toast he'd proposed, getting
along as well together as I'd known they would. I
moved my attention to one of the windows as I sipped
my javi, watching dark walls rush by no more than six
inches from the car. They hadn't told us how long a
trip we'd be making, and I really hoped that was because the time would be too short to be worth mentioning. With problems of real importance waiting for
me to get home, I wanted that job over with as soon
as possible.

"And now that you've been fortified, why don't you try that apology on Inky?" Lidra's voice came, back to sounding amused. "I'd be more than happy to spend this vacation entertaining you myself, but Chal said he sees very poor health ahead for me if I do more than flirt with you and daydream. I'd hate putting my health in jeopardy, so Inky's your only other chance. I know you don't find her very interesting, so I guess you'll have to force yourself."

"Well, we all have to sacrifice *something* on a joint vacation, for the sake, of course, of the others with us," Serendel agreed in a solemn voice, probably looking just as sober. "I'm sure most men run screaming from the sight of Inky, but I'm strong enough to hold my ground and stick it out. Closing my eyes every now and then should help, at least until I get used to her looks. After that, she may not even notice I'm forcing myself."

"No wonder you don't mind entering the arena to answer a challenge," Chal said to him, his tone dryly amused. "If that's the sort of thing you say to every woman you meet, you have to be safer *in* the arena than out of it."

"Well, she didn't seem to like hearing me say I found her attractive," Serendel protested, and I could hear that innocence again in his voice. "If she prefers being told she's an eyesore, who am I to deny it to her? I try to give all women what they like best, without passing judgment on their taste."

"Did you hear that, Inky?" Lidra said with a very heavy leer in her voice. "A man who gives women what *they* want instead of what he wants. You'd better grab him quick before he gets away."

"Yes, I heard what he said, and I couldn't be more delighted," I answered, continuing to watch the unending black outside the window. "Since what I want most is to be left alone, I'm glad to hear I'll be getting it. Repeating yourself a dozen times or more can be unbelievably boring."

"Look, I really do apologize for what I did a few minutes ago," Serendel said as I sipped at my javi, sounding seriously serious as he stepped closer to my chair. "The truth of the matter is I *wasn't* trying to take advantage of you, but I *was* trying to play on your sympathies. I've found that some women—hesitate—when it comes to getting involved with me, and that because of the number of women I've already been involved with. I thought if I made you feel sorry for me you would let me know if you considered me at all interesting, and then we could go on from there. If I had really been trying to take advantage of you, would I have been so fast to drop the act? Wouldn't I have kept on with it, at least until I'd gotten what I wanted?"

"I don't know," I answered, finally moving my eyes back to look up at him. "Would you have?"

A flash of frustration showed in his gaze, brief but fair-to-middling intense, the sort of thing no professional con artist would ever have let himself show. *Push the mark off-balance and keep her there* was the standard way of doing it, make her question herself rather than you. I'd been taught more than basic tactics even before I was out of lower school, a self-defense course given gratis by some of Seero's vast multitude of friends. My teachers had all been experienced professionals, but "talented amateur" was the best that could be said about Serendel. He'd conned me once, and I wasn't in the mood to give him a second shot at it.

"Come on, Inky, you're being unreasonable," Lidra protested, glancing uncomfortably at Serendel. "You're acting like he's trying to apologize for attempted assassination. You know he was looking in your direction even before we got here, so you can't possibly believe he's handing you a line. Give the guy a chance!"

"You give him a chance," I said, getting out of my chair to head toward the drink dispenser. "I'm not here just to fill in his empty time until he reaches the next group of dancing girls. If there's a law written somewhere that says I have to associate with him, show it to me. If there doesn't happen to be that kind of law, leave me the hell alone."

I put my cup in the slot and pressed for a refill of

the javi, hearing the heavy silence my last remarks had produced. After having given me her full approval, Lidra was obviously not very happy that I refused to fall swooning at the feet of her idol, but that was just too bad about her. They were all expecting me to let that big jerk treat me any way he pleased and simply be grateful for the attention, but I'd be damned if I would. They all had so much in common it was sickening; since the choice was mine I'd be staying out of it, and they could all have fun sickening each other.

"It might be a good idea to talk about something else for a while," Chal's voice came after a minute, trying to smooth the awkwardness out of the moment. "This is supposed to be a vacation, after all, so let's just relax and enjoy ourselves. Have you ever been here before, Serendel?"

"No, this is my first visit," the man answered after the briefest of hesitations, apparently agreeing with Chal about a change of subjects. "There aren't many places I can go to get away from the general public for a while, but this promises to be one of them. My business manager contacted them for me, and was told that the number of people on each tour session is deliberately kept small, to encourage those people to join in on the action as a part of it. Their workers, who stage the scenes in the Mists, either stay in character no matter who comes past them as a guest, or they get fired. If I can spend my time enjoying the tour rather than being one of its main attractions, I'll probably become a regular visitor."

"Lidra and I have never been here before either," Chal said, and I heard them moving around as though they were sitting down. I, myself, was in the middle of going back to my original chair with my freshened cup of javi, pleased that they finally seemed to be leaving me alone. "As a matter of fact Lidra and I met on the liner coming here, the same liner you were on. Since we're both fans of yours, it worked out very well in bringing us even closer together."

"How about your other friend over there?" Serendel asked as I sat down all alone, his tone not quite as friendly as it had been. "Did either of you know Smudge before you met on the liner?"

"Ah—that's 'Inky,' and no, we didn't," Lidra said hastily when Chal stayed silent, something odd in her voice. "We all became friends on the liner, especially after we found out we were all going to the same place. Inky isn't very happy to be here, because vacationing in the Mists was her friend's idea, her friend got sick at the last minute, and the Mists people refused to return Inky's deposit. She came alone rather than simply lose the money, but she really is determined not to enjoy herself. Knowing that, you may be able to understand now why she's being somewhat unfriendly."

"What I think I understand even better is why her friend got sick," was the terribly clever reply, the words dry and spoken clearly enough so that everyone could hear them. "Under similar circumstances, I might do the same myself."

They went on to talk about other things after that, but I had stopped listening. As I sipped my javi, it had come to me how familiar that situation seemed, and then I remembered an incident in upper school that I thought I'd forgotten completely. All schools have their in-sets and exclusive power groups, and mine was no different; those of us who had little or no interest in that sort of flock nonsense simply left them to their games and went about our own business. I'd had no intentions of ever getting involved with those people—until one of them decided to do me a favor.

I sighed as I crossed my legs in the comfortable chair, remembering how excited my best friend had been when I was asked to a dance by the boy who was the star member of the most exclusive of the in-groups. They were the ones who had the money and the social position, and the boy had decided that my guardian, Seero, had enough money to justify my being included in their group. The fact that he was also hot to try scoring with me had helped him make that important a decision, but I hadn't known about that part of it; I'd thought he was simply interested in me as a person. Seero had chuckled at my excitement and had told me to go for it, and my best friend had decided it was the most marvelous thing that could ever have happened to me. If I'd had any sense I would have refused, but with my best friend urging me on I ended up accepting.

The dance itself had been a little on the boring side, but I'd had fun when some of the older members of the group tried making me feel uncomfortable by discussing all the places they'd been. Much to their dismay it had turned out *I'd* been to all those places too, and a number of others besides. When I'd mentioned I'd even been on a run through the wilds they'd all gasped, and for the next hour I'd been flooded with questions about the time. My escort had been absolutely delighted that he'd chosen so well in a partner for the dance, but only because I hadn't mentioned the strokes that had taken Seero and me to all those places, or the reason we'd had to make the wilds run. There aren't any strokes to be made in the wilds, but there are other things.

When the dance was over, my escort had taken me home in his expensive new sports model—or at least he was supposed to have taken me home. What he'd actually done was end us up in a really bad neighborhood, parked in a deserted shopping-traffic lane, and then had pleasantly announced the way I was going to thank him for taking me to the dance. When I'd announced back that he must have had too much of the mixed-fruit punch he hadn't been amused, and had then proceeded to explain my choice. Either I gave him what he wanted or I got out and walked home, or at least tried to walk home. In that neighborhood there was no guarantee I would make it without losing a lot more than he was asking for, but the choice was completely mine. His grin of enjoyment had twisted his handsome face into a leering glimpse of his true nature, but the grin had lasted only until I got out of his sports model and slammed the door hard enough to crack its paint job.

As an added statement to the sort he was, he actually drove away and left me there. I'd waited until he was completely out of sight, and then I'd followed one of the dark, uneasily-deserted streets to the place of business of one of Seero's friends. The woman had been furious over what had been done to me, and had had one of her largest bouncers drive me home. My former escort had been right about the sort of things that could happen to a girl alone in a neighborhood like that, but I hadn't been as alone as he'd thought. Thanks to Seero and the shadow-life he'd shared with me, I hadn't had to do anything I would have found extremely distasteful, and I hadn't been harmed because of the refusal I would have made in any event.

After that I'd stayed as far away as possible from exclusive in-groups, and hadn't even paid attention when my escort of that night had begun having expensive, embarrassing accidents. Seero had been really angry over what the boy had tried to force me into, and Seero had had an awful lot of friends. My own best friend had tried telling me I'd been an idiot, that what the boy had asked for would have been a small price to pay for admission to their group, and not long after that she'd found someone else to be friends with. The someone else had already been accepted on the fringes of the group my ex-friend had had so much interest in, and only then had I understood that she'd wanted me accepted so that *she* could have an associated acceptance. Finding that out had really gotten me mad, and I'd sworn never to let myself be put in a situation like that again.

I stirred in my seat as I heard the laughter coming from those I shared the car with, the people who had so very much in common. It was a shame Serendel would have to be dumped when we got to where we had work to do, but Lidra and Chal would just have to live with it. Once we were finished they'd be able to find him again, of course, and I'd be able to get out of there and go back to work that really needed doing. I had no interest in belonging to in-groups—of any kind—and once I was back home I'd never have to be bothered by them again.

I was just finishing my third cup of javi when the car began slowing down from a headlong rush. There was still nothing but featureless black walls around us when we reached an easy gliding pace, and then suddenly there was an open area of lights and color that looked very much like the one we'd left. As the car came to a smooth and uneventful stop I was able to see the one difference between there and the place we'd started, the sign on the wall that was now to the right of the stairs we faced. The sign read, "The Mists of Llexis," and as the doors opened there was another boy dressed as a page to greet us.

"Welcome, gentle travelers, welcome to the Mists of Llexis," the boy said, watching as we approached the doors from where we'd been when the car had stopped. "I'm here to take you to your journey scout, who will then get you settled in your accommodations in this part of the city. Please follow me."

Chal and Lidra stepped through the doorway without hesitation, following as requested, but Serendel didn't go with them. He stopped beside the door instead, looked down at me with those cold gray eyes, then gestured me out ahead of him with a small, sardonic bow. I was tempted to say thanks anyway, but I'd rather not have you behind me, but it really wasn't worth the effort. Rather than saying anything at all, I simply walked past him as though he weren't there, glancing around before moving after the three who had already begun climbing the stairs. That multi-colored area had the same panels with things behind them that the first place had had, but there still wasn't any way for me to check them out.

The climb up wasn't as long as the climb down had been, which was a lucky thing for Lidra. She was already breathing heavily when we reached the top, but at least she wasn't gasping. Our page paused then to let us look around, which was really very wise of him. If he'd just continued on he would have found himself alone, and not because any of us, including Lidra, needed to rest. There had been some stray wisps of fog on the stairs as we'd rounded the last turn near the top, finding it thickening the higher we went, but it hadn't prepared us for what we finally moved up into.

All around us was swirling gray fog, roiling mists that refused us sight of the sky, and the sun, and even the ground we stood on. The only things that *were* visible were the items that had been built in and for the Mists, things like buildings. Not far from where we stood, on our left, was a line of buildings and stores and shops and stalls, all of it glowing faintly as though the construction material had been the very sun that the fog refused sight of, a sun that had been reduced to individual pieces of its spectrum. Reds and yellows and greens and blues glowed faintly through the gray of the fog, coloring small patches of the mist, looking like ghosts of things that were bright and real. Some-one clattered past us on a greenly-glowing cart, what was drawing the cart invisible in the fog, and finally our page decided he'd waited long enough.

"This way now, travelers, if you please," he said in a very firm tone, apparently having experience with needing to be firm. "Your journey scout is waiting for you in the assistance booth right over there. If at any time during your tour you happen to need help and your scout isn't available, simply go to one of those booths. There will be someone on duty at all times, and anyone you speak to will be glad to help."

We were being led off to the right during all that, in a direction that seemed to take us through a gap in other stalls, shops and buildings, toward a structure that was brighter than all the glowing objects around it. It looked very much like a slender pyramid built of cold, blue-white fire, and was obviously made to be easily visible in all directions. I tried to watch where I was putting my feet as I walked, and for that reason noticed the ground beneath us was cobblestoned in wide blocks, every fourth block glowing the way the buildings did. Strangely enough the mist felt warm and dry rather than damp as I passed through it, just as though someone had blotted up whatever moisture might have originally been present. I might have felt *too* warm if I'd been wearing normal clothing, which could have been one of the reasons we'd been given costumes.

It took only a couple of minutes to walk to the pyr-amid, and during that time a number of other people appeared out of the fog, passed us, then disappeared again. Only one of them was dressed in the same sort of leather costume the male members of our group wore, and that one strolled along being followed by men in short-skirted tunics of cloth. The one in leather paid no real attention to the ones in cloth, just as though he were allowing them the honor of being near him, but still didn't find it necessary to acknowledge their existence. The rest of the passersby wore nothing but cloth, walked alone, and moved so slowly they seemed to have all the time in the universe. Everyone we'd seen was moving slowly, except for our newest page.

"And here we are, gentle travelers," our page said, opening a door in the side of the pyramid that faced us, then leading the way inside. "Allow me to present Velix, the journey scout who will look after you during your stay in the Mists."

"Words fail me to describe my delight in meeting you, lords and ladies," the scout said as we stopped just inside the doorway to stare at him, the comment most definitely on the dry side. "As you may have noticed from the release you all signed, during your stay here in the Mists, my suggestions are your commands. You go nowhere and do nothing without my express permission, or the one place you *will* go is back to the port to wait for your liner. Your time in the Mists will be the most unusual vacation you've ever had, but if you don't obey me it can also be the most dangerous. Since you're paying for fun rather than harm, let's make sure that's what you get, eh? Are we all clear on how it will work?"

He looked around at each of us, calm arrogance and authority in the bright eyes that touched us, but he didn't get the sort of immediate agreement he was obviously looking for. I didn't know what was keeping the others quiet, but I was still too busy staring at him to have time to react to what he'd said. He was sitting calmly in the middle of the booth floor, paying no attention to the page behind him or the one who had brought us there, apparently also unaware of the fog that swirled around all of us, fighting with the bright lighting inside the booth. Sitting on his haunches his head was as high as mine, his beaked nose and mouth giving his dark eyes an even fiercer look. If I hadn't had other things to take my attention I might have wondered how he spoke our language so easily, but the impatient swishing of his long, tufted tail was too distracting. That tail led back up to a dark yellow body that was positively huge, and it was possible to see how well-muscled it was even with the folded dark green wings covering his back. I couldn't quite tell if his mane was fur or feathers, but it came more than halfway down his huge chest, toward four feet that were rather clearly taloned.

I had been expecting our journey scout to be an older version of the pages, but what he had turned out to be was a nonhuman Griddenth.

Chapter 8

"For the amount of money I'm being charged, I expect to have *some* say in what I see and do," Lidra remarked at last, the first of us to come out of it. "Paying for the privilege of being bossed around isn't my idea of a fun vacation, Velix, and I think my attorneys will see it the way I do. I agreed to obey the rules of the Mists in the release I signed, but I never agreed to become a puppet or a slave. If that's the way *you* intend interpreting the release, you'd better get one of your bosses in here to discuss the point with us."

"I'm afraid I'll have to go along with the lady," Serendel put in as the Griddenth glared at Lidra, the man's words sounding almost amused. "I'll be more than happy to have your advice and guidance, but I don't obey *anyone* without question. If that's the way you intend running this tour, you'd better find a different group to do it with."

"So I've been blessed with not one but two free souls this time around," the Griddenth growled, looking between Lidra and Serendel, his bearing now much more aristocratic and even less distantly familiar than it had been. "You both seem to think I'm exaggerating the danger and playing tyrant for the fun of it, but that's only because you've never been through here before. You're the ones who decide which way you'll go after the set tour areas are visited and what you'll do when you get there, but I'm the one who tells you whether it's smart to go that way or do as you intend. That point doesn't happen to be subject to debate with me *or* my superiors, and if you can't accept it you'll simply have to leave. Now, which way will it be: do you stay, or do you go back where you came from?''

He set the question flatly in front of them, no doubt at all in any part of his bearing, and Lidra, at least, seemed more than simply annoyed. Considering the fact that we *couldn't* just turn around and go back, she wasn't free to push the matter too far, not if there was any chance at all the management of the Mists would back Velix. As a matter of fact she'd already made more of a fuss than she should have; if they thought we were likely to cause trouble, they'd watch us more closely than we'd find comfortable or convenient. I saw her lips tighten in angry determination, as though she'd just decided not to let herself be pushed around, and if I'd had the time I would have groaned. Since I didn't have the time, what I did instead was step forward before she put all our feet in it.

''What difference can it possibly make who decides what?'' I asked, addressing most of the question to Lidra while hoping she'd understand what I was really saying. ''Maybe you and Chal expect to have a good time here, but for my part I've come for no more than a single reason. If I listen to them and do exactly as they say and still don't enjoy myself, they can't very well complain I didn't go along, now can they?''

She had her eyes on me by the time I'd finished, and this time I could see frustration in them instead of the previous looking-for-a-fight. She'd read my message ten and zero and was wishing she could argue, but wasn't dim enough to think she really could. Behind her to the left Chal stood with nothing but blandness in his expression, but if that wasn't a hint of relief in his eyes, I've never seen the emotion. No more than seconds went by while Lidra swallowed the bitter pill, and then she nodded with no indication of defeat whatsoever.

''You know, Inky, you've made a very good point,'' she said, then moved her gaze directly to the Griddenth. ''It *will* be a much stronger stand if we go along with their absurd demands, and our vacation is ruined because of it. My lawyers have won any number of

cases like that, but the position does require full co-
operation. I'll have to be very careful to see that I do
exactly what Velix says—within reason, of course."

"Your graciousness is an inspiration to us all,
Lady," Velix said with an infinitesimal bow of his
head, sarcasm dripping from every word. "I look forward to our association during this tour. And what
decision have *you* made, lord Serendel?"

With our own problem solved I found myself hoping
the fighter would stick to his previous stance and turn
around and leave, but no such luck. He smiled faintly,
possibly at the realization that Velix had recognized
him but hadn't shown it in any way other than using
his name, and then he shrugged.

"I can't afford the time leaving and going somewhere else would cost me," he said, sounding no more
apologetic or defeated than Lidra had. "I'm here so
I'll be staying here, but it's only fair to warn you about
one important point. If I'm told *why* I shouldn't be
doing something I'll most likely go along with the rec-
ommendation, but if I'm simply given an order I tend
to get annoyed. You really should understand that I,
unlike the lady, rarely hand over my annoyances to
lawyers. When people understand I prefer dealing with
them myself, I find a much smaller number of annoyances to deal with."

"Hardly surprising," the Griddenth commented,
and I would have sworn he'd developed the same sort
of faint smile worn by the man. "When one refuses
to accept petty annoyances, one finds fewer of them
offered. I'm sure we'll strike a balance acceptable to
both of us. Are there any other questions or protests
waiting their turn to be placed or lodged?"

He looked around at all of us again, giving it plenty
of time rather than none at all, but even though Lidra
stirred where she stood, no one took him up on his
offer of an argument. I had the feeling he was neatly
reestablishing his authority, and when no one challenged it he nodded his head and stood.

"We'll go on to your accommodations, then, and on
the way I'll explain what your places are in this town,"
he said, briefly shaking out his wings as he moved

toward us. "The period of time is taken from the planet Llexis' distant past, and although they all consider it fact-bound history, the rest of the Empire tends to think of it more as fanciful imagination. Llexians like to believe their distant ancestors had the ability to do magic."

"I've heard that before," Chal put in as we followed our scout back into the fog, leaving the two pages behind in the booth. "I used to wonder how they could believe that in the face of logic and reason, and then I found out. They think the ability was lost somewhere along the road to advanced civilization, that whatever caused the talent to do magic atrophied like the appendix some members of our race once had. It's been theorized that the appendix allowed the human animal to take nutrition from the bark of trees, but once they developed a hunting and farming culture to replace simple gathering, they no longer had a need for it. It was . . ."

"Exactly, exactly," Velix interrupted courteously but hastily, happily heading off what promised to be a *very* long lecture on comparative biology. "Our people felt the belief would do very well here in the Mists, and this town is the result of that conviction. Those who wear plain cloth are commoners, those in leather like that worn by you gentlemen are upper class lords, and those in glowing robes are magicians. You ladies are also dressed as members of the upper class, and that's the way you'll all be treated—*except* by the other members of the upper class."

"Sounds to me like the rivalry was somewhat intense," Serendel commented, apparently interested. I, myself, was more interested in something I'd noticed about Velix, a fact that could turn out to be very handy later on. As I walked beside him through the ever-present fog, the sound of his talons clicking against the cobblestones was very clear. If he didn't have some way of muting that sound, we'd never have to wonder whether or not he was in the immediate vicinity. Engaging in frowned-upon activities went easier and more successfully with a break like that, but before we relied on the theory it would have to be tested.

"The rivalry was more than 'somewhat' intense," Velix said to Serendel, now apparently amused. "Every member of the upper class was ready, at a moment's notice, to insult or destroy any other member. The only thing that kept it from being a time of constant, all-out warfare was the presence of the magicians. Every lord had a magician backing his House, and the strength of his magician determined what he could and couldn't do against the others. After you've rested, you gentlemen will have the chance to choose magicians of your own."

"What about 'we ladies'?" Lidra asked at once, taking her attention from a pinkly-glowing house on the left that seemed to have a lot of windows, all of them lit. "Don't we get to choose magicians for our own Houses?"

"Alas, dear lady, the period of time didn't work that way," Velix answered as he turned his head to her, his amusement perfectly clear under the sorrowful tone he'd adopted. "Only lords were permitted to be heads of Households, never a lady alone. The ladies were another popular point of contention for the lords, and may well have been the most popular. If a lady struck a lord's fancy he simply claimed her, and the strength of his magician determined whether or not he got to keep her. You two ladies will certainly be claimed almost immediately, and if the magicians chosen by the lords who accompany you aren't powerful enough, you'll need to accede to the wishes of the claiming lord. If the chosen magicians prove more powerful than their adversaries, you'll be the undisputed property of the lord accompanying you. That's the way the game works, and I believe both of you ladies indicated complete willingness to comply in your releases."

"But what if we don't *have* a lord accompanying us?" I said, finally finding something of my own to argue about. "I agreed to go along with the game where the people working here are concerned, but nothing was said about my having to be stuck with some other guest like myself. If something *had* been said, I would have had the chance to enter a refusal, just the way I'm doing now."

"My dear young lady, we *do* have experience in arranging these matters," Velix said as he this time looked at me, superior and almost condescending reproof in his voice. "If there had been no other acceptable guest to add to your party, one of our own would have been added to balance your numbers. With lord Serendel available, however, the effort became unnecessary. For you, *he's* the lord accompanying you."

I thought I heard a sound like swallowed laughter, but when I turned my head fast to the right, the fighter was looking down at me with the blandest expression I'd ever seen. When he saw me looking at him he shrugged just a little, his small headshake adding to the impression of total resignation in the face of complete helplessness, a defeat accepted even before battle had been joined. I'm sure he thought he was being really cute, but I was in no mood to be the butt of anyone's joke.

"As I said, I never agreed to let myself get stuck with some stranger," I told Velix as I turned back to look at him, even less friendliness in my tone than there had been. "Since there isn't anyone acceptable around to be my lord, I'll just have to do without one."

"No one *acceptable?*" the Griddenth echoed in near outrage, those bright, dark eyes glaring at me. "My dear young woman, have you any idea what you're saying? Don't you know—"

He broke off in the middle of the sentence, obviously fighting to keep from talking about things his job didn't allow him to talk about, and then he got a firmer grip on himself.

"All right, I think it's fairly clear that whatever gods there may be are displeased with me," he said, a strong determination to cope now in his tone. "Nevertheless, I think I'll be best off ignoring that and simply going ahead as though they weren't. If you intend arguing the term 'acceptable,' young lady, you ought to know how these matters are judged. A court will poll a hundred women from your own home world, and if three-quarters of them or more disagree with your decision, the court will find against you. You will

be told that we had every right to eject you from the
Mists for breach of contract, and not only won't you
be relieved of the necessity for paying us the full
amount charged, you'll also be given the burden of
paying court costs. And just in case you're uncertain
as to how the poll will turn out, I'll let you in on a
little secret. One of the larger glad program networks
already did a poll about three months ago, using the
top five winners as their offering and every woman
between the ages of sixteen and ninety on every planet
the network broadcast to as their base. Based on the
results of that poll, and bearing in mind the fact that
even women who weren't regular viewers of arena
events were counted in, my advice to you would be to
not waste your time and money."

"I seriously doubt whether any court can tell me I
have to like what everyone else likes," I countered,
feeling the need to dent his heavy satisfaction a little,
but more concerned with a different point he'd mentioned. "My planet has laws guaranteeing my right to
my own taste in things as long as no one else is affected by my choice, but I don't understand why you're
being so unbending about this. Why would I be ejected
from the tour if all I did was refuse to associate with
someone in my own group?"

"The answer to that, dear lady, is that a choice of
such a sort on your part would affect many more people than just yourself," he answered with a sigh, stopping where we were in the fog to look directly at me.
"Based on the answers given in your release, certain
specifics were arranged for this group's tour, and lord
Serendel was added to it. If you try changing your
mind now, after everything has been arranged, our tour
plans are ruined and so is lord Serendel's vacation.
With that in view our only option would be to eject
you, replace you with one of our own people, and then
charge you for the time lost. You would also be expected to pay for the tour as though you'd taken it,
and if it came down to going to court, your signatures
of agreement on the release would make the term 'acceptable' a matter of general opinion rather than a specific. Do you understand what I'm saying, or must I

go through it again more slowly and in greater detail? I'll be happy to go over it as many times as you like, but I really must have an answer from you now. If you insist on keeping to your refusal, I have to see about sending you back and bringing one of our workers in to replace you."

I didn't answer him immediately, but not because I didn't understand him or was worried about having to pay for a tour I hadn't taken. My hesitation was based entirely on the apparent fact that if I refused to go along with their game, they'd kick me out without waiting for another reason. Having to go back home immediately rather than after a delay would not be my idea of a heartbreaking outcome, but that would leave Lidra and Chal in a bind after I'd given my word to help them. I stood there for a minute without being able to see any way out of the mess, and then Chal decided to do for me what I'd done for Lidra.

"Come on, Inky, you don't want to spoil *our* vacation, too," he coaxed. "If you aren't here with us we'll have a miserable time no matter how much fun it turns out to be, so try to be reasonable. And I'll tell you what: if it happens that Serendel's magician is stronger than a claimant's and you make an effort to get along with the winner but can't, you and Lidra can trade lords for a while. You don't consider *me* unacceptable, do you?"

He gave me a smile with the question, emphasizing the personal and deemphasizing the fact that he'd reminded me I was needed, and because he was looking at me he missed the peculiar expression that Lidra briefly showed. She'd agreed completely with the first part of his speech, but when she realized he'd offered himself in the place of Serendel, she hadn't seemed to like the idea. Considering the way she supposedly felt about the big fighter her reaction was very interesting, but I had no time at all to think about it. Velix seemed even more pleased with Chal's offer, and quickly added some urging of his own.

"And you really must remember that a lord is needed no place but here, in the Mists of Llexis," he said, settling his wings flatter in a very comfortable way. "Once we move on to the next place on your tour, the scenario will be entirely different."

"And it *could* turn out that my—lord—picks a magician who can't cut it," I added my own oar, trying to sound as though that possibility in itself made it worth taking a chance. "All right, I'll agree to give it a try, and if the try doesn't work I'll go for the swap. As long as there isn't some rule or regulation against swapping."

I looked at Velix as I said that, daring him to even hint there was, but all I got was a headshake and the suggestion of a smile of amusement. I thought that would be the end of the subject, but someone else turned out to have a question.

"Now that the point's been mentioned, how *do* we pick our magicians?" Serendel asked, totally placid and not even glancing in my direction. "I want to make sure, you understand, that I don't pick anything but the best available."

He gave our journey scout a very innocent smile then, and I think if Velix had been human he would have had to rub at his face while he coughed into his hand. The Griddenth found Serendel amusing, but I still didn't.

"We'll discuss the matter of choosing after you've all rested," Velix's answer came in a familiarly bland and innocent way, as he leaned back on his haunches to gesture behind us with one taloned forepaw. "The guest house right there is where you'll be introduced to the magicians, so the stop is essential. After that you'll plunge right into upper class society, and will be given accommodations at the palace any time you want them. The activites go on nonstop over there, and you're free to go on with them as long as you feel yourselves able. My humble advice to you is to take full advantage of this stop to restore yourselves."

After having stressed the word "humble" he got back to his feet and moved through our line to lead the way into the guest house, leaving behind him the distinct impression that he was doing all in his power to keep from insulting us with orders rather than suggestions. I'd never met a Griddenth before getting to that

planet, even though they'd been full members of the
Empire for more than a hundred years. If they were
all as arrogant and sarcastic as Velix, though, it was
fairly clear I hadn't missed much.

We followed our scout through the front door of the
guest house and were met just inside by two people, a
man and a woman, in the cloth outfits of the lower
class. They greeted us warmly, told us we could have
anything we wanted just by asking for it, then led us
through the large entrance room to a stairway going
up. There were a lot of lamps lit all around the room
and on the wall by the stairs, but their numbers didn't
help that much against the thick fog hanging everywhere. The guest house seemed to be made entirely of
wood with heavy leather furniture standing around
waiting to be used, but the fog turned everything into
a suggestion of itself, insubstantial-looking and therefore possibly unreal.

We were taken to the second floor and shown to
rooms, one for each of us and no nonsense about sharing between lords and their ladies. The man who had
opened the room for me urged me to look around while
he got Lidra settled, and if there was anything I wanted
he would be available very shortly to supply it. The
first thing I looked at was him leaving and closing the
door as he went, wondering if his offer was really as
broad as he'd made it sound. He was definitely on the
handsome side and hadn't looked bad in his short cloth
outfit, but for some reason I couldn't generate much
interest in taking him up on the suggestion he might
have been making. I wasn't on that trip for the purpose
of having fun, and the urge to get on with it was beginning to grow stronger than it had been.

I did take the time to look around the room, and was
unsurprised to find a fully equipped bathroom behind
one of the doors. What did surprise me was finding
my luggage behind the door that hid a closet, and I
couldn't help noticing that it hadn't been unpacked. It
seemed to have been sent along with me in case I
needed something from it, but otherwise could simply
be ignored. Since I didn't need anything right then I
ignored it, but felt a little better knowing my bodysuits

were handy if I wanted one. I was looking forward to it not being very long before I was able to get down to work, and that would be when I wanted one.

My temporary accommodations were moderate in size, with a large bed opposite the door to the hall, three leather chairs scattered around the room, the bathroom and closet doors in the wall to the left, and three wide windows in the wall to the right. All the windows showed was more fog with ghost-lights appearing here and there in it, the same sort of fog that shared the room with me, the stuff I was beginning to get tired of looking at. I went to the bed and sat down on it, wondering what you were supposed to do during that rest time if you didn't feel like resting. The bedcover seemed to be svalk, comfortable but not terribly interesting even though the color was a pretty rose. I lay down on it for a while, counted wounded minutes dragging themselves by, then finally sat up again. Even more lame time limped past, possibly a year or two, and then a knock came at my door.

"Who is it?" I asked, wondering if it was the man who had brought me to the room, coming back to re-offer his suggestion in case I was bored. I still wasn't interested in that sort of a distraction, but I needn't have worried. The door opened to admit Chal, carrying what looked like a blue flame in a small, round copper dish, and when he closed the door behind himself he turned to face me with a grin.

"Isn't this the wildest thing you've ever seen?" he asked as he came toward me, sounding like a little boy with a brand-new gadgettoy. "That woman is the most brilliantly creative person I've ever met, male *or* female. I can't get rid of the delightful feeling that I'm in the middle of a children's adventure book."

"If we end up getting caught doing the wrong thing, I doubt if you'll have trouble losing the feeling," I commented, trying to be as specific and yet obscure as it was possible to be. I didn't know why he was suddenly acting as though we didn't have to watch what we said, but it didn't seem wise to go along with him in it.

"Oh, you don't have to worry about anyone overhearing us," he said as he sat at the foot of the bed opposite me, just as though he'd read my mind. "As long as this flame stays blue, there aren't any listening devices operating near us and we can speak as we like. If anyone tries eavesdropping with nothing but ears, they'll find our conversation is too low for them to hear. If the flame suddenly turns orange, though, we'd better be fast about finding something innocent to discuss."

"That's one of Lidra's devices?" I asked in surprise, finally understanding what he'd been talking about. "It doesn't look like anything but a plain copper bowl, and a small one at that. How can it do all that?"

"You're asking me?" he came back with a snort of amusement, giving me a wide grin as he set the bowl down between us. "When it comes to electronics, I know flipping the switch up turns it on and down turns it off. If it doesn't have an on/off switch, which this doesn't, I usually ignore it entirely. That saves me from having to admit how far beyond me it is."

"You and me both," I muttered, leaning forward a little to peer at the bowl and the blue flame it held. "Isn't it too hot to just set down on svalk like that? If we start a fire, we'll have to explain how it happened."

"It isn't hot at all," he said, still enjoying whatever my expression must have been like. "No matter how real it looks, that flame isn't a flame, and it isn't burning. I had to put my hand in it before I believed that, but there's really nothing there. Go ahead and try it for yourself."

"I'd rather take your word for it," I denied, sitting straight again. "With the way *my* luck's been going, I'd probably find out it only burns females. How did Lidra smuggle something like that in here?"

"She simply tossed it into her luggage," Chal said with a chuckle, leaning back against the padded footboard. Serendel had complained about having trouble with the skirt of his costume, but even leaning back Chal wasn't having the same. "She tells anyone who asks that it's an ashtray for puffers, and even has the puffers to prove she indulges. She isn't anything like an habitual smoker, but every now and then she has one. She brought it to my room to explain how it works, then suggested I show it to you.''

"Your being here is *her* idea?'' I asked with brows high, finding myself distracted at last from the copper bowl and its nonflame. "After the offer you made me, that's about the last thing I would have expected her to do. Is she trying to show how broadminded she is, or that she doesn't really care?''

"Neither,'' he answered with a good deal of satisfaction, folding his arms as he looked at me. "You had to be told there was a way to speak freely when we had to, and I had something to pass on that I didn't want overheard. That made it my place to come in here, but not with company. If Lidra had come with me without our inviting Serendel to join us, it wouldn't have looked right. And if the time comes that you want to speak to one or both of us in private, just make some comment about puffers. We'll get the message and be with you as quickly as possible.''

"Puffers,'' I acknowledged with a nod, certain that he knew he hadn't really answered my question. "And what was it you felt you had to pass on in private?''

"I wanted you and Lidra to know about some of the things I brought along to help us,'' he answered, his expression now more businesslike. "According to what Velix said I expect us to be offered a lot of partying, and there's no reason for us to arouse suspicion by refusing to join in. If there's a lot of drinking going on, for instance, I can give you something to take beforehand to keep you sober no matter how much you swallow, or I can give you something afterward that will sober you up in about fifteen minutes. If we have to stay awake for long periods of time you have the same choice, something to keep you awake, alert and refreshed, or something to make you that way when you're dead on your feet. We'll be smartest eating as much as we can as often as we're able, but if for some reason provisions become unavailable, I can take care of that, too. In addition to those I also have a good supply of pain-killers, antibiotics, sleep-assists, and the like, and all of it's compatible with the biosphere around us. My initial research made sure of that, but I double-checked with the entrance officials here just to be on the safe side. We may need to take time to recover from the strain afterward, but for the short time we'll be using the compounds, we should sustain no lasting physical damage."

"And you brought it in as your own medication," I said with another nod, remembering when he'd mentioned it to the Customs officials. "I hadn't expected something like that, and I have to admit I'm impressed. Do you happen to have something to take against the possibility of sudden, extreme nausea?"

He frowned briefly at that, at first taking the question seriously, and then he understood what I meant.

"I'm really sorry you've decided you'll be feeling that way with Serendel," he said, his light eyes examining me soberly. "I still don't really understand what went on between you two, or why you refused to accept his apology."

"What went on was that he tried to con me, and apologizing for something like that is never more than an extension of the con," I said, turning to stand a thick pillow against the headboard for me to lean against. Chal had been polite enough not to put his curiosity as a question, which meant I didn't mind answering what he hadn't asked. "I also don't like being done favors, and that's what Serendel's attention feels like to me. The big man has graciously decided to give the little girl a giant thrill, but the little girl isn't interested in buying. The man who raised me taught me that people who grant you favors aren't worth knowing; only the ones who are willing to *exchange* favors think of themselves as dealing with equals rather than doormats."

"I really do think you're misjudging Serendel," he said with a sigh, shifting a little against the footboard. "I'm willing to bet more than one of the top fighters are like that, but I don't think he is. If I'm right, though, you'll probably find it out for yourself. The man you mentioned, the one who raised you—he sounds like an extraordinary person."

"He was," I said, smiling just a little at the memories all the ruthless killing in the Empire couldn't destroy. "There was a time right after my mother died that I pretended Seero was my father, taking the trouble to raise and protect me even though he didn't want to acknowledge me. He *wasn't* my biological father, but by the time I was able to admit that to myself, it no longer mattered. He proved himself my father with everything he said and did, and the fact that we shared no common blood made it better than if we had. He didn't *have* to take care of me, he *wanted* to; if that didn't make him my father, nothing in the universe *including* blood would have."

"I see I was right about him being extraordinary," Chal said with a smile, and then the smile faded. "I—don't quite know how to ask this without insulting you, but there's something I've been very curious about. If the man who raised you was so special, and everything you've said confirms that—how did you end up in the—unusual—occupation you've reportedly become so good at?"

"That must be the most tactful way of putting it I've ever heard," I said with a grin, finding his open embarrassment amusing. "Seero told me right at the beginning that there were two kinds of people: those who would understand what we were doing, and those who wouldn't. He said I'd know which were which by the way they approached the subject, and damned if he wasn't right as usual."

"I hope that means you think I'm one who would," he said, a wry expression showing that was probably the result of my grin. "I really meant what I said about not wanting to insult you, so if you'd rather not talk about it all you have to do is say so. On the other hand my curiosity *is* close to killing me, so . . ."

". . . so why don't I save your life by giving you a chance to understand," I finished for him with a chuckle when he just let the last word trail off. "It so happens I do think you're the type to understand, but I also think you have the right to make up your own mind about it. Let's start with the way Seero first explained it to me, when I asked him why he took things

rather than working for them the way my mother had.
I was very young at the time, and he knew I wasn't
judging or criticizing, only asking.''

"Just the way I'm doing,'' Chal put in, abruptly
looking very virtuous despite the amusement in his
eyes.

"Yes, just the way you're doing, sweetheart,'' I
agreed with the sort of oil you use on a child when
you think it's too young to understand it's being patronized. Chal winced and held his hands up in surrender, admitting defeat and letting me go on.

"Seero took me out onto the dining terrace, sat me
down with a soft drink the two of us shared, and then
told me gently that the Empire wasn't the fair, just
place everyone liked to pretend it was. There were
people who worked hard for what they had and others
who tried to take those things away from them, but
not all of those who took were arrested, tried and put
in a cell. Some were too clever or competent to be
caught by the police, but by far the largest number of
them *bought* their way out of trouble. Some did the
buying with the jobs they held, as politicians or judges
or maybe even as police. Others used part of the money
they stole to buy themselves out of trouble *with* politicians or judges or police, using what they took to
keep themselves in a position to take even more. The
honest police couldn't touch them because the honest
police had to work within the law, and it was almost
impossible to have them do that and still expect them
to get anywhere. That made the bad people think they
were something special, that they had the *right* to keep
stealing from innocent people and getting away with
it. Seero said he didn't blame them for thinking that,
but he didn't agree.''

"Don't tell me *that's* who you took from!'' Chal
said with sudden delight, sitting up away from the
footboard. "You and he went after the crooks who
stole and got away with it?''

"Yes, but it's not quite the virtue you're trying to
make it sound like,'' I answered, smiling only faintly
at his enthusiasm. "No matter who the targets of our
stroking were, it was still stealing and against the law.

We ended up being responsible for quite a few of the
supposedly untouchable getting caught, because when
we cleaned them out we forced them to go back to the
well before it was really safe, thereby setting them up.
We even helped put the skids to small Twilight Houses
on behalf of larger Houses, to keep the small-fry from
growing up and carving out pieces of their own terri-
tory. But that, Chal, doesn't mean we weren't stealing. It only means we stole from those who had no
legitimate claim to what they had. Seero refused to
start training me until I proved to him I understood the
point. We might have been stealing only from scum,
but if we'd gotten caught *we* would have been the ones
who ended up in a cell.''

"If you ask *me,* you were both making too much of
the point,'' he said, and damned if he wasn't acting
stiff-necked and offended on Seero's and my behalf.
"If the law can't touch somebody, does that mean
they're entitled to get away with what they do? No
matter who gets hurt? I don't happen to believe that,
which is one of the reasons I'm here right now. The
S.I. isn't as helpless as planetary officials are, and I'll
bet *they* don't think you did wrong, either.''

"Don't make bets you can't afford to lose,'' I told
him, remembering what that S.I. man Filster had said
to me. "Most people can't be bothered with differen-
tiating between one thief and the next, and you can't
really blame them. Stealing *is* stealing, no matter how
well you justify it. Seero and I simply felt that whatever ends we accomplished made the rest of it worthwhile; I'm just glad you're one of the few who agree.''

"Damned right I agree,'' he huffed as he leaned
back again, still touchy but beginning to calm down.
"People who take advantage of the helpless set their
own rules for the game, and have no call to complain
when others play by those rules. If they're as helpless
before you and the man who raised you as others are
before them, who could have the gall to say it's unfair? And—ah—I think I've been very insensitive. It's
only just come through to me from the way you were
speaking— The man Seero is dead?''

"Yes, he's dead,'' I said, looking down away from

Chal to keep the whole thing from flooding over me again. Every time I met someone I liked, my first urge was to drag them home and introduce them to Seero, to let them see for themselves how wonderful he was. Even after almost a year, I still hadn't learned not to do that. Somehow I didn't think I would ever learn not to.

"Inky, I'm sorry," Chal said, and the tone of his voice was compassion rather than pity. "I didn't mean to bring the pain back to you, not for the sake of nothing but curiosity. I can see I should have kept my big mouth closed."

"No, Chal, it wasn't your fault," I said, looking back to his very serious face and forcing a smile. "You couldn't have known, and talking about it just helps to remind me that it's all being taken care of. But I've also been reminded of something else, and since we're into asking each other openly direct questions I'm going to repeat one to you: *why* didn't Lidra mind your coming here to talk to me alone?"

"I never said she didn't mind," he corrected me, a faint look of satisfaction suddenly back on his face. I didn't know if he realized I was changing subjects on purpose, but he didn't seem reluctant to cooperate in the effort. "What I said was that Lidra understood why she couldn't come with me and suggested that I come alone, not that she didn't mind staying behind. But that's not all she was bothered by, only I didn't see it until she came to my room."

"She isn't as happy about the swap as she expected to be," I guessed, positive that had something to do with it. "She thinks Serendel might not be attracted to her, and she doesn't want her idol yawning in her face."

"Inky, Lidra's not like that at all," he protested, moving around again where he sat, his expression now faintly hurt. "She knows Serendel is too much of a decent person to do something like that to her, and it isn't even the fact that she knows he prefers you. When she came into my room she was so quiet I almost didn't recognize her, and although I could see she really didn't want me coming in here alone, she forced herself to tell me I had to. We all have a job to do, and Lidra knows that has to come first.''

"Then what could her problem possibly be?'' I demanded, sitting up away from the pillow. "I thought she was jealous over the offer you made, but what you're describing doesn't sound like jealousy.''

"I'm hoping it's better than jealousy,'' he said, and now he was back to grinning faintly, a definite twinkle in his light eyes. "I have a feeling the first part of Lidra's problem is that she isn't quite as—eager—to have sex with every acceptable male in sight as she pretends to be. It wasn't until she realized I was seriously attracted to her that she let me come closer than arm's length, and just between the two of us, I'm not very used to that. I may not be a fighter like Serendel, but I seem to attract women almost as easily as he does. When Lidra told me she wanted children I agreed to father at least one of them, but nothing was discussed about any sort of relationship beyond that, and I never told her I didn't want her getting involved with Serendel. I didn't have the right to tell her something like that, especially not without specific agreements between us.''

"But—then I don't understand at all,'' I protested, really feeling confused. "She kept insisting she would do just about anything to get Serendel into bed, and now that she practically has him there she's trying to turn and run the other way. And why isn't she at least faintly annoyed that you offered to swap her for me? More than once I had the impression she was looking at you like private property.''

"I think she realized she hasn't done anything to give her the right to look at me that way,'' he answered, and again that satisfaction was there. "I'm convinced she didn't offer anything in the way of a relationship because she's been hurt in the past, quite a few times, and didn't want it happening again. I thought she understood how deep my interest in her goes, but now I can see she's been deliberately letting it slide right past her. And I didn't swap Lidra for you; I swapped Serendel for me, and that Lidra *does* understand.''

"I'm glad *someone's* following what's happening," I muttered, leaning back on the pillow again to give him what I like to think of as a baleful stare. "What's the difference who got swapped for whom? We're still talking about the same swap, aren't we?"

"Oh no, we're not," he came back, grinning at my annoyance. "Lidra realizes I used the opportunity of a near-crisis to not only smooth things over for you, but to also give her what she kept insisting she wanted. I don't think anyone's ever done that for her before, and I'm certain she didn't expect it to be done this time either. She's been very careful to maintain the attitude that says there's nothing between us but an agreement to make a child, all the while loudly exclaiming how acceptable she found Serendel. I'm sure she does consider him acceptable, but only in a distant, biological way."

"You mean she kept drooling out loud over Serendel because she never expected to end up anywhere near him," I said slowly as the light finally came, distantly knowing Seero would have understood a good deal sooner. "And she barely glanced in *your* direction because you were right there and closer than arm's reach, able to hurt her badly if she showed the least sign of interest going deeper than plain sex. Now she's trapped because Serendel and I aren't getting along, and she may even be put into the position of having to sleep with him. Chal, you have to do something! Hitting her with a problem like that just isn't fair."

"You have to remember how unfair a place the Empire really is," he answered with a smile for the way I was sitting straight again, then held up a hand to cut off the immediate protest I began. "Inky, Lidra certainly does have a terrible problem, but it's nothing I can help her with. If I work very hard and manage to convince her I want her on a more permanent basis than the one she's offering, she may come around to agreeing to go along with it, but she'll never really believe it. She has to decide on taking one last chance of letting her own feelings out, and give *me* the chance to respond to them. That way she'll be able to accept what I'm offering, and won't ever have to wonder if it's the truth. If I don't make her do that, then we'll never have anything worthwhile between us.''

''Worthwhile,'' I echoed, wondering how so inno-cent-sounding a word could be responsible for so many difficulties. ''And just what do you consider that to be, Chal? What is it you want happening between you and Lidra?''

''I want us to make a life together,'' he answered very simply, his warm, happy smile turning him even more handsome than usual. ''I've always found it very convenient having so many women attracted to me; it gave me the chance to look carefully for the one I wanted. I was certain I would find her some day, and when I met Lidra I knew that some day had come. We share so many pastime interests we might as well be the same person, but our major career paths are so widely separated that one can never intrude on the other. Since she's as brilliant in her field as I am in mine, our children will have the potential of being just about anything they please. Our house can have two labs, one for her, one for me, and I'll never have to worry about her coming into mine to 'straighten a lit-tle.' There are all sorts of benefits in marrying a highly intelligent woman, and that's just the best of them.''

By then he was grinning at me, the joke he'd made trying to turn the situation funny rather than touching, but I couldn't see it that way. His intentions seemed like the most wonderful thing I'd ever heard, the sort of romantic drivel you laugh at in books, but can't quite laugh at in real life. I found myself envying Lidra instead of feeling sorry for her, as it seemed fairly clear that Chal had no intentions of letting her get away. I spent a very short instant wondering what that would be like, and then I smiled at him.

''I hope it works out the way you want it to,'' I told him, and I was sure he could see I wasn't just saying that. ''I suppose I'd also better hope now that it doesn't come down to my having to swap Serendel for you. That would just make things harder all around.''

''Not at all,'' he said with a continuing grin, begin-ning to get back to his feet. ''The swap might be just the thing to push Lidra past that blind spot of hers. If

she wants my attention while not having to give anyone else hers, she'll have to talk to me. I'm sure she
feels about me the way I feel about her; all I have to
do now is get her to admit it.''

"All," I repeated with a laugh, watching as he re-
trieved the copper bowl with its blue fire from the bed.
"I'm glad my end of this three-way partnership is the
easy one; the only thing I have to do is get us into a
place people don't want us getting into. Security systems are a lot easier to get past than emotional defenses.''

"You may be right, but emotional defenses are all
I'm equipped to handle," he answered with a chuckle,
then sobered just a little. "And speaking of emotions,
if Serendel wasn't truly sorry for his misjudgment in
his conversation with you, he ought to leave the arena
and take up acting. He was trying to make associating
with him easier for you by evoking faint pity first and
then humor, but you reacted in a way he wasn't expecting. He said if he'd known you had the soul of a
female glad, he wouldn't have worried about your being afraid of him.''

"Well, he's right about my not being afraid of
him," I said with a snort, leaning back against the
pillow again. "As far as the rest of it goes, though, I
don't *want* associating with him made any easier. Bottom line is, I don't intend associating with him at all.
There's the faint possibility I may have to sleep with
him, but that doesn't mean I have to talk to him.''

"Inky, don't make the mistake of offering him a
challenge," Chal warned, now completely serious.
"He ignores that sort of thing from noncombatants,
but he seems to have classified you differently. If you
annoy him too badly, you may find him reacting in the
mental set that makes him a very successful fighter. If
you find you need to talk about that or anything else,
just come to my room. Lidra is next to you on the
right, I'm beyond her, and Serendel is beyond me.
Right now, I'd better get back to where I belong.''

I nodded to show I agreed he'd already been in my
room long enough as far as possible suspicion went,
and once he was gone I was able to look down at my

hands without being bothered by someone who had
obviously studied the mental sciences as well as the
biological ones. I didn't feel uncomfortable, exactly,
most certainly not where that big fool Serendel was
involved, but I didn't quite understand what Chal had
meant when he'd said the fighter had classified me as
other than a noncombatant. I didn't like the sound of
it any more than I liked the man himself, and snorted
out loud at the thought of how solicitous he'd been of
my feelings. I wasn't afraid of him or anyone, and if
I had to prove it there on Joelare the way I had on
Gryphon, I would.

I sat up to lay the pillow flat, then stretched out,
wondering in annoyed impatience just how long a time
we'd be wasting in ''rest.'' If it turned out to be too
long, they'd find themselves in possession of a complaint they couldn't simply gloss over. Having a guest
dying of boredom was very bad press, and if they knew
what was good for them they'd try hard to avoid it.

Chapter 9

Our rest time was long enough for me to fall asleep for a while, which didn't turn out to be as unwelcome as I'd thought it would. When I woke I had enough time to stretch comfortably while I considered getting up, and then soft, pleasant music began playing in the room. The music went on only long enough to wake me if I'd been asleep, and then a woman's voice announced that my presence was requested in the dining room downstairs at my earliest convenience. Once the voice had stopped I wondered very briefly what they would do if I simply turned over and went back to sleep, but I was only curious, not interested in trying to find out. I yawned and stretched a second time, then got up to use the bathroom.

As expected, even sleeping in the svalk costume hadn't wrinkled it, so all I had to do was throw a little cold water on my face and brush my hair, and then I was ready to go. The hall outside my door was deserted when I walked out into it, and I couldn't help noticing how eerie the fog made everything look. There had been just as much fog inside my room, but there had also been a lot more light and the presence of windows. For some reason having fog around when there were also windows was less disturbing, but I hadn't any idea why that should be. I raised my head a little to show the fog I wasn't afraid of *it* either, and then moved deliberately through it toward the stairs leading down.

When I reached the lobby it was also deserted, but a glowing sign hanging in midair showed an arrow indicating the dining room somewhere off to the left around the staircase. I walked through the fog into the next room, expecting it to be just as empty as the lobby, but found instead that the next hovering arrow, still pointing left, also indicated a group of people. Our trusty journey scout Velix stood between Chal and Serendel, talking to them as he indicated four men seated in large, ornate wooden chairs which stood side by side in front of the wall the two men and Velix faced. The seated four had long white hair and beards, eyes which glittered even from where I was, and wore ankle-length, long-sleeved robes that glowed even more strongly than the lights and signs around us. None of the four looked at the men who were examining them, instead gazing straight ahead while resting their arms on the chair arms, and as I came up behind those who were observing them I was able to hear what Velix was saying.

" . . . are the ones you'll be choosing among for your personal magicians," the Griddenth told the two men, sounding very firm. "Whether or not there are others available makes no difference at all, lord Serendel. These four are representatives of the available talent, and it's up to you gentlemen to each choose the one you think will serve you best. You may each ask one question of any two of them, and then you must state your choice. Since lord Serendel got down here first and therefore gets to choose first, lord Chal may ask his questions first."

"That's your idea of giving me a break?" Chal said with wry amusement, his eyes still moving among the four who were seated. "How am I supposed to know what to ask them?"

"You're supposed to ask them questions which will tell you whether or not you want their protection," Velix answered, less wry and more amused. "Look at them carefully, remember what their purpose will be, and then choose two to question. I can't be any more specific than that, or it won't be fair."

"*I'd* consider it fair," Chal came back in a way that made Serendel chuckle, and then he shook his head. "Well, if I have to, I suppose I might as well get on with it. You said to ignore the fact that they don't seem to be paying attention, and simply address the one I want to talk to? All right, then I'm addressing you, sir, the gentleman on the extreme left. Who's the most powerful magician among you four?''

''I am,'' the man addressed answered, sounding considerably younger than his appearance suggested. He'd answered without hesitation, but he hadn't even glanced at Chal.

''Since I don't get to choose first, maybe I shouldn't have asked that question,'' Chal said, looking to his right at Velix with raised brows. ''What do I do now?''

''I would strongly suggest asking your second question,'' the Griddenth answered, now apparently even more amused. ''You don't get involved much with gameplaying, do you, lord Chal?''

''I don't have the spare time most of it requires,'' Chal said, suspecting the Griddenth was trying to tell him something, but not knowing what. ''I can't think of anything to ask that would better my first try, so all I can do is save Serendel the trouble and confirm what I've already been told. You, sir, second from the left. Who's the most powerful magician among you four?''

''I am,'' the second long-bearded man answered with as little hesitation as the first, also sounding equally as positive. He also made no attempt to look at Chal, but this time Chal was returning the compliment.

''I'll bet I wasted both of my questions, didn't I?'' he asked Velix as he stared at the Griddenth, sounding more excited and enthusiastic than depressed over having messed up. ''It didn't matter that I asked what I did, because it doesn't help Serendel any more than it helped me. Am I right?''

''In a way, you certainly are, lord Chal,'' Velix answered, his wings moving a little with his amusement. ''At the very least, as far as your own efforts go, you *have* wasted your questions. Let's see if lord Serendel can do any better.''

I joined the two of them in looking at the fighter, but probably unlike them I was hoping he would *not* do better. For his part Serendel was staring narrow-eyed at each of the four magicians, but rather than simply looking them over, he seemed to be searching for something in particular. After a minute or so his inspection ended, and a faint smile raised the ends of that long red mustache.

"I believe you said they would all tell the truth, at least as far as *they* see it," he stated to rather than asked Velix, only glancing at the Griddenth long enough to see his nod of confirmation. "In that case, I'll address my first question to the one here in front of me, on the far right. After yourself, who's the most powerful magician in this group of four?"

"After me, the most powerful is Jejin," the man answered at once, still staring off into space somewhere but giving me the distinct impression he was beginning to be amused. Serendel nodded as though he'd gotten exactly the answer he'd been looking for, and then his eyes moved to one of the ones Chal had already questioned.

"You, second from the left," he said, his tone a good deal less respectful than Chal's had been. "Which one of you four is Jejin?"

"Jejin sits beside me to my left," the man answered, and I would have put money on the fact that he was enjoying himself as much as the other one had. Serendel nodded again, this time with that faint smile he liked so much, and then he was looking directly at Velix.

"Since first choice is mine, that's the one I want," he said, calm satisfaction in the decision. "The one named Jejin, who I believe is sitting second from the right. Do I have to do anything beyond stating the choice?"

"No, but I'd say lord Chal is curious as to why you did it the way you did," Velix answered, his tufted tail flicking back and forth. "You don't owe him an answer unless you want to give one, and you certainly don't have to say anything until he's made a choice of his own."

"But I can comment if I want to, which it so happens I do," Serendel summed up, then looked at his fellow tourist. "Chal, we were told twice to look them

over, and when I finally heard the hint and followed
it, I noticed something interesting. They're all wearing
the same *kind* of clothes, but not the same quality.
They may all consider their own power the strongest,
but if it isn't so, which it probably isn't, how other
people see them is the most telling point. The strongest will pull down more wealth than the others, so he
should be dressed better than them. I asked who the
second strongest was, got an answer that should have
been true, then double-checked it against appearances.
The two matched, so I made my choice."

"Damned if you aren't right," Chal muttered, this
time looking at the four magicians with purpose rather
than aimlessly. "The one you picked is better dressed
than any of the other three. And you *did* get use out
of my wasted questions, by realizing that they can't
be trusted to speak anything but opinion when it comes
to themselves. I appreciate the help, my friend, and
I'll use it to choose that one."

Chal pointed to the magician on our far left, the one
he'd spoken to first, the one who, after the fighter's
choice, was dressed in the best quality robe. It came
to me to wonder if that was how Llexian magicians
really had shown off their status spots, with more material acquisitions rather than fewer, but I didn't mention the point. My nemesis seemed to have overlooked
the consideration, and I wouldn't have wanted to bring
it up even if Velix hadn't already started going back
to his take-charge guidance.

"Now that the choosing is taken care of, my lords,
you and your ladies and your magicians are free to
have your meal," the Griddenth said, just short of
purring. "When you've finished eating I'll conduct you
all to the nearest palace and its revelries, where you'll
certainly have opportunity to test the wisdom in your
choices of magicians. If you'll follow me?"

The two designated magicians had gotten out of their
chairs to join our little group, and when Velix moved
off to the left leading Chal and Serendel, they followed
along behind. I hesitated for a moment, wondering how
Lidra was supposed to find us, then glanced around to
discover that she already had. She stood a few feet

back from where we'd all been, a phantom of a ghost in the swirling fog, an odd, secret smile on her face as she watched the men moving behind Velix. She seemed more calmly amused than in the grip of the sort of disturbance Chal had described earlier, and when she saw me looking at her she actually grinned and winked. If she'd had her copper bowl I would have asked her what she found so funny, but without it all I could do was join her in adding to the parade behind Velix.

The room the magicians had been sitting in was wider than it was long, and the doors in the short left-hand wall were double with servants to see to their opening. We sailed on through as though we had just bought the place, and once into the next room we could see two long tables facing one another across a space of about ten feet. There were three heavy chairs set at the outer sides of each table, and a servant stood behind each of the six chairs. Velix stopped short of the tables, then nodded toward the one on the right.

"That one is for you and yours, lord Serendel, and the one to the left is yours, lord Chal," he said, his head moving around as though he were making sure everything had been set up right. "There will be entertainment during the meal, but I would advise using part of the time for getting acquainted with your newly acquired magicians. I'll rejoin you all after you've eaten."

He glanced at the two men he'd been talking to, again giving them the chance to ask any questions they might have, then moved off to the far right when they didn't take him up on the offer. As soon as he was gone from among us, the servants came forward to welcome us while deftly herding us to our respective places, and I found myself being seated first, in the center chair of the right-hand table. Through the fog I could see Lidra was being given the same honor at her own table, but I still would have made a fuss if I'd thought it would do any good. My digestion would have been considerably improved if the magician had been seated between me and Serendel instead of to my left with the fighter on my right, but our hosts obviously didn't want it like that. Since I hadn't been given a choice there was nothing I could do but sit back in the padded, thronelike chair and pretend I was as comfortable as it's possible to be.

"I feel as if I'm starving," Serendel said as he settled himself in his place, glancing at me and the magician both. "I haven't eaten since early this morning on the liner, not even so much as a snack in the car that brought us here. When was the last time you and the others got something to eat?"

The question he'd put was casual small talk, nothing of earth-shattering importance—but also nothing the magician could be expected to answer. It looked like the companion who had been forced on me was trying to break the conversational ice, but that sort of thing isn't hard to get around.

"We all had a snack during Customs inspection," I answered without even glancing at him, then turned my head to the magician with a smile. "How long has it been since the last time you were chosen to be the protector of a visiting House?" I asked as though really interested. "And are you truly as pleased to be included in on this meal as you look?"

"I'm delighted to be included in on this meal, and as soon as they bring out the food you'll understand why," he answered in a light and easy voice accompanied by a return smile, apparently all through with staring off into the distance. "As far as being chosen as a protector goes, I'm picked at least as often as any of the others, but rarely for so—distinguished—a House. I may be putting my foot in it by saying this, but—am I wrong in thinking you don't agree with me about how much of an honor it is?"

He was examining me with guileless, light blue eyes, waiting for an answer to his admittedly baldfaced question, most of his expression hidden behind that long white beard. I really wasn't much interested in going into detail on my dissenting opinion, but someone else proved more than happy to jump in for me.

"The lady feels I insulted her," Serendel supplied in the same calm and easy tone that he'd used earlier, drawing the magician's gaze. "All I thought I was doing was soothing the nervousness many women feel in my presence, but apparently she doesn't see it like that. She's decided I insulted her on purpose, and isn't interested in hearing any statements to the— Ah, here comes the first of the food."

He interrupted his own story to watch the approach of four tray-bearers, three carrying tureens and tiny cups and spoons, the fourth carrying nine empty bowls and nine regular-sized spoons. The tureen-bearers put their burdens down on the far side of the table opposite us, paying no attention to the golden cloth covering the table, and with the help of the servants who stood behind our chairs, we very quickly had three tiny cups standing in front of each of us, samples of the different sorts of soup which had been brought. As other servants came by to drop off baskets of more kinds of bread than I knew there were, the servant who had been carrying the bowls stepped in front of the three soup-men.

"Gentles, please taste our offerings and indicate which of them you find most pleasing," he said, performing a general bow that was apparently meant for us all. "Should you find two or even three equally as pleasing, simply instruct your personal servant to fetch you some of each. Three or none, the choice is, of course, yours."

He bowed again before going back to his tray, and the annoyance I'd been feeling with the fighter sitting next to me spread to cover the Mists people almost as thickly. Giving us soup before offering anything more substantial wasn't too obvious a ploy to cut our appetites for and possible consumption of more expensive dishes, and that idea was a perfect kicker to Serendel's attempt at showing just how unreasonable I was being. If I hadn't realized just how hungry I was I would have ignored the soup samples the way I was still ignoring the fighter, but the smells coming out of the three tiny sample cups were just too good to resist. I knew I *had* to taste all of them, and then I might be able to get back at Velix's bosses by refusing all three.

After tasting the samples, the best I could do was

settle on just one of the three. I couldn't remember ever tasting soup that good even at the very expensive resorts Seero and I had visited over the years, but I wasn't ready to admit I might be wrong about the scam the Mists people were trying to run. Seeing the chilled fruit and cheese and even more hot baked goods added to our table let me stay suspicious, but once they began bringing out the meats and vegetables and gravies—and wines—I decided I might be wise dropping all thoughts of a scam. We were urged to try as much of as many different dishes as we liked, and despite the soup I found I wasn't reluctant to go along with the suggestions. I felt as though I were eating ten times more than I ever had in my life, but I enjoyed every bite without also feeling that I was about to explode. When I finally finished I was most aware of satisfaction, that and the impression that I was now prepared to get on to other things.

"That has to be the best meal I've ever eaten," Serendel announced once his wine glass had been refilled for the twentieth time, a pleasant nod of thanks for the servant who had poured. There hadn't been any conversation while the food had held our attention, but there *had* been music as well as dancers who spun gracefully between the tables. The dancers had been mostly female, which was probably why I'd had the opportunity of noticing how little the magician had eaten in comparison to the fighter. Our bearded friend hadn't been shy about helping himself, but even my capacity had been greater than his. I wondered if the difference meant anything, but couldn't think of any way it might.

"There's never any stinting when it comes to a feast of greeting," the magician—Jejin, that was his name— said in answer, his own wine glass still more than half full and close to his hand. "You won't go hungry in any of the Mists, but this one is far and away the best. Before the meal, lord Serendel, you were saying something about many women being nervous in your presence. I think you understand there are certain things I can't mention here and now, but with those things in mind even though absent from tongue, I must confess

I don't understand why that would be. I should think
you would find it the complete opposite.''

"Most people think it's the complete opposite,'' the
glad answered, faint amusement in the gray gaze he
rested on Jejin, his body relaxed back in its chair except for the hand that gently swirled the wine in its
glass prison. "There are enough amateur wigglers and
hot crazies around to give that impression, but you
can't lump them in under the general heading of
'women.' They may be female, but they're not interested in what you might want to say to them, only in
what you can do for them, in bed or in supplying pres-
tige. Those who *can* be listed under the heading of
women are capable of occasionally doing something
really unusual, like carrying on an intelligent conversation.''

The dryness in his voice made Jejin chuckle, but I
was busy paying more attention to the newest dancers
performing in the space between the tables. One male
and one female they were, and their costumes were
definitely on the skimpy side.

"Yes, men of action aren't supposed to be interested in something as unusual as conversation,'' the
magician agreed, his appreciation of the comment still
clear. "Some observers seem to be afraid that if they're
allowed that, the next things they might take an interest in could be the unthinkable realms of poetry or
music or literature. I can see that, but what I can't see
is why you maintain women are nervous in your presence. Is conversation with you considered that much
of a danger?''

"You forget it's not supposed to be conversation
that I'm interested in,'' Serendel returned, just short
of sounding like a martyr. "A woman finds herself
face to face with me, suddenly remembers all those
things everyone *'knows'* are true about people like me,
and that's the end of any chance at conversation. Calm
friendliness changes so fast to nervous tension that
you'd need an open lens to catch the action, and all
because they're afraid I won't be able to keep from
attacking them.''

"And men say women aren't perceptive,'' I mur-

mured to myself, still keeping my eyes and attention
on the dancers. I knew I shouldn't have cut the hook
from the dangling fishing line, but the temptation had
been too heavy to resist. I was supposed to have been
filling up with pity for the poor little misunderstood
fighter, but it hadn't quite worked out that way. I understood him better than he knew, and if he decided
to argue I could always cite Chal as my authority.
Rather than argument a lot of silence came from my
right, and then there was a throat-clearing sound from
my left.

"I beg your pardon, my lady, but are you saying
you agree with those who judge from nothing but idle
gossip?" Jejin asked, his tone a good deal more diplomatic than his words. "Were you afraid lord Serendel would attack you before you and he began
arguing?"

"I was never 'afraid' of *anything* in connection with
lord Serendel," I came back, shifting in my chair as I
glanced at the bearded man in annoyance. "It so happens I don't believe in being afraid of things, or people
either for that matter. If all your friend wanted out of
me was a little conversation, why was he so interested
in choosing the strongest magician available? Is that
what 'lords' win in this section of the Mists, the right
to *talk* to the lady of their choice?"

"If that's what would please them most,"Jejin began to say in counterargument, making it sound no
more than reasonable and to be expected, but that was
as far as he got. A sound like the hissing of vexation
through teeth came from my right, and then I had unexpected support on my side of the disagreement.

"The lady is absolutely right, Jejin," Serendel said
in what was nearly a growl, drawing my attention as
well as the magician's. "All I want from her is the
use of her body, and that's what I intend getting. What
do I have to know or do, to be sure no one succeeds
in claiming her from me?"

"You have very little more to do than has already
been done," the bearded man said with the faintest of
hesitations while I glared at the miserable beast of a
fighter. "If you're challenged by another lord, you

simply order me to protect what's yours. If my powers are stronger than those of the magician I go up against, you win. If they aren't, you lose.''

''Can't you tell beforehand which of you is stronger?'' the fighter demanded, completely ignoring the way I was looking at him. ''Haven't you been here long enough to have been tested against most if not all of the others?''

''It doesn't work that way,'' Jejin answered, shifting just a little under the cold gray stare he was getting. ''The magicians here come in grades of ability, and if your original choice is someone from the lowest grades, you might as well give up the idea of winning against anyone of higher ability. If your choice brings you someone of high ability, that in itself should guarantee success in most cases. The only time difficulty arises is when your challenger's magician is of the same caliber as your own. There's always uncertainty when two master magicians face one another, so the meetings are usually governed by pure chance. But that's a circumstance covering the meeting of equals, which only happens occasionally. It really isn't worth getting too upset about.''

By that time the bearded man's voice was nearly trembling, and the sweat beaded on his forehead wasn't being caused by the closeness of the room. He was obviously required to tell Serendel just what he had been telling him, but what the fighter wanted to hear was how he could win, not the reasons why he might lose.

''Then maybe we can find something I *should* get upset about,'' he said in that same near-growl, his eyes refusing to turn Jejin loose. ''That list of grades we were just discussing—on what part of the list does *your* name appear?''

''I—I'm the strongest magician of them all,'' the man mumbled in the faintest of voices, close to being terrified at having to give an answer that was obviously required of him. Serendel's head went up when he heard it, those gray eyes growing even colder, but I'd had enough of that nonsense.

''Stop it!'' I snapped to the fighter, the anger in my

voice enough to finally get his attention. "Can't you
see you're not supposed to find out how good or bad
he is until after the first challenge? And where the hell
do you come off giving *him* a hard time? It wasn't *his*
idea to be chosen, it was yours! If you're mad at me
and looking to start a fight because of it, start the fight
with *me,* not some innocent bystander! I said I wasn't
afraid of you, and I meant it!"

"Yes, you did say that, didn't you?" he murmured,
most of the coldness gone from his eyes as he leaned
back to stare at me. "It obviously slipped my mind
that you have the soul of a female glad, but I'll try not
to let it happen again. And for the second time, the
lady is absolutely right, Jejin. I *was* taking my mad at
her out on you, and I apologize. None of this stupidity
is any fault of yours."

"Thank you for understanding that, lord Serendel,"
the magician answered, vast relief in the words. "The
explanations we're required to give are designed to
keep guests in eager suspense, but it's clear they
weren't anticipating guests like yourself. And my most
heartfelt thanks to *you,* lady Dalisse, for interceding
on my behalf. I'm afraid my bravery isn't quite on a
par with yours."

"Don't tell me you're someone who believes all that
idle gossip about how untrustworthy fighters are?" I
asked with inch-thick innocence, turning my head in
time to see the magician flinch over having his own
words fed back to him. "Don't you know they're men
of iron self-control, who have absolutely no need of
the handlers it's been suggested they shouldn't be allowed to walk around without? Were you afraid of the
man *before* he started flexing a bad temper in your
direction?"

"Of course he was afraid of me," the fighter answered for Jejin in a very neutral way, the ghost of
guilty agreement flashing briefly in the bearded man's
eyes. "Everyone with sense is afraid of a man—or
woman—whose career is based on the ability to kill.
Any other reaction is the result of never having thought
the thing through. But don't forget, Jejin, it wasn't
bravery that made her defend you. Without fear brav-

ery isn't possible, and she isn't afraid of me. And you should also know that she prefers her nickname, so please don't call her lady Dalisse. Call her lady Smudge.''

"That's Inky, not Smudge," I said with a growl of my own, turning again to send daggers toward the big fool. "Don't pretend you don't know that, because I heard you being corrected once before. And in any event, what the name is or isn't doesn't concern you. My nickname is reserved for the use of *friends,* and you don't happen to qualify."

"Why are you acting so outraged?" he asked with brows raised high, the innocent child being unjustly accused. "Didn't you just now say that if I wanted to start a fight, you were the one I ought to be starting it with? Don't you consider being insulted a good way to start a fight?"

"Oh, it's a wonderful way," I agreed as I seethed, hating the grin he couldn't quite swallow—not to mention the chuckling Jejin was doing. "The only problem I can see is that it isn't quite fair on my end. There are so many things about *you* open to comment, I'm having trouble deciding which to use first. Maybe I ought to settle for asking how you can speak so clearly with your foot constantly in your mouth. If you doubt the contention, just remember how many times you've had to apologize over the last few days."

"At least I'm bright enough to recognize those times apology is called for," he came back as he straightened in his chair, a good deal of his amusement having dissolved. "That's more than can be said for other people at this table, specifically other female people. You . . ."

"My lords and ladies, may I have your attention please," a voice suddenly came to interrupt the fighter, and I reluctantly looked away from the argument to see Velix standing in the space between the tables, a replacement for the dancers I hadn't seen leave. "If you're all quite finished with your meal, we can leave for the palace now. Nibbles and drinks will also be available there, and I have transportation outside befitting those of your station. Please rise now and follow me.''

"Just a minute," I called as I stood, making no effort to look at the fighter again. "Is that transportation one of your ironclad requirements, or is it possible to *walk* off part of that meal I just swallowed? I'm not worried about getting lost in the fog. If I have to ride in anything right now, it's much more likely I'll have being sick to worry about."

Most especially from the company, I added to myself as Velix paused, wishing I could read the Griddenth's expression. If he refused my request and I ended up anywhere near Serendel in whatever we were supposed to ride in, everyone else was in danger of ending up knee-deep in spilled blood. Lidra wasn't the only one who had managed to smuggle something past Customs and the clothes change, and another five minutes of arguing with that stupid glad would guarantee everyone's finding out just what that something was. Serendel and Jejin got to their feet the way the three people at the other table did, and Velix looked around at us all before performing a gesture that was very like a shrug.

"I meant to mention this once we'd reached the lobby, but since the point has been raised I might as well go into it now," he said, sounding calm and undisturbed. "It so happens you do have the choice of walking, but not through the heavy mists in the street. Anyone not thoroughly familiar with this area couldn't help getting lost, that's why another route was prepared. It reaches the palace by means of an underground passage, and although the passageway isn't used very often, it's not really possible to become lost in it. I, unfortunately, must stay aboveground with the transportation, but any of you wishing to use the passageway may certainly do so."

"Then that works out really well," I said before anyone else could jump in. "You'll go along with my fellow travelers in the transportation, and I'll have the passageway and a little time to myself. Every now and then I need to be alone, and this seems the perfect

opportunity to satisfy the need. No one objects, I
hope?''

I'd.tried making the request sound like sweet reason
incarnate, primarily to have a strong basis for protest
if the mighty Serendel decided to open his mighty
mouth in disagreement. I'd stated a need and had asked
for everyone's help in seeing to it; if the fighter tried
arguing *he* would be the unreasonable one, and his
suitability as an acceptable companion would begin
losing all those legs it had been standing on. I waited
with a friendly smile on my face, not really looking at
the way Chal and Lidra exchanged a silent glance, and
then Velix gave that sort-of shrug again.

"Apparently no one does object," he said, deliberately looking around as he said it. "The passageway
is all yours then, and we'll meet again when you reach
the palace. We'll all walk to the lobby together, and
then go our separate ways."

The servants pulled the chairs out of everyone's way
to make it easier to leave the tables, and I followed
after Velix without even a single glance behind me.
As I passed Jejin, I noticed a faint frown on his face,
but I didn't ask him the reason for it and he didn't
volunteer any data. I was too delighted at the thought
of getting away from that glad to wonder why the magician was unhappy, and then it occurred to me our
reasons might be exactly the same. I was happy to get
away even for a little while, but that meant Jejin would
be all alone with Serendel until I rejoined them. If he
was as afraid of the fighter as he'd claimed to be, my
not being there as a buffer would make the time a good
deal less than pleasant for him.

Getting back to the lobby didn't take very long, and
we hadn't gone more than a couple of steps before
Velix stopped and turned to look at me.

"Our transportation lies through the doors straight
ahead, the doors you all came in by," he said, gesturing behind himself with his head. "Your point of
departure, dear lady, lies behind you to your left,
through that portal. A servant will be here in a moment
to open it for you."

I wondered why I needed anyone to open a door for

me, but once I'd turned to look I began to understand. Portal Velix had called it and portal it was, a heavy, metal-bound wooden door that had a large ring of metal on the left, halfway up. If I wasn't mistaken, it was the thick ring that was used to open the door, and with the swirls of mist all around it it really did look as though it hadn't been opened in a while. I wasn't actually beginning to have second thoughts about going through the door, not with the alternative being what it was, but the arrival of two big men ended the time I had even to toy with the consideration.

"Very good, men, just as prompt as ever," Velix said to the new arrivals, watching them walk to the door. "There's only one to go through this time, and then you can close it again."

"Close it again?" I asked as the two men put hands to the ring and shoulders to the wood, then began pushing with all their strength. "You mean you're just going to—close that behind me?"

"Well, of course," Velix said with an indulgent chuckle, his bright, dark eyes faintly amused. "We can't very well leave it open, not with the number of other guests around. We really do need to keep track of all of you for safety's sake, and if we left that door open, half our charges would disappear through it, just to find out if it really does go where we say it goes. Surely you can appreciate the problem."

"Surely," I said in a voice that sounded very hollow to me, which is why I said no more than the single word. I hadn't known I was going to be closed behind a door I had no chance of opening again, but it was much too late to back out by refusing to go. I'd look and feel like a complete idiot, and I knew I'd rather die than give Serendel the satisfaction of that. I'd just walk as fast as I could until I got to the other end of the passageway, and then it would all be behind me.

"When you reach the palace, the servants there, stationed inside the portal, will open it for you," Velix said, his tail moving in sharp arcs in contrast to the smoothness of his tone. "I believe the opening is wide enough for you to fit through rather easily now. . . ."

He let the sentence trail off as he moved closer to

examine the efforts of the two men, and when I made myself follow I could see he was right. They'd pushed the door more than halfway open, and behind it and them I could see mist-shrouded stairs that trended downward. Through the fog I could also see the faint glow of intermittent light, which meant there was no reason including dangerous dark to keep me from getting started. My lips felt the least bit dry when my tongue wet them, but then I realized there was really nothing to be nervous about. I was being sent through that door in front of witnesses, so if anything happened to me the Mists people would be liable. It was like crossing a street in the middle of ground traffic; no matter how badly the drivers wanted to hit you, none of them would or their insurance would go up. I was safe and I knew it, so I simply stepped through the opening without the slightest worry.

Chapter 10

The lack of worry lasted until that impossible door was pulled slowly and silently shut behind me, then the lack of worry became conspicuously absent. The back of the door was completely smooth, with nothing for anyone without talons like Velix's to get a grip on, and somehow it seemed out of character for the thing to have opened and closed without making a sound. By rights there should have been the eerie scream of protesting hinges, much like the moaning cries of lost, tormented souls . . .

"Are you completely out of your mind, or just a little on the weird side?" I demanded in a hiss, talking to myself the way I deserved to be talked to. "If you do any more of that, you'll be having hysterics even before you've gone down the stairs! I thought you were supposed to be the one who wasn't afraid of things."

I conceded that an excellent point had been made, then took a deep breath and looked around a little more. Between the fog and the plain, stonelike material of walls, steps and ceiling, there wasn't much of anything to see, so I simply started going down the stairs.

By the time I reached the bottom of the flight, I was certain I'd gone lower than the level of the transportation system that had brought us to that section of the Mists. The descent had been long, tedious, dizzy-making, boring—but it hadn't been hard on me physically even when I'd jumped down one section of the steps. I'd done the jumping because I'd been curious about what the steps were made of, which wasn't stone even though it looked like it. The material was unexpectedly springy while still being very firm, and the sharp edges of the steps were anything but sharp. It came to me that I probably couldn't hurt myself on the stuff even if I tried, and when I looked more closely at the walls I saw they were made of the same material. I realized the Mists people really were being cautious about my safety, and after that felt a lot better about continuing down.

The ever-present fog didn't thin at the bottom the way I'd been hoping it would, but the passageway I found before me was wide enough and almost well-enough lit to make that a minor problem. As I began walking I noticed there wasn't a sound anywhere, nothing but the very soft, very faint scuff of my sandals against the not-stone of the passageway floor. Even right on top of it I could barely hear it, and that gave me an odd sense of being absolutely alone. The thought was disturbing, and I didn't understand why that should be. I'd been alone before, most especially on strokings, but I'd never felt the way I did right then.

The only thing I could do about the feeling was shrug, so I shrugged and just kept going. The passageway took me straight ahead for a while, and then it began curving first right, then left, then right again. After another few minutes it was a toss-up as to which way the curve would go, and that no matter which way the previous curve had gone. I wasn't completely sure, but I was beginning to think the light was a little less than it had been, and the passageway walls looked somehow different. The fog hung too thick around the walls for me to see them at all easily, but I was sure there was something different about them. If I'd stopped to examine them I might have found out what, but I didn't stop. I just kept going while trying to look everywhere at once.

"This is stupid," I whispered to myself, the words coming out with a lot less sound than I'd wanted them to have. "There's nothing here, not even a shadow. Why are you so nervous?"

I would have enjoyed being able to answer that

question, but I couldn't think of an answer. The fog was just as warm and dry as it had been all along, but it seemed to be threatening to go chill and dank at any moment. The mist-diffused light was trying to hide the fact that it was slowly fading, the walls were sneakily changing in some way, and even though I'd been trying not to admit it, I thought I heard small sounds both behind and ahead of me where there had been nothing but silence earlier. Velix had said the passageway wasn't used very often, but although it had felt empty when I'd first begun walking, it didn't feel that way any longer. I *knew* something was down there with me, I just didn't know what.

"And wouldn't it be nice if we could keep it like that," I muttered to myself, still looking around at fog-covered nothing. If the passageway was usually empty, something could have moved in and made the area its home; it was possible the stretch *had* been safe, but now no longer was. I looked around again, remembered that one of the reasons the S.I. had sent me to that world was to keep me away from traps that had been set and waiting, and almost laughed. There wasn't a day or night I wouldn't have preferred facing Twi House traps to what was right then in front of me, but it was much too late to make that sort of a choice.

The urge to laugh didn't last any time at all, especially once I'd turned the sharpest bend yet and found something like a fairly large room beyond it. To be honest it was more of a chamber than a room, circular, completely undecorated, fog-blurred not-stone with an archway leading out of it again on the far side. I stopped just inside the entrance archway to look around, but the curving walls to left and right were too obscured by the mist for anything but vague outlines to be seen. I decided it must have been meant as a rest area for those using the passageway, and might even have comfortable benches near the walls for anyone who wanted to sit down and rest a while. Since sitting and relaxing was the last thing I wanted to do, I began crossing the area to the only other way out of there. I suppose if I'd stopped to think about it, I would have realized that that was the perfect time and place for the lights to go out.

I froze almost in midstride in the thick, ominous blackness, my heart thudding so loud I would have missed the sound of a ten-foot-tall behemoth charging at me, my imagination immediately sending a lot more than one of them in my direction. I was even sure there were other things creeping at me, and that thought was much worse than the idea of being charged. How all those attackers were supposed to see me in that endless, enveloping dark was beside the point; things like that *never* had trouble finding their victims in the dark, something *everybody* knew. I was sure I heard faint sounds all around me, and if I hadn't been beyond movement of any sort, I would have trembled like someone trying to stand upright in an earthquake.

That was when the lights came on again, too faint to be anywhere near the level I wanted, but at least a thousand times better than absolute dark. It couldn't have been more than a minute that I'd been without light, but while it was happening it had felt like ages and eons and time without end. I forced some spittle down my very dry throat, so relieved to find nothing in creeping distance that the feeling was indescribable, my mind grabbing wildly at the thought that the loss of light had only been a brief, meaningless, power outage. Nothing sinister, nothing trying to get me—and then I finally looked up to see what had become of the previously solid walls.

"That's not possible," I breathed as I looked frantically around, but it wasn't just possible, it had already happened. Instead of one archway leading into the room and one leading out, the walls were now covered with archways, some lit, some as black as the darkness I'd so recently been through. The passageways I could see were riddled with crevasses and openings, places where anything or anyone could lurk unseen, none of them as smooth-walled as what I'd walked past to get there. I didn't know which way I'd come in, couldn't tell which passageway led out again, but knew beyond the faintest doubt that if I chose the wrong one I'd deeply regret it.

And then I heard a sound I wasn't at all unsure about, a sound that froze the blood in my veins and almost brought a whimper to my throat. Something was moving in the darkest passageway to my right, something that shuffled and dragged part of itself, something that breathed with a gargling, burbling sound, something that was definitely coming toward the chamber I stood in. Dizziness swept over me, and the need to be violently sick, and it was all I could do to fumble out the tiny palm dagger I had sheathed high up on my right thigh. The weapon was too small to be useful against anything but people, which meant it would be no help at all against whatever was coming out of the passageway. I held the useless dagger in a fist of whitened knuckles, and began backing away from the passageway without light. I backed three steps, four steps, still seeing nothing in that dark, only hearing it—and then I backed into something that was definitely not a wall.

At that moment quite a lot of me was ready to pass out, but what was left refused to do anything that suicidal. I may have screamed as I whirled around, but I certainly brought the palm dagger around with me, sweeping up at the belly of whatever might be there. It was one of the movements I'd been carefully taught, a crippling swipe even if it failed to be lethal, but the blow never landed. A thought-fast hand wrapped around my wrist, stopping the attack cold, and then I was staring stupidly up into the face of the fighter Serendel.

"I know you said you wanted to be alone," he drawled, "but I didn't think you'd go to these lengths to be sure you were. If I let you go, will you put that thing back where it came from?"

His glance was for the palm dagger, and I realized he was one of the very few people who had seen it who didn't consider it a harmless toy. I'd found it possible more than once to say it was a nail file, but the ones who had believed that weren't professional glads. The one who was still had his fingers closed tight around my wrist, undoubtedly waiting for me to agree to his offer, but that wasn't going to happen.

"I'm not putting it away until I'm out of here," I said, the words unbelievably steady in comparison with how I felt. "There's something heading this way from that darkened passage, and if you think I'm going to meet it emptyhanded, you're out of your mind."

"What do you mean, 'something' heading this way?" he asked with a frown, his eyes and attention immediately on the section of room I'd mentioned. "If there's anyone there it has to be one of the Mists people, but I don't hear or see a thing. Are you sure you didn't imagine it?"

"My imagination most prefers supplying horrors without adding details," I answered, pulling my hand out of his loosened grip before turning to eye the guilty passageway. "What I heard moving along in there may have been imagination, but it certainly wasn't mine. And now that you mention it, I don't hear it anymore either."

"It probably decided to take its stroll in a different direction, one where it would run less of a risk of getting sliced into strips," he said, a faint amusement now in his voice. "If I'd known you were that well armed, I might not have started that insult exchange. Female glads can be pushed only to a certain point, and then they'll use whatever they might be carrying."

"I'm not a female glad," I told him sourly, giving him no more than a glance. "And don't bother trying to pretend you're afraid of me with a weapon in my hand. I saw just how afraid you were when I accidentally attacked you. What are you doing here?"

"I'm walking to the palace," he answered, making it sound absolutely usual and routine. "I was in no more of a mood to ride than you were, but I felt I'd crowded you enough for one day. I waited until you were well on your way before having them open that door again, and then I started out. I really didn't expect to meet you on the way, but I can't say I'm disappointed that I did."

I looked over at him then, to see the very open, frank and sincere expression he wore. None of it was overdone or in any way phony-looking, but for some reason I didn't believe him. His gray eyes rested on me with easy unconcern, which just seemed to add to all the rest.

"You enjoy arguing so much you're happy you caught up to me?" I asked, wondering if it was my previous annoyance that was making me so suspicious. "Now I know why you became a fighter. You must consider being in the arena the ultimate party."

"It keeps me out of barroom brawls," he offered with a faint grin, his long red mustache moving with his lips. "And it isn't the prospect of more argument that makes me happy to see you. Don't forget that I'm after your body."

My first response to that was to come back with something smart, but despite being able to think of any number of things to say, I somehow couldn't bring myself to say them. Even if the accusation I'd made was true, it was hardly so unusual and despicable a thing that I'd had to make it sound like perversion. As far as females went, I wasn't too close to being an eyesore, which meant most healthy males looked at me with one and the same idea. It wasn't a novel concept, it certainly wasn't insulting, and I had the distinct impression that if Seero had been around to hear me say what I had, his anger would not have been aimed at Serendel. I found myself hoping it was too dim in that place for the warmth in my cheeks to show, but just in case I found an excuse to turn away from the fighter.

"Have you any idea which of those passageways is the right one to use?" I asked, very busily examining the archways in question. "When I first got here there was only a single way out, but now I can't tell which one it was."

"I have the feeling this place was originally supposed to be part of the show, but so few people went for it they decided to turn it off," he said, making no further mention of the subject I'd avoided so gracefully. "The first part of the walk was so boring I thought I'd fall asleep on my feet, and then everything suddenly changed. Maybe they realized they'd forgotten to turn on the special effects, and decided to go along with 'Better late than never.' If that's true, then

it doesn't much matter which passageway we take.
They should all lead to the same place.''

"What kind of 'show' could they be putting on?'' I
asked, confused and faintly disturbed. Just before
reaching the chamber I remembered thinking the walls
of the passage looked different, but hadn't been able
to figure out different in what way. If Serendel was
right—and it was hard to argue the point—then the
difference in the walls meant they were *supposed* to
change. "What could they have in mind that this sort
of special effects would be called for?''

"They're probably trying to make us think we have
to hunt for the way out,'' he answered, looking around
with faint amusement. "You know, make the right
choice or wander around forever. Some of those passageways may make the walk a little longer, but I'm
sure they all lead to the palace eventually. Why don't
you choose one, and we'll see if I'm right.''

"As long as there's light, I don't care one way or
the other,'' I said, frowning at the choices he'd given
me. "This place reminds me a little too much of a
certain section of the wilds on Gryphon. How about
that one?''

"That one it is,'' he agreed, beginning to walk with
me toward the passageway I'd pointed to, but he was
suddenly giving *me* more attention than the direction
in which we were going. "You've been through the
wilds on Gryphon? I was there myself once, so I think
you'll know I'm not joking when I say I'm impressed.
It isn't a place for tourists.''

"Well, most of it wasn't all *that* bad,'' I said, for
some reason embarrassed by how serious he sounded,
finding it easier watching the passage we were about
to enter than looking up at him. "We had a couple of
guides who had as much experience with the area as
it's possible to get and they were both well-armed, so
the trouble was kept to a minimum. The worst part
was going through the mountain caverns to get to the
other side of the range; that was where we lost one of
the guides, and the rest of us weren't sure *we'd* make
it either. If it was possible to fly in rather than needing

to go overland on wheels or on foot—but of course they won't allow that."

"Not when you never know who'll be taken over and who won't be," he agreed, distaste now coloring his tone. "They told me pilots have almost no chance of resisting the mental attack, even if they've gone in on foot before with nothing happening. The muties hate each other as much as they hate humankind, but they apparently band together if there's a chance of getting an air vehicle. I'm told as soon as they get one, they crash it in the middle of one of the cities."

"It had to happen three times before the planetary officials got the idea and banned air traffic into the area," I said, spending only a little disgust on people who'd been dead even before I'd been born. "The planet was settled because the muties lived nowhere but in the wilds, but they should have expected trouble when they found it impossible to sign treaties or agreements with any of them. I suppose they were feeling too superior and advanced to worry about trouble, so people had to pay with their lives before they understood more advanced doesn't mean indestructible. I hate stupidity like that, but it seems to be the common curse of humans everywhere."

"Which is one of the reasons why I like the way my home planet sees to the problem," he said, dividing his glance between me and the crevasses and folds of the walls we were passing. "No matter what you want to do on Rober Tay, you have to prove you're the best one for the job. Not that you want the job more than anyone else, but that you're also the best. If you want to work in the government, you and your opponent or opponents don't run for election, you all do the job for a year in simulation by interactive computer programs, facing the same problems actually faced by the one who *is* doing the job. If one of your moves is so wild and brainless it leads to a crisis, you're immediately disqualified. If all you do is play it safe by taking no chances not backed by precedent, you're disqualified. You have to show imagination and ability, otherwise you have no business involving yourself in other people's lives."

"Gryphon isn't quite that advanced," I said, deciding I liked the way his planet did it. "Our people still think it's possible to make an unknown stranger into a good leader by pushing a lever in a voting machine. Or by taking the word of his or her party as to how competent the candidate is. After all the times they got duds instead of doers, you'd think they'd have learned their lesson."

"Change is the hardest thing for people to accept," he said, sounding a good deal more tolerant than I was feeling. "The established way of doing something might not be the best way, but what guarantee is there that a new way won't be a lot worse? You have to be in a position where *nothing* could be worse than what you have, and then change becomes the best of all options. Not the most eagerly accepted, just the best."

"You know, that's very deep," I said with a small laugh, looking up to his face where he walked beside me. "You sound more like a philosopher or a psychologist than a—"

"Than a mindless, bloodthirsty glad?" he finished when I didn't, more amusement in him than anything else. For my part I was back to being painfully embarrassed, but silently cursing the big, flapping mouth I come equipped with didn't call the words back. It also didn't help me understand why he wasn't feeling insulted, as he had every right to be.

"Despite a lot of people's opinions to the contrary, there really is no law that keeps a fighter from being able to think," he went on, his grin wider than it had been, probably because of whatever my expression was like. "I wasn't forced into becoming a glad, I made the career choice as soon as I was old enough to understand what the choice entailed. It was a field that suited my temperament perfectly, one that kept me from ending up fighting society instead of other born fighters like myself. I began training when I was very young, just the way everyone on my world is encouraged to do even if they never intend going near an arena, but that doesn't mean I stopped going to school. I enjoyed school almost as much as I enjoyed training, and I like to believe I may have stopped going now, but I haven't stopped learning."

"Maybe there's a law keeping *me* from thinking," I suggested, feeling even worse than I had earlier. "It might not be an excuse for the way I've been behaving, but at least it would be a reason."

"I can think of a better reason than that," he said with a chuckle, accepting my halfhearted and fully inadequate apology as though it been perfect instead. "All those people who kept telling you how wonderful I was—they turned the mistake I made into a crime of gigantic proportions. If they'd left you alone, you would have seen for yourself that I'd just been stupid in my estimation of you. Instead of that they kept trying to insist I was too marvelous to do *anything* wrong, which you knew damned well was a lie. And you don't like having people telling you who to associate with, do you."

The last was a statement rather than a question, those gray eyes still faintly amused as they looked down at me. I could see he was sharing a joke rather than laughing at me, and I couldn't help smiling myself.

"No, as a matter of fact I *don't* like having people telling me who to associate with," I agreed. "And I'll bet you paid a *lot* of attention in school to courses on psychology. An awful lot."

"Enough to know when it becomes time to keep quiet," he said as he laughed, understanding immediately that I'd caught him trying to play me again. "Let's see if there's any more to their show than making us think that we're lost."

The suggestion was a very sensible one, so we both began putting it into effect. The passageway we walked along almost seemed to be hovering menacingly, but with the presence of someone there besides myself, the menace wasn't as—menacing—as it had been. I grudgingly sheathed my palm dagger and we walked on through the fog for a while, following the twists and turns of the passageway, and then Serendel said something or other that was no more than conversational. I know I answered him in a way that made him chuckle and say something else, but I really wasn't paying attention to the chit-chat. I'd begun hearing small noises from some of the openings in the walls we were passing, but I couldn't tell what they were. Very soft noises that stop as soon as you try listening to them are annoying, but in a place like that they're something else as well.

"You're not listening to me, are you?" Serendel said abruptly, but his voice was filled with curiosity rather than annoyance or anger. "Is something wrong?"

"I think someone's starting to exercise their imagination again," I muttered, silently cursing all that fog and darkness. "There's movement of some sort going on in those unlit openings, but I'm damned if I know what's doing the moving."

"I haven't heard a thing," he said, now sounding puzzled. "Of course, I also haven't been listening. Maybe the problem is that this place does remind you too much of the caverns under the mountains in the wilds. Is this any help?"

"This" was his arm coming gently but firmly around my shoulders, a gesture I hadn't been expecting. Startled, I looked up at him, seeing the faint, calm smile in his gray eyes, and that told me he really *was* asking whether or not I minded. He wasn't expecting me to mind, but the attitude was more a matter of assurance than arrogance, a mature outlook of serene confidence. I remembered the times in school and afterward when boys and men had done the same, most of them self-conscious, nervous or aggressive, all of them using the gesture as an opening move toward taking more. None of them had asked, not even the nervous ones, and this time I somehow knew the arm around me wasn't meant as an opening gesture. The man I looked up at didn't need gestures of that sort, an obvious truth that managed to make me inexplicably uncomfortable again.

"If this is the way you usually guard yourself against possible attack, remind me to bet on the other guy the next time you fight," I said, holding the words as steady as I could. His hand was so very warm on my arm, and my left shoulder touched one of the leather straps on his otherwise bare chest, and that was the closest we'd come to one another since our very first meeting. Thought of that time made me laugh just a little, breaking the mood of embarrassment, which in turn let me add, "And is this supposed to make me feel better? The last time we were this close I was nearly trampled."

"You're in absolutely no danger of that now," he said with an answering laugh and a grin, enjoying the comment. "I usually limit the number of times I trample any one woman, just to keep the rest from getting jealous. If I trampled *you* more than once, I'd have to do it to all of them."

"I hope you know you're not really kidding," I said, remembering Lidra's comments on the subject. "And I also hope you know you have my sincere sympathies. Living with something like that would drive me crazy in no time."

"If you do your best to win the loaf, you can't complain when the crust comes along with it," he said in a very *pious* way, deliberately making it sound like an ancient adage I wasn't old enough to have learned. I stuck my tongue out at him while making a very rude noise, and his grin came back doubled. "But it happens to be true," he protested through a laugh, and then the arm around me tightened. "And you can't deny there are occasional compensations. If I wasn't who I am, you might have been able to get away with calling me unsuitable as a companion for this tour. Then I'd really need someone's sympathy."

His grin eased off as his head began lowering toward mine, his intention obvious, and I wasn't surprised to find I didn't mind the thought of kissing him. He was more than just a handsome hunk of meat; at the very least he was acceptable to have vacation fun with, and I began to raise my own face, when—

"What the *hell?*" he exclaimed as I whirled away from him, the palm dagger already in my hand. "What are you doing?"

"Damn it, something pinched me," I answered with a snarl, my eyes searching the thick, swirling fog. "I know men come equipped with more than two hands, but I really don't think it was you. Am I wrong?''

"No," he said with a frown I could hear, also undoubtedly searching the fog. "But how could anything have pinched you? If anyone had been behind you, I would have seen them."

"If you're going to suggest it's my imagination again, let me assure you it never works overtime without getting paid," I responded sourly, reluctantly giving up the useless search as I turned back to him. "There's something weird going on here, something we're just not—"

The word I'd been going to use was "seeing," but suddenly it no longer fit. There, just beyond Serendel's left shoulder, was a six-inch line of dark blue, a streak that stood out clearly against the gray of the fog. The streak was just hovering in the air, unsupported and all alone, and if it's possible for a six-inch blue line to laugh at someone, that damned line was laughing at *me*.

"If I end up paranoid, I won't have to wonder why," I muttered as I resheathed the obviously useless palm dagger, more than aware of the strange look I was getting from Serendel. "Turn very slowly that way, and *then* tell me I'm imagining things."

His brows went up as though he thought I was becoming a candidate for protective restraint, but he still turned slowly to his left as I'd suggested with my nod. I felt grimly pleased that he hadn't hesitated, but the pleasure dissolved fast when the line began moving with him, just enough to keep out of his range of vision. The damned thing really was playing games, and I was so instantly furious I'm surprised I didn't start foaming at the mouth. If Serendel didn't see the thing he'd *never* believe me, and the thing was making very sure the fighter didn't see it.

"Is this where I get to say you're imagining things?" the man in front of me remarked mildly, turning back after having examined nothing but fog. "Now let's see, where were we?"

Very suddenly both of his arms were around me, holding me tight against him, and before I could make a single sound he had taken my lips with his. I struggled to get free, damned if I was going to be kissed in front of a line with a warped sense of humor, but struggling abruptly became entirely unnecessary. The arms that had closed around me quickly opened again, and Serendel's head drew back as he voiced a wordless shout.

"Damn it, something bit me!" he growled, turning completely around to reexamine the fog that had shown him nothing only a minute earlier. "I'd love to be able to blame *you,* but girls *don't* come equipped with more than two hands."

"Remind me to introduce you to some of the girls *I* know," I said, trying not to laugh out loud at the way I'd been vindicated. "Are you sure it wasn't my imagination? Some people feel it can be very vivid."

"Is vivid supposed to include having teeth?" he asked, fists to hips as he glared around. "I don't like being attacked from behind, and especially don't like having that attacker then refuse to face me. Do you still see whatever it was you saw?"

"It was a thin blue line, and no, I don't," I responded, also looking all around in the fog. "When you missed it, it hid behind you, but I don't see it now. Are we going to search for it?"

"Search where?" he asked, finally turning back to show me heavy annoyance—aimed elsewhere. "The thing could be hiding ten feet away from us, but with this fog we'd never know it. Our best bet is to just keep going—and have a little talk with our—hosts— when we get to the palace."

"You knock 'em down, and I'll stomp on 'em," I agreed with a laugh I couldn't hold back, looking up at his continuing anger. "I didn't like where I got pinched any more than you like—ah—the way you were bitten."

"The *way* I was bitten," he repeated, surrendering to a grin that refused to be denied. "I like women who are diplomatic. Let's go get 'em."

We resumed our walk up the passageway, and although I was still able to hear sounds from the darkened openings, there was no sign of interfering blue lines. The passage continued to twist and turn as it pleased, but absolutely nothing happened. My companion and I were trying to be very alert, but boredom and nothingness will wear down sharpness faster than any number of attacks. After about fifteen minutes we reached a stretch of wall with fewer openings than there had been, and suddenly I was no longer walking ahead but was being pulled around and folded into Serendel's arms.

"I think we've earned a short break," he said as he held me to him, his voice very, very low. "If they don't know about it they can't bother us, and this looks like a perfect place."

His head lowered and his lips touched mine, briefly testing the waters, so to speak. The waters were fine as my smile and return kiss proved, and then our lips were touching with less brevity and more sustained interest. He held me to him with my hands against his chest, his arms delightfully tight around me, one of his hands to my hair. Our bodies moved closer to one another, the taste of warmth rising, and then—

"Slig!" I yelled, and "Slime-wiggling jark!" Serendel snarled, the two of us pulling away to whirl around in murder-rage. This time there were two of them, one blue line hovering behind each of us, and although I didn't know what had happened to the fighter, I knew damned well what had been done to me. It was the next step up from pinching, the sort of long-finger effort that was usually the trademark of sidewalk idlers, and the only other time it had happened to me I'd gone after the doer with a length of two-by-four that had been lying handily about. Not only was there no handy wood this time, I had the definite feeling it wouldn't have done any good even if there had been.

"The damned things are laughing at us!" Serendel growled, probably still glaring at his the way I was doing with mine, making me feel less paranoid. "I wasn't wrong, they *are* trying to keep us apart. What in hell are they?"

"Part of whatever game our hosts are playing," I answered, jumping forward fast to try grabbing my line. My hand closed on nothing as the line darted up and away, which made me feel better despite the miss. If getting my hands on it wouldn't have done any good, the line would have had no reason to dodge. Since it *had* dodged, *I* now had reason to try again, at a time it would hopefully not be expecting the grab.

"I've now gotten to the point of not liking the game at *all,*" the fighter said very flatly, his voice slightly raised as though he spoke not only to me and the lines, but also to whoever else might be listening in. "Everyone's entitled to fair warning, so I'll say it once clearly, and then I won't bother again: stop the game and cancel any other plans you have in regard to me and the lady in this place, or you're the ones who will be responsible for what happens. You won't be able to say you didn't know. Come on, Dalisse."

He took my arm and went marching up the passageway again, ignoring the two blue lines we left hovering behind us. The lines now seemed more unsure than amused, and if that was true I couldn't say I blamed them. The fighter was so angry his gray eyes were frozen slow-sparks, which made me decide to tell him some other time that I didn't like being called Dalisse. Right then my most central concern was keeping up with him without running.

After a couple of minutes Serendel slowed down, but more because he'd gotten his anger under control than because it was any less. He made no attempt to look behind us to see if the lines were following, but I didn't have the same unspokenly-deadly image to maintain. I looked back a few times without making any attempt to hide what I was doing, and finally glanced at Serendel.

"I don't know if it means anything, but they aren't following," I told him. "Or at least I can't see them following. Maybe they'll be smart and take your advice."

"They'd better be that smart, because it wasn't advice," he came back without looking at me, all of the growl gone from his voice but the faintest of shadows. "Doing things like that to people isn't the joke some consider it, especially when there's a lady involved.

My parents taught me manners while I was growing up; if theirs didn't do the same for them, it's more than time the oversight was corrected.''

I lapsed back into silence at that, not quite sure what to say. The fighter was angry, all right, but not for the reasons I'd thought and he wasn't only angry. He also seemed to be indignant and outraged, in large measure on *my* behalf. A reaction like that wasn't something I'd expected from a virtual stranger, especially not one I'd exchanged more argument with than conversation. Obviously there *was* more to Serendel than just being a brainless glad, and he'd been very right: if people had left us alone, I might have found that out sooner.

Once again we just kept walking, something that was beginning to be really boring. I felt as though we'd already come miles, and there was no knowing how far we had left to go. Serendel didn't seem interested in more conversation, and I agreed with that. When two people begin getting to know each other, the personal items they exchange are meant for each other, not an audience. We'd had more than enough proof that someone was keeping track of us; if they really were also listening in, the rest of our conversation could wait.

Possibly another ten minutes went by, and then I began noticing different sounds coming from the darkened openings we passed, with some not confined to the openings. I hadn't realized it sooner but the fog also seemed to be thickening, which made seeing more than a few feet beyond us just about impossible. Some of the noises sounded like dragging, some shuffling, a few like scrapes, and one or two were nothing but strange breathing. At first I considered the whole thing stupid, but when the noises began sounding closer and there was still nothing in view to account for them, *I* began thinking about changing my mind.

"I think it's safe to assume my warning was heard and believed," Serendel said suddenly, almost making me jump. "Since I didn't like the first game, they've decided to play a different one."

"Do you think they'd listen if I said *I* didn't like *this* one?" I asked, the words very nearly a mutter. "I know I don't have your standing or size, but I am supposed to be a paying customer.''

''I hope you're not taking any of this seriously,'' he returned, and there was no doubt he was back to being amused. ''Strange noises in the dark, breathing out of the fog—it's the sort of thing you use to frighten little children.''

''Little children aren't the only ones smart enough to distrust what prefers hiding out of easy sight,'' I told him with a glance, disliking the faint grin he was wearing. ''And there's a big difference between fright and caution, something someone in your position ought to know.''

''That's right, you're the one who isn't afraid of anything,'' he said, and if he didn't sound even more amused it was only because he was consciously refraining. ''Believe it or not, I'm glad you reminded me about that. Now I don't have to spend any time reassuring you, or protecting you, or anything like what I'd have to do with a different woman. It feels good having a companion rather than a dependent.''

With that he pounded me on the back a couple of times, not quite hard enough to knock me down, but certainly with brother-and-equal vigor. When I glared at him he chuckled, wordlessly admitting he was the kind who never passed up an opportunity for teasing, which told me I'd be wasting my time getting mad. He fully intended pulling my leg until it came off in his hand, and people like that are beyond help. All you can do is shake your head at them and sigh, and then get on with what you were doing before they started their nonsense.

Which meant I went back to wondering just what the hell *was* making those noises, and even more to the point, why they were being made. They couldn't *seriously* be expecting to scare anyone, not even if it did sound like dead bodies and whatever had made them dead were just out of sight, waiting to add one or two more to their group. The fog was really thick at that point, cutting down visibility to arm's length or less, and the fighter beside me was giving most of his attention to the ground under our feet. Since he was doing that my own area of responsibility became obvious, and that was why I kept a close watch on the fog all around. If anything was going to jump out at us in attack, it would find at least *one* of us on guard.

Our having to move so slowly made it seem as though we spent a really long time in the extra-thick fog, but it couldn't have been much more than another ten minutes before our range of sight began expanding again. The fog thinned rather than receded, and when we were finally able to look all around, most of my companion's amusement thinned with the mist.

"This doesn't look anything like the passageway we were in," he said with a frown, staring at the much wider area we suddenly found all around us. "As a matter of fact, it doesn't look like anywhere I'd ever choose to be. Could we have taken a wrong turn?"

"Through all that completely transparent fog?" I asked with a snort, no happier than he was. "Of course we couldn't have taken a wrong turn. This must be part of the palace."

At that point it was his turn to make a sound of ridicule, all due to what we were seeing more and more of as the fog thinned. The walls of the area had wide, uneven gaps rather than archways, and where there wasn't a gap it was possible to see some sort of long, drooping, creeping plant growing on the wall surface. What looked to be trails of slime could be seen under the plants, and here and there the floor had matching trails. Even though I didn't want to, I looked up toward the ceiling, and was indecently relieved to see that it was just ceiling with some mist below it. If those plants had been on the ceiling as well, even someone Serendel's size couldn't have kept me from stampeding out of there.

"If this is the palace, I'm going back the way we came," Serendel said, turning slowly to look all around himself. "That ragged gap behind us must be the way we came in, but I'd like to know how much more of this we're supposed to . . ."

His voice trailed off because he had heard the same thing I had, the sudden sharpening of a sound that had probably been hovering just below the level of our conscious awareness for the last couple of minutes. It was the sound of deep, body-racking, heartbroken sobbing, the voice clearly a woman's, also clearly coming closer. For some reason it was difficult deciding from what direction the crying was coming, but it was definitely getting closer. It got nearer and nearer, louder and more like a totally shattered soul, and then, with what seemed like no warning despite all the sobbing, the woman was there in the room with us.

I think every drop of blood in my body froze at her appearance. It wasn't the fact that she and her floor-length gown were as white as the fog was gray, or even that she was surrounded by at least a dozen of those dark blue lines, all of them taking turns stroking and touching her. What turned my stomach upside down and aimed it at my mouth was the fact that the sobbing woman held her arms out toward us as though begging for our help, but she couldn't also stretch out her hands. Her arms ended where her wrists should have been, nothing but stumps without proper finishing.

"I can't find them," the sobbing woman said, looking at us from where she'd stopped, at least twenty feet away. Her voice was muffled by the crying but was also unbelievably clear, as though the words and the woman herself were no more than inches away.

"I can't find them," she said, sounding like a little girl who had lost her brand-new birthday boots. "They took them and won't give them back, and now what am I going to do?"

Serendel made no more effort to answer the question than I did, but he stood staring at the woman with no visible sign of the shuddering storm I could feel inside *me*. I would have loved being able to say something smart, but at that point I couldn't even get my heart to stop the exploding it considered beating. Although I don't know what I would have done with it, I was wishing I could make myself reach for the palm dagger—and that's when we began hearing the laughter.

Have you ever heard someone who was really insane, laughing in chilling delight at something you have no hope of seeing the humor in? The laughter we

heard then was very much like that, and then all the
ragged openings behind and around the woman were
filled with hideous creatures, showing themselves as
the ones who were laughing. Two of them, one to the
left and one to the right, each held a slender white
hand, and even as we watched they approached the
woman with their burdens. They were humanoid in
shape but horribly twisted and malformed, wearing
rags rather than clothing, and when they reached the
woman they each set a severed hand at the end of a
stump of a wrist. The woman's sobbing trailed off
when they began their grisly attempt at reconstruction,
and once it was done she began to laugh the way the
others were doing. I couldn't see what there was to
laugh about—until she held up arms and hands that
were complete.

"Oh, thank you, thank you for giving them back,"
she sang, beside herself with joy, and then her horrible
white eyes returned to Serendel and me. "Now you
can take *theirs!*"

A chorus of insane laughter greeted the suggestion,
and then all of the creatures were producing very long,
very sharp-looking knives from somewhere. Every one
of them was staring straight at Serendel and me, and
then they began moving toward us.

I wasn't exactly frozen in place any longer, but I
might as well have been, for all I could figure out what
to do. My palm dagger was useless against the knives
the creatures were holding, and even if there had been
some definite place to run to, I didn't want those *things*
coming right behind me. Running was a bad idea and
I had nothing to stand and fight with, all of which
meant I might as well have been frozen in shock for
all the good being relatively free did me. I took a step
back from the slowly advancing creatures, watching
as many of them as I could while I frantically tried to
think of *something*—and then something happened that
was even more unexpected than what had already occurred.

I hadn't forgotten about the man who stood only a
few feet away and ahead of me on my right, but despite Serendel's size and training, I couldn't see that

he had any more of a chance to accomplish something
than I did. Numbers and weapons tend to negate size
and skill, but our intended attackers were due for a
shock. They, like me, had thought the fighter was un-
armed, but suddenly, unbelievably, he proved he was
anything but.

The fighter took one short step forward and his right
hand reached left, but rather than finding nothing but
air his fingers seemed to close around something. He
drew his fist up and away, as though he unsheathed
that giant sword I'd seen him wearing on the liner,
and then I had to rub my eyes and blink very hard
because he *was* holding the sword! I hadn't the faintest
idea of where it could have come from, but there was
no doubt that it was there; he wrapped both of his fists
around its hilt, set himself as he held it up before him,
then grinned that faint, deadly grin at the advancing
creatures.

Formerly advancing creatures. When I looked at
them again, they were as still as paintings, decorations
for the room that had been posed staring at the gleam-
ing sword held by a man who had proven he was very
good at using it. Even the woman was staring in
shocked silence, and then one of the creatures swallowed hard.

"Shit," he muttered, and the word rang hollowly
but clearly all over the room. "That *is* Serendel, and
he sure as hell *does* have his multi-sword with him. I
don't know about the rest of you, but I didn't take this
job to get sliced into sections. I think it's time for my
javi break."

With the last of his words the creature turned and
began striding back the way he had come, suddenly
looking more like a man in costume than a malformed
monster. The rest of the creatures lost no time following his example, some almost tripping over their own
feet in their hurry, and in less than a minute only the
woman was left. She looked as though she wanted to
call to the creatures to wait for her, but there turned
out to be something she had to say instead.

"The—the way up into the palace is just through
there, sir," she quavered, pointing with a long-

fingered hand toward the largest gap on our right as
she backed away. "I'm sorry we— I mean, it's only
what we're supposed to— Please don't be angry—"

Serendel's lack of response finally got to her, and
she turned and ran into the nearest wall gap as though
she was being chased, her hands holding up the bottom
of her gown. I was seriously tempted to let myself
collapse into a heap on the floor, but couldn't do it
with all that slime they'd spread around.

"And that's another benefit to having people know
who you are and what you can do," the fighter said
with heavy satisfaction when the woman was out of
sight. "Their own game ended as soon as they saw I
was about to start one of my own, and that's just what
I wanted. They couldn't— Hey, are you all right?"

His question obviously referred to the way I stood
there with my eyes closed and one hand to my head,
the rest of me trying to get the sour taste out of my
mouth. If the scene Serendel had broken up was the
Mists people's idea of fun, there'd be no pretense
about it when I hated the rest of the tour.

"We'd better get you up into the palace where you
can sit down for a while," the fighter said as his arm
went around me, nothing at all patronizing in his tone.
"I'm as mindless as they are for not understanding
how you'd take this nonsense. Come on, it shouldn't
be far."

I opened my eyes to see his concerned face looking
down at me, but he didn't know the half of it. I felt
very pale as we took the gap pointed out by the woman
in white, a corridor that turned out to be no more than
fifteen feet long. On the other side of it was another
room with a stairway leading up, but it was a normal
room with normal walls and floor, and two normal,
human men.

"Is the lady all right?" one of the men said when
he saw us, the other frowning and coming forward
with the first. "Was there an accident? Does she need
a doctor?"

"All she needs is to sit down for a while, and what
happened was no accident," Serendel told them in a
very hard voice, one that stopped the men before they

reached us. "Don't you people have sense enough to check the home planets of your guests before you pull childish jokes on them? If I hadn't been there, someone could have been very seriously hurt."

"I—don't understand," the same man said, exchanging a bewildered glance with his friend. "The passageways scene is an extremely popular one with guests, especially the very end. What could home planets have to do with any of that?"

"The lady comes from Gryphon, and Gryphon has the wilds," Serendel answered, still sounding very unfriendly. "Anyone who has ever been in the wilds knows that the fastest way to get killed is to doubt what you're seeing, no matter how fantastically unreal it looks. Some part of the seeming fantasy will always be real, and if you don't figure out which part that is, you'll never get another chance. The lady has been through one of the worst sections of the wilds, and because of that everything she just went through was real rather than a joke. Is there any way up to the palace besides that stairway?"

"Certainly, sir, there's an emergency lift right over here," the second man said hastily when the first just stood with his mouth open, looking almost as pale as I felt. "Please follow me and I'll accompany you aboveground, and then pass on what happened to my superiors. I know they'll be very upset, and they'll also want to apologize to the lady."

"Give me a couple of minutes, and I'll be glad to tell you what they can do with their apologies," I managed to say, making the second man look very unhappy. He pressed a section of the not-stone wall and a part of it slid aside to reveal a small lift-car, then moved into the car to hold the door open while Serendel helped me in after the man. The fighter's sword had disappeared again, back to wherever it had come from, I supposed, but I wasn't quite up to wondering where that was. What I needed right then was a good, stiff drink, or maybe two or three drinks of the sort that bring you alive again. I still had the fun of the palace to look forward to, and I could hardly wait.

Chapter 11

The man who was accompanying us aboveground had the choice of letting the lift move as fast as it could, or setting it to a much more leisurely pace. I'm not quite sure why he opted for the slower rise, but by the time we got to the top and the door opened, I'd pulled myself together enough to stand without help. I hadn't realized just how hard I'd been hit until it began wearing off, and I didn't know yet whether or not to be angry. I'd have to speak to Lidra first, in private, and then I'd be able to decide.

The open door let us out into what looked like a private alcove off a much larger room, part of which could be seen through the crystal-like walls of the alcove. Besides being absolutely enormous, the area beyond was filled with fountains, and crystal staircases, and couches and servants and music and partying people, none of which caused crowding in any of the parts I could see. It looked as if someone had roofed over an acre or more, fog and all, of course, but nobody seemed to be minding the fog. The scene was so opulently compelling it was hard to look away from, at least until Chal, Lidra and Velix came hurrying up to us.

"Inky, are you all right?" Lidra demanded as she reached me, more outraged than the ones who had asked the same question before her. "These people must substitute this fog for their brains, always assuming, of course, they had any brains to begin with. I think a doctor should look you over."

"I could have used one down below to restart my

heart, but I'm over that now," I told her, pretending I didn't see how carefully Chal was studying me. "If I had any wishes coming I'd wish I was still a smoker, though. A drink and a puffer and a quiet place to sit down for a couple of minutes are things I would enjoy right now."

"Well, I can take care of the puffer," Lidra said, turning to look at a Velix who was on the verge of hovering behind her. "Do you think anyone in this place is up to supplying the rest, O faithful and capable journey scout? If not, I'm not above opening doors until I find what I want."

"There's certainly no need for something like that," the Griddenth answered stiffly, trying to balance his annoyance with Lidra and his concern for me. "There's a ladies' retiring room just up the corridor here which should do nicely, and I can have drinks brought to you there. If there's anything else you'd like, just ask for it."

"How about the head of whoever thought up that cute idea for the passageway?" I muttered as Velix fussed his way past me to show where the "ladies' retiring area" was. The Griddenth's wings were threatening to start flapping, his fur was practically on end, and he ignored my comment in a way that made me think he wanted the same thing. I hadn't expected him to be that upset over what had happened to me, and couldn't understand why he was.

Velix led the way to the right of the lift, away from the area beyond the crystal wall, and stopped a few feet down in front of an archway on the left surrounded by opaque pink crystal walls. The pink was obviously a sign to be read as girls only, which most of the men with us seemed ready to go along with. The sole exception to that was someone I'd forgotten I was still being held around by, but Lidra noticed and stopped just short of the archway.

"It's all right, Winner, you can trust her in my care for a little while," she said to Serendel as she put a hand on my arm, smiling up at him warmly. "Before you know it, I'll have her back to you just the way she was."

"Anything but that," the fighter murmured only loud enough for me to hear, giving me the job of keeping myself from laughing out loud, then he raised his voice to a normal level. "I'm not doubting your trustworthiness, Lidra, but I can supervise her sitting down and putting her feet up just as easily as you can. She and I were getting acquainted when this happened, so we can use the time she rests up to go on with it."

I knew I couldn't very well talk privately with Lidra if the fighter was there, and Lidra, of course, had to know the same. The only problem was, she didn't *look* like she knew it; instead of arguing, all she did was smile again.

"Well, if that's the case, then come on in with us," she invited pleasantly, her eyes sparkling as her hand tightened on my arm. "Come on, Inky."

I stepped forward with her, feeling as confused as I ever had, but it was only a moment before I understood completely. Lidra and I moved through the archway without any difficulty, but Serendel stopped so abruptly it looked like he'd run into a brick wall. I'd heard about exclusionary gender screens but had never seen one before, not even in the resorts Seero and I had stayed at. The area was open only to those who were biologically female, and the way Lidra chuckled softly as she led me deeper inside said she'd known the screen was there.

"I'm glad you two are finally getting along so well, but I really don't think ten or fifteen minutes of being apart will ruin anything," she said, directing me around the corner to the left. "We'll let the men explain the facts of life to him, and in the meantime you and I can sit down and rest a little. We may have ridden here rather than walked, but once we arrived they started giving us the Grand Tour. You won't believe how big this place is until you see it for yourself."

There was a very pleasant, pinkly-lit resting area around the corner we'd turned, one with etched crystal walls and soft carpeting and svalk-covered lounge couches and one mirrored wall. Beyond the etched crystal I could see the man who had ridden up with us

in the lift and the Griddenth Velix, both working to
soothe a very annoyed Serendel. Nothing of what any
of them were saying came through, but it was possible
to see that even the two previously-chosen magicians
were now there.

"And here come our drinks," Lidra said, nodding
toward the female servant who was circling the group
of men with her tray held carefully away from them.
"One-way walls are fun, but you're not in here to
stand and sight-see through one. Sit down on that
lounge-couch, and close your eyes for a minute."

I let her urge me down with my back to the one-way
wall, then closed my eyes as she'd suggested. I didn't
really *need* to do any of that, but if she and I were
going to speak privately, there had to be an overt reason for our being alone. I heard the female servant
come in and put her tray down, and then she offered
to stay and help Lidra take care of me. Lidra told her
it would probably be a couple of minutes before I was
up to taking *anything* from Mists people including their
help, and happily the woman didn't argue. I heard her
leave, heard Lidra sit down, and then a minute or so
later there was the clink of glasses.

"Okay, you can have your drink and conversation
now," Lidra said, and I opened my eyes to see her
holding out a filled glass toward me. "This place is
completely clean, although that girl who came in
wasn't. As long as we're careful to watch for any
new arrivals, there shouldn't be a problem. You didn't
really want a puffer, did you?"

"No," I answered with a shake of my head, taking
the glass being held out to me. The wine in it was a
very pale orange, and although it was smooth going
down, it caused my blood to surge a little in greeting.
I could have done without the drink, but as I leaned
back on the couch I admitted to myself I was glad I
had it.

"What in hell did they put you through down
there?" Lidra asked, and I saw that she held a lit puffer
as well as a glass of her own. I admired her dedication
to her image, but certainly didn't envy it. "All we
were told was that you'd had some sort of unexpected

trouble. It couldn't have had anything to do with the reason you chose this place to vacation, could it?''

"That's what I'm trying to figure out," I answered, sipping at my wine as I answered her real question about the assignment. "Serendel thought I was scared gray because I believed everything going on was real. It's true that someone who has been through the wilds on my world tends to come away believing that everything they see after that, no matter how strange, is real, but after a while the belief fades. Their cute little horror show may have shaken me a little, but it wasn't until the very end that it took me by the throat. Lidra, the woman who was the first to show herself to us had both hands cut off at the wrists.''

The girl sat in silence staring at me, both the puffer and her drink forgotten. I'd thought I might have to explain what the symbolism meant, but the way she'd paled a little showed she understood without explanations. The very old, very standard way of punishing thieves was the removal of one or both hands, and from the time I'd first heard of that, at a relatively young age, I'd had periodic nightmares about it. It hadn't been enough to make me let Seero down by not joining in his private social protest, but I also had never mentioned the point to him.

"You think they may have been warning you off," Lidra said at last, the sentence a statement she was weighing the truth of. "It presupposes the fact that they know who and what you are as well as the reason why you're here, and although not impossible, the consideration is highly unlikely. If they know about you they know about Chal and me, which means they would have warned all of us and that hasn't happened. Are you disagreeing with anything I'm saying?''

"I'm not disagreeing with anything that comes out rational and levelheaded rather than scared gray," I told her, feeling a great deal of relief. "I couldn't think about this thing, all I could do was look for a corner to shiver in. I agree it isn't very likely for them to know anything yet, so as long as you and Chal are left alone, I can be indignant instead of shaky.''

"If anyone ever did something like that to *me,* I'd

be a hell of a lot more than shaky," she said with a definite shudder, now beyond considering the matter professionally and into the realm of the personal. "I'm not joking when I say I think the whole thing is a nauseating coincidence, but I wonder if I can ask a very intrusive question. What would you do if it *wasn't* a coincidence? What would happen if they really were warning you off?"

"That's two questions," I pointed out, raising my wine glass, hesitating, then putting it down again before looking bleakly at a very sober Lidra. "What I'd *want* to do is run not walk to the nearest exit, then take a liner going any place at all. What I *would* do, unfortunately, is pretend I didn't know what they were talking about, then set the stroking for as soon as it was possible to schedule. Once I commit to something I'm stuck with seeing it through, especially if it can't be done without me. Maybe you and Chal would be interested in a quick course on lifting and stroking for fun and profit."

"I don't think so," she said with a laugh, some sort of satisfaction in her light eyes. "The first rule you learn in this business is not to try spreading over into someone else's specialty. If it was possible for you to be as good as they are, you would have been given the training before you were sent out. It looks like it's a good thing luck is on our side, though. With Serendel around for you to stand next to, your nerves shouldn't be spending too much time regretting your commitment."

"What do you mean, stand *next* to?" I asked with a snort, this time swallowing more of the wine without changing my mind. "The place I stood was *behind* him, a position I can't possibly recommend too highly. Those make-believe monsters the woman sent against us had *knives*, and no matter how idiotically melodramatic everyone else considered the scene, I thought sure we'd had it. That was when Serendel pulled his sword out of thin air, and if I'd been capable of speech I would have thanked every god ever conceived of."

"I don't think you're as over your time in those wilds as you believe you are," she said, her smile less amused than sharing. "And Serendel didn't pull his sword out of thin air, he didn't have to. It's a multi-sword, after all, so all he did was shift it full-in and overt, bringing it on-line instead of off. He probably wouldn't have done it if he hadn't been considering you, but I'll bet those monsters changed their minds in a hurry. People tend to forget multi-sword wielders are never without the weapon once they win the right to use it; being reminded the hard way is just a little unsettling."

"Most especially in the bowel and bladder regions," I said, wondering if I should ask, then decided I might as well. "I know I'm going to sound ignorant as hell, and I won't even *try* to find out how you know this place is clear while the serving woman wasn't, but—what was that you said about the multi-sword? That on-line instead of off made it sound like a computer printer."

"In a manner of speaking, that's not too far from what it is," she said with a laugh, reaching to the crystal carafe of wine still on the tray and refilling both of our glasses. "If I could show you the math it would be much easier to understand, not to mention explain. Multi-swords are quasi-paradimensional constructs made to manifest fully, partially or negatively in a specific mathematical locus. If you want to think of them as computer analogs with sharp edges and a point you won't be wrong, but you also won't be completely right. They're very complex in nature, which is one of the reasons why their usage is so limited, and teams all over the Empire are working on their basic principle to find out where it can take us. The breakthrough was made by an arena buff, who was trying to make a weapon worthy of use by Winners. He made the weapon and was delighted with the accomplishment, and never once stopped to consider what else he had done. I hear the various research teams use his name as a curse word; they lost two years of work through having to find out about the breakthrough from an arena telecast accidently viewed by someone who could appreciate what he was seeing."

"Well, at least I can understand that part of it," I

said, shaking my head. "I've also come across the idea that a 'negative manifestation' is considered positive and measurable to the sorts who use the kind of math that has no numbers, but if you don't mind I'd rather not think about things like that. I tend to picture people with nets chasing after invisible glow-flits."

"Well, of course they use nets," she said, a straight-faced, reasonable expression all over her. "You can't catch an invisible glow-flit without using a net."

"Since I don't doubt you're one of those who do it on a regular basis, I'll take your word for it," I told her, the dryness in my tone making her grin. "I also won't be surprised if I hear people have started chasing *you* with nets. How much longer do you think it'll be before we get close enough to our objective to get to work?"

"I think we may very well be within range when we get to our next tour area," she said, controlled eagerness quickly taking the place of playful teasing as she leaned forward. "We're closer now than we were at the port, and the route we're on is supposed to swing us right by there. I'll check again once we get to the designated area, and if we seem close enough you can do a physical check. *If* you can find some way of shaking yourself loose from Serendel."

The last of her words were filled with sudden disturbance, as though she hadn't considered the point sooner, and she leaned back again on her couch looking thoughtful. It was nice to see her matchmaking enthusiasm dimmed, but that didn't solve the problem.

"I'm glad you finally noticed," I said, watching her take a last drag on her puffer before she dumped it in the couch slot provided for the purpose. "I think it would have been easier if he and I had stayed enemies, but it's too late for that now. If I started snarling at him again after what he just helped me get through, even his great-aunt Nellie would be suspicious. When the time comes, you and Chal will have to divert him."

"If we can," she answered doubtfully, still looking bothered. "In case the point went past you, it took an exclusion field to separate you two a few minutes ago. All we can hope is that he was just feeling very pro-

tective because of the way you reacted to the passageway game, and will back off on his own once he sees
you're all right. That's not too much to hope for, is
it?''

"You're asking me?" I said with a sound of ridicule, taking a last sip of the wine before returning the
glass to the tray. "You and Chal are supposed to be
the experts on that particular glad, and I don't like
infringing on other people's areas of expertise. I'm
going to use the facilities in the next room, and then I
think we ought to rejoin the others.''

"Before Serendel finds a way in *here,*" she said,
gesturing with her chin toward the wall behind me. I
got off the couch and turned to look, and at first I
couldn't see anything but the fighter standing with
folded arms, staring at the wall he wasn't able to get
through. It took a moment before I noticed the look in
his cold gray eyes, and then I suddenly understood
what Lidra was talking about.

"I'll hurry," I said, and began to do exactly that.
If there was ever a man calmly considering which point
of an annoying obstruction he was very soon going to
be attacking first . . .

When Lidra and I walked out of the comfort area,
no one was there but Serendel. Everyone else seemed
to have vanished, and we found out to where when the
fighter came over to join us.

"Chal and the magicians are in the men's area down
there on the right, Velix and the man from below went
somewhere to file a report, and that leaves me," he
said, answering our question before we asked it out
loud, and then his eyes came to me. "You're looking
a lot better than you were, but you weren't in there
very long. Would you like to find some place else to
sit down, preferably some place with equal access?"

"I think I'd rather see what this place has in the
way of diversions first," I answered, using Lidra's
theory as a basis for the response. If Serendel would
ease off as soon as his worry about me did the same,
I intended being as recovered as possible as quickly as
reasonable. Letting him get into the habit of sticking
close would be stupid, and I had the feeling there

would be enough stupidity on our project without my deliberately adding to it.

"If she gets tired too quickly, she can always change her mind," Lidra put in when the fighter hesitated, his expression saying he wasn't sure he ought to agree with that reckless a decision. "She wasn't physically hurt, after all, not the way *you've* been hurt from time to time, and even though you undoubtedly heal faster than she does, you have to consider where she's starting . . ."

"Hold it," the glad interrupted quickly, raising a palm in Lidra's direction. "I should have asked this as soon as I saw you, and would have mentioned it before you went into the rest area if I hadn't been caught by surprise. Did you spend any more time telling her how great I am? If you did, I just may turn very violent."

"Relax, my friend, she didn't say a word," I answered for a bewildered Lidra, finding it impossible to hide how funny I thought the situation was. "I haven't decided to walk around because I'm trying to avoid being alone with you. What I'm trying to do is find a little fun *I* can appreciate, the sort of thing everyone keeps assuring me this place is loaded with. If you don't think you can handle something like that, just say so. I still have the option of trading you in for Chal."

"You can't exercise that option until after you've tried me," he said with a faint grin, finally less intense than he had been, the amusement reaching even to the gray eyes looking down at me. "I'll go get the others, and then we can start searching for that fun."

He turned and moved off toward the blue-walled area farther down on the right, and once he reached it and disappeared inside, Lidra put a hand on my arm.

"What in hell was *that* all about?" She demanded in a hiss, still wide-eyed and confused. "If I ever wondered how his opponents must feel, I'll never have to wonder again."

"I don't think he actually would have killed you," I said with a laugh, perversely pleased with the way that had gone. "If you'd said anything nice about him he might have broken some of your bones, but I really don't think he would have killed you. After all, you *are* one of his biggest fans."

"I can see I stepped into some sort of private joke," she said as she sighed, smart enough to give up asking for an explanation she could see she wouldn't be getting. "If you decide to trade him for Chal after all, give me a couple of minutes of prior warning, will you? That will give me time to formulate the questions I want to ask while I can still think. After that, *he'll* be the one to find out how his opponents tend to feel."

Her eyes were on the place where the fighter had disappeared, a lip-licking expression of hopeful anticipation on her face, and I didn't understand that. According to Chal she didn't *want* Serendel the way she claimed she did, but that wasn't what I was getting from looking at her. I spent a minute wrestling with the question of whether or not to pry, and even though it wasn't true hesitation I still lost the opportunity. The four men we were waiting for came out of the rest area, and we no longer had time for the discussion of delicate subjects.

"I've been led to believe there are ladies out here who are interested in finding some fun," Chal said as he came up to us, his grin wider than Serendel's. "If that turns out to be true, we're pleased to inform you that we know two lords interested in the same. May we be of service, ladies?"

"Only if you mean that in all senses of the word," Lidra answered with a grin of her own, reaching over to take Chal's arm. "So far the only things we've gotten out of this trip are one new outfit each and a moderately lavish meal, but we expect that to change. If it doesn't, we'll be the ones who change—to a vacation spot where the fun times aren't quite so well hidden."

"I have the definite feeling the second half of that doesn't include us, Serendel," Chal said to the fighter with an expression of anxiety no one above the age of two would have believed. "We'd better hurry up and find something to change their minds, or you and I will be left with no one but each other."

"I like you, Chal, but I don't like you *that* much,"

Serendel said with a chuckle as he came closer to me, then took my right arm to put around his left, the way Lidra held Chal. "I'm sure there's something in this place to divert the ladies, and if it turns out there isn't, we'll just have to—improvise. Jejin—is it beyond your range of duties to act as a guide for us?"

"I'm supposed to be more of a silent companion, lord Serendel, but there's nothing to keep me from commenting on some of the things you stroll past," the magician answered, he and Chal's man both smiling under their beards. "We're also meant to answer questions put to us, so if you see something you'd like explained, simply ask. There shouldn't be too much of that sort of thing, as most of the diversions in the palace are no more complicated than they look."

"In that case, let's get started," Chal said to us all, then led off with Lidra. His magician moved to follow along behind him, and Jejin kept his place behind us.

It wasn't more than a dozen steps to the end of the alcove area, and then we were suddenly in the midst of a giant structure of crystal and mirrors and mist. I'm sure the mirrors helped to add to the impression of size, as did the fact that the second floor didn't start until where the third floor should have been, but it *was* large to begin with. Chandeliers hung from the thirty-foot ceiling, multicolored glowings that lightened and tinted the mist, fountains gurgled happily as their contents poured endlessly from various beautifully-cast statues, and people wandered everywhere. Most groups were six-people big and some larger, but few, if the man was in leather and the woman in svalk, were smaller than three.

"Now, that's something you two ought to know about," Chal said as he stopped and turned to Serendel and me. "The first thing Lidra and I were told about when we got here was those fountains. Do you see all those goblets around the rims, almost as though they were decorations? Well, they're not decorations, because the fountains aren't filled with water. That's wine they're throwing about so casually, and anyone who wants some is free to help himself. Why don't we start by helping ourselves?"

My companion thought Chal had come up with a great idea, so we all went to the nearest fountain and started to help ourselves. Serendel took a goblet and tried to hold it in the froth of spray coming out of the gills of some sort of water beast, but after a few seconds it was clear he was getting more wine on his hand and arm than in the goblet. I'd chosen the heavier stream coming out of the statue's mouth, so I had enough to drink in no time at all. When I pulled the goblet back I sipped from it, then raised my brows.

"Hey, this isn't bad at all," I told the fighter, turning to watch his much less successful efforts. "If you ever get any, you'll probably like it. Do you think that fish is a fan of yours, and doesn't want to see you drinking?"

"If it is, it'll just have to close its eyes," the fighter came back, paying more determined attention to what he was doing than to the words he spoke. "I'm here on vacation, and I'll be damned if I'll let people—or fish—tell me what to do. I have enough of that when I'm in training."

"At your meager size, I can understand how everyone coming by must push you around," I said with a nod of compassion, smiling inwardly when he gave up on the froth and switched to the stream *I'd* used. "You really should hire someone to protect you."

"I've considered the idea," he agreed solemnly, finally pulling back a filled goblet. "I'd need somebody who was tough, preferably armed, and wasn't afraid of anything. Would you like a job?"

"I'll have to check my employment schedule," I answered, seeing the amusement in his eyes as he sipped at his wine. "I'm in such demand as a bodyguard that I'm just about booked solid, which I'm sure you can understand. If I find any uncommitted time, I'll let you know."

"My poor abused body will be grateful," he said with a chuckle, then shifted the goblet to his left hand in order to shake the right and hold the arm away from him. "I'd also be grateful for something to take care of this mess. Wine in the mouth is a treat for the palate; on an arm, all it is is sticky."

"That small fountain over there has nothing but water," Jejin said from behind us, waiting until we turned
before pointing in the proper direction. "There are also
towels to be found in its base, as this sort of thing
happens on a regular basis."

"Then let's take advantage of it," Serendel said,
immediately starting for the pretty little spout and ba-
sin to the left of the fountain we'd gotten the wine
from. "We still have fun to find, and I'd like the use
of my arm while we're looking. Just in case I have to
improvise, you understand."

The grin he sent to me said he now had another
subject to tease about, and as I followed along I made
a mental note to thank Chal for that. People who consider teasing their second calling in life don't *need* to
be handed a subject by those around them; they do
well enough finding ammunition on their own. Jejin
chuckled softly as he followed in turn, but that was
only because he knew he was hardly likely to be made
victim in my place.

As soon as Serendel reached the water fountain, he
put down his goblet of wine and began washing his
arm. Just to save time I bent to look for the towels
that were supposed to be in the base, saw immediately
which carved panel was supposed to be slid back, and
uncovered the hidden cache without any trouble. I did
have to put my own wine aside in order to pull out
one of the giant monsters folded fluffily inside, and
then I had to stand in order to open it.

"I think they were anticipating bathing orgies," I
said as I unfolded about a quarter of that bright yellow
towel. "This thing is big enough for half a dozen people all at once, and may even be a tent in disguise. If
you aren't careful, you could get lost in it."

"Only if you're there to get lost with me," the
fighter said, coming over to put his now-clean-but-wet
arm into the towel. "Getting lost all alone is never
any fun."

Those gray eyes were looking down at me with only
a hint of amusement, and it actually took a minute or
two before I realized he was just standing there while
I used the towel to dry his arm. Finding that out was

somewhat embarrassing, mainly because I also found I *wanted* to do the drying. It has also occurred to me to wonder what drying the rest of him would be like, and that was even more embarrassing. I was sure the eyes watching me knew exactly what I was thinking, but I was saved from having to retreat in total fluster by the intervention of Jejin.

"The towel can be left right there, in front of the fountain," the magician said, drawing Serendel's gaze and thereby earning my profound, undying gratitude. "The servants will take care of it in a minute, and you two still have all the palace to see. What do you think you'd like to do first? Have a snack to go with the wine? Buy slaves at the auction? Gamble with some of the other lords? Watch the races or other athletic events? There are also shows, and music, and . . ."

The man's voice went on and on, listing our choices, but I'd dropped the towel, turned away to retrieve my wine, and was right then busy sipping it. I didn't know about the fighter, but the one thing *I* was interested in hadn't been on Jejin's list. I didn't know what was wrong with me, suddenly wanting a man so badly my hands were nearly trembling with the effort not to let it show. The wine undoubtedly had something to do with it, but I was used to having more capacity than that, and more resistance to the beast called male. Most men were fun to be with, but I'd never experienced the—draw—I did with Serendel, the urge to be somewhere alone with him without mindless blue lines around to spoil things. . . .

"And now, my lady, you may consider yourself claimed," a smug voice said suddenly, bringing me abruptly out of my thoughts. I looked up to see that I'd apparently drifted away from the water fountain to an open section of the floor, and there was a strange man in leather standing about five feet in front of me. He was the one who had spoken, and as an apparent emphasis he gestured to the robed magician on his right. That worthy stood with one hand up, and in the hand was a glittering rope of light. I looked down again to see that the light stretched from him to me and around my waist, a special effect that was mildly impressive. I remembered then what Velix had said about my being subject to claiming, but I really wasn't in the mood for that.

"Why don't you find someone else to claim?" I suggested with a smile, an attempt to show the handsome newcomer that it wasn't him I was refusing. "We've only just gotten here, and I haven't even had a chance to look around."

"You may have that chance once I'm done enjoying your favors," he answered with a grin, the way he looked me over turning it more into a leer. "The choice in the matter is mine, lovely lady, as you are. You will now accompany me to a privacy chamber, where I may take pleasure from my claim choice."

I was about to tell him exactly what he could take and also what he could do with it, when I was interrupted by something I hadn't been expecting. The string of light around my waist tightened to a point where I could actually feel it, and then it began tugging me forward. A glance at the magician showed that he was the one pulling on the light, but the grinning man in leather was the one I was being pulled toward.

"Damn it, I said I'm not interested!" I snapped to the man, trying to dig in nonexistent sandal heels. "You can't just drag me off as though my opinion doesn't count."

"Alas, dear lady, but your interest and opinion do *not* count," he said, really enjoying the game he was playing. "Here, your lord may do with you as he pleases, and at the moment *I* am your lord."

"But not for much longer," another voice said, this time from behind me, and suddenly I felt the countertug of another rope of light. A glance back showed Jejin holding the second rope, and Serendel, of course, had been the one who had spoken.

"You mean to challenge my claim?" the man in leather asked the fighter, scorn in his voice and ridicule on his face. "With the aid of the least magician in these precincts? You could not possibly have chosen worse, my friend, and you will certainly shame yourself if you continue. For your own sake I advise you to withdraw the challenge, and accept a quiet defeat rather than a public one.''

"The only time to accept defeat is when you're dead," Serendel returned flatly, erasing the smirk from the other man's face with the softness of his words. "And if Jejin was all that bad, you wouldn't be trying to *talk* me out of the win. The woman was mine when this first started, and she'll still be mine when it's over. Magician, defend my property."

The other man was scowling by the time Serendel finished his speech, and had obviously decided against wasting any more words. His gesture to his own magician was even more curt than the fighter's command had been, but it managed to serve the purpose. The two magicians moved to face each other to my left, both of them taking the straight parts of their strings of light with them. I discovered that the loops around my waist had been left when I tried to turn and walk away, finding out only then that I was still being held in place. My anger flipped up a notch at that, right into the spitting-furious range; your lord can do as he pleases with you, and magician defend my *property?*

The two men to my right who were so eager to win me weren't even looking in my direction, but instead were giving all their attention to their magicians. The gray-bearded figures had shortened their light-strings as they faced one another, and then suddenly the strange magician sent his string flaring toward Jejin. The end of the string widened immediately into a cone mouth that reached for Serendel's servant, but Jejin wasn't asleep or in any way unready. His own string widened and flashed to intercept the first, which it did with no difficulty at all but with lots of pretty sparks. The two widened strings fought each other with coruscating colors that lit the swirling, ever-present fog, and groups of people who had only been passing by stopped to watch the duel of powers.

If I'd been in a better mood I might have enjoyed the show, but then again I might not have. The two magicians made a real production out of it, first one of them gaining an edge only to lose it, then it was

the other's turn. I stood there with my arms folded,
waiting to see which of my admirers would be the one
to learn just how well I enjoyed being treated like a
stick of furniture, and then the soon-to-be lucky man
was decided on. Jejin's string-cone of light began
forcing the other magician's string back, and as it lost
ground it also lost size and strength. The second magician struggled, bringing up his left hand in an effort
to brace the right, but it wasn't any good. His light
retreated so far back it became no more than a shortened string, and then the remaining string and one of
the loops around my waist abruptly winked out. Jejin's
cone touched the other magician from head to foot,
and when it retreated back to a simple string form, the
second magician stood as still as a carving.

"Mind rot!" the other man in leather snarled, stalk-
ing over to stare at his magician before turning again
to scowl at Serendel. "He's out for a full turn at least,
perhaps even two! You must surely now be well-
pleased with yourself!"

"Why shouldn't I be?" the fighter returned, his faint
grin intended for the purpose of making things worse
for the other. "I wasn't the one who started this by
trying to appropriate someone else's woman. Next time
stop to think about it first."

The small crowd watching the goings-on laughed,
which got to the losing side even more. He turned
again and stalked away, looking as though he intended
finding someone smaller than him to beat up on, and
that ended the show completely. As the crowd began
to disperse, Jejin and Serendel both moved closer to
me.

"That must have been terrible for him," the fighter
said to the magician when they reached me, his grin
now wider. "Having your man beaten by the least magician in these precincts is embarrassing. Did he really
think I'd believe him?"

"A certain number do believe, and I'm sure he was
hoping you'd be one of them," Jejin answered with a
chuckle. "He knows I'm rated stronger than his own
magician, but he's one of those who really enjoy the
laws of this land. Your lady took his fancy so he de-

cided to take *her,* trusting to luck that her companion would allow himself to be talked into backing down. Now he has to wait at least the minimum time before his magician comes out of it, and until then he can't claim any women at all. I have the feeling he'll be finding the wait a long one no matter how short it turns out to be.''

"Serves him right for being fool enough to think I'd hand over what was mine without a fight," Serendel said in a voice filled with satisfaction, then his attention turned to me. He started to say something, noticed my expression before any of it got said, and then that teasing look was back in his eye. "Watch it, Jejin," he warned, trying to sound nervous. "I think we're about to have a second confrontation. I hope you're not too tired to protect me."

"You're as funny as a shuttle crash," I growled, arms still folded as I gave him a frozen stare. "How could a man be afraid of something that's 'his'? Jejin, take this stupid child's toy off me. I don't like being tied, even with real, honest-to-gosh light."

For some reason the man hadn't canceled his special effects, and the string he had taken to fight with was now reattached to the loop around my waist. It was a cute gimmick to amuse the tourists, but there was at least one tourist who had had enough of it.

"My dear lady, I will be more than happy to release you," the magician answered, his tone very neutral. "We'll see it done as quickly as I have the command from your lord."

I immediately switched a thawed and furious gaze to the man who was pretending to be a magician, but he didn't even have the decency to avoid my eyes. It's all a game, his calm expression seemed to be trying to tell me, no one's serious, so there's no reason to get upset. I could understand that, I really could, but accepting something intellectually, I was learning, wasn't the same as accepting it emotionally.

"Then there should be no problem," I said as evenly as I could, trying to calm the emotional anger. "I'm sure my—noble and generous lord won't consider hes-

itating even a moment. Will you, O noble and generous lord?"

I looked again at Serendel, working to keep as much
of the desire for bloody dismemberment out of the stare
as possible, but I don't think I did very well. His grin
widened as he gazed down at me, and then he was
shaking his head.

"I don't know if I can go along with that," he denied, the doubt deliberately added. "Since I won you
I *am* your lord, but you don't seem ready to believe
it. I think I need a demonstration of some sort concerning your sincerity of purpose, your purity of intent. In other words, what'll you give me if I have you
turned loose?"

He was teasing me again, I could see from his grin
that he wasn't completely serious, but that was only
on an intellectual level. Emotionally I reacted just the
way he very obviously wanted me to, with enough
outrage to build a ten-floor office building out of. I
tried calling him names, making obscene observations,
and flatly refusing all at the same time, which means
I stood there gabbling and foaming with nothing at all
intelligible coming through. Jejin glanced at my
clenched fists, then looked away with a pained expression on his face, but the red-headed fighter decided it was time for deep concern.

"Damn it, Jejin, now look what I've done," Serendel said, the gleam in his eyes wiping out all effort
toward self-condemnation. "I said something wrong,
and now the poor little thing is upset. The least I can
do to make up for it is to take her some place quiet to
calm down. Where did you say those privacy chambers are?"

"Oh, now I *am* going to commit murder!" I snarled,
telling nothing but the absolute truth. All I wanted to
do was get my hands on him to rip and tear, but he
was only warped and twisted, not suicidal. As soon as
I started for him, he ducked out of my reach, then
came forward again fast, and suddenly I was being
lifted from the floor on his shoulder. I screamed in
rage and tried to struggle free again, but the grip of
his arm around my legs kept me from doing it.

"We're all ready to follow you, Jejin," the miserable monster said lightly to the magician, totally ignoring the way I was pounding on his back with my fists. "The chambers are spaced around the supporting walls of this fountain room, you said?"

"And, for the convenience of guests, also on the floor above," the man answered, sounding reluctantly amused but still amused. "I see a number of unoccupied chambers in this direction, lord Serendel, so you can have your choice from among them. Clear crystal walls means vacant, heavy swirling fog means occupied. Once you enter a chamber the fog will close off all view of you and your lady, but you must say aloud whether or not you want the room left open. The words 'open' or 'closed' will either allow others to enter and join you or give you complete privacy, whichever you prefer. Also, of course, any chamber where entry is not barred may be entered by you if you so desire."

The beast carrying me simply made a noise of acknowledging receipt of the information, nothing of a comment on it one way or another. Jejin had obviously been giving him a prepared speech, something I'd had no trouble telling even through my continued struggles, and had no need of a specific answer. The "lord" would decide which way he wanted it, without needing to consult anyone else. I growled and kicked and pounded harder at the heavily-muscled back under my fists, but all I accomplished was to give the people we passed something to laugh at. They thought the sight of the big glad carrying me across the wide floor a riot, and even Chal and Lidra, left behind after the magical confrontation, seemed to be sharing in the general amusement.

Needless to say, I was not viewing Serendel's actions with a big grin and a hearty knee-slap. I had the feeling I was doing more damage to my hands than I was to the back I kept beating on, but that didn't stop me from struggling all the way across the very wide room. I found out we'd arrived where we were going when we passed a Jejin who was pointedly not looking at me, and then I saw the crystal-walled doorway we'd just passed through. As soon as we cleared it heavy fog began cutting off all sight of the fountain room beyond, and then I heard the single word, "Closed."

"If you think that'll do you any good, you're even more feebleminded than you look," I announced, giving the back I'd been attacking an extra hard thump. "I want out of here, and I want it *now.* "

"That's too bad about you," he said, sounding completely unconcerned as he continued crossing what seemed to be a room decorated in crystal and blue. Crystal benches with blue svalk cushions, crystal tables with carved blue knick-knacks, blue carpeting and crystal walls. Our forward progress was slowed and then stopped by something I couldn't see from where I was slung over his shoulder, and then my outrage was replaced by true fury. A big hand hit my backside three times, the shoulder I was on dipped, and suddenly I was falling toward damned-if-I-knew-what. The next second I hit something soft, and even though I was flat on my back I tried to go into action. My right hand darted for the palm dagger in its sheath as I tried to struggle to sitting, but as fast as I'd moved it wasn't quite fast enough. An oversized hand flashed to my wrist, a big body forced me flat again with my right arm above my head, and then those gray eyes were looking down at me from little more than a foot away.

"Do you intend turning this attack thing into a habit?" the beast asked in a very mild way, the look in his eyes no more than curious. "If you do, I strongly suggest a reconsideration of the decision. Someone could get hurt."

"I'll think about it *after* someone gets hurt," I grunted, fighting to get my wrist out of the unmoving metal grip that had wrapped all the way around it. "A touch or two of red would do wonders for the color scheme of this room. I consider it a matter of principle to help out like that whenever I can."

"I have the feeling your 'matter of principle' stems more from that very brief smacking you just got," he said, those eyes unmoving from my face. "You're of the opinion you can beat on me as much as you like, but I'm not entitled to give back any of it? Did I miss the announcement of the law making me a public punching bag?''

"I'm not the one who forcibly carried *you* in here," I returned heatedly, even more outraged over his colossal nerve. "Maybe your reputation lets you push other people around, but I'm not other people! If I have to use this dagger before I can walk out of here I'll do it, because I *am* going to walk out of here. Either let me go this instant, or don't complain later about what happens to you.''

"I can understand not liking to be told what to do, but letting the attitude rule you to the exclusion of all reason isn't very smart," he said, the words a little harder than they'd been until then, the look in his eyes matching. "You were told about the game they're playing here and you twice agreed to go along with it, but as soon as it came to living up to the commitment, you forgot all about it and got insulted instead. If I hadn't carried you in here, you would have forced them to throw you out of the Mists, and if you walk out again without doing as you said you would, the same thing will happen. Is that what you really want? To have to pay for a vacation you won't be allowed to continue with?''

I moved just a little in discomfort under that cold gray stare, finally remembering what Velix had said to me—and what I had said in return. The fighter had something of a point, but conceding it didn't mean I liked it.

"There are some emotional reactions none of us can help responding to," I answered, trying not to feel as defensive as I might have sounded. "If you hadn't teased me about it I probably could have kept quiet, but that consideration didn't do anything to stop you. Now it looks like there's only one thing I can do: stay in here long enough to keep them from getting suspicious, and then trade you for Chal. After that you'll get everything you want and then some.''

"I don't think so," he disagreed immediately, doing nothing in the way of turning me loose. "The deal you made was to try me first, and go for the swap only if you didn't like what you got. Sitting around waiting out a sufficient amount of time will negate the deal, and the next thing you'll be doing is going back to the port.''

"There's no way they can know that all I did was sit around," I came back with a snort, trying to move my wrist in his hand. "Unless they have this place bugged they'll think everything is just fine, so will you please let go of me?''

"There's *one* way they can know what you did," he said, a faint smile turning the corners of his mouth. "Would you like to guess what that one way is?''

"You would *tell* them?" I demanded, the outrage coming back to me the instant I understood what he meant. "You would do something that low and dirty? But of course you would, why am I even asking?''

"Stop feeling so self-righteously put upon," he said, the dryness coming close to setting exasperation in his voice. "This is *my* vacation you're trying to ruin, and all because you don't know how to keep your word. What gives you the right to ask me to lie for you? The warm and gracious way you've been treating me since the first time we met? Somehow I don't think so."

I wanted to give back the same kind of lecture he was giving me, but I was having trouble figuring out a properly adequate response. I didn't see anything wrong in not keeping a word I'd been forced to give, and I'd certainly had cause to be less than friendly toward him, but he was twisting everything around. He claimed to be the one who was being harmed, but I had a feeling his true reasons were something else entirely.

"I may be mistaken, but I think you *like* the idea of owning a woman," I stated, voicing the dirty suspicion that had come to me. "You don't give a damn whether or not *I* like it, you're just enjoying the situation. If you weren't, you wouldn't be so morally intent on holding me to my word. Tell me I'm wrong.''

"Of course you're not wrong," he answered, his grin back and strong. "I don't mind dealing with women who are free to do as they like, so why should I mind dealing with ones who aren't? Equality of interest is my philosophy, equality in everything. And it isn't the thought of owning just any woman I'm enjoying, it's the thought of owning you. Are you going to keep the word you gave, or are you going to accept being thrown out?''

"You know damned well I don't want to be thrown out," I growled, moving my wrist in his hand again as I silently admitted I couldn't *allow* myself to be thrown out. "I can't stop you from doing anything you please even though I don't please the same, which means you're about to do something that's beneath any real man. If you're that desperate go ahead and get it done, and afterward you can hold your breath until I thank you. That way you'll end up matching this room perfectly."

"I don't look all that good in blue," he said, his grin widening as he got what I meant. "And I think you'd be surprised to find out how few men, real or otherwise, would hesitate over accepting the temporary ownership of a desirable woman. Permanent ownership would be boring and more trouble than fun, but short-term owning is another story entirely. Especially if the woman is one whose body you really want."

He gave me enough time to redden at his teasing, and then he lowered his lips to mine with a gentle kiss. The last thing I wanted was something like that, but bracing myself to hate the whole episode didn't do well against gentleness. It's force that bracing works best against, and aside from the way he was refusing to allow me to use my palm dagger on him, the man wasn't forcing me to do anything. He kissed me gently, his free hand stroking my hair, for all the world making it seem as though being there was my own choice. After a moment it came to me that I *had* chosen to be there, and in all fairness had to admit I was trapped by circumstance rather than by the effort of the fighter. If not for that S.I. job I could have done as I pleased, up to and including walking away from the man. After another moment I remembered how interested I'd been in finding some place quiet where Serendel and I could kiss without being interrupted, and my resentments over everything he'd insisted on began melting away.

It's strange the way some kissing keeps you from noticing how much time is going by, especially when the kissing becomes two-sided rather than an individual effort. I don't know when I started kissing him back, and also don't know how long I spent doing it; when he finally raised his head to end the time, all I knew was that I'd never experienced the same with any other man.

"Considering the amount of time I've been wanting to do that, you didn't have much chance of talking me into lying for you," he said with a smile, still stroking my hair. "I really have no intention of hurting you, you know, no matter what you've heard about glads and their nasty, bestial ways. Most of us save the bestiality for the arena, and those of us who don't either end up in a cell, or all alone in the bathroom. Word spreads faster among fans than anywhere else, and the honestly vicious ones don't have more than a handful of followers. Do you believe what I'm saying?"

"I never thought about it one way or the other," I answered honestly, feeling almost unbearably shy as I realized he was telling me exactly what he intended doing. "Is it safe to say I'll soon be finding out first hand?"

"Very soon," he agreed with a faint grin, moving his hand from my hair to my face. "It's a lucky thing for me you're a woman who isn't afraid of anything, not even a fighter with a reputation like mine. I find it very comforting."

He gave me a quick kiss with that, then let me go as he stood up again. Unfortunately for my peace of mind he took my dagger before he stood, and I sat up slowly with the partial wish that I still had it. What I sat on was a giant couch quilted with blue svalk, big enough to accommodate four people Serendel's size, big enough to make me feel almost lost on it. It wasn't that I didn't trust the glad, only that he brought me very strange sensations, and I couldn't quite look at what he was doing where he stood. It was nice that he was comforted, but the fact that he was getting out of the leather outfit didn't make me feel the same.

"Now that's a lot better," he said as he came back
onto the couch next to me, to sit as I was doing. "That
leather may look authentic to the costumers in this
place, but I'll bet any amount you care to name that
the original outfits were totally different. This stuff is
a little too stiff to wear comfortably, and not boiled
properly to be adequate protection. It's good for nothing but show—or taking someone's eyes out with those
shoulder pieces. Is something bothering you?"

By the time he asked the question I had inadver-
tently glanced at him, which meant I was less bothered
than I had been. Instead of being stark naked under
the leather the way he'd hinted he was, he wore a very
brief pair of shorts that were like a male model's bathing trunks. For some silly reason I felt better having
him like that, but I still found very little in the way of
comfort in the situation. His body was really massive
with muscle, the sort that comes with strength rather
than empty exercising, and even in the face of all his
assurances I still couldn't help realizing he was like
no man I'd ever been with before.

"Of course nothing is bothering me," I answered
after the briefest hesitation, very aware of how close
he was. "I haven't been a child for quite a number of
years now."

"I didn't say anything about considering you a
child," he returned, his right hand coming to my back
under my hair. "If I'd thought you were a child, I
would have *sent* you to bed, not taken you there.
You've been taken to bed by men before, haven't
you?"

"I used to think so," I muttered, trying to understand why it was all I could do to keep from pulling
away from his hand, and then I raised my voice a
little. "What I meant was, of course I've had sex with
men before. There's nothing to it, really, and most of
the time it's fun."

"You sound like you're trying to talk me into it,"
he said with a chuckle, his hand sliding across my
back to curve around my right arm. "I know most
people consider me shy and hesitant, but I don't really
need convincing. If you're sure there isn't anything

bothering you, why don't you try relaxing a little? Here, let's make both of us a bit more comfortable.''

The next thing I knew both of his hands were on my shoulders, and then the wide straps of the top of my costume were being slid gently down my arms. The effort almost immediately turned me as bare-chested as he was, and before I could even begin to react, he had wrapped me in this arms and had stretched us out on our sides on the couch.

''Ah, yes, this is a lot better,'' he said as he settled me more closely to him, my breasts tight against his chest. ''There have been times I've gotten to bed so tired that even falling asleep seemed like too much of an effort, but there's no such thing as being too tired to cuddle.''

''Cuddle?'' I echoed, looking up at him without being able to decide whether I wanted to raise my eyebrows or lower them. ''Are you sure that's the word you wanted to use? And are you sure you're a fighter and not a ladies' hairdresser?''

''Stop being a little snob,'' he said in a stern way, but I could see the amusement lurking in his eyes. ''Fighters have just as much right to enjoy cuddling as hairdressers do, and maybe even more if you stop to think which group would do better if the right had to be fought for. I happen to like cuddling with certain girls, and I don't mind saying so. Do you have anybody you'd like to bring over to tell me I *shouldn't* be saying it?''

''I think the twelve-foot Monster of Isak is busy right now, so I'll have to get back to you,'' I muttered, feeling very firmly put in my place. ''The biggest problem in acceptance of that is trying to picture a glad 'snuggling.' It's not exactly the sort of scene that comes first and most easily to mind.''

''I'm not responsible for your prejudices,'' he said, that faint, now-familiar grin visible again. ''If you ever hear me tell someone I like snuggling in the arena, that's when you can lodge a protest. When it comes to what I do in bed, no one has a say but me.''

''How about your bed partner?'' I asked, suddenly

aware of the arms around me in a different way. "Do you get the say over her as well?"

"Usually," he agreed with a widening grin, then quickly tightened his hold on me as I began pulling away. "But only because that's the way most of my bed partners prefer it. You'll never find me telling the woman I'm in bed with that her preferences are wrong. Something like that could take the friendliness out of the occasion."

"You mean there are actually women in this universe who feel friendly toward you?" I asked, utterly delighted to find that he was teasing me again. "And here I thought you inspired nothing but lust."

"Life is tough for those of us who are sex objects, but you learn to take the bad with the good," he allowed in a way that was just short of noble. "Women by the thousands come after me and force me into bed, and all I can do is accommodate their preferences. After that, I find this change of pace very refreshing."

I started to ask what change of pace he was talking about, and then I remembered: as long as we were in that particular section of the Mists, his was the only opinion that counted. I could see from the gleam in his gray eyes that I was supposed to get wild and try to start another fight with him, but it had finally gotten through to my temper that he was enjoying the reaction far too much for it to be smart letting it go on. If my getting mad was his version of fun, then mad was the last thing I should be getting.

"Oh, I understand now," I exclaimed, turning my right hand to put it on the chest I was being held against. "What you're all that tired of is being in charge, and what you'd like is to have someone else take over. Why didn't you say so right away? I'll be glad to take over."

The gray eyes looking at me turned briefly startled as he began shaking his head, *that* close to telling me I had it wrong. I knew he didn't want me in charge as well as he did, but I fully intended making him say it so that *I* could laugh for a change. I waited for the protest and disagreement, already enjoying what I would hear—and then I heard something I neither enjoyed nor particularly understood.

"You know, you may not have a bad idea there," he said slowly, his head nodding as the agreement in his voice strengthened. "As a matter of fact, the more I think about it the more I like the way it sounds. You're absolutely right about what I need, so let's do it that way."

He let me go and lay back flat on the couch, tucking his hands behind his head as he grinned. I was sure he couldn't be serious—or at least almost sure—but I didn't know whether to go along with the joke or tell him to stop messing around.

"Well, what are you waiting for?" he prompted, not moving an inch out of the position he'd taken. "You said you'd be glad to be in charge, so let's see some of that gladness. Or are you afraid?"

"I'm not afraid of anything," I snapped, stung by his mockery and moved out of indecision. "If it's female aggressiveness you're looking for, consider it found."

I twisted around and put my hands to his chest, then took his lips with a lot more strength and passion than *he'd* used. He made no effort to stop me, or even to try taking over direction of what I was doing; all he did was cooperate completely by returning the kiss he was getting. It went on for a short while, the warmth of his body and lips slowly coming through to my awareness, my doubts and hesitations melting away a good deal more quickly. I found myself running eager hands over the hardness of him, and also found that something was definitely missing.

"I hate breaking in on your rest," I said between shortened kisses, "but I'd like to be held and touched, too. Do you want me to send for a servant to show you how it's done?"

"If I practice a little, I should be able to figure it out," he answered with a chuckle, and then his arms were around me, his hands moving in silent appreciation of what they touched. It felt so good I almost moaned, and the heat coming to fiery life all through me was startling. Sex had always been something I could take or leave alone, something pleasant to be indulged in with a pleasant partner. With Serendel there was nothing easy or meaningless about the situation, and very briefly part of me tried to become frightened. I couldn't afford to be involved with anything that *wasn't* meaningless, and I remembered what Chal had said back on the liner. The fighter was that strange kind of man who would not touch certain women unless he was serious about them. That was the part that tried to frighten me, but with Serendel's hands touching and stroking everywhere, the fear was drowned beneath waves of churning desire. I wanted him no matter what, and he seemed to feel the same about me.

We spent half of forever kissing and touching, at least five or ten minutes, and then the glad could no longer control himself. Rather than me working on him, I suddenly found myself on my back with him crouching above me, his shorts having disappeared somewhere without my noticing their departure. I laughed as he held me down, knowing I'd won the point of who would be in charge after all, and then he was entering me and there was nothing left to laugh at. His presence inside me was sheer bliss and the very beginning of desire fulfilled, and when his face came to take a kiss he found one already waiting for him. He held me tight as he stroked and kissed me, my fists locked in his hair, and I had truly never experienced anything that wonderful before in my entire life.

Chapter 12

After it was over I refused to move for a while, partly because I didn't know if I *could* move. Every ounce of strength seemed to have been briefly drained out of my body, but it was a marvelous draining that I didn't want to lose the sensation of. I'd just learned that it takes a man's efforts to turn sex into love-making for a woman, and I also wanted to spend some time silently demanding why more men weren't familiar with the technique. I'd lived with Tris for more than half a year, and although the time had been pleasant it had never been as good as what I'd just experienced with Serendel.

"As soon as you don't need me as a pillow any more, be sure to let me know," the object of my thoughts said from above my head. "This chamber has a tiled bathing tub in the back righthand corner, and it won't hurt either of us to use it."

"You're an unfeeling, inhuman slave driver," I mumbled into his chest, refraining from asking why he was holding me so tight if he was all that anxious to get up. "Not to mention the fact that you cheat. If that was your idea of me being in charge, I'd hate to see what your being in charge is like."

"So I lied," he admitted without hesitation, the cheerful dismissal a rumble I could hear in his chest. "I don't mind lying in a good cause, and anyone in this room who tries claiming what we just shared *wasn't* a good cause will find herself in a very tight spot."

"As tight a spot as the one *you* found yourself in?"

I asked with wide-eyed innocence, raising my head to look at him. "Some men seem to consider being in a tight spot fun, but you're not silly enough to be one of them, are you?"

"Absolutely not," he agreed very solemnly with a slow shake of his head. "Abstinence and decorum are the very cornerstones of my life. The other two are honesty and reticence, and by the way— when you're ready to go again, just give me a wink."

"You forgot to include reluctance and hesitation among your cornerstones," I said with a laugh, running one hand over the light hair on his chest. "How does a wink go again?"

"You're trying to ruin me, that's what you're doing," he said with narrowed eyes, pointing a finger at me. "You're in the pay of Farison, and you're trying to make sure I can't walk when it comes time to face him. I knew it as soon as I met you, but the evil plan won't work. You won't find me in your bed more than five or six times a day, and I'll be throwing you out into the street a good half hour before any fight between us is scheduled. Even if it isn't scheduled for another five or ten years."

The last sentence of his teasing came out with very little of the lightness of the previous nonsense, and I suddenly felt the weight of those gray eyes on me, making his words more than they'd been all by themselves. I wanted very much to look away, to listen to the fear inside telling me I couldn't afford to get involved with a man, but I had to admit it was too late for sensible advice. There was something about the man who held me that I just couldn't turn away from, and his own obvious interest made my heart thump and my blood sing. Trite reactions for a situation I'd never anticipated or imagined, but trite doesn't mean it can't be wonderful.

"Serendel," I said with a smile, holding to his gaze with complete willingness. "I think I'll have to remember that name for a while. Do you have something I can write it down on?"

"If you make it Seren, you might be able to remember it without writing it down," he answered with a grin, one big hand coming to stroke my hair. "That's what my baby sister used to call me, after deciding the full name was too formal. She was my favorite sister, and I'd really like having you call me the same."

"*Was* your favorite sister?" I asked, reluctant to put the question but wanting to know. "Did something happen?"

"She was killed," he answered, his eyes going momentarily inhuman, and then a smile banished the deep, terrible cold. "But I think she really would have liked you, and wouldn't have minded your using her version of my name. Your own name, though, probably would have given her problems. Even she wouldn't have been able to do much with Smudge."

"I'll smudge *you*," I said with a growl, getting to my knees beside him in order to reach his throat more easily. "I'm about to strangle you, and you can't say you don't deserve it. When you take a girl to bed, the least you can do is remember her name while she's still *in* that bed. Afterward it isn't necessary, but *during* it is. It's a shame you didn't learn that soon enough to save you."

He grinned while I wrapped my fingers around his throat and tried to squeeze, and very quickly it became clear why he was grinning. His neck was so massive I could barely get my hands around it, and squeezing against the cords was completely impossible. If I'd been seriously interested in doing him harm, I would have been out of luck.

"Out of the goodness of my heart, I've decided to spare you," I announced after a minute's worth of useless effort, looking down at his amusement. "I certainly hope you've learned your lesson, since the next woman you take to bed might not be as generous."

"I don't think I'll have to worry about that for a while," he said, and then his arms were around me, pulling me down and holding me close. "For a time there will only be one woman sharing my bed, and who knows? As generous as she is, I might get lucky enough to have her agree to extending the time. She and I haven't known each other long, but some things don't take very long in developing. All I can hope is that they take a whole lot longer before ending. Maybe even a lifetime long.''

He started to lean up with a kiss, but I was already coming down with one, the only answer I could make to what he'd said. I think everyone wonders what love will be like, how it will feel, how they'll react, and how they'll know it if they do come across it. I'd had those same questions myself, but as I held Seren's face between my hands while kissing him, I knew the answers and many more besides. I was already three-quarters in love with him, I had just been told he felt the same about me, and there *were* no other questions. All the answers in the universe were mine, and I would use them to solve any problem that tried to come along.

We spent some time simply kissing, and then we went together to the bathing tub Seren had mentioned. It was almost big enough to swim in, more than large enough for the two of us, and while we bathed we talked. Seren told me about his family and I told him about Seero, and with everything the two of us wanted to share we almost missed seeing the blinking blue light over a panel of the wall to the left of the pool. A closer inspection showed us a hand plate in the panel, and pressing the hand plate brought to view a small closet space which contained a fresh leather outfit for him and a fresh svalk costume in yellow for me. I was about to take the fresh clothing, but Seren just grinned and told me to leave it there for the moment, then took my hand and dragged me back to the couch. We'd made the mistake of drying each other after getting out of the pool, and I was more than willing to let the clothing wait. Somehow the second time was even better than the first, and the minutes passed by without either of us noticing.

When we finally got out of that chamber, we discovered that Lidra and Chal were in one of their own. Jejin told us that Chal's magician had bested the one representing a challenger for Lidra, and Chal had then carried Lidra off just the way Seren had done with me. Jejin grinned and said he thought a new tradition may well have been started, and we laughed at the idea with him, then all three of us went looking for drinks and entertainment. The shows being put on were absolutely marvelous, and when Lidra and Chal got around to joining us, they thought so too.

After that a lot of our time at the palace was blurry, but we seemed able to go on and on without rest and the partying around us never stopped. Twice Seren was challenged for me and twice Jejin won without trouble, but the third time his hesitation and uncertainty were horribly obvious. Jejin knew something about the rival magician that we didn't, and when Seren read his expression he didn't hesitate. The fighter seemed to be remembering the way Chal had lost Lidra in one challenge, and although the loss had only been a temporary one, he didn't appear prepared to accept the same. Despite what were probably rules to the contrary, Seren approached the man who had challenged him, spoke very quietly, then took a step back. None of us knew what the fighter had said, but the other man paled, apologized for bothering us, then hurried away with a very puzzled magician trailing behind him. After that episode, no one came with a challenge again.

More than once Seren and I made use of the privacy chambers, and there finally came a time when we fell asleep after making love instead of returning to the partying. When I woke again, I had the feeling quite a lot of time had passed; I was back to being able to see clearly what was around me, and I also felt well-rested and ready to get up. When Seren awoke, I had my mind changed for me about the getting up part, and I was more than happy to cooperate. I couldn't seem to get enough of the man, in bed or out, and was no longer even interested in complaining about the way he teased me. Very early on I'd contracted the teasing disease myself, and thereafter worked at giving as good as I got.

We left the chamber to find that a breakfastish meal would be served to us as soon as Chal and Lidra joined us, and that made me feel odd. The fog both inside and out hadn't changed at all, which made it seem as though we were still living the same day we'd started on, no matter how long it was stretching. The thought upset me just a little, but before I could find a reason for the reaction Chal and Lidra came up, and we all went for our meal. We had been given over into the care of servants, and our magicians were nowhere in sight. When they didn't join us for the meal, we decided their jobs might have been finished, and they'd gone back to offer themselves to the next batch of tourists. They never did show up again, and aside from wishing they'd at least said good-bye, we quickly forgot about them.

We weren't far from finishing when Velix arrived, confirming our speculation on the possibility of a change in the offing, but he stood to one side of the room until the floor show was over. The man and woman dancing were dressed in the rags and chains of slaves, and at intervals during the meal the man had stopped the dance by capturing and holding the woman in one way or another, and then had asked Chal and Seren what they wanted him to do with her. The man wore a big grin at those times despite the look he was getting from the girl he held, and seemed only faintly disappointed when his first requests resulted in nothing more than an order to go back to dancing. He seemed to know that the "lords" would not be refusing him forever, and he was right.

The third time he asked he was told to go ahead and have some fun, and even though Lidra and I tried talking Chal and Seren out of it, the two men refused to change their minds. The girl's dancing had been more and more deliberately provocative, they insisted, and they were simply seeing that she got what she'd asked for. Since the man put her to the floor right there in front of our knee table we all saw her getting what she'd asked for, and the way she quickly switched from indignation to enjoyment was very unsettling. I didn't know how Lidra was looking at it, but even though I was trying to be annoyed with Seren, I was also suddenly very hot for him. I tried not to let it show, but his grin said he knew all about it and was simply waiting until I attacked him. I would have enjoyed being able to laugh in his face, but I knew as well as he did that that attack would not be unreasonably long in coming.

When the man and woman finally left the floor, Velix came to stand in front of our long, low table and look down at us with a smile in his eyes that was very close to a smirk. It was a really lucky thing that Griddenths don't show expressions on their beaked faces, or those like the journey scout would sometimes end up as trophies on den walls.

"I see, my lords and ladies, that you've reached a certain appreciation of this area of the Mists," he said, the words just short of being a purr. "I trust there will be no further need for discussions on legal actions or swaps?"

His dark eyes touched Lidra and me as he said that, and Seren chuckled with the satisfaction of a man who knows he has nothing to worry about. That combined with his earlier grin *really* annoyed me, so I decided it was time to dent some smugness.

"Of course there's no further need for discussion on those topics," I said, smiling sweetly at the Griddenth. "I was promised I could swap if I wanted to, so there's nothing left to be talked about. After all, you don't expect a girl to stay with a man who can't even remember her name, do you?"

The feathers around Velix's face puffed out and his head went up, but that was nothing in comparison to Seren's squawk of surprise. He'd had a really good time calling me Smudge at every opportunity, but he suddenly seemed to be regretting the fun. When I transferred my icky smile to the glad, he tried to explain that he'd only been kidding and hadn't understood that it was really bothering me, but before the rush of words could reach an end, they were interrupted by Velix.

"Am I to take it, my lady, that you're now insisting on indulging in the swap?" the Griddenth demanded, his wings moving in short snaps as he spoke. "I'm well aware of the fact that the choice was granted you, but I was under the impression . . ."

"Dalisse, you can't be serious," Seren interrupted in turn, reaching over to take my hand, actual worry in his gray eyes. "I thought we'd agreed there was something more going on between us than simple vacation fun. Was I wrong?''

"Of course you weren't wrong," I answered, squeezing the big hand that held mine, my smile now warm and loving. "You know I feel the same way about you.''

"Then why are you insisting on swapping me for Chal?" he asked, complete confusion turning his expression bewildered. "If you're feeling as satisfied as I am, why do you want to . . .''

"Who said I'm insisting on the swap?" I put with great innocence, taking my own turn at interrupting. "All *I* said was there was no need for further discussion on the point, and then I made a personal opinion observation about men who can't remember the names of the girls they're with. Since you don't happen to be one of that sort, whyever would you think the observation referred to you?''

There was a long ten seconds of silence after my question, and then Lidra and Chal, who sat to Seren's left, both started laughing at the same time. A noise like a strangled growl came from Velix where he stood, an obvious attempt to smother reluctant amusement, but there was still one reaction to come. I'd been smiling pleasantly at Seren, and after a moment of staring at me with narrowed eyes, he produced a faint smile of his own.

"I'm going to get even for that," he said in a very warm, pleasant way, reaching over to gently pat my cheek. "You did it on purpose to scare the hell out of me, so there's no way you'll be getting away with it. When it happens, don't say you didn't ask for it.''

I laughed and immediately began trying to talk him out of the threat, while Lidra and Chal tried to get details on what he intended doing. He smiled and shook his head quietly at all of us, pretending to be determined to carry through on dire plans he wasn't about to divulge, and then Velix was breaking in on the silliness.

"My lords and ladies, please give me your attention," he insisted, probably enjoying playing the wet blanket. "I've come here to tell you that you're now scheduled to move on to the next Mists area on your tour. There are new costumes you must first change into, and then I will lead you to your transportation. The changing rooms are this way, so if you'll please follow me, we can be on our way.''

He fussed at us until we got to our feet, and then led the way through a quiet back door in the eating room that opened on a long, deserted corridor filled with more quiet doors. Each of us was herded into a separate room, and in mine I found my original luggage, a wide, padded bench, a mirrored wall, and my new costume hanging on two hooks of a blank wall. The first hook held a floor-length gown in palest rose that was completely transparent, and the second a matching floor-length cloak that closed at the left shoulder and was completely slit down both sides. I later discovered that the two layers of light, delicate material put together made the costume completely opaque, but even as I began getting out of the svalk outfit I'd gotten used to so easily, I wondered what sort of area we were heading for next.

The material of the gown came up to my throat and down to my toes while leaving my arms bare, but the mirror wall told me complete nakedness would be considered by most as being more modest. Despite all the time we'd spent in the inhibition-relaxing atmosphere of the palace, I put my hands to the form-fitting gown where it hugged my waist above my hips, and wondered if I had the nerve to wear it. That gown was an invitation to attack if I'd ever seen one, and being attacked doesn't happen to be one of my major aims in life. I added the cloak out of sheer desperation (no pun intended), and that was when I discovered how well the two went together. I felt something of relief at that, but only a small something. There would certainly come a time when the cloak would have to be taken off, and if it turned out to be a public occasion I was definitely not looking forward to it.

I was sitting on the padded bench and staring down at the toes of the rose svalk slippers that had replaced my lace-up sandals, when a scraping knock came at my door. I'd been trying to decide how much trouble

I'd be given if I changed out of the gown and cloak
into one of my bodysuits, but there'd been no way of
knowing. I'd been told I didn't *have* to wear the costumes, but just in case Velix decided to come at me
with threats again, it seemed wiser to wait with the
decision to balk until we were a little closer to the
objective we'd come there to reach. We'd also be
closer to the end of the tour by then, which seemed to
be stretching on an awfully long time. . . .

"It's time to leave, my lady," Velix's voice came
through the door after the scraping knock. "Are you
ready?"

Instead of answering I sighed, then got up to go to
the door. The Griddenth waited in the corridor just
outside, and my three traveling companions were already with him, Lidra in lilac, Chal in black, Seren in
brown. The two men showed hose and tunics through
the slits of their solid cloaks, and my first thought was
about how unfair that was. It would have been a perfect point to complain about, except that I suddenly
realized Lidra had been given the same kind of outfit
I had, and she had a good deal more than modesty
areas to hide. I glanced at her to see if she was showing signs of upset, didn't find any, then had to give up
on the effort. Velix was already leading the way up
the corridor away from the door we'd come in by, and
there was nothing to do but follow along with the others.

The end of the long corridor held a door, and a servant opened it for us to allow unimpeded access to the
mists of outdoors. The fog in the streets was a good
deal thicker than that which floated indoors, but not so
thick that we weren't able to see the large coach waiting for us at the curb. Six shadow-shapes of large an-
imals we couldn't quite see were attached at the front
of the coach, and another servant stood by to open the
coach door for us.

"This vehicle will take you to the Mists of Bulm,
and I will be there to greet you," Velix said, nodding
toward the coach and the servant opening the door.
"It would give me greater pleasure to accompany you,
of course, but my body shape unhappily forbids such

accompaniment. Please relax and enjoy the trip, and
rest assured that it will be quite brief.''

None of us felt the need to comment on that, so
Velix stepped aside to give us access to the coach.
Lidra, standing ahead of me, moved forward first, and
even with the help of Chal and the servant quickly
proved how awkward it was getting into a high vehicle
while wearing a long gown and a long cloak. I wasn't
looking forward to my own time trying, and that may
be why I let myself be distracted by a sound coming
from our left, the sound of another coach arriving. It
pulled up to the curb, a servant hurried over from the
palace door that stood there, and then the people inside
were being helped out. I stared at them with a frown,
wondering where I'd seen them before, wondering why
their arrival at that time seemed totally wrong, and
then it hit me.

Those were the four other people we'd gone through
Customs with, the four who had decided to stay over-
night at the castle.

But we'd already been in the Mists for days. Why
were they only just arriving? Could they have started
elsewhere? *Was* there anywhere else to start from? If
there was, why had Velix given us such a hard time
when Lidra and I had protested the setup in that area?
Wouldn't it have been easier simply sending us to the
alternate starting location? I couldn't figure out what
was happening, and then I did something that turned
simple confusion into numbed shock. For the first time
since I'd entered the Mists, I remembered the watch
I'd been given and looked down at it.

To find that according to the timepiece, no more
than half a day had passed. All that time spent ca-
rousing in the palace had taken no more than hours.

"Inky, are you all right?" Seren asked suddenly,
putting an arm around my shoulders. "It's hard to tell
in this fog, but you look like you just went pale."

"By rights I should have gone albino," I muttered
in answer, then raised my eyes to look at Velix. "But
maybe there's a simpler solution to my questions than
the outlandishness that almost knocked me over.

Maybe something has simply gone wrong with my watch."

"My dear lady, how very observant you are," Velix said with a purr while my companions checked their own watches and came up with a variety of exclamations. "You've deduced that time moves at a different rate here in the Mists, and the only accurate measurement of it is the watch on your wrist. That, of course, is the reason our prearranged plans couldn't be changed once you'd arrived here. Acclimatization to the condition takes a bit of time, and too much of it would have passed here if we'd needed to bring in one of our own. As most of our guests take much longer noticing the anomaly, I really must congratulate you."

"But how could that be?" Chal protested, dividing his stare between his watch and the journey scout. "I've never heard of time moving at different rates on a single planet, and if it's true it couldn't be kept secret. Out of all the thousands of tourists you get, at least *one* would have said something to somebody!"

"Not if they didn't remember the phenomenon once they were free of its effects," Velix answered, smooth amusement now very much with him. "Leaving the Mists means leaving most of the memory of it as well, which is why the secret has been kept for as long as it has. One man managed to take it out with him in an utterly ingenious way, and he was the one who convinced others to help him build the Mists of the Ages. I doubt there are as many as half a dozen who know the truth, and employees—not to mention guests—are certainly not numbered among them. All you'll take out with you will be the sketchily detailed memory of a wonderful time, which is exactly what the rest of us take. And now, if you please, the coachman is waiting."

With Lidra already inside the coach I was helped in next, and then the two men of our party joined us. Chal sat next to Lidra and Seren next to me, and none of us said a word until the coach lurched to a start and we pulled away from the palace. At that point Chal stirred in his seat, then shook his head.

"I don't buy it," he stated, knowing we would have

no trouble following him; what we'd just learned was occupying the thoughts of all of us. "I don't claim to know more about this anomaly than the people who discovered it, but I can't accept the different time rate theory. It could be that our biological processes have been speeded up by something in the fog, but that has nothing to do with what *they're* claiming."

"I don't really understand either point," Seren said, looking at Chal with distraction in his eyes. "The idea of a different time rate isn't easily swallowed without the context of alternate dimensions wrapped tightly around it, but no one has said anything about other dimensions. The idea of biological changes—isn't that reaching just as far?"

"Not really," Chal denied, his mind busily chewing at the question. "We take things all the time that affect or adjust our metabolisms, and usually think nothing of it. If these mists slow us down to the point where we're living days in comparison to hours outside, that's only an extreme extension of something we're already well familiar with."

"Slow us down?" I echoed, feeling more confused than ever. "If we're living days to hours, wouldn't it be speeding us up? I mean, don't you have to move faster to cram more into the same amount of time?"

"Yes, our bodies would be moving faster, but our perceptions would have to slow down," Chal said, just as though he intended starting a lecture, but then his expression went peculiar. "I'd like to make that clearer for you, but I don't think I can do it without getting really technical. How much biology have you had, Inky?"

"The level I left it was above the birds and the bees, but about three miles below what you're talking about," I said with a wave of my hand, dismissing his question. "You'd be wasting your time, Chal, and all I'd get out of it would be a headache. Let's just say we spent what felt like more than two days living through half a day of time, and let it go at that."

Chal nodded and Seren agreed with a wordless sound, but that was hardly the end of it. Lidra hadn't said anything and really seemed to be lost in her

thoughts, and the two men went back to silent speculation while I did the same. It was a fantastic idea to
kick around, and the air-conditioned interior of the
coach kept us comfortable while we thought. Part of
me wanted to consider how the new information would
affect the job we had to do for S.I., but the rest of me
refused to consider the matter. Chal and Lidra were
the big brains of our threesome, and I was just along
to find and open things. They could take care of the
problem, while I spent my time thinking about all the
extra hours and days I'd have with Seren.

The silence stretched on for an amount of time that
was probably laughing at us, and then Seren stirred
and sighed. If I'd had to guess about the sigh, I would
have bet he was giving up on understanding what was
happening, and I considered that very wise of him. I
was fairly sure it would take even Chal and Lidra more
than a few minutes to figure out which way was fast
forward, so for the rest of us to try was a complete
waste of time. The fighter shifted until he had put his
right arm around me, and then he gestured toward the
window on his left.

"It looks like we were so distracted, we missed
leaving the city," he said. "There's nothing out there
now but fog and shapes shaped like bushes and trees.
I wonder what the new area will be like—and if we'll
enjoy it as much as we enjoyed the last one."

"We'll probably be forced to play kiddy games, and
made to sleep in segregated dormitories," I said, feeling his faint grin all the way down to my slippered
toes. "All the girls will have dragons for chaperones,
and all the boys will die of frustration."

"Not this boy," he said with a chuckle, leaning
down to kiss my ear. "Any dragon who gets in my
way will need heavy-duty medical insurance. And ever
since you and Lidra came out of your changing rooms,
I've been curious. What sort of costumes do you have
on under those cloaks?"

"Oh—nothing terribly special," I said as casually
as I could, suddenly understanding why there had been
four changing rooms instead of two. With two, there
would most likely have been a delay in leaving, and I

could just picture Seren's reaction the first time he saw me in the gown alone, without the cloak. If I was very lucky we also would be alone; I didn't know how he felt about it, but public exhibitions didn't fit in well with my private inhibitions.

"What sort of nothing terribly special?" he pursued, bringing his free hand to my bare left arm. "I love this color they keep giving you, it goes so well with the black of your hair. How about one peek under the cloak?"

I looked up at him quickly, having the feeling I recognized the tone in his voice, and unfortunately I was right. There was a definite gleam in the gray eyes looking down at me, which meant he'd already come to certain conclusions.

"But I can't give you a peek," I said, keeping my voice very, very reasonable. "I gave my word not to, and going back on your word isn't very nice. You don't want to make a liar out of me, do you?"

"Absolutely not," he agreed very solemnly—without losing anything of the gleam. "I'd never sink so low as to make a liar out of anyone. I'm not trying to be a pest about it, but before we left the palace I had a glimpse of that gown material where it showed through the side slit of your cloak, and since then I've been—curious. How about if I take a peek on my own?"

"Don't you dare!" I hissed as his hand left my arm to finger the edge of the cloak's front panel, his grin beginning to widen. "Seren, leave it alone!"

"Why are you blushing like that, Smudge?" he asked in a very innocent way, the arm around my shoulders keeping me from shifting away. "I know you're not naked under there, and even if you were it wouldn't matter. I've already seen you naked, so it would hardly be anything new. You know how I enjoy looking at you, so come on—just a little peek."

'You do, and I'll pop you one in the nose," I said with all the elegant hauteur I was capable of, trying hard to make him know I meant it. "We're not alone in this coach, and I'll be damned if I put on a show even for people I'm friendly with. I intend waiting until we get where we're going before I start the fun games again; if you don't care to wait, you're on your own.''

"I don't think you have much to worry about in the way of an audience," he answered with a small laugh, gesturing with his head toward the coach seat opposite ours. "They've been busy with their own concerns for a couple of minutes now, so you might as well think of us as being alone.''

I looked over to Chal and Lidra, and was surprised to find that they were holding each other around and exchanging light, brief kisses. Staring is an intrusion in a situation like that, so I almost looked immediately away again—until I saw the way Lidra's lips were moving between the kisses. She and Chal were talking rather than necking, and the fact that I couldn't hear any of it said she was guarding the conversation with one of her devices. That, of course, meant it was business, which also meant it was up to me to distract Seren away from what they were doing.

"This still doesn't match my definition of being alone, but I do have to say I'm disappointed," I told the big man to my left, bringing my eyes back to him with a small sigh. "Here you sit, bothering me about peeking, while Chal gets right down to more interesting topics. Maybe I should have gone for the swap after all.''

"You're a cruel, heartless woman, but this one time you may be right," he allowed with a thoughtful look, then abruptly reached his left arm down and slid it under my knees. With his right arm already around me, it was no more than seconds before I was seated on his lap, and then pulled tight against his chest. "Well?" he demanded in pretend impatience. "What are you waiting for? You know I'm too weak to stop you from kissing me half to death.''

"Never let it be said I'd pass on a chance to take advantage of the helpless," I said with a laugh, then put my arms around his neck and began taking advantage. His lips were so reluctant I was almost overwhelmed, but since I was kissing him for the sake of the job, I just had to put up with it. The sacrifices I had to make for S.I. were getting worse and worse, but I felt sure I was strong enough to stand up under the pressure.

The sensation of the coach slowing down brought an end to the time, and in one way it was a very good thing. Seren's hands had been moving under my cloak while we kissed, and I discovered I was about five minutes away from not caring *who* might be watching us. There was no possible doubt he felt exactly the same, and I was certain the only thing holding him back was the knowledge of my reluctance. The ride ended before the reluctance did, which, I suppose, can be considered the good thing; the reverse of the coin was the way I cursed under my breath, reviling whoever was responsible for arranging such damned short trips.

"Looks like we get tents this time," Seren observed in a murmur, his big hand still moving over my bottom. "I wonder how fast they'll show us which is ours."

"It better be immediately, or I'll pick one on my own," I murmured back, fighting to withdraw at least part of myself from the mindless demand of my body that I'd nearly merged with. I wanted Seren so badly the itch was almost driving me crazy, and I wasn't in any mood to accept delays.

After a moment of inner struggle I was able to straighten on his lap, and that's when I saw his choice of the word "tent" was somewhat inaccurate. What we'd pulled into the middle of was a collection of pavilions, wide, brightly-colored almost-buildings that glowed prettily through the mist. Light spilled out of the front of most of those pavilions, and people dressed in our current costumes moved here and there through the camp.

"Look, there's Velix," Chal said, pointing out the window toward the front of the coach. He and Lidra faced the direction in which we'd been going, and Seren and I faced where we'd come from. Some people might have protested having to ride backward in the second-class seats, but Seren and I had been occupied with other concerns.

"And Velix isn't alone," Lidra added, leaning toward Chal to get a better view. "He has four men and
two women with him, all dressed the way we are. I
wonder what's going to be happening?"

"It won't be long before we find out," Seren said,
also looking out the window. "We're stopping right
in front of them."

Which was just what we were doing. The coach
came to a complete stop, one of the men stepped forward to open the door, and Velix moved closer to look
up at us with a tail-flourish.

"My lords and ladies, welcome to the Mists of
Bulm," the Griddenth announced, a purr of satisfaction again in his voice. "All the arrangements have
been made, so if you'll join us now we can get you
settled. The ladies first, if you please."

Since I was closest to the door I got to be the first
one out, and two of the men took my arms to help me
down. Once I was on the ground they urged me out of
the way, and with all those people there I could understand why they didn't want another immediately
underfoot. The man on my right asked if I was having
a good time, and when I'd assured him I hadn't been
horribly bored, the one on my left asked if there had
been anything about the palace I hadn't liked. I thought
briefly about the question and couldn't come up with
much, and then I suddenly noticed we were still walking. The pavilions we'd stopped among, the people,
the coach—all had disappeared behind us in the fog,
and when I tried to stop and turn around, the hands on
my arms tightened gently but irresistibly! They'd distracted me until we were far enough away from the
others, and now they weren't going to let me go!

Chapter 13

Automatically I began to struggle, having no idea where those men were taking me or why, but the one on my right seemed to be expecting the reaction.

"No, no, it's perfectly all right, sweet damsel," he said with a reassuring smile, he and the other still moving me forward through the mist. "Your companions will be along shortly so we have to get you settled first, or you'll all lose half the fun of it. There's no real danger, of course, especially not with us leading you along, and it isn't very far."

"Are you sure I'm not being kidnapped?" I asked, trying to keep the tremor out of my voice. I'd suddenly remembered the real reason I was in the Mists, and my heart was pounding at the thought that someone had found out.

"But of course you're being kidnapped," the second man answered with a laugh, causing the first to grin. "That's the whole basis of the Mists of Bulm. The damsels are kidnapped by outlaws and monsters and ogres, and the men have to find and rescue them. After that you can reward your hero or not, just as you like, and can even request a different hero if the first takes too long finding you. The men also have the option of getting a different damsel to rescue if they don't like the reward they're given after the first time, so you might keep that in mind."

The first man chuckled but didn't add anything, and I was too relieved to put in anything of my own. Being kidnapped for the purposes of their ongoing game was a hell of a lot better than being found out and taken prisoner, no matter *how* silly the idea would have been all by itself. Under the gown I still had my palm dagger, but I really had no interest in finding a need to use it.

We continued on through the fog for a while, and I wondered how the men knew where they were going until I spotted the button in the right ear of the one to my left. After that I noticed the other man touching his own right ear, which I took to mean he had a button like the first. They were being guided through the fog by others who had instruments capable of penetrating the fog's obscurity, but realizing that didn't do much in the way of making me feel better. If there were instruments around capable of detecting people moving through the fog, the job my teammates and I would be doing had just become harder.

True to the word I'd been given, our destination *wasn't* very far. A large shape loomed in the mists ahead of us, and when we moved closer it took on more of the outlines of a broken-down, gloomy mansion. I was led over a small bridge and then up a badly-kept path of stones, and then we were at a heavy wooden door that hung open and half off its frame. Getting through the doorway was a one-at-a-time operation, and once we were inside I didn't consider the accomplishment worth the effort. Thick cobwebs hung everywhere with only an occasional candle to light them, what furniture there was stood sheet-covered like ghosts, and the dust of years was so thick it could have been mistaken for carpeting. We had come into a wide, round entrance hall, and after giving me a chance to look around at the ghastly mess, my two companions again urged me forward.

"This place looks like it was cleaned by someone with my housekeeping abilities," I remarked, not very pleased at the idea of a more detailed tour. "Are you sure this is where we're supposed to be?"

"Positive," the man on my left chuckled, enjoying my uneasiness. "This first time you won't be hidden too well, so your rescuing hero should have very little trouble finding you. The second time won't be as easy as the first and the third won't be as easy as the second, and so on until he's tearing this place apart. If at any time he *doesn't* find you, you get a special prize and he has to pay a penalty. The women always enjoy the prize, but the men never feel the same about the penalty. Right in here, please.''

"Here" was a room to the left, off the back of the entrance hall. Its double doors were still on their hinges, but there was a protesting scream from those hinges when the doors were opened by my companions, to reveal what seemed to be a large, pillared dining hall. Weak candlelight showed a long table toward the rear of the room, dust-covered, cobwebby half-eaten food still on it, skeletons occupying the high-backed chairs around it. Some of the skeletons still held goblets, as though they were about to raise them in a toast, and I was so busy watching to make sure I wouldn't be taken anywhere near them or the table, I didn't immediately notice it when we stopped. We were about halfway between the entrance doors and the grisly feast scene, and two solid-sounding clicks brought my attention quickly back to my immediate vicinity.

"What are you doing?'' I demanded with more hysteria than I would have preferred, trying to get my wrists loose from the cuffs that had been closed around them. I'd been backed up against one of the pillars with the doors on my left and that table on my right, and my wrists had been set into soft plastic cuffs held by the rounded pillar from the rear. The gentle cuffs weren't hurting me, but I still couldn't bring my arms forward or step away from the pillar.

"Don't worry, sweet damsel, we're just chaining you,'' the man on my left said, now distracted by the need to check what he and his friend had done. "If you aren't chained or locked up somehow, you wouldn't need to wait for a hero to save you, now would you? We'll be getting on back now, but first I want to tell you not to worry when you hear strange noises. The monster who kidnapped you is prowling around the mansion, waiting to pounce on anyone who tries rescuing you. Or, once your hero gets here, the monster will try to devour you before you can be rescued. There are three or four different ways it can go, and we never know which it'll be. Just be patient, and remember: this is all in fun. No one will be getting hurt, so you have nothing to worry about.''

He and his friend both smiled reassuring smiles at me, but they weren't as ready to leave as the first one had said. Instead of turning away he reached to the clasp on my left shoulder, opened the cloak, then pulled it away.

''Hot damn,'' the second one breathed as he stared at me, ignoring the sound of protest I'd made when the cloak had been taken. ''Sweet damsel, if you decide you don't like the way your first hero operates, you just tell them you want me instead. I guarantee you won't end up disappointed.''

The first man laughed at what his friend had said, his expression clearly supporting the opinion, but rather than adding anything of his own he slapped his friend's shoulder and the two of them turned away. The second man turned twice to look back at me before he and the other went through the door, and then, with more squealing from the hinges, I was finally alone. I pulled angrily at the cuffs that held me, embarrassed and annoyed at the way the cloak had been taken, but not all that surprised. A minute of thought said the ''heroes'' had to have an immediate reward for finding the missing damsels, and the costume we'd been dressed in was it.

Despite the nasty, gloomy atmosphere of the room I was chained in, I soon found myself more bored than frightened. There isn't much fun in standing chained to a pillar, and after having been warned, the creaking, ominous sounds I heard every once in a while weren't in any way attention-takers. The only thought occupying me was the question of how long it would take Seren to find me, how long it would be before I could give him his reward. The coach ride was still sharp in my memory, and it wasn't only boredom that shifted me from foot to foot in front of the pillar.

About fifteen or twenty minutes went by, and then I heard a sound that was less of a creak and more like the slow approach of footsteps. I was immediately sure

it was Seren and then just as immediately not quite as
sure, especially since the footsteps weren't hurrying.
I waited with faintly pounding heart while the steps
came up to the room's doors, heard them pause, and
then one of the doors wailed at being opened. A large
shape loomed in the open doorway, making me pull at
the cuffs that held me in place, and then the shape was
in the room and walking toward me.

"Yes, I can see now that they were right," Seren's
voice came with amusement in it, while I tried to re-
swallow my heart. "They said I wouldn't be disappointed when I found my damsel in distress, and they
were absolutely right. I'll just have to have some words
with them about waiting so long before putting you in
that costume."

"If you'll reel in your eyeballs, you'll find it easier
opening these cuffs on my wrists," I said, suddenly in
even more of a hurry to be free. Seren had looked at
me more than once in the time we'd been together, but
never with the slow gleam he was showing right then.
I had time to notice his cloak was gone and he'd been
given a play sword that looked like tin, but that was
all I had time to notice.

"Why the rush?" he asked almost laconically, stopping in front of me to grin and inspect. "At first I
didn't think much of the way this place was decorated,
but I've suddenly changed my mind. Could that gown
be svalk?"

He reached a big hand out toward me, and although
I tried avoiding it, the cuffs held me in place while his
fingers closed gently around my left breast. When he
began to stroke me I moaned, feeling as though I had
been turned into a sun.

"Seren, please, you're killing me," I begged, having no idea why he as doing that to me. "Take the
cuffs off so we can go and find a tent to use. If you
don't do it fast, I'll be nothing but a pile of ashes."

"Oh, I think you look stronger than that," he returned with a chuckle, his hand leaving my breast to
slide down to my waist. "I'd be willing to bet you're
strong enough to last through hours of this—just the
way you were strong enough to pretend you wanted a

swap a little while ago. Do you remember pretending you wanted a swap?''

"It was just a joke!" I wailed, pulling again at the cuffs as his hand slid down over my hip to my thigh. "Please, Seren, it was only a joke! Don't keep me like this for hours!"

"Well, it's possible you might be able to make me change my mind," he allowed, but there was a lot of deliberate doubt in with the words. "Why don't we see how well you do with convincing, and then we'll see if there's reason to think about changes."

He leaned down to give me the chance to reach him with a kiss, but he didn't stop touching me and he certainly didn't try opening those cuffs. I reached to his mouth with mine and kissed him with more fervor than I had at any time before, really trying to get him to change his mind. I was fairly certain he was only teasing me about keeping me like that for hours, but it had suddenly come to me that he could be absolutely serious. I didn't like the way he was getting even for what I'd done to *him*, but just then I couldn't find it in me to argue the point.

"That was very nice," he said as he ended the kiss, grinning at the way I tried not to let his lips go. "The next thing we have to do is . . ."

His words were cut off as both doors to the room were slammed open, and a heart-stopping roar suddenly came. Seren whirled around, his hand immediately going for his swordbelt, and then, unexpectedly, he laughed.

"Would you believe I almost forgot company was coming?" he said, relaxing out of a readiness stance. "That must be the fellow who's supposed to have kidnapped you."

He stepped aside to the right to point at the new arrival, and being reminded that we were still in the middle of a game didn't make sight of the thing any easier to take. What had just come in was about eight feet tall, built like a man and proportionally made, except for the fact that its arms were too long. It had dark, greasy hair on its uneven skull and over most of its body, its eyes were very light and downright crazy-looking, and its mouth hung open to allow the drool to drip down its chin to the floor. It wore nothing of clothing and carried no weapons, but its fingers opened and closed to show sharp, talonlike claws. It stood just inside the doorway to stare at us stupidly for a minute, then it grinned and uncovered two rows of yellow, pointed teeth and began a slow, shuffling advance.

"Seren, are you sure that thing isn't serious?" I asked nervously, pulling for the thousandth time at the cuffs that still hadn't been opened. "I don't like the way it's looking at me."

"There's nothing wrong with the way it's looking at you," Seren answered with a laugh, glancing back to me as he drew and raised his toy kiddy-sword. "It's exactly the same way *I* was looking at you. What I have to do now is touch him with my magic blade, and he'll instantly fall over dead. After that we can get back to what we were doing when we were so rudely interrupted."

He glanced at me again with a grin, then began striding toward the horror coming shufflingly at us, enjoying the game in a way I couldn't seem to match. I didn't like the looks of that monster, I didn't like being chained to a pillar, and I didn't like the fact that Seren would get to do all the defending. I've always had this thing about needing to make my own efforts toward self-defense, even if the guy next to me *is* able to do it better. There's nothing worse than standing around letting someone else be responsible for your safety; if they decide they'd be happier doing something else, you've had it.

"Sorry, friend monster, but that delicious damsel is mine," Seren said, closing the last few feet between him and the horror. "I can't blame you for wanting her, but—"

He reached out to touch the thing with his kiddy-blade, which should have, according to the rules, made it fall over dead. Instead of falling, alive *or* dead, the thing looked down at Seren, seemed to see him for the first time, and uttered a snarling growl that caused my blood to stand still. One giant, filthy hand flashed out to grab the toy blade that had touched it, the fingers

closed to crumple the blade like foil, and then the other
arm swung light-speed fast to catch Seren hard in a
backhanded roundhouse that sent him flying off to my
far left as though he were a tiny child. At that point I
considered screaming, discovered that I couldn't, then
saw that the thing had begun shuffling toward me
again, that slobbering grin wider than before.

"If this is a game, I want my marbles back so I can
go home," I muttered, too white-faced scared to know
what I was saying. All I did know was that the thing
coming toward me wasn't playing, not the way those
creatures in the passageway leading to the palace had
been. The stink that came forward with it supported
the theory, since the ones playing monster underground hadn't had a like aroma. It wasn't hard to see
we now had serious trouble, especially after what it
had done to Seren. If it had all been part of the fun
time we were supposed to be having, it wouldn't have
hurt a guest like that. And Seren *had* been hurt, even
though I couldn't bring myself to think about how
badly.

The giant monstrosity shuffled closer and closer
while I tried frantically to get even one wrist free of
those cuffs, and then the problem was solved for me.
The entire time I'd been imagining having those talons
sunk deep into my flesh as soon as the thing was near
enough, but my body wasn't what was first reached
for. The giant stopped about three feet in front of me,
reached out with both knuckle-dragging arms, and
closed its hands on the chains holding me to the pillar.
One grunting pull and the stone of the pillar gave with
a sharp-rumbling crack as though it were made of hard-
packed sand instead, and the chains that had been set
so deep were no longer seated where they had been. I
suddenly *knew* that the monstrosity wanted to wait until it had gotten back to its lair before it started on its
newest meal, and then I was being dragged by the
wrists away from the pillar, toward the doors the thing
had come in by.

Having had a number of unpleasant experiences with
very close calls in my life, I'd almost gotten to the
point of envying the old-fashioned sort of book-

heroine, the kind who handled nasty situations by fainting, thereby leaving it to the broad-chested hero to get her out of the soup. When the monstrosity began dragging me out of the room, I would have greatly enjoyed fainting, but my own broad-chested hero was down in the shadows somewhere, I still had this need to do something to protect *myself*, and my wrists were finally close enough together for me to reach the cuffs on them. It took a moment or so of groping before I located the release points by feel, and then two pushes later I was finally free.

But only of the chains. The monstrosity didn't seem to be terribly bright, but the combination of the empty cuffs hitting the floor and the loss of my resisting weight at the other end of what it was pulling did manage to let it know its snack was trying to do a fade. It stopped lumbering forward and started to turn back with a growl, and the idea about fainting began looking better and better. I was already backing away from the thing, but there was no real place of safety in that room. I might have found it possible to dart past the misshapen form to the doors out, but I'd already seen once how fast it could move—and I wasn't about to leave Seren there, alone and hurt, to be a substitute meal.

When the thing turned and saw me free it snarled even louder, dropped the useless chains, then began coming back after me. I swallowed hard, but kept backing away—and then I heard a sound from my left that was so compelling even the lumbering monster was attracted by it. It was almost like the sound of soft singing, but nothing that a human voice had ever produced. There was joy in the gentle song, and delight and eagerness, and when I turned my head to see what was producing it I found myself very surprised and a little shocked.

Seren stood just at the edge of the shadows, both fists wrapped around the hilt of his multi-sword, a sword that was fully activated to perform as it was born to do. What had shocked me was the realization that I had never seen the sword completely alive before, not when Seren had been working out on the liner, and not even when he'd drawn it in the underground passage, against the pretend monsters. Both of those times the fighter had been playing, but just then he was deadly serious. He knew as well as I that the monstrosity was real, and I could see that his efforts were going to be the same.

The thing snarled with rage when it saw Seren standing there, but it seemed to be faintly puzzled by what he held. The sword's blade had a very faint glow in the dimness, something that would be invisible in normal lighting, and what could be seen of the jeweled hilt around and between Seren's hands was a blaze of almost-living light. The sword continued to sing its song of eagerness, and that seemed to help the monstrosity make up its mind. It apparently had no idea what the sword was, but it suddenly decided it wanted it.

It was strange to see the way the thing began moving toward Seren, one long arm reaching out in the direction of his multi-sword, a distracted snarl for the man who held the weapon. The monstrosity wanted the bright, pretty thing the man held, and it was going to take it. The thing was almost childlike in its behavior, and that was the phrase that rang a bell of memory for me. I remembered reading or hearing about a race of semi-humanoids that had been found inhabiting a newly discovered planet with high background radiation. The race had been described in long, pedantic words that translated to misshapenly ugly, of moronic intelligence, and easily moved to murderous rages. The only faintly redeeming quality seemed to have been a childlike curiosity for bright, new things, but that didn't change how dangerous the race was. They were meateaters, which turned out to mean *any* meat including vanquished foes of their own race, or careless researchers working with some of them. . . .

I shuddered as I watched the thing shuffling toward Seren, finally understanding how I'd known I was going to be its next meal. My subconscious had identified the thing before the rest of me had, and I only hoped the fighter knew what it was facing. How the thing had gotten into the Mists was something I had

no idea about, but if Seren's resolve weakened at the
sight of its fascination with his pretty sword . . .

But it didn't. Just as I was trying to decide what to
say in warning to the fighter, the creature got close
enough to reach a hand out to the sword, at the same
time raising its other arm in the sort of backswing blow
it had caught the glad with the first time. Seren ducked
both the grab and the blow and then swung his sword
across the thing's middle, apparently intending to cut
it in half. I fully expected that to be the end of the
fight, but the monstrosity was much faster than its
usual lumbering gait led you to believe. It jumped back
with the speed it had used the first time it had struck
at Seren, and rather than be cut in half it was just
opened from side to side.

The roar the thing sounded was both deafening and
paralyzing, equally as bad as the sight of the blood
pouring out of the wound it had received. Pain and
outrage seemed to madden it, and with another roar it
attacked the smaller being that had dared to hurt it,
clearly intending to catch the offender and tear him
apart. Seren moved even faster than the monstrosity to
get out of its way, swinging at an arm as he went, and
the thing roared out its hatred even as more blood began flowing from its filthy body.

That was the start of it, but minutes went by and the
end came no closer to being in sight. Due to the very
long arms the monstrosity had, Seren couldn't close
with the thing, not and expect to keep away from hands
that wanted to tear him apart. He tried for those hands
and arms as he kept out of reach, but the thing wasn't
too stupid to understand what he was trying and moved
at its fastest to keep it from happening. It couldn't stop
itself from being wounded over and over, but the loss
of all that blood wasn't slowing it the way it should
have. Seren's sword sang with delight every time it bit
deep, but it wasn't able to reach anything vital on the
giant creature.

During that time *I* wasn't able to do anything but
stand and watch, moving now and then to keep well
away from the area of action. The creature seemed to
have forgotten all about me, which would have been

a benefit for our side if I could have come up with a way of using the edge. Watching the fight hadn't been fun; it had been terrifying, knowing as I did that nothing could stop it short of the death of one of the participants. In the arena Seren could lose but still live if he were no more than badly wounded, but even if he died he wouldn't be *eaten* afterward. I was also well aware of the fact that if *he* lost I would quickly share his fate, which meant I had to do something to help or I would have no complaint coming afterward. If all you do is stand around and watch your side go down, you deserve whatever happens to you because of it.

Which truth finally made me begin to look around seriously. If there was nothing obvious for me to do, I'd have to find something unobvious. The main trouble was the room was so bare and dark, containing nothing I could use as a weapon, nothing I could handle easily enough to make my presence felt. Even the chairs the skeletons sat in around the cobwebbed table were too big and heavy to be swung, otherwise I could have—

My desperate thoughts stopped still when I looked up toward the darkened ceiling of the room, to see the very large, round, wooden chandelier hanging above the table. None of the dozens of candles ranged around its outer and inner circles were lit, which was why it had taken me so long to see the thing. Having found the one I quickly looked for others, and sure enough, here and there around the room, unlit candles were supported by the same kind of wooden circles. The fight had moved, at various times, under at least three of them, and right then seemed to be heading in the general direction of a fourth. If I could just get up on the thing—!

I would do what? I stood chewing my lip with one hand to my hair, racking my brain for an idea, and then I saw the chains the monstrosity had pulled out of the pillar, then dropped to the floor. The chains were light enough for me to use as a weapon, especially if I attacked from an unexpected direction, and the distraction might even be enough to allow Seren to finally close with the creature. It was at the very

least worth a try, but even as I hurried over to pick up
the chains, I still didn't know how I was going to reach
the chandelier. It was a good twelve feet or more above
my head, and although my standing high-jump was
better than what most people can accomplish, I hadn't
learned to fly going *up*, only when coming down. I
had to reach it, but I didn't know how!

Seren and the creature were still going at it when I
began to look around, and the way they were moving
told me I didn't have much time. If I wasn't already
up in the air before they got in range I would be wasting my time, and possibly even our lives. I needed
something to bring me a few feet higher off the floor,
something that wouldn't be easily noticed when the
fight reached that area of the room. Something, something—

I was moving around the fringes of the darker area
of the room when I saw it, hidden in shadow and invisible from more than a couple of feet away. A sturdy-
looking box that had no business being in a room like
that, but one that was two feet wide, at least three and
a half long, and about eight inches thick. I didn't know
what it was or what it was doing there, but I knew at
once that if it could be counted on to hold my weight
even for a little while, it would be enough to get me
where I wanted to go. Without wasting another minute
I lifted its more-massive-than-weighty weight, and
carried it over to where I needed it.

By the time I put it down, the still-weak but stronger
candlelight had shown me why something that had no
business in that room had been lying around in the
shadowed darkness. The contents of the box was sten-
ciled on each of its sides, and those contents were
"cobweb curtains and strings." The room was undoubtedly fixed after each time it was used, and having
the phony cobwebs that handy undoubtedly saved quite
a lot of effort. I gave silent thanks that someone was
too lazy to want to walk back and forth to a storeroom
every time the chamber had to be redecorated, and
then paid attention to standing the box firmly on its
end.

Before I could try climbing up on it I had to take

the back of that stupid, see-through gown skirt, pull
the bottom of it through my legs and anchor it in the
front of my belt, then hook the two lengths of chain
together and wrap them a few times around my waist
before awkwardly tying them in place. I was working
frantically to move as fast as possible because of how
close the fight was getting, and also trying very hard
not to look at the combatants. A glance earlier had
shown me four long, ragged lines of red down Seren's
left shirt sleeve, letting me know the creature had gotten some of its own back. I didn't want to think about
Seren's being hurt; I was close to trembling at sharing
the pain he must be feeling, and the last thing I could
afford to do was tremble.

As soon as I was set, I climbed carefully up onto
the box, trying not to let the extra weight of the chain
around my waist over-balance me. I could almost hear
the creaking protest of the box as it gave a little under
my weight, but I didn't listen to that any more than I
listened to the screaming voice inside my head that
kept ranting that I hadn't checked how well-anchored
the chandelier was in the ceiling. I had no way of
checking the chandelier and knew damned well the
box was not about to hold me for longer than moments, so I had no time to listen to screaming or protests or even to the sound of nearing battle. All I could
do was stand crouched on the box for the seconds I
needed to set myself, then unfolded upward with the
powerful spring used by cats. I went up in the air and
at the height of my rise stretched out long to make it
go farther yet, and then my fingers were closing on
the outer circle of the chandelier.

I think I held my breath for a few seconds, but although the chandelier began swinging it didn't even
threaten to pull out of the ceiling. I pulled my legs up
fast to hook my knees over the outer circle, and then
I was riding the swing upside down, settled in place
and ready to see if I could do what I'd planned. The
box I'd stood on was back to being flat on the floor
from my launching kick, which meant it ought to be
well enough out of the way as far as being a telltale
clue went. As I swung and watched the fighters draw-

ing nearer, I began unwrapping the chain from around my waist.

For the most part Seren was leading the monstrosity toward me, one step forward in attack and three steps backward in retreat doing the job of leading. Hanging by my knees from the chandelier put me only two or three feet above the creature's head, but I noticed with a good deal of relief that the thing seemed totally unaware of anyone but Seren. It was bleeding from so many places I found it incredible that it still lived and moved, but the snarling hatred it showed was most likely what kept it going. The small thing holding the bright object was what had hurt it, and it seemed determined to end its enemy's life before it let itself die.

I made a loop in the center of the chain and hung as still as possible while I held it, waiting and trying to quiet as much as I could of the chandelier's swing. If the fixture had been anchored at only one place the swing and tilt of it would have been extreme, but luck had been with me in that the chandelier was set into the shadow-lost ceiling at six points instead, three from the outer circle and three from the inner. From the feel of it the candleholder was heavy, a piece of good luck if I'd ever seen one. If it had been flimsy instead, my hanging on it like that would have surely pulled it out of the ceiling.

I'd been in a hurry to get up to my ambush point, but it seemed to take forever before the two fighters were under me. My heart nearly stopped when Seren's foot hit the box while he was backing, making me think he was going to trip and fall, but then he kicked it out of his way without missing a step and everything was all right again. He backed and drew the monster forward, one step, then another, and then the endless waiting was over. It was directly below me where I could drop the loop of chain over its head to land around its neck, and then I drew the ends up and back with all my strength.

If I'd ever wondered what it would be like to put a rope on a wild animal, that was when I got my answer. The creature roared out its fury and tried to pull free, but it pulled from side to side instead of down, as though it didn't know from which direction it was being attacked. I held on through the initial explosion, not knowing how long I'd be able to do it, and then the creature finally looked up. When it saw me its light, mad eyes went absolutely feral, it screamed again in a greater rage than before, and lifted those terrifyingly long arms toward me. It would have no trouble reaching me, neither with its hands *nor* its talons, and when it pulled the chain out of my frantic grip I echoed its scream and closed my eyes as tight as I could. It was so close I could smell its foulness like a miasma of doom, and I hung there waiting to be clawed to the bone or pulled down and eaten. Through my own scream and its snarling I thought I heard a song of exultation, and then—

And then there was a sound like an axe into a tree, a bat against a hanging rug, a cleaver into meat. The monstrosity's snarls went suddenly choked, as though the chain I'd put around its neck had finally cut off its air, and rather than being touched I heard two or three shuffling steps, as though the thing were leaving rather than staying to attack. The steps ended in a terrible clatter, a sound I'd been longing to hear since that insanity first began, and I opened my eyes to see Seren standing over a creature that had been nearly cut in half. The sword in his hand pulsed with victory, but its glow was diminished by smears of gore, and he himself diminished by near exhaustion. His chest heaved as he pulled in acres of air, and then his eyes raised to me where I hung.

"What in hell are you doing up *there?*" he asked with the beginnings of a grin, starting to walk toward me. "Are you trying to kill yourself?"

I opened my mouth to join him in the teasing, but upside down grins aren't as infectious as the regular sort, and even upside down I could see that his arm was still bleeding. I put my hands over my mouth to keep a moaning sob from escaping, and all at once I couldn't stand hanging there any longer. I arched up to grip the chandelier with my hands and unhooked my knees, but before I could drop to the floor I felt two arms closing around my legs. I braced against those arms and shifted my hands to the shoulders below me, and then Seren was sliding me to the floor but not letting me go.

"It's all right, it's all over now," he murmured as I clung to him, the trembling finally taking over completely. "Thanks to you it's dead, and now we can get out of here."

I came out of it enough to notice that his multi-sword was gone again, and then he was leading me around the monstrosity's unmoving body toward the ruined doors of the room. I held him around with both arms as we walked, but only his right arm curved around me. The left hung at his side in its torn and bloody sleeve, and it was all I could do to keep from babbling out an apology. My mind seemed to have been waiting for the fight to be over, and once it was I'd been treated to the clearest thinking I'd managed yet.

The monstrosity hadn't been part of the game, it had really meant to kill me. Things like that creature didn't turn up by accident, so that meant its presence was deliberate. Seren had been hurt fighting it, which meant his pain was my fault.

Somehow, some way, I'd made a mistake, and the Mists people knew what I was there for.

Chapter 14

When we got outside the supposedly old and haunted mansion, there was a man in costume sitting on the ground and smoking. He put the puffer out and got to his feet as soon as he heard us, turned to give us a hearty greeting, and saw Seren's arm. No one who worked in the Mists had anything like a tan, but the man's face still paled enough to be noticeable and he hurried forward, stuttering out questions about the "accident." He also seemed to think I was supporting Seren instead of it being the other way around; when he offered himself in place of me, Seren waved him away with a faint smile, saying he'd rather lean on a woman than a man any day. The Mists worker didn't find the comment any more amusing than I did, but still didn't argue. Instead he began leading us into the fog, obviously anxious to get us back to people and help as soon as possible.

When we were back among the tents I asked him to take us to where the rest of our party was, and he didn't hesitate even a moment. He was determined to take us wherever we wanted to go and then get the "accident" reported, and in that he lucked out. We were approaching a large tent that seemed to be violet and black in color, when Velix materialized out of the fog to our right.

"Ah, lord Serendel and lady Dalisse," he purred, swishing his tail as he came closer. "Back so soon? Didn't any of the second floor rooms suit you? I hadn't thought—"

We never did find out what the Griddenth hadn't

thought. His words ended abruptly as he finally took a good look at us, and then the man who had led us there began unburdening himself.

"Sir, there's been an accident of some sort," he blurted, just as though Velix hadn't already seen the blood himself. "If you'll take over here, I'll go and get one of the doctors."

"Stop wasting time talking, and do it," the Grid-denth snapped, moving even nearer to study the wounded arm. "How did this happen, lord Serendel? What kind of accident could have caused something like that?"

"No kind of accident," Seren answered flatly, speaking freely now that the worker had run off into the fog. "What in hell is going on here, Velix? If I hadn't been the one with Dalisse, she would probably be dead now. There was a—thing—in place of the play monster I was supposed to rescue her from, and it almost got the two of us. If this is the Mists' idea of a good time, I'd like to file a dissenting opinion."

"I've never heard of anything like it," the Grid-denth answered, incapable of looking pale but not of sounding shaken. "I'll report the incident at once, of course, and then we'll be able to get to the bottom of it. Everything will be settled to your complete satisfaction, and if it turns out to be in any way our fault, reparations will be full and unstinting. Why don't I show you to your own pavilion now, and you can lie down until the doctor gets here."

"We'd rather be with other people," I interrupted to say, uncertain as to how far Velix could be trusted. "And since Chal is supposed to know something about medicine, we're going to let *him* take care of Seren. If we need one of your doctors, we'll let you know. If you don't hear from us, don't send one."

Velix opened his mouth, probably to argue, then his bright, dark eyes looked at me again. His wings were moving in agitation and so was his tail, and finally he shook his head.

"I can understand your suspicion right now, and don't quite blame you," he said, the talons on his right front leg crunching into the ground. "If I were to come to the belief I'd been attacked, I would feel the same. It's up to us to prove no such thing happened, which we'll do with all possible speed. Until then, I ask only one thing of you: if lord Chal finds the wounds beyond his ability to deal with, please send for one of our doctors at once. Lord Serendel has no need of being in further jeopardy.''

He waited until I'd nodded to show my agreement with his condition, and then he turned and trotted away into the fog. At that point Seren and I were free to continue on into the tent, and that was when I noticed I was being leaned on more than I was being helped along. Moving through the svalk entrance curtains brought us into a small, empty room of violet svalk, and the sudden extra weight on my shoulder combined with the emptiness to bring me close to panic.

"Chal! Lidra!" I called in desperation, looking up to see how ashen the fighter had grown. "Where are you? Hurry, I need you fast!"

Seren was trying to force himself to stand straight again when one of the curtains parted to allow the arrival of my two co-workers, and Chal took no more than a single glance before moving past Lidra in a rush to get over to us.

"What happened?" he demanded even as he took Seren's weight from me, nothing left of his easygoing manner. "Never mind, I'll find out about that later. Right now I've got to see to that arm."

He began helping Seren toward the curtain he'd come in by, and even before they'd gone, Lidra was over next to me with an arm around my shoulders. Once the svalk had fallen closed behind the two men, the blond woman urged me toward another curtain on the left. We moved through it to find a room filled with soft lighting, violet cushions on light brown plush, and small tables holding various items. Lidra sat me down on the floor next to one of the tables, took a decanter of wine from it and filled a goblet, then handed the goblet to me. She walked away while I sat there simply holding the thing, and when she came back she had her copper bowl with its blue flame.

"All right, what happened?" she asked as she settled on the floor near me, her voice as businesslike as Chal's had been. "Before you answer, take a good swallow of that wine. You look like you're in shock."

"I *am* in shock, and wine won't do anything to help," I answered, not even up to taking a deep breath. "They tried to kill me, Lidra, and that means they know about me. I think I should have gone to my own tent to keep from involving you and Chal, but Seren was hurt and I didn't want to give them another chance at him while he was weak, and—oh, Lidra, he could have died, and it would have been all my fault!"

I put the goblet aside to bury my face in my hands, and the next moment Lidra was there, holding me to her. She spent a minute soothing the tears she knew were on the inside, and then she patted my shoulder.

"Never mind about involving Chal and me, you were right to come here," she said, sounding absolutely certain. "If they do know about you we're already under suspicion, and with these people being suspicious seems to mean they act. Just relax now, and tell me exactly what happened."

I let her coax me into telling her all about it, and by the time I was through I was feeling a little better. I still hated myself for getting Seren involved, but at least I was somewhat beyond the breast-beating stage.

". . . so the thing couldn't possibly have gotten there by mistake," I finished up, sipping again at the wine that I really did need. "I don't know where or how I could have slipped, but it's fairly obvious I did. And I don't understand how they could be so open about it. Did they expect to be able to write our deaths off as an accident?"

"Maybe they intended writing off two disappearances," she said with a shrug, part of her attention on the blue flame in the bowl near us. "Now that they have a dead monster instead, it'll probably turn out the thing escaped into the Mists from a zoological institute or something, and Serendel is in line for a reward for stopping it. Why didn't they mention it sooner? Why, to keep people from panicking, of course. I wonder what would have happened if Chal

and I had gone out fun-seeking the way you and Serendel did.''

''They might have had four disappearances to write
off,'' I said, and then looked at her curiously. ''Now
that you mention it, why *didn't* you and Chal end up
in that mansion? I was on my way there so fast I didn't
even get to ask to use a ladies' room. From what my
escorts said, I had the impression you were supposed
to be kidnapped at the same time I was.''

''That's probably the way they planned it,'' she said
with a nod, and then she grinned. ''Fortunately for our
two-thirds of the team, I planned differently. I really
will have to remember to thank someone for this costume. If not for that, I'm sure I would have been right
there with you.''

I looked at her when she mentioned her costume,
and for the first time noticed that she was still wearing
her cloak. That was when I remembered all that equipment she carried, and I began to understand.

''You've got it,'' she said, apparently seeing the
answer in my expression. ''You may look good enough
to eat in that thing, but anyone trying to take a bite
out of me would probably be electrocuted. I couldn't
afford to wear that gown, not when I knew damned
well they'd be taking the cloak, but I also couldn't
afford to refuse. I compromised by putting a bodysuit
on underneath as a just in case, then arranged to be
horribly ill from that coach ride. I was almost in a faint
even before I left the coach, so naturally we were
shown immediately to our pavilion.''

''I knew there was a benefit in being the fainting
kind of heroine,'' I said with a sigh. ''It's too bad I
didn't try it myself right from the start. What are we
going to do now?''

''We're going to wait until Chal takes care of Serendel, and then the four of us are going to eat a very
careful dinner,'' she said, reaching over to pour a goblet of wine for herself. ''After that we'll put Serendel
to bed, pretend to do the same with ourselves, but in
reality we'll be waiting until everyone thinks we're
asleep. Once that happens we'll sneak out of this tent,
avoid any watchers or guards, and go find that infor-

mation we're after. It so happens we're almost on top of their headquarters building, which means the wait is over. As soon as we have what we need, we'll call down those Empire troops to help us avoid any more 'accidents.' "

"I think I like the sound of that," I said, nodding at her easy smile. "I'd like it better if we were calling down the troops *before* we went in, but I suppose you can't have everything. And once it's all over, Seren won't be in any more danger."

"At least until he goes back to the arena," she said, sipping at her wine as annoyance flared in her eyes. "I can't get over the nerve and stupidity of those people, thinking a fighter of Serendel's caliber could be brushed aside while they did anything they pleased to you. It's a good thing for them he wasn't hurt all that badly, or they'd have *me* to deal with once our job was done. It isn't every man I'd consider sharing a bed with for more than fooling around, and if they'd harmed the one I lust after most right now, I would have made sure they heartily regretted it."

"Lidra, I don't understand you!" I said with all the exasperation I was feeling, too drained to be at all diplomatic. "One minute you're panting after Seren, the next Chal tells me you're in a panic at the thought of catching him, and now you're saying you want him again. Aren't you ever going to make up your mind?"

"But Inky, I *have* made up my mind," she said with a laugh, apparently in no way reluctant to discuss the point. "If I could, I'd attack Serendel, knock him down, then ravage him unmercifully, but it so happens I can't and not because of his size. There are more important considerations, one of which is the word I used to describe my feelings for him. He's a great fighter and a really nice person, but all I feel for him is lust."

"You're under the impression you've explained something?" I said, still staring at her. "What difference does the word you're using make? Words have only a very little to do with how you feel and what you do."

"That only goes for certain words," she said comfortably, sipping again at her wine. " 'Lust' is the word you use for someone who attracts you physically, which is what I feel for Serendel. The word to describe what I feel for Chal, though, is love.''

This time, words of all sort were missing from my stare, and she laughed in amusement.

"I can see he must have told you his theory about how reluctant I am to admit to that feeling,'' she said, almost smiling to herself. "I've been regretting the need to continue letting him believe that, but we aren't on our own time here. Once the job is over we can talk about anything we like, and the first thing *I'll* be talking about is the fact that it isn't men in general I've learned to distrust and not commit myself to— only the men I work with.''

I suppose I must have started getting it then; as she looked at me she nodded with another smile.

"I see you're remembering the incident I told you about, the one where my so-called partner ran out on me,'' she said. "That wasn't the first time it happened, and it wasn't the worst story I could have told. They usually look for specific talents to send along on these things, paying no attention at all to the personalities behind the talent. I kept Chal at arm's length at first because I didn't know him and wasn't about to get stuck the way I had in the past. I think I was a little shocked at how easy it was to *get* to know him, but at the same time I was impressed. He's nothing short of brilliant as well as physically attractive, and I've been looking around for an acceptable father for my children for quite some time. At first, that was the only real interest I had in him.''

"From what you just said, it looks like that changed,'' I put in. "I'd also like to know why whatever happened turned you so on again-off again about Seren.''

"Inky, try to understand that *I'm* not the one whose feelings have changed,'' she said, the words gentle and patient. "It wasn't until Chal offered to swap himself for Serendel that I understood what he was really doing and feeling, and at first I wasn't sure I liked it. Chal was giving me a chance to have the man of my hottest dreams—but only if I gave him up for it. I discovered right then I'd take Serendel under any condition but that particular one, and that Chal was more important to me than any casual fling. He may not realize it, but what he was doing was feeling jealous enough to demand I choose between him and Serendel. The demand was gentle in accordance with his basic nature, but it was still there. It bothered me when I spoke to him in his room in our first lodging in the Mists, but it didn't take long before I had the matter resolved. I never expected to find a man to father my children and someone I could live with both in the same body, but now that I have I'm not about to let him get away.''

"I think Chal will be very glad to hear that," I said with a grin of my own, really pleased that things would work out right between them. "Now all we have to do is live long enough to get out of this place, preferably with what we came for. And since Seren won't be really safe until it's over, I wish we could leave right now. This isn't in any way his job; it isn't fair for him to get hurt because of it.''

"You two have really and finally started doing it right," she said, a bright twinkle in her eyes. "I wonder if—"

She broke off and immediately reached for her copper bowl, startling me a little, but then I heard what she probably had, the sound of someone approaching the hanging into the room, and understood. I suppose I was expecting Chal or one of the Mists people, but when the svalk was moved aside, it was Seren I saw coming in. I had the goblet down and was on my feet so fast I couldn't remember doing any of it, and then I was standing in front of him.

"Are you all right?" I asked, not very evenly, looking at his bandage-covered arm. "Seren, I'm so sorry . . .''

"For what?" he asked with his usual grin, reaching out to put his arms around me. "Saving both our lives? I don't know how you got up where you did, but I've never been so glad to see an upside-down woman in my life. If you hadn't distracted that thing, I might not have been able to get past those arms before it cornered me. And I thought *I* was fast. Was it able to hurt you before I cut it down?''

''It didn't have the time,'' I reassured the worry in his eyes, putting my hands against his chest. ''You look better than you did, but are you *sure* you're all right?''

''The only thing bothering me right now is the fact that I didn't meet Chal years ago,'' he said, his grin back and widened. ''No more bleeding, no more pain, no more exhaustion—I'm just afraid he may be into black magic.''

''Where I come from it's called medicine, not magic,'' Chal put in with a chuckle, showing he'd come into the room behind Seren even though I hadn't seen him. ''I know you're feeling better, Serendel, but you can add 'no more fighting' to your list, at least until you've had a chance to rest. You may be in marvelous physical condition, but there's no sense in overdoing it.''

''He isn't seriously hurt, then?'' Lidra asked from behind me, while I laughed softly at the terribly-suffering expression Seren had put on where Chal couldn't see it. Being mothered is worse when it comes from a fussy doctor; members of the medical tribe don't believe in taking chances—which is probably a damned good thing for those of us who can't be bothered with worrying about it.

''No, despite the way his arm was laid open, and despite a number of bumps and bruises, he isn't seriously hurt,'' Chal answered Lidra as he walked over to her. ''But how is Inky? Does she need to be looked at?''

''Only by the one who's already looking at her,'' Lidra said with a chuckle, a rustle accompanying the words as though she took Chal's arm. ''Since you and I have things to talk about, why don't we shift over to your part of the pavilion? I seriously doubt that Inky and Serendel are interested in talking, at least not with us. Or were you planning on sticking around to watch, just to make sure he doesn't overdo it?''

''I think Inky can be trusted not to be too rough with

him,'' Chal came back with a laugh that was a little on the embarrassed side. ''Let's go get to all those things we have to talk about.''

I heard them moving around us to leave the room, but I couldn't seem to look away from the gray eyes gazing down at me. Seren was smiling faintly as his hand stroked my hair, and once Lidra and Chal were gone he shook his head a little.

''No doubt about it,'' he said very softly, his left arm tightening around me. ''I've just had the best win of my career. You do know the way it's supposed to go, don't you?''

''The way what's supposed to go?'' I asked, beginning to feel confused. ''I don't . . .''

''The way the rescue business goes,'' he interrupted, amusement dancing in his eyes. ''When a fair damsel is rescued from a terrible monster, the hero who rescues her is entitled to her hand. I had the feeling you didn't know that, so I wanted to be very sure you got it straight. Do you understand now?''

I had no words to answer that with, all I could do was put my hand up and touch his face. I'd very recently had to admit to myself that I loved him so much I was willing to be anything he wanted me to be. I could see right then that he knew that, and had therefore been very careful to state just exactly what he did want. He could have asked for anything, and yet he'd chosen to ask for—

''Oh, Seren,'' I whispered, feeling tears of happiness rolling down my cheeks. ''Are you sure?''

''Positive,'' he answered with that wonderful smile, one finger coming to wipe away the tears. ''Now, about that *other* reward I was supposed to get for rescuing you . . .''

I had only a moment to laugh before he leaned down to kiss me, and after that there was nothing to laugh at, only marvelous things to enjoy.

Seren's lovemaking always robbed me of awareness as far as the passage of time went, so it was something of a surprise when I heard loud, deliberate, throat-clearing sounds outside the hanging leading to the rest of the tent. Seren stopped kissing me, and turned his head over his shoulder without letting me go.

"She abused me terribly, Chal," he said, apparently having recognized the identity of the throat-clearer. "She sneered at my honorable, weakening wounds, then had her will with me. Everything you did for me is now undone."

"Seren!" I protested with a push against his chest, feeling my cheeks getting warm. He was grinning at how awful he'd made me sound, but I was still the one who was being held down by a beast of a fighter who didn't want to hear anything about taking it easy. I'd made the mistake a few minutes earlier of suggesting he might not be strong enough to go again, and had gotten taken prisoner for it.

"Oh, you poor thing," Lidra's voice came, her laughter mixing with Chal's. "We were going to invite you two to join us for a meal, but now it looks like only Inky will be able to eat it. What do you think we ought to get for him, Chal? Wouldn't broth be easier for him to digest than that beautiful roast with all the trimmings? And we'll have to find someone to give his portion to. . . ."

"Hold onto that food!" Seren called as I laughed, finally letting me go. "I just had a sudden unlapse, which may or may not be the opposite of relapse, but I'm too hungry to care. My lady and I will be with you as soon as we can throw some clothes on."

He stood and then reached down to pull me to my feet, pausing in the middle of his rush to fold me in his arms and give me a lovely kiss that was a promise of more to come later. As he turned away to find his clothes, I couldn't help feeling very strange. "My lady," he'd said, *his* lady, he'd meant, something I never thought I'd love hearing. Being his lady was the most wonderful thing that had ever happened to me, and I'd never find fault with the word again.

Seren had more to get into than I did, so I waited until he was ready and then we went looking for Lidra and Chal together. I had put that see-through gown back on only because Seren liked it—and because it was sure to make our eventual dessert even sweeter.

I'd always been a lover of desserts, but Seren's brand was my absolute favorite.

"Come on over and dig in, you two," Lidra called when we entered the predominantly brown room that was ostensibly Chal's, she and the third of our team already seated on the plush carpeting near what looked like a giant picnic spread. "This food is so good, I'll need all the help I can get not to eat every crumb myself."

"And food isn't the only thing we ordered," Chal said as I sat down next to him on his left, his hand pointing with none of the carelessness his words held. "Right over there are your personal things, fetched from the pavilion that was supposed to be yours. As soon as we're sure Serendel's wounds won't be developing complications, you and your luggage can move back where you belong."

Seren was too busy looking over the food to even glance at the corner of the room where our things lay, but Chal seemed very determined that *I* take a peek. I turned a little in a hopefully casual way, saw my bag and Seren's larger amount of possessions—then spotted what Chal had wanted me to see. Lidra's copper bowl stood very near my luggage, almost hidden by it, in fact, and the flame that wasn't a flame had been ignited.

The only problem was, the flame was orange rather than blue.

"You'd better hurry up and start filling a plate, Inky," Lidra said as I turned back away from the device that said our conversation was being electronically eavesdropped on. "If you don't get a move on, Serendel will have it all down his throat before you even get a look. I'd say taste instead of look, but tasting it will be even more unlikely."

"But I have to regain my strength, don't I?" Seren protested plaintively without slowing down on piling up his plate. "And this little girl next to me may not look it, but she's absolutely insatiable. That's another reason why I need my six thousand calories."

"Seren!" I said the way I had earlier, the warmth in my cheeks increasing with Chal's grin, and then I finally registered what else had been said, "Six *thousand* calories? You intend eating enough for a week or more?"

"Six thousand calories is what I eat a *day*," he answered, glancing up to flash me a grin. "Why do you think fighters make so much money, but usually end up with so little left over? Those grocery bills are murder."

We all laughed at that one, then went on to eating and talking and generally enjoying the time. I forced myself to forget that we were being listened to and simply went along with the joking; after all, when you stop to think about it, there wasn't much else I could do.

The meal wound down to a friendly close, and Seren and I went back to the room that was Lidra's. The first thing the fighter did was sweep me into his arms and kiss me, and then he looked down at me quizzically.

"Why didn't you tell Chal and Lidra we're no longer just good friends?" he asked, faint disturbance behind the question. "I waited the entire meal for you to make the grand announcement, but you never did."

"I've decided I can't afford to keep you," I answered as I leaned against him, not about to explain how I'd be damned if I said anything that important with enemies listening. "Six thousand calories a *day!* I'd be broke in no time!"

"It'll be tough, but I think I can come up with enough to keep us fed," he said with a grin, then let the humor fade. "Are you sure you haven't changed your mind?"

"Positive," I said, putting my arms as far around him as they would go. "And I'm waiting for a really special time to make the announcement, like when we're finally out of this fog. Besides, you don't want to ruin the rest of Lidra's vacation, do you?"

"Certainly not," he agreed, and this time the grin stayed with him. "And there's something else to consider. If she finds out now I won't be single much longer, she might make up her mind to take advantage of her last chance and attack me. Normally I might not mind with a woman like Lidra, but somehow I have the feeling she's stronger than I am. You'll protect me from her, won't you?''

"Oh, you poor thing, of course I will," I said with a laugh, wondering how I ever enjoyed life without him. "Don't you be afraid, Inky's here to take care of everything."

"That's Smudge, not Inky," he murmured, lowering his head to kiss me. "Never saw a woman before who couldn't remember her own name."

It took him about five more minutes, and then my name wasn't the only thing I couldn't remember.

My eyes opened fast when a hand shook me a little, but it was only Chal gesturing quiet and urging me silently to follow him. Seren was sound asleep beside me on the plush carpeting, and I certainly agreed that we didn't want to wake him. I got to my feet without making any noise and followed Chal out of the room, leaving my costume gown where it had been thrown. For what was ahead I wanted a bodysuit, which was undoubtedly why Chal and Lidra had had my clothing brought to their tent.

"Your bag's over there," Lidra whispered as soon as she saw me, gesturing to a place to her left. "Are you feeling better after your nap?"

"I'm feeling better, but not because of the nap," I answered in a matching whisper, giving her a wink as I moved toward my things. "Are you sure we're speaking low enough to keep them from picking up what we're saying?"

"I'm blanking their receiver, so if we wanted to we could shout," she came back, following me over and watching as I opened the bag. "The reason we're whispering is your roommate. It would be the least bit awkward having him wake up just now. Besides, we're all supposed to be sound asleep from what they put into our food. Showing them we're not might ruin their good mood."

"What do you mean, what they put into our food?" I demanded in a hiss, holding the suit I'd pulled out of the bag. "If I was drugged, why don't I feel anything?"

"Mainly because you weren't drugged," she said, gesturing at me to hurry up and get dressed. "Chal tested every dish they sent us, found the drug, and gave us all neutralizers in our first glasses of wine. We considered skipping the neutralizer with Serendel, but we didn't want to leave him helpless, so instead we whisper. Hurry it up, will you? I have all the watchers spotted, and a clear path out of here already plotted. I don't want to have to do it a second time."

She walked away from me to pick up a small oblong something that looked like a makeup case and opened it, but somehow I had the feeling it wasn't a makeup case. Since she and Chal were already dressed in dark bodysuits, I hurried up and got into mine, then began assembling my kit from the pieces scattered all over my bag.

I don't think it took more than ten minutes before I was ready, and I joined my teammates by a brand-new, knife-made door in time to see Chal finish up a quick check of his own kit. I didn't know what he had packed to take along, but I doubted that that was the first time he'd checked it. Lidra looked at me, nodded in answer to my own nod, and then—

"Did somebody really throw a party without inviting *me?*" a voice asked from behind us, one of the last voices we'd hoped to hear. "Now my feelings are hurt, and I just may cry."

"I *knew* we should have skipped his dose of neutralizer," Lidra growled under her breath, then turned with Chal and me to look at Seren. "Why, look, guys, he's awake after all, but I'll bet he's still tired. We're just going out for a short stroll before calling it a night, Serendel, which means we'll be back in no time at all. Why don't you see to setting out nightcaps while we're gone, and by then we'll be here to drink them."

"So all you're doing is going for a short stroll," Seren said, folding his arms across a still-bare chest. All he'd put on was his hose, which also left him barefooted. "A late-night stroll through fog so thick that it doesn't even let you know it *is* night, and all of you dressed in dark bodysuits. I don't think there's anyone

I know who doesn't stroll at night in the fog in a dark bodysuit.''

"You've had a long, painful day, Serendel," Chal said, his voice professionally smooth and soothing. "When we're overtired, we sometimes start imagining things, and that's the time we're best off going back to bed and sleeping it off. By the time you wake up, you'll be ready to laugh at all this."

"I think I'm ready to laugh now," Seren said, those gray eyes totally uncompromising, and then he shrugged. "But I do have to remember you're the doctor, don't I? Okay, I'll take your advice and go back to what I'm using for a bed. Come on, Smudge. I need you more to help me fall asleep than they need your company on a stroll."

He put a hand out toward me where I stood between Lidra and Chal, but all I could do was stare at him. We didn't have the *time* for me to coax him back asleep, not when we didn't know when our enemies would be by to check on how well their drug had worked. We had to get what we were after and then call in the troops, and only at that point would we be able to put our feet up and relax.

"Seren, *please* go back to the room," I said at last, giving up on the wasted effort of trying to fool him. "There's something we have to do, and then we can tell you all about it. And once we're through, you can bet there won't be any more 'accidents.' "

"But no guarantees about it beforehand, especially for you," he said in a growl, those eyes now on *me*. "If you think I'm letting you just walk out of here into who-knows-what, you're the one who needs lots of rest. I want to know what you three are up to, and I want to know *now*."

"What's your authority for making that demand?" Lidra said calmly while Chal and I exchanged glances over the flat finality in Seren's voice. "Considering the fact that we're associates of Stellar Intelligence, your credentials would have to be awfully impressive to justify asking us anything at all. I think you'd better just go back to your room and . . ."

"Stellar Intelligence!" Seren interrupted with sudden excitement. "I *knew* there was something going on in this place! Tell me why you're here."

"You have a very bad case of selective deafness," Lidra answered with a frown, nothing left in her manner of the adoring fan. "I've *already* told you we don't have to answer . . ."

"You don't have to give away the information for nothing," Seren said, interrupting again but back to showing calm. "I'll tell you first why *I'm* here, and then you can return the favor. Is it a deal?"

"I don't know," Lidra said at once, but now she was looking interested rather than impatient. "If what you say is relevant to the reason we're here, it may be to our benefit to join forces. If not, you go back to your room and sit there quietly until you're told you can come out. How does *that* deal grab you?"

"In the same way and place that thing in the mansion tried for," Seren answered dryly, clearly a good deal less than pleased. "And I'm beginning to understand how Velix felt about you when we first got here. You're not giving me any choice at all, but I don't think your backers would appreciate it if I argued. All right, me first and then *maybe* you. Why don't we sit down, just in case you happen to get the urge to add something once I'm through."

He began folding to the floor without waiting for agreement, and after a very brief hesitation Lidra followed suit. I could see she was probably thinking what I was, that Seren might *need* to sit down after all that blood he'd lost, and it shouldn't hurt anything. Since we were going to listen anyway, we might as well do it in comfort. Chal and I chose our own pieces of floor carpet while I wished I could sit over near Seren instead, and once we were all settled the fighter immediately started in.

"About a month ago, I got a frantic call from my mother," he began, looking from one to the other of us but mostly toward Lidra. "She hadn't wanted to bother me, but something seemed to have happened to my older brother. Jalry had always been the hard-working, industrious sort who never bought something just for the hell of it, and always paid his bills early.

He also kept in touch with the family on a regular basis, not because he had to but because he was a full, loving member of it. My mother told me he had gone on vacation with some friends, and not only had he been late getting back, weeks had passed without her hearing a word from him. When she tried calling him instead, he laughed off her worry but turned down a weekend invitation to dinner. He was too busy, he told her, and after that cut the call short."

"Let me guess where he vacationed," Lidra said, glancing past me to Chal, who was suddenly looking very attentive.

"Of course it was here," Seren said, in some way expecting the comment and showing heavy satisfaction with it. "As soon as I got free I went to visit my brother, and I could't believe the change in him. He wasn't working hard anymore; he was hardly working, and his few quiet, carefully-chosen friends had become an army of loud-mouthed, lazy-looking office louts. There had to be over a thousand people working in the building where his office was, and half of them must have dropped by in the short time I was there—including the man who owned the company Jalry works for. When they saw he had a visitor they apologized for interrupting—all of them *including* his boss—and said they'd come back at another time. What really got me was Jalry's insisting there was nothing wrong or different about him, and the fact that he was *annoyed* over his visitors' having to leave. Before then he had always been delighted when I was able to steal the time for a visit with him. 'My infamous kid brother' was what he called me, and he usually said it with all the pride in the universe. When I tried pressing for some answers, he turned ugly and told me to go back to hacking people apart instead of bothering my elders, and then he asked me to leave."

Seren was looking drawn and hurt, but all I could do was put my hands over my face to keep from having to see it. I'd heard Chal's sigh, showing he understood what the problem was as well as I did, but he'd have to be the one to tell Seren. I was faintly surprised he didn't already know, but when you live the clean, straight life yourself, you sometimes miss the signals whispering from a shadow source.

"So you came here to find out what happened to change him like that," Lidra summed up, and I couldn't tell from her neutral tone whether or not she understood. "Do you think what you've found so far could account for it?"

"Not in any age this place offers," Seren answered with a snort, now sounding coldly angry. "My brother has never been late going to or getting back from anything in his life, at least not until he came here. I know they did something to change him to what he is now, and I'm going to find it with or without your help."

"The only thing charging around will get you is killed," Chal said, weariness creeping through his attempt at soothing. "Your information has forced me to certain tentative conclusions I don't like at all, but I'm afraid I won't be given any more choice in the matter than you were. Lidra, I think we'd better let him join us, especially now. We may very well end up needing more protection than we can provide for ourselves, and if they've linked up Serendel's name with his brother's, he may have to face their attentions alone. If he comes with us, we can mutually share the burden of protection."

"They shouldn't have linked me up with my brother," Seren put in before Lidra could say anything. "He came here using our family name, Etree, and glads never use a family name. That's why I was so surprised over that attack. They shouldn't have known why I was here, but it sure as hell looked like they did. But let's discuss those conclusions you've drawn, Chal. I haven't been able to come up with a thing."

"They might not have had any trouble at all linking you up with your brother," Lidra said, taking her turn at interrupting while I uncovered my eyes to see how thoughtful she'd grown. "Assuming they did something to your brother—not a hard assumption to swallow—they ought to have him on a list somewhere, along with the names of others they did something to. If it were me, I'd run an automatic check on everyone making a reservation here, looking for a tie-in to a name on my list. *I* knew what your family name was, from old publicity releases when you first started winning. How hard would it have been for *them* to get the information, most especially if they're as thorough as they seem to be?''

"About as hard as checking arena stats," Seren answered with a lot of self-disgust and a headshake of annoyance. "And I never even thought of it. I can see now how effective a secret agent I make. I float happily along in blithe ignorance, and almost get Smudge killed right along with me. If they gave out crowns for super intelligence, I'd deserve at least five or six.''

"We're still not sure *whose* fault that attack was," I said before anyone else could jump in, hating the way he was blaming only himself. "You may remember my trying to apologize to you afterward, even though I couldn't tell you why. We're here to check out a number of reports, ones like the story you just told us, and others that seem to be connected. It's more than possible *I* did something that got them suspicious, and it was me they were trying to get rid of. That would mean it wasn't your fault at all, and you were no more than an innocent bystander.''

"Or they could have combined separate suspicions and decided to take you both out just to be on the safe side," Lidra said while Seren gave me a look of gratitude that made me feel warm inside. "Sitting here speculating in order to find out where the blame belongs is a waste of time we don't have. We've got to make our next move before they make theirs, so we'd better get with it. If you're coming with us, Serendel, you'd better let Chal lend you one of his bodysuits.''

"There's one last thing we have to talk about first," Chal said as Seren nodded and began getting to his feet. "I usually keep my theories to myself until they become fact, but this time I don't think I can afford to do that. The extra time spent in the Mists by Serendel's brother and the other people we have reports on, the so-called time anomaly found here, the lack of complete bodies for those who died here, the radical character change Serendel described—we're going to have to be very careful about walking into traps we may not be able to get out of again.''

"You're not talking about any ordinary traps, are you?'' Lidra said while Seren settled back down, her voice not quite as steady as it had been. "What do you think it is we have to be on the lookout for?''

"Serendel, I'm sorry, but it looks like your brother's been addicted to a controlled substance of some sort,'' Chal said with pity in his voice, not ignoring Lidra but trying to get the bad news out and said as fast as possible. "I also had the feeling Inky recognized the symptoms as soon as I did.''

"He's right,'' I told the stunned, disbelieving look in Seren's eyes, hurting for his hurt but also trying to save him the pain that would come from a refusal to accept the truth. "Seren, Chal is telling you he's hooked, but you're the one who told *us* he's also dealing. All those people who came to see him, the ones who didn't stay while you were there? They were buyers, my love, customers who couldn't conduct business in front of witnesses. I'd say your brother's boss is one of those customers, and is fronting for him by letting him deal out of his office. That's why he doesn't have to do any regular work in order to keep from getting fired.''

"It can't be true!'' Seren whispered harshly, one hand closed tight in his hair, his face wearing a look of agony. "Jalry always hated the idea of drugs! I could believe him capable of the coldblooded murder of a child as easily as the thought of him being on something. And selling? Even if he somehow got hooked himself, there's no way he would ever take others down with him! He'd consider it *his* problem to solve *alone*, and would turn himself in for treatment. See, that's why you have to be wrong! If someone had forced him into addiction, he would have turned himself in to get off it!''

His suddenly hopeful, grasping-at-straws expression was like a knife inside me, and I simply couldn't stay where I was any longer. I rose and moved over to sit beside him, but before I could take him around he grasped me to him, as though I were a life-preserver he needed to keep from drowning. I spread my arms out as far as possible to give what support I could, knowing he wasn't about to get the agreement he was looking for.

"From what you said of your brother earlier, I'd expect him to do nothing *but* turn himself in," Chal told him, gently but nevertheless relentlessly. "The double fact that not only hasn't he done so but is also selling to others—*that's* what scares me the most. Every drug affects a user's personality, but one that changes the personality so completely and radically— there's never been anything like it on any planet in the Empire. Some drugs force their users to change life-time habits because the drug use just doesn't fit in with those habits, but that's just a matter of putting the use ahead of all other considerations. If your brother had tried to *hide* his addiction, I could understand and ac-cept it as a normal reaction. Taking the drug himself and selling it to others almost openly is nothing like normal."

"Not to mention the fact that large-scale dealers are never users themselves," I put in, beginning to be frightened by what I was hearing. "Seren, if there were that many people trying to buy from your brother, he shouldn't be hooked himself. Higher-ups in that busi-ness know better than to trust twitches in positions of responsibility, so there has to be something more in-volved. Since it has to involve what the drug does to people, I'm afraid to ask what it is."

"I'd say we already know certain facts about the drug," Chal pointed out, glancing at a Lidra who was listening intently. "For starters it takes time to estab-lish a hold in its victim, or there would hardly be so many people who were late getting back from their vacations. Even with the help of the accelerated me-tabolisms produced by this fog, those people were still late. If not for the fog they probably couldn't hook *anyone* soon enough to produce significant character changes, so the drug has to be given time to work. We also know it either doesn't work with some people, or quickly kills them. Those partial bodies returned of

those who died—no blood left to test, and only deliberately provided uncontaminated tissue samples.''

"But none of that tells us how dangerous an initial
dose is," Lidra said, finally putting in her own oar.
"For all we know a single exposure to it sets you up
for wanting more, and that's what you meant by traps.
Instead of setting off alarms or tripping deadfalls, a
mistake on our part could mean immediate exposure
to whatever it is they use. It might be a good idea if
you changed your mind about coming with us, Serendel.''

"You think staying here is a guarantee of safety?"
Seren asked with a snort, tightening his hold on me.
"If they sent that thing in to the mansion to tear me
up, what's to stop them from doing the same thing
here? And if Smudge is going to be part of anything
dangerous, *I'm* going to be right there next to her.
They may have hurt my brother, but I'm not about to
let them do the same to my lady. Where did you say
that bodysuit was?''

"This way," Chal told him, getting to his feet.
"And while you're dressing, I'll tell you what drugs
we have working on *our* team.''

Seren hugged me, then got up to follow Chal, and I
just sat there a minute before moving over to Lidra to
see what she was doing. For someone about to go much
deeper into a very dangerous situation, I felt just like
a woman without a worry in the world.

Chapter 15

Lidra had our observers respotted by the time Seren was dressed and ready, so we wasted no more time in leaving the tent. Our electronics expert had us all keep close together until we were well past the line of those who were supposed to be watching us, and then we were able to relax a little, but not too much. We still had to stay reasonably close to keep from losing each other in the fog, but aside from that our only chore was following Lidra. She followed whatever it was that her non-makeup case told her, which sent us through the swirling gray mist quickly and surely. It was eerily silent in the fog, more silent than I'd noticed sooner, a heavy hush that forced us to join with silence of our own.

We walked for fifteen or twenty minutes, and during that time I squashed the idea part of me was getting that we were going nowhere by testing the ring I'd been given back on Gryphon. I held my arm straight out ahead then squeezed my hand into a fist, and sure enough, the central "jewel" on my ring lit up to show we actually were going in the right direction. It was an interesting toy I played with for a minute, then forgot about again; Lidra had the real thing rather than a toy, and I truthfully didn't begrudge it to her. My only feeling was that I was happy I hadn't had to find my way through the fog alone, using nothing but the toy.

After the fifteen or twenty minutes Lidra stopped, but our eyes were able to give us no reason for her doing that. We still stood in the middle of nothing but fog, but Seren let my hand go when our guide turned and gestured me over.

"We're still a couple of hundred feet away from the building, but the approach to it starts just ahead," she told me when I reached her, her voice held deliberately low. "I'll bring us to the edge of the approach, but after that you'd better take over."

"Let's have a look," I said, keeping my voice as low as hers. "I have to see something before I can decide what to do about it."

She nodded and led off again, but more slowly than she'd moved before. After only a few yards she stopped again, but this time I didn't have to ask why. A neat walk of polycrete lay just before us, about five feet wide and lined on both sides with low, decorative railings, or at least the railings were supposed to be taken as decorative. I saw something else in them, and in the walk as well.

"Lidra, those railings have to be switched off," I said in an even lower voice, not moving from where I'd stopped. "At the very least they'll let everyone know we're here, and I have the feeling they do other things as well. Can you use that thing to locate a control box?"

"I can do better than that," she answered in a mutter, tapping tiny keys in the non-case. "I can override their control box, and turn the thing off. Just give me a minute."

"Set it on neutral instead of turning it off," I said at once, looking at the railings again. "Some systems have an independent circuit alarm set to scream if the system is switched off at the wrong time. Something tells me this is one of them."

I caught her distracted nod out of the corner of my eye, so I didn't say anything else. The system setup reminded me of something, but exactly what that something was insisted on remaining stuck in the back of my memory.

It took Lidra more than the minute she'd asked for, but not an unreasonable amount of time more. When she looked up to give me a nod that said it was done, I accepted the assurance despite being not very happy about it. Seero had carefully taught me to rely on no one's efforts but my own, a precaution that had become an ingrained habit. I didn't like having to take Lidra's word that the security system was neutralized, but at that time and place there was no other choice.

"All right, I want everyone to listen carefully," I said to my three companions, still keeping my voice down. "We'll be moving toward that building we still can't quite see through the fog in single file, me first and the rest of you following. You step where I do, as close as possible to the rail without touching it. Anyone who sets foot in the middle of that walk will activate a pressure alarm, and that's one that usually can't be turned off from the outside. Let's go, but let's be *careful*."

I got three nods of compliance before I turned away from them, but Seren's expression had been somewhat on the puzzled side. He didn't seem to understand what my part in all that was, which meant I'd have some explaining to do once we were out of there. I felt the least bit nervous about that, but then the nervousness went away. If Chal had been one of those who understood, Seren would certainly be.

Going up the walk beside the railing let me see how the ground dropped away to the right as it probably did to the left, beyond the approach the Mists people wanted everyone to use. I moved forward with every sense I had stretched to the limit, trying to feel what was around and ahead of us, but it wasn't until we were almost to the building that some sense of unease brought me to a stop. The railing was still turned off as far as being active goes, but it felt like there was *something*. . . .

"Lidra, are you getting any activity readings at all?" I asked, turning my head to speak softly over my shoulder. "I'm getting the impression we're about to walk into something, but I can't tell what."

"Everything's showing inert as far as my board is concerned," she answered, frowning as she tapped tiny buttons. "Are you sure it isn't just a case of nerves?"

"When I'm working, the only nerves that operate are the specialized ones," I came back, really under-

standing for the first time why they'd needed *me* on
that job, and not just Lidra and her instruments. "The
rest of you stay right here for now, and pass back the
word that I'd prefer if none of you even shifted in
place. I'll be back as soon as I find out what's been
left in our path."

I turned back away from her but didn't immediately
begin moving, and not because I was waiting for her
to pass on the information and instructions I'd given.
Moving forward at any pace at all was going to be
dangerous, and in situations like that it's best to think
before you creep. I took a moment of thinking time,
decided that creeping actually would be my best bet,
and so went down to all fours. More often than not
that turns out to be the most all-around useful position
to assume, most especially when you can't see as well
as you'd like.

I could feel the warm, dry fog swirling all around
me as I slid my hands forward through it, my fingertips
brushing the ground before I committed my weight to
my palms. Behind me everyone was standing absolutely still, withholding the distractions of speech and
movement, their thoughts alone moving with me in
support. At times like that it felt as though every nerve
ending in my body had come alive to sense what lay
around me, and it was almost as though my surround-
ings knew that and responded. The polycrete was
smooth and even, angled strangely but otherwise perfectly normal, and I moved forward three uneventful
feet, and then five—

And that's when my fingertips brushed it, the faint
rise in the approach ramp, a bump less than an inch
high but at least ten inches wide. I froze in place while
I studied it, and then I reached beyond to find the line
that was invisible to the eye but not to the touch. There
would be a second line to match the first, of course,
but not for at least three feet more, and maybe not
even for five or six. I reached into my kit for the tiny
spray can I carried, hoping the location of the second
line would be something we never discovered, and
used the faintly luminous paint inside the can to mark
both sides of the ten inch rise. Once that was done I

got to my feet again, and gestured over Lidra and the
others.

"Whatever you do, don't step *between* those
splotches of paint," I explained in a whisper, seeing
that Chal and Seren were straining to hear from their
places behind Lidra. "There's a pressure bar under
that slight rise in the polycrete, which probably stays
locked closed while the railing is in an activated state.
Deactivating the railing, even into neutral, releases the
lock on the bar and turns *its* mechanism active. It isn't
electronic so it doesn't register as active, but springs
and balances were used a lot of years before people
knew there even *was* such a thing as electronics. It's
there to be stepped on, so let's be sure not to oblige."

"What happens if someone does step on it?" Lidra
asked, looking quietly shaken. People who live in the
world of electronics are too often blind when they're
taken out of it.

"Stepping on it will cause the section of the ramp
above it to drop open, probably after a few seconds'
delay so that the victim is directly over the opening,"
I answered, deciding it was not time to be gentle or
considerate of her feelings. "The drop either takes you
down to the ground in a hurry, or into a lower level
of that building already prepared against your arrival.
I hope you're not interested in finding out which."

She shivered and shook her head, giving me a faint
smile to show she was upset but still handling it, and
then gestured me on again. I returned her smile and
gave her my back again, then paused very briefly before stepping wide over the bump. It shouldn't have
been possible to spring the trap without stepping on
the bar, but people are notorious for tinkering with
things and changing their "possibles" entirely. All I
could do was go ahead like before, hoping hard our
enemy was too lazy or unimaginative to have tampered
with the basic idea; if they hadn't been, I'd be the first
to find out about it.

Fifteen feet beyond the bump I stopped again, this
time to let everyone catch up. The trap area should
have been well behind us at that point, and I didn't
sense anything ahead. Instead what I saw was the front

entrance of the building, sitting quietly less than five feet away.

"It's code-guarded," Lidra whispered as she stopped behind me, most of her attention on her noncase. "I'll have to neutralize that before you can work on the lock, but it looks like we might be in luck. You don't code-guard a door when people are going to be using it, so maybe it *is* middle of the night right now."

"If so, there could be security patrols around," I pointed out, wanting her to forget about that middle-of-the-night idea. Honest people consider the middle of the night the best time to do something dishonest, a time when no one will be around to see them do it. Once you get that idea in your head you unconsciously tend to relax, and relaxation is less than half a step from sloppiness. We couldn't *afford* to be sloppy in that place, not if we wanted to get out of it again alive.

"Security patrols, right," Lidra said in a faint voice, taking an instant to glance at me before going back to what she was doing. I knew she was shaken again, and was as glad to see that as the fact of her still being able to handle it. If she was afraid, she would be that much more careful, and that was exactly what I wanted.

While Lidra worked on the code-guard, I spent my time looking around, so when I got her whispered go-ahead I opened my kit and went straight for my next job. I wouldn't have been surprised to find another drop-trap right in front of the doors, but if they had one, it was too well concealed for me to pick up on it. The door lock was to the left of the section of transparent doors, behind a square of hinged stone that couldn't have been anything *but* that, and was sickeningly easy to open. It was a tenet of my profession that the easier the lock, the worse there is waiting for you on the inside, and that was a reminder I didn't really need. Instead of worrying about it, though, I listened for the hiss of releasing mag-locks, reclosed the square of stone when I heard it, then gestured the others after me through the nearest door.

Lidra whispered us all to a stop just inside a wide lobby area, one that was faintly lit all around by nightstrips high on the walls. There wasn't much in the way of mist inside the very modern building, the blowers at the doors accounting for that. We all stood quietly while Lidra consulted her silent assistant, and after a not very short time she looked up.

"I've neutralized every spy-device and blocking-lock in range of us, and set up an automatic program to do the same for all external systems as we move deeper into the building," she told us, her expression almost grim. "That still leaves not only things like that bump outside, but also the fact that I can detect life somewhere in the building. The range is too extreme so I'm not sure where, but they're probably a security patrol like Inky suggested there might be. I think we'd better continue to be very, very careful."

None of us argued with that conclusion, and once Lidra showed me the direction we wanted to go in, I led out again with the others back to following in single file. Five corridors radiated out of the entrance hall, each with a quiet sign on the wall beside it, but the signs were composed of alphabet soup that didn't have meaning for anyone who didn't work there. Lidra was still following that homing device planted by S.I. efforts, and once we reached it we could decide where to go from there.

The corridor we took ran straight back away from the entrance hall, no curves involved but any number of crossing corridors. The building was only one story high so there also didn't seem to be any staircases, but that made things harder rather than easier. What we wanted were the executive offices, and in buildings with multiple floors the higher-ups were almost invariably higher up. In one-story affairs they could be in the middle of everything or down at the end, with no way of telling which without checking. After walking a few minutes I began looking behind some of the doors we were passing, all of which opened without any fuss at all. Unfortunately what I found behind them wasn't what I was looking for, so all we could do was continue on.

We had passed another cross-corridor and Lidra told me we weren't far from the source of the homing signal, when I finally began seeing what I'd been looking for. The doors in that area were beginning to be farther apart, and opening one of them showed carpeting and drapes that were part of a decor rather than just stuck in to fill up empty spaces. It looked like we'd found the executive area, and when Lidra pointed to a door on the left as the one containing our signal, I opened it to find as little as I'd expected to. The doors on the left were still close together, so only the ones on the right belonged to executives.

The end of our search came about five minutes later, with a door that wasn't simply closed. I was working on the theory that the information we needed would be kept close among the upper echelon, at the very top or near it, so that's where we had to look first. If it turned out to be in another location entirely we would be out of luck, but the time to worry about something like that is when the possibility becomes a reality. Right then I noticed that the only door for some distance up and back on the right had a separate lock arrangement, which made me feel a good deal better. The presence of a lock means there's something worthwhile sitting behind it, and worthwhile was what we were after.

With the help of a couple of tools from my kit, the lock became a past problem. It was a lot more complex than the one at the entrance to the building, but sometimes more complex is easier, and it certainly did more to ease my mind. I made the others wait while I looked around inside by myself, then I gestured them in and relocked the door behind them. If that wasn't the place we wanted, we were in the wrong building, and I didn't think we were in the wrong building.

"Inky, are you sure there's anything here to find?" Lidra asked in a low voice, looking around slowly the way the other two were doing. "It's nothing but a very expensively furnished office."

Meaning it was also very sparsely furnished, that being the current style. You didn't put much in, but what you did put had to be very expensive and in exquisitely good taste. The large room had a wide, empty desk, four upholstered chairs, a wall bar to the left, a

handmade tree in a carved pot to the right, glowing
nightstrips on the walls in a rainfall pattern, and nothing much else.

"Maybe there's a wall safe or something behind one
of those paintings," Chal suggested, eyeing the artwork that theme-matched the glowing rainfall of the
walls. "If it were me, I think I'd use that storm-cloud
scene. It's big enough to hide three safes."

"If you ever need a safe spot, Chal, please talk to
me about it first," I said, trying not to sound *too* critical. "That painting is so obvious, it probably has an
independent circuit-alarm attached to it. I *know* what
we need is in here, but it isn't in any ordinary wall
safe."

Lidra nodded wryly to show I was right about the
circuit-alarm, but by then I was back to paying more
attention to the room than to my companions. There
was a safe spot hidden in there *somewhere*, but the
question was *where* . . .

I had only just begun merging with the pattern of
the windowless room, not yet up to checking the ceiling, when the obvious answer slunk its way in. That
handmade tree in its very expensive pot—it was an
umbrella tree of some sort which supposedly meshed
in with the office theme, but it wasn't in the right *place*
for a theme-merge. It made the room unbalanced where
it stood, and there was no reason for it to be there,
unless—

I walked quickly over to the thing, but slowed as I
approached so that I could find the proper angle for
looking past. I stopped short when I caught the shim-
mer, eased around to get more of it in view, and when
I had both the near and the far edges turned my attention to the painting that had taken Chal's eye. The
storm scene hung not far from where the tree stood,
and that had to be where the control area was.

I heard Lidra's breath suck in when I made for the
painting, but at least she didn't try telling me not to
set off the circuit-alarm. I found which way the thing
was set to slide without touching it, then reached for
the opposite side and pulled instead. The painting
swung to the right and revealed the controls I'd been

expecting, and no more than a moment's checking of
the circuitry with a meter from my kit showed the circuit-alarm had to be left activated if the safe spot was
to be reached. Having no argument with that meant I
only had a single toggle to flip, so I flipped it and
turned away from the controls. Lidra gasped again,
and then she was moving closer.

"How did you know to do that?" she asked softly,
obviously impressed by the accomplishment. "The
second signal was so well masked by the circuit-alarm,
my board never even picked it up!"

"When you know it's there, there's a limit to how
long it can hide," I said, inspecting the flat, two-
dimensional picture of a tree on a cupboard-sized door.
That was the safe spot, of course, and it was anchored
into the floor as many of them were. That was why
the tree hadn't been stood elsewhere, which meant the
safe spot had been there longer than the room theme.
"Don't touch anything until I say you can, and make
sure your board doesn't help me. There don't seem to
be any more locks or traps, but I want to make sure."

Lidra nodded as she tapped keys again, but the cautioning turned out to be unnecessary. The safe spot
opened to show shelves filled with reports and files,
stored information that couldn't be reached by the best
computer break-in expert ever born. The data wasn't
in a computer, which made it safer than it would have
been if it was.

"We'd better see how fast we can find out if that's
what we need," Lidra said as Chal moved forward
toward the cache of possible treasure. "Those life
readings I picked up earlier are closer to us now, and
it won't be many minutes before they're right on top
of us. It might even help to have someone listening at
the door."

I thought I saw Lidra glance at me before she moved
forward to help Chal, but just then I was too busy
staring at something in confusion to know for certain.
On a top shelf of the safe spot, all alone in their stand,
were two large vials of something that looked somehow familiar. The contents were a bright pink that
shimmered very faintly in the dimness, and I could

have sworn I'd seen something like them somewhere else, at a different place and time. I was trying to remember where that could be, when Chal's low exclamation distracted me.

"This is it!" he said excitedly, using a tiny hand-beam to make reading easier. "Just give me a few minutes, and I'll know what, if anything, we want to take with us."

Which meant a guard at the door was definitely going to be necessary. Lidra was ignoring her board in favor of helping Chal, and just because the door was locked didn't mean we couldn't be surprised. I gave up pushing for a memory that would come in its own time and turned back to the door, and was actually surprised to see a large figure already there. I shook my head as I walked over to Seren, then grinned up at him.

"Would you believe I actually forgot you were with us?" I asked very softly, wishing it wasn't the wrong place for him to put his arms around me. "It must be because you're so small and unimpressive-looking, the kind of man no one ever notices in a crowd."

"Yeah, that must be it," he answered, but the words were distracted and completely without amusement, as were his eyes and expression. For an instant I thought he was insulted over being forgotten, but before I could apologize seriously he was going on. "Smudge, Lidra said you three are associated with S.I.," he stumbled, apparently searching carefully for what he wanted to ask. "That means you all work for S.I., doesn't it, on a regular basis as agents of theirs?"

"Seren, it means we only work for S.I. sometimes," I answered, wondering why he wanted to know. "Lidra's done this more than Chal or I have, and as a matter of fact this is my first assignment from them. If you were worrying over how often I find myself with the bad guys sending horrible things to attack me, you really have nothing to . . ."

"Then where did you learn to do all—that?" he interrupted with a motion of his hand, his gray eyes strangely cold in the dimness. "The way you opened all those doors, and led us over that trap instead of

into it, and were able to find that safe as though someone had told you where it was— You didn't only just
learn all that, it had to come from years of experience
and practice. If you aren't an agent for S.I., then what
are you?''

He asked his question and just waited, assuming
nothing, being as fair about it as I'd known he'd be. I
would have preferred a different place and time for that
particular discussion, but since the point had been
raised I would answer it, and then the matter would
be behind us.

"Seren, my love, what I am is a thief," I said,
finding my voice almost as steady as I wanted it to be.
"I know it sounds terrible when put that baldly, but
that's what I am. Seero raised me and trained me to
do what he did, to get back at all those who think
they're above the law, and that's who I steal from.
I'm very good in my profession, as good as you are
in yours, and that's why S.I. sent me along on this
job. It was . . .''

"You're a *thief?*" he said, sounding and looking
utterly repelled as he backed a step from the hand I
tried to put to his chest. "You pretended to be someone decent, but you're actually a *thief?*"

"Seren, please," I said as my insides began to twist
with a terrible fear. "I only steal from those who deserve it, those who are bigger thieves than I could ever
be! Please don't look at me like that, I'm still the same
person I was! Just because I . . .''

"How can you say there's nothing different about
you?" he demanded, those gray eyes burning me down
where I stood. "You steal, don't you, no matter who
it is you steal from? Stealing is stealing, which means
you're nothing but a dirty *thief!* I wish to hell I'd never
laid eyes on you!"

He began to turn away from me, the disgust on his
face so clear I thought I would be sick just from seeing
it, but I couldn't let it simply end like that.

"Please don't say you really mean that," I begged,
feeling the tears of terror begin to fill my eyes, my
hand reaching quickly for his arm. "Hearing it so suddenly was a shock for you, but once you think about

it you'll find it easier to understand. I love you, Seren, and I . . .''

"Don't call me that!" he snapped, pulling his arm away from my fingers as his eyes blazed down at me. "Seren is a name my baby sister gave me, and she was *killed* by a thief! I don't ever want to hear you fouling the name again by speaking it! And above that don't ever try touching me again, or I won't be responsible for what happens.''

He looked at me one last time before striding away toward Lidra and Chal, but my sight was too blurred by tears to know what he'd put in the look. I turned around to stare at a dim and blurry door, finding it impossible to believe my world could have died so quickly and without warning, but I knew beyond doubt that it had. In the blink of an eye his love had turned to hatred, and I simply couldn't bear it. I'd thought he would understand but he hadn't, and there wasn't anything I could say or do to change that.

I wanted desperately to be somewhere where I could sob out the unbelievable pain I felt with no one to hear it, but there wasn't any place like that around. It suddenly came to me that even though I couldn't leave, I also couldn't stand being in that room any longer. Beyond the door was a corridor where I could at least be alone, and I suddenly had to have *that* at the very least. I smeared the tears from my eyes with the back of one hand as I reached for my kit, and it was only a moment before the lock was open and I could do the same with the door. I stepped into the corridor as my fingers put the picks away in my kit, my mind too full of other things to pay attention to anything else, and then—

"Hey, you!" a voice shouted from fifty feet away up the corridor, bringing my head around with a jerk. "Stop right where you are and don't twitch a muscle! If you don't have a pass, you're in deep shit!''

Three men in uniforms were beginning to run toward me, men who *had* to be the security patrol Lidra had spotted earlier. I stood frozen in place, too shocked to do anything but obey, and then I heard Lidra call frantically from inside the room.

"Inky, quick!" she hissed over the sound of running footsteps. "Get back inside here! I'm going to use the screen!"

A glance showed me the way she tapped at her board, undoubtedly calling up the privacy screen that turned her invisible. Chal and Seren were already close beside her, showing the screen would be up in seconds, which meant I *couldn't* go back in there and join them. The guards would know there was no other way out of the room, and if they couldn't find me they would start to search. Since it was my fault we'd been discovered in the first place, there was no sense in taking the others down with me. Instead of reentering the room, I turned away from the approaching guards and ran like hell.

The footsteps behind me faltered very briefly, and then they came on again, all three sets. That told me Lidra had gotten her screen up in time, so I could forget about the people I'd almost betrayed and simply concentrate on running. I didn't expect to get away, wouldn't have known where to go even if I did, but the farther away I got, the more of a chance the others would have. The men behind me shouted and yelled, threats and orders coming from all three, and then they must have realized I had no intentions of stopping no matter *what* they said. A few seconds of silence went by and then the air suddenly blurred to my right, a whining tingle reaching through my bodysuit to flip every nerve on the right side of my body. I flinched away to the left, my mouth suddenly dry when I realized they were using stunners, but there was really no place to go. The offices were dead-ends and the nearest cross-corridor was too far ahead, and then I heard another whine—

Chapter 16

I came out of it slowly and painfully, at first not knowing where I was or what had happened, and then it all came back. I'd walked right under the noses of a security patrol and had been captured, and now the enemy had me. It was pitch dark wherever I was, but I didn't need light to know I was tied down to what I was lying on, and I didn't hurt so much that I couldn't tell I'd been stripped naked. The whatever under me seemed to be made of metal, but the bindings on my wrists and ankles had more of the feel of leather.

"Am I supposed to care?" I whispered into the darkness, making no attempt to see if I could free myself. My body hurt from what the stunner had done to me and probably from the fall I'd taken as well, but I just didn't care. Seren was disgusted by me, hated me so much he didn't even want me to speak his name, and almost the first thing my memory had shown me when I'd awakened was the sight of his face. He'd been so repelled, so utterly sickened, and he'd wanted nothing further to do with me or my love.

"And can you really blame him?" I asked myself, choking the words out into the dark. He came from a happy, normal family that had been touched by tragedy because of someone like me; could I expect him to put all that out of his mind just for my sake? It would have been unreasonable to expect that, but—

But I loved him so much! And he'd turned away from me in hate and never wanted to see me again, and all *I* wanted was to die! The tears started again and this time the sobbing came with them, but even

then my miserable life refused to end. It just dragged
on and on while I cried into the dark, a dark I hoped
I would never again be taken out of.

The crying lasted for a long time, and once it
stopped it left behind an even greater lack of caring
than I'd felt when I'd awakened. My life could go on
the way it had been going before I met Seren, but I
just didn't care if it did or ended instead. I lay in the
dark in a numb, unthinking state, more aware of inner
pain than outer, and after an unmeasured length of
time a pinpoint of light began glowing above me. It
brightened slowly, slowly, until it began illuminating
everything around me, bringing to view a rather large
room of stone with no windows and only two doors.
One of the doors was in the wall to my right and one
in the wall beyond my feet, and when I turned my head
away from them in disinterest, I nearly found myself
shocked enough to feel it.

On the wall to my left, about ten or fifteen feet away
from the table I lay on, the chained, unmoving body
of a Griddenth hung. The body's taloned feet had been
smashed, its wings had been torn, blood covered
feathers and fur alike, and the beaked mouth had
been knocked out of alignment. It was a horrible, sick-
making sight that almost reached through to me, most
especially since I was certain the Griddenth was Velix.

"That's what comes from trying to poke your nose
in where it doesn't belong," a voice said from my
right, a voice I seemed to know. "Let it be a lesson
to you when it comes to answering questions as well,
and maybe you won't end up the same way."

By that time I was looking at the man who spoke,
and even though his voice was familiar, I couldn't
place his face. He was somewhere in his thirties with
brown hair and light eyes, and he wore ordinary slacks
and shoes of black and a light orange shirt.

"You don't recognize me, do you?" he asked with
a grin, moving away from the opened door to allow in
two other men. "Would it help if I said I considered
you very brave, lady Dalisse?"

"Jejin?" I said with a good deal of confusion, finally able to connect the voice. The face was still the

face of a stranger, what with the long white beard
gone.

"Jejin isn't really my name, but you can use it for
the sake of our discussion," he said, stopping beside
the table to look down at me. "I have a few questions
for you, and you'll save yourself a lot of pain and
terror if you answer them quickly and truthfully.
Where are your friends hiding, and what are you all
up to?"

"Why are you bothering to ask?" I said, feeling
more confused than ever. "If I'm not mistaken, there
are any number of drugs that can get you all the answers you want."

"But none that work here in the Mists," he corrected, his light eyes looking put out over that. "It's
the reason we have to resort to other methods when
we find someone we think ought to be questioned. This
is too big and important an operation to take any
chances at all, even if we still thought you were innocent. But you aren't innocent, are you, and wasn't
it lucky I was there for another reason when you made
your slip."

"What slip are you talking about?" I asked, trying
to ignore the fact that his finger had come to my throat
with his questions, and his eyes were taking on an
unpleasant glint.

"I was playing magician to keep an eye on that mus-
clebound hulk of a glad," he answered, running his
finger across my throat as he spoke. "We knew his
brother was one of our spores, but we weren't entirely
convinced he had come here with the idea of poking
around. If he hadn't chosen me himself, I would have
had to substitute myself for whichever magician he *did*
choose, but he was very cooperative. The way he was
sniffing after *you* really set us wondering, and then we
got a present we hadn't been expecting: we discovered
you had a practiced eye when it came to finding hidden
panels. You remember the wine fountain in the palace,
and the need for wash water and a towel afterward?
Guests always have to be shown where those towels
are, but you found them all by yourself."

At that point I certainly did remember the towels,

and the fact that I'd noticed only vaguely how well-hidden they were. And Jejin had been no more than a few feet away when I'd committed that stupidity, another fact I'd been too busy to notice.

"And so we arranged for you to be introduced to our resident ogre," the man above me went on, his finger still moving back and forth. "We fully expected you to become a tragic accident victim, of course, and if the glad happened to end up a corpse by trying to save you, well, wouldn't that have been just too bad? We had everything planned and then we put the two of you right in it—but no one had remembered about that cursed multi-sword. The two of you got away and were able to rejoin your other friends, and that's when we began having everything go wrong. That Griddenth was useful to us, but when he came here shouting that he may have been guilty of starting that passageway incident, but he had nothing to do with the serious attack and was damned well going to find out who had, we had to close his mouth. We knew nothing about the scare you had in the passageway and cared even less, but the ogre attack wasn't quite as easy to explain away."

He was looking down at me with a glare that made all his troubles my fault, and I could see where he wasn't far wrong. I seemed to cause trouble for almost everyone I met, but hopefully that would not be going on much longer.

"And then we found you right in our headquarters building, stunned by a security patrol, but already having gotten into almost every secret place we had," he continued. "We knew then that we should have made absolutely certain you died in the mansion set, but it was far too late for should-have-beens. Some of our files are missing, and so are your three good friends. Where are they, girl, and what made you all try this break-in? Did you know what you were after, or were you shooting in the dark?"

"I don't know *where* the others are," I told him, feeling my interest in the conversation drain away. "If you haven't caught them I couldn't be happier, which means I'm not about to do anything that would change that state of affairs. Since you don't have any drugs to use on me, you might as well go and bother someone else. As far as you're concerned, I'm all out of answers.''

"Dear, brave, sweet lady Dalisse," the man calling himself Jejin said, a faint smile twisting the corners of his mouth. "I'd so hoped you would be intelligent instead, but obviously that's not meant to be. You *will* tell me what I want to know, that and everything else you can think of, as much as I care to listen to. Do try to remember that this is no one's fault but your own.''

He took his finger away from my throat and moved along the table toward my feet, but not because *he* intended doing anything. He was simply making room for the two men who had come into the room with him, men who stationed themselves to either side of me. They carried small, heavy-looking leather cases which they placed on the floor and opened, and after flipping a few switches inside the cases, they straightened with copper-glinting wires in their hands. The wires were insulated where the men held them, and the insulation wound all the way down to connections in the cases.

"It's too bad I can't give you one more chance," Jejin said while I looked back and forth between the two men, belatedly pulling at the leather holding my wrists tight to the table above my head. "Once they turn on their pet devices, my friends have to be allowed to use them. If you've decided you've changed your mind, tell me what I want to know as fast as you can before they start. That won't stop them from hurting you, but if you tell the truth they might not hurt you quite as long."

I licked my lips while the rest of me trembled, terror beginning to grow inside me. I *had* to keep from telling them what they wanted, or my teammates were as dead as I would undoubtedly be. Death was something I would have greeted happily and warmly just then, but it wasn't death they meant to give me first. It was pain they would give me, and I had to have the strength to take it without breaking. Death would come in its own good time, and that's the thought I had to cling to and remember. I tried, I honestly and truly tried, but only seconds after they started I wasn't able to do anything but scream.

The smell under my nose made me cough and turn my head away, and just that quickly and easily the agony was back. I moaned with the terrible burning flare of it and almost fainted again, but whatever had brought me back to consciousness wouldn't let it happen.

"You poor little girl, you're hurting so very badly, aren't you?" Jejin's voice came in my right ear, his hand slicking back my sweat-soaked hair. "You were begging for help just a minute ago, but surely you know there's no way help can get to you. Even if you had confederates waiting in a ship just off-planet, and even if you were able to contact them, they'd never understand what you were trying to say. You're living at a different rate than they are, so transmission from the Mists is impossible. *I'm* the only one who can help you, which I'll do the minute you answer my questions. Where are your friends hiding, and why can't we find them?"

You can't find them because they're invisible, I wanted to say, but even swimming in searing pain I knew better than to say anything at all. One comment would lead to another and then it would all come out, which just might happen anyway. My throat was raw from all the screaming I'd done, screaming caused by having burning hot wires pushed into my body. I'd been sick from the pain and I'd fainted from the pain, but my tormentors simply wiped me off or woke me up, then continued with what they were doing. The only thing they didn't bother with was the sweat covering me everywhere, that and the small trickles of blood. The sweat mixed with the blood and burned even more into the wounds, and that was a good thing as far as they were concerned.

"I have something to make it all stop hurting," Jejin said, a friendly coaxing in his voice. "If you tell me what I want to know I'll give it to you, and then the agony will be gone for good."

Right along with me, I thought, having no strength left to open my eyes. I could feel the ring on my right hand, the ring I was supposed to call for help with, but even pressing the jewels in the prescribed way would bring nothing but disappointment. My sense of time was messed up by the mists, which meant I'd never be able to send the proper signal. I didn't know if it should be faster or slower, how much faster or slower, or how much longer I could hold out. I needed the pain to stop for good, needed it very badly, and if it didn't stop soon—

"No, please, not again!" I screamed in a cracked voice, writhing as a flame was slid inside my outer thigh. "I can't stand any more, you *have* to stop!"

"I'm afraid, dear lady, that stopping isn't on our schedule," Jejin said, pleased anticipation in his voice. "As a matter of fact we've left the best places for last, the places where you'll feel the pain even more than you have until now. Delicate, soft and tender places those are, and after we're done you'll never feel pleasure in them again."

"No!" I screamed, totally beside myself as his finger touched between my thighs, one of the places I hadn't known they were deliberately ignoring. "You can't do that to me, you can't! I'll die if you hurt me there! Seren! Don't let them do it! Seren, I'm begging you!"

I was so terrified I didn't even know what I was saying, and all I could do was throw the strength of panic against leather straps that refused to part. I screamed again and fought to get loose—and then it finally came through that I wasn't the only one screaming. I forced my eyes open to look wildly around—and couldn't believe at first that I wasn't hallucinating.

Both doors to the room had been thrown open, and men in uniform were pouring in—led by Seren with his multi-sword in his fists. One of the two men who had been hurting me made the mistake of running toward Seren in an effort to get away, and he didn't live long enough to realize the error. His head flew from his shoulders without Seren even breaking stride, and then the fighter had reached Jejin where he trembled against the left wall. The ex-magician was trying to unwrap something and put it in his mouth, but Seren knocked that something out of his hands and then knocked Jejin over the head. The Mists man crumpled to the floor and lay still, and I knew he would wake up to regret that he hadn't been killed.

The screaming I'd heard was coming from the third man who had been captured by some of the uniformed men, but I paid almost no attention to that. Despite the soul-eating pain still washing over me I laughed where I lay, knowing my love had come to save me again, knowing his own love was soon to be mine again. I watched him with shining eyes as he turned away from the unconscious Jejin—then felt worse agony than anything the enemy had given me when his eyes slid past me as he began making his way out of the room. He didn't even stop to find out how badly I was hurt, didn't even want to look at me long enough to see if I was going to live. He just kept going and disappeared through the door, and then Chal was standing next to the table to my right.

"Dear lord, Inky, look what they've done to you!" he said in a trembling voice, reaching immediately for the leather holding my wrists. "We've got to get you out of this, and into decent medical facilities as soon as possible! Some of you men give me a hand here! This woman has to be . . ."

His voice trailed off as the blackness began forming behind my eyes again, and my last thought was a fervent prayer that I never wake up.

It took a very long while before all the confusion passed or settled down, and by then I knew that prayers were never answered. I'd awakened the first time on board a ship that didn't seem to be a liner, but hadn't been clear enough to recognize the uniforms I saw. By the time I was awake enough to know I was in a planetary hospital, I was also awake enough to know I was still alive. I ached just about all over and was bandaged like a first-aid practice dummy, but there was no doubt about my being alive. Even if that wasn't what I'd wanted to be.

"Well, *you're* looking better than you did," a cheery voice said, and a female nurse entered my room carrying a tray. "This breakfast will probably change *that* in a hurry, but it really is good for you no matter what it tastes like. And why don't we get a little light into this place?"

She put the tray down near me then went to the window, and a sweep of her hand later there was bright sunshine pouring into the room. I squinted against the brightness, finding it totally out of place, but the nurse never noticed. She used a button to raise the top half of my bed, swung the tray in front of me on a lift field, then left the room.

Once she was gone I pushed the tray back again, lowered the bed, then spent my time hurting and thinking about what I had lost. Velix had said we wouldn't remember the details of what we did in the Mists, but in my case he was wrong. I remembered all of it, even the parts I didn't want to remember, even the fact that he'd never know he'd been wrong. I was back on a planet and still alive, and it was clear vacation time was over. I had my own planet to get back to, and something important to finish, and it really no longer mattered to me whether or not I would survive its completion. As a matter of fact I'd be happier if I didn't; what I wanted most in the world—after seeing that Seero's death was paid for—was to follow after Seero, to find out if there really was a place we would meet again. I needed very badly to cry out my hurt against him, and have him show me how to bear it for the rest of eternity.

The trouble started when I refused the medication they tried to give me, after refusing the food they wanted me to eat. They lectured and threatened, telling me how much I would hurt and how weak I would get if I didn't cooperate, but I didn't feel like cooperating. When they finally went looking for a doctor to add his own lecture to theirs, I forced myself out of bed, ignored the dizziness, then looked for and found the bodysuit I was hoping would be in the closet. Get-

ting dressed was painful but didn't take very long, and
ditto for finding the floor's exit stairs. I made my way
slowly to the ground floor, having no idea where I was
going besides out of there, and then the question was
answered for me. Two men were waiting in the stair-
well at the bottom, and both of them grinned at me.

"I think Raksall just made some money again," one
of them said, his expression showing how amused he
was. "We're here to help you find your way to her
office, and to make sure you don't get lost on the way.
You weren't supposed to be out of here for quite a
while yet, but since you're going for a stroll, you might
as well stroll with us."

The other one was just as amused and just as alert,
but it didn't make any difference. It seemed I was back
on Gryphon, and that would save me some time and
effort. I shrugged in answer to their unspoken question, and simply went with them.

Despite it being early afternoon, Raksall really was
in her office—with an officious-looking Filster sitting
in a chair next to her desk. One of the men who had
brought me there had called ahead, but I hadn't heard
what was said. When I walked through Raksall's door,
I didn't so much hesitate as pause to catch my breath,
but the S.I. woman misinterpreted the halt.

"Now, Inky, don't be upset at Filster's being here,"
she said at once, raising a calming hand. "He's just
finished going through most of the reports that were
filed, and he wanted to tell you what a good job he
thinks you did."

"What an efficient, satisfactory and extremely pro-
ductive job you did," Filster corrected with care, giving me a narrow smile as I lowered myself into a chair.
"Not only did you perform with all of your ability on
our behalf, you even made it possible for your teammates to have the time to summon the assistance you
all needed. That was truly fine work, and you've vindicated the computer's decision to make use of you."

"Ah, Lidra tells me you may not know how she
called the troops down and then found where they were
holding you," Raksall said hastily, probably because
of Filster's final, highly flattering comment. "She and

Chal explained about the anomaly that ruined your time sense, but Chal says you should have no trouble remembering everything that happened. Is he right?''

I nodded with all the interest I was feeling, not to mention the pain from the trip up there, and she took the answer as though it were the height of enthusiasm.

''Then unconsciousness *is* the key,'' she said, nodding happily. ''Chal theorized that it might be, and you're the last one we had to check. He tried to explain how the rapid readaptation of the metabolism in the conscious individual slurred the memory that was linked in and active, but I'm afraid I missed most of what he said. He doesn't *try* to talk above people's heads, but in his position it can't come out any other way.''

''One cannot expect the brilliant to lower themselves,'' Filster put in, narrow and stiff as ever. ''The same, of course, goes for Lidra, who programmed her board with an equation that solved the anomaly, and was therefore able to contact the orbiting troop ship.''

''But let's not forget it was Inky's discovery of the anomaly in the first place that let Lidra know she'd need a conversion formula,'' Raksall came back at him, smooth satisfaction in her tone. ''They made an all-around excellent team, and if the troops homing in on Lidra's signal hadn't had to spend some time adapting to the mists, they would have reached Inky a good deal sooner. She did still have her ring on, you know, so her location under the headquarters building wasn't difficult to find.''

''The delay wasn't all that critical, considering the prisoners they were able to take at the end of it,'' Filster said, thumbing through some of the papers he held. ''The number of hours hardly matter, when you consider what we were able to learn. That one calling himself Jejin, for instance . . .''

''Filster, what's wrong with you?'' Raksall snapped, her eyes on me in a worried way. When the man had mentioned the delay he considered so acceptable, what had gone on during those hours had suddenly come back to me all at once. ''How can you sit there and say what they did to Inky doesn't matter? She wasn't simply locked up during all that time, she was being *tortured!* Her being able to hold out was the only thing that *got* you those valuable prisoners!''

Filster looked up with a frown, blinked when he saw my face, then went back to the papers he was holding to search for one in particular. When he found it he spent a few moments reading, and when he finally looked up again he was definitely pale.

''I—somehow missed that the first time through,'' he said, his eyes clinging to my face. ''Electronically heated wires—such barbarism should be punished to the fullest extent of the law— I had no idea— And after you allowed yourself to be captured so the others would find it possible to escape—''

His words broke off and didn't resume, his pain-filled stare refusing to leave me, but it didn't matter. Whether his opinion of me had changed or not, it simply didn't matter.

''Well, at least it wasn't all for nothing,'' Raksall said, leaning back in her chair while she pretended not to see Filster's reaction. ''The problem we found is considerably more far-reaching and critical than simple fraud, and we've only begun probing through the first few layers. Unraveling it all will take everything we can come up with.''

''Yes, well, with all those addicts,'' Filster said, finally pulling himself together enough to go back to his papers. ''The ones addicted in the Mists go on to addict others, but the drug isn't being *charged* for. And there's the fact that if there *is* some sort of counter or antidote for its influence, it might well be found right here on this world. The computer is suggesting the core group running this thing makes a habit of establishing a headquarters in ordinarily inaccessible locations, like the Mists of the Ages on Joelare and the wilds here on Gryphon. It's a shame we haven't been able to learn exactly how many headquarters locations they have.''

''Or what they're really up to,'' Raksall said, then she leaned forward and put her forearms on the desk. ''Inky, you're still not looking very well, and even though I knew you'd be out of that hospital before they wanted to let you go, I think you'd be better off going back now. I know just how badly they hurt you, and you won't be over it for quite a while. Go back and let them take care of you.''

"You really must, you know," Filster put in, looking at me soberly. "Anyone going into the wilds must be in absolutely peak condition just to survive, not to mention function efficiently. It won't be long, so . . ."

"I'm not going into the wilds," I said, the words forced out of me by the internal shudder I felt. I was beginning to feel really sick, and the pain was flashing through my body like an asteroids-warning beacon. I knew I had to get out of there, so I forced myself to my feet and started through the doorway, but Raksall and Filster came right behind me.

"Inky, you're just not up to thinking about it now," Raksall said, a mixture of pleading and coaxing in her voice. "Once you've recovered you'll understand how badly they'll need your ability, just the way they did in the Mists."

"This is of vital importance, young miss," Filster put in his own oar, his voice now sounding anxious. "The original Situation had been reclassified as an A Prime Emergency, something none of us can ignore. Your sense of duty and honor . . ."

"I have no honor," I interrupted without turning, stopping for a minute to let the dizziness pass. "I'm a thief, and thieves *have* no honor. Just leave me alone."

"Leave you alone to desert your teammates?" another voice asked, a strong male voice. "You know you're not the kind to do that, Inky. If you were, I never would have asked you for a date."

It took some effort to turn, but once I did I saw that big blond field agent I'd met at the beginning of that mess, standing behind and to my left in front of an open office. He grinned at me in a way I vaguely remembered, but I had nothing to say to him. All I wanted was to get out of there, but before I could turn back toward the exit three people came out of the office behind him. Two of them were Chal and Lidra, staring at me with hurt in their eyes, and the third, of

course, was Serendel. I realized they'd probably re-
cruited him to be one of their associate workers, but
that was hardly surprising. What *was* faintly surprising
was the fact that this time he looked straight at me,
and his expression was a careful neutrality. He seemed
to have gotten control of himself, but I couldn't say
the same about me. Instead of returning his gaze I
completed my previous intention to turn away, but the
big blond agent couldn't let it lie.

"We'll have time for that date before we leave for
the wilds, Inky," he said, his voice strong and steady
and persuasive. "You'll go back to the hospital and
let them help you, and then we'll . . ."

"I won't go into the wilds," I said again, my own
voice weak but no less determined. "I won't have any
more to do with you people at all, and I want you to
leave me alone."

"We're not 'you people' any more, Inky," the man
persisted, the calm in his voice unchanged. "You're
one of us now, a full member with privileges earned
the hard way, and you can't expect to simply walk
away. We won't let you walk away."

"There's only one thing I am," I said, wishing I
could sit down right where I was. "Tell the man what
I am, Mr. Filster, just the way you said it to me."

"My dear young woman!" Filster protested, his
voice tinged with distress. "What I said then was
before I knew you, before I realized what you were
truly . . ."

"Tell him!" I repeated harshly, aware that everyone
in the office had stopped to watch and listen. "It's the
complete, unglorified truth, so I want you to tell him!
What am I, Mr. Filster?"

"A—a thief," the man whispered, the words torn
out of him bringing pain to his voice. "Your talent is
stealing, young miss, and you're nothing but a thief."

"Thank you, Mr. Filster," I said, looking down
from all the pity and compassion I could see in the
faces of those who listened. That should have been the
end of it, but unfortunately it wasn't.

"If you're nothing but a thief, then we don't have
to spend much time worrying about your feelings,"

the blond agent said, his voice having turned hard. "If you prefer having it put another way, you can join us on the assignment, or you can be sent to a detention cell. Does the assignment sound a little more attractive now?"

"Fieran!" Raksall exclaimed in shock, the only sound in the entire office. "You can't mean that! Don't you know . . ."

"I know everything I have to," the man Fieran came back, his tone still remorseless. "What about it, Inky? The assignment has started to look a little better now, hasn't it?"

"No, it hasn't," I answered flatly, a heavy knot of satisfaction inside me due to the fact that my friends were long gone and no longer at risk. "I won't go into the wilds with anybody, most especially not with you and them. Either arrest me, or let me go."

"Now you're giving *me* a choice," the blond Fieran said, his tone suddenly odd. "Are you sure you won't change your mind?"

"Positive," I answered, the need to leave having grown absolutely critical. I didn't much care where I went, as long as it turned out to be some place other than there. I started moving, vaguely wondering how far I would get before I passed out, but the question never came up.

"If that's the way you feel, I really have no choice at all," the blond man's voice came after me, the tone filled with more authority than it had previously held. "As the Agent in Charge of this star sector, I hereby arrest you for actions damaging to the general public. You two men take her away."

An uproar began all around, but that's exactly what the men who had brought me there did.

DAW

Presenting JOHN NORMAN in DAW editions . . .

Attention:

DAW COLLECTORS

Many readers of DAW Books have written requesting information on early titles and book numbers to assist in the collection of DAW editions since the first of our titles appeared in April 1972.

We have prepared a several-pages-long list of all DAW titles, giving their sequence numbers, original and current order numbers, and ISBN numbers. And of course the authors and book titles, as well as reissues.

If you think that this list will be of help, you may have a copy by writing to the address below and enclosing one dollar in stamps or currency to cover the handling and postage costs.

DAW BOOKS, INC.
DEPT. C
1633 Broadway
New York, N.Y. 10019